P9-BVC-543

I Need; I Want

Bill Liggins

I NEED; I WANT

Author Credits: William A. Liggins Jr.

Cover art is by 123RF.com
Pink stage background by: kittiyaporn1027 (123RF)
Male singer by: wavebreakmediamicro (123RF).
Woman singing by: blendevo (123RF).

iUniverse books may be ordered through booksellers or by contacting:

iUniverse
1663 Liberty Drive
Bloomington, IN 47403
www.iuniverse.com
1-800-Authors (1-800-288-4677)

ISBN: 978-1-5320-4910-1 (sc)
ISBN: 978-1-5320-4911-8 (e)

Library of Congress Control Number: 2018905621

Print information available on the last page.

iUniverse rev. date: 10/16/2018

Chapter 1

"I need acknowledgment. I want the energy from that. I need truth. I want to be believed. I need to cry sometimes. I want to be able to cry. I need to break out of this rut. I want -- I want -- I want to feel free to be angry."

"Feel free, Matt," a firm female voice said from the surrounding darkness. "What are you angry about? You're angry because --"

"Awe shit, Shelley."

"Go on. I'm angry because --"

"I'm angry because --" Matt took a deep breath and began pacing on the harshly lit stage. "I'm angry about my career. I'm angry at this industry. I'm angry about this exercise -- about not having any options outside of acting. I'm angry because sometimes I can't seem to think clearly. I'm angry because I'm impatient. I'm angry because -- because -- because -- I'm angry." Matt paused when he heard some of the other actors chuckling. "I'm angry --"

"Okay, Matt. Cut!" A middle aged, blond woman with reading glasses halfway down her nose, stepped into the stage lights. She was short, but heavy. Matt towered over Shelley, but she was still an intimidating presence for him and all the other professional actors in her workshop. Shelley smiled, and gave Matt an encouraging nod. "Very good."

"Thanks." Matt walked off the side of the stage, and leaned on a table along the wall. A woman's golden-brown hand reached out and lightly scratched the side of his bald head. When feeling her ticklish touch, an easy, dimpled smile sprouted on his face.

"Still angry?" she asked him, in a slight English accent.

Matt shook his head, and turned to the stunning young actress next to him.

"Who's next?" Shelley asked. She removed her glasses, turned toward the other seventeen actors sitting in the darkness. No one raised their hand, but Shelley locked her eyes on one of them, the actress ticking Matt's copper-toned scalp. "Kayla! We haven't heard from you in a while. Come on up. I need; I want."

Kayla turned toward the stage. "Bloody hell," she whispered. She reluctantly left Matt, and strolled toward the black platform.

Matt sipped on a bottle of water while watching her, appreciating her tight denims and her shifting hips.

When Kayla reached center-stage, the first place she looked was to Matt who gave her a reassuring wink, and that dimpled smile. Kayla then faced the dark audience.

"Let's go, Kayla. I need; I want. Action!" Shelley stepped back into the darkness.

Kayla nervously rubbed her left hip and suddenly felt chilly. "I need -- I need --" She smiled and shrugged. "I need to have a need." Kayla stood there silently with her eyes wide open, shaking her head as if she had exhausted her emotions. She shrugged again.

Shelley slapped her clipboard on her lap. "Come on, Kayla."

"I'm just not a needy person."

"Are you being honest with yourself?"

"Yes, I am."

Shelley uncrossed her legs, set her clipboard aside and gently nibbled on her pencil. "Kayla? Honey, we all have needs and wants, dreams and hurts. I want you to take a moment to search yourself mentally. And I want honesty this time."

"Okay." Kayla lowered her head and closed her eyes. She shifted her stance and rubbed her hip again. She snickered. "I need to pee."

Lip flapping chuckles peppered the silence. Shelley turned and shushed the audience. Turning back to the stage, she said, "Better. Give me more."

Kayla lifted her head and opened her eyes. "I want to go to the bathroom?"

"Good. You can't yet. More please."

"I need -- I need --" Kayla lowered her head, then shrugged, flinging her hands out to the side. "I need --" She lifted her head and stared at Shelley. "I need?"

Shelley leaned forward in her chair. "What's the problem?"

"I just don't have any needs."

"You need food? You need to breathe?"

"But I'm doing that," Kayla said.

"You need love? -- Maybe sex?"

Kayla glanced at Matt, then turned her eyes downward. "That's taken care of."

"Do you want success?" Shelley asked.

"Of course."

"Good. Do you need success?"

"Sure."

"Oh my God. You have a need and a want. Why?"

"Huh?"

"Why do you have that need and want?" Shelley asked.

"Because, I don't want to fail?"

"Because, it's a choice you make!" Shelley turned back to the rest of the actors. "That's all this exercise is about -- to help you find choices within yourselves -- little buttons you can push during a scene that can evoke real emotions. This is not a psychological group session here, but I am trying to open your eyes to the work professionals like Whitaker, Damon, and Streep have to do to stay as good as they are. Your emotions are just as much of an instrument as your body. Just like violins in a symphony orchestra, we're running the scales here. You know, doe-re-me-fa-so-la-tee-doe or something like that. To keep your instrument strong, you have to do this regularly." She turned back to the stage. "Kayla?"

"Yes."

"Honey, what happens inside when you think about your father?"

A stress furrow appeared on Kayla's forehead. She blinked her eyes more rapidly. "It hurts of course."

"It hurts bad, doesn't it?"

"Yes."

"Especially when you think about how he died too soon. Especially when you think about how he'll never be a grandfather to your children. Kayla, your children won't have your father as a grandfather. All these years you could have used a daddy, and he wasn't there. You were denied your father's love. Kayla, he'll never dance with you at your wedding. In a future wedding you won't have anyone to give you away, will you?"

Kayla lowered her head. "No." She sniffed.

"He's gone, Kayla. It was a senseless murder, but that was ten years ago, Kayla. You have to get over it, Kayla. Get on with your life, Kayla. That's what people tell you, don't they?"

"Sometimes."

"And what do you say to them?"

She sniffed and rubbed her right eye. "It still hurts. I can't get over that."

"I need; I want, Kayla! Quickly!"

Kayla rocked slightly while rubbing her hip again. She couldn't look at Shelley or anyone. She sniffed again.

"Kayla, I need; I want," Shelley repeated. Kayla remained silent, but Shelley stayed on her. "Kayla, your father's gone. Get over it, will ya. Get on with your life."

Kayla stared angrily at Shelley. "I still want my daddy back! That'll never change."

Shelley met Kayla's gaze and said, "I need?"

Kayla's eyes softened before closing tightly. "I need him sooo – badly. I want -- to talk to him -- to hold him. Sometimes, I really need that. I do. I do need that. I miss his cologne, his laugh. I miss my family time. I want my daddy. I want my daddy. I want him --" Her voice became a whisper. A grimace pulled her mouth wide. Tears hung on her eyelashes before falling to the floor. She stood center-stage alone in the harsh lights, motionless and fully vulnerable.

Matt impulsively took a half a step toward her, but Shelley halted him.

"Cut!" Shelley stood and stepped into the stage lights with Kayla, then slowly pulled her into a gentle, sympathetic embrace. "Good work," she whispered. "I know this is tough, but you'll need to know your internal buttons. Your father's only one. As you advance in your career, you'll find more and more." Kayla wiped her face and nodded. Shelley looked up to her eyes. "You okay?" Kayla nodded to her. "All right. Go pee, honey." Kayla chuckled and wiped more tears from her eyes and face. Shelley smiled and embraced her again.

Kayla walked off the stage toward the restroom.

Shelley turned, then eyed the other actors. "Who's next? Albert! Get up here!"

"Awe shit," Albert said from the back. A middle-aged white man with silver hair and faintly deranged eyes stood, and walked slowly to the front. As Albert passed Shelley, he gave her a playful punch in the shoulder. He stood center stage with a sarcastic grin on his face. "Please, be gentle with me."

"Shut-up. I need; I want, Albert. Action!" Shelley picked up her clipboard and sat.

Kayla entered the small restroom and glanced at the toilet which appeared more abused than neglected. After seeing it, she decided she could wait. Kayla turned toward the mirror over the sink and adjusted her hair. She stared at her face -- a face only she thought could be prettier. *Can I make it?* While other young actors held the deluded confidence of predestined stardom, doubts flourished in Kayla's mind. *Why am I going through this? How much longer can I give myself?*

Kayla sighed and wiped her eyes. A man's scream from outside pulled her attention away from the mirror. She straightened her blouse and walked out the door. Another primal scream paused her steps. She looked up at the stage, and saw Albert on the floor banging his hands and feet like a temperamental infant screaming at the top of his lungs.

"What the –," she whispered.

Kayla circled behind the other actors in the audience, avoiding Shelley, and walked up to Matt who reached out to hold her hand.

"You okay?" he asked.

"Yeah, but what's this with Albert?"

"More Eric Morris technique."

As Albert's screaming tantrum held their attention, Matt stepped behind Kayla and held her waist. Upon feeling Matt against her, she briefly and discreetly swayed her hips in response.

Albert continued screaming and pounding until he heard Shelley's voice.

"Cut! All right, Albert. Good work."

He rolled over and sat-up. "Thank you for stripping me of my dignity."

"Shut up and sit down," Shelley said. "If you're afraid to look foolish, you'll never be a complete actor." As Albert hurried by Shelley, she slapped him on the butt then took a glimpse at her watch. "Let's take ten. We have two scenes to get to before ten. We have *Hitch* with Dom and Norm. And *Extremities* with Niki and Jenny."

Ybor City's streets still glistened from an early evening shower, the moisture filling the air with heavy humidity. Festival lights arched over Seventh Avenue and on the narrow sidewalks under them, people strolled with few aims that evening except to eat, drink, and gaze at the window displays of antique and pop-art shops. Music sounded from all directions from the many bars with live acts.

It was eleven o'clock, and though this was a weeknight, the sidewalk crowds hadn't thinned. The bars and pizzerias remained crowded. Carlotta's was one such place. The noise level inside made it hard to talk without shouting, but this was Albert's kind of place, an audience hall where he and seven of his fellow actors could decompress after the pressures of an evening in Shelley's Professional Actors Studio.

With another primal scream, Albert held up a mug of beer and gulped a mouthful. "HOOOOOO! I'M FEELIN' GOOODDD!"

Kayla noticed the stares from other tables. "Shhhhh. You want other people to think we're bloody cracked or something?"

"We are, baby. We are. Screamin' our brains out, that's what'll make us stars. Shelley says so, right? HOOOOOOO!"

Matt took a slice of the huge pizza in front of them. "Yeah, we're cracked. We're cracked because we're here in Tampa. Can't get big time credibility here."

"Now I wouldn't say that," Albert said. "Remember Milo?"

"Milo?"

"Yeah."

"Oh yeah. Milo Stankavich," Jenny, one of the other actors, said. "A few years ago."

"He started in the workshop with me," Albert said.

"He must have left before me and Kayla joined," Matt said.

"Probably. Anyway, Milo got a few bit parts in Miami and Orlando, and some L-A producer called him for a featured role in a little production called *Now You See Me.*"

"Really? I loved that movie," Kayla said. "Which one was he?"

"He was one of the FBI agents," Albert said. "Anyway, build up your credits, make contacts, and maybe they'll call you west too. Milo's out there as a working actor."

"What about you?" Jenny asked.

"Me? Baby, I've been there and back -- spent years in Hollywood and didn't like it. It's colder, more dangerous, and the ground shakes every now and then. I'm doin' all right here in Tampa. I usually land three commercials a year. And I can do as many plays as I want."

"That's easy for you and Milo, but auditions for my type are rare in Florida," Matt said.

"Oh yeah? And what type are you?" Albert knew what Matt was talking about but asked anyway.

"A typical All-American descendant of mother Africa with a taste of Italian, a pinch of Irish, and a sprinkle of German. You know -- that type."

"Oh? You're black?"

"True."

"Oh my God. Matt's black." He turned to Kayla. "Say, did you know your boyfriend's black?" Kayla smiled and nodded. Albert's eyes grew wider in mock shock. "Hello? Just a moment. Kayla? Are you black too?" Kayla nodded. "Sweet Dixie Jesus, what is happenin' here? Black presidents -- black golf champions -- now black actors?"

"All right – all right --" A smile broke out on Matt's face.

"Are there any other black actors at this table?" Albert asked. One of the other actors raised his hand. "Gary? Nooooo. You're black?"

"Actually, I'm Irish -- you know, the blacks of Europe?"

Albert sneered at him. "Shut-up, Gary."

"Okay, you trying to make a point or what?" Matt asked.

Albert calmed himself and leaned back in his chair. "A point?"

"Yeah."

Albert took another swallow of his beer. "The point is -- is – well, I really don't have a point. Just life. Look, I like you, kid -- and consider you a friend." Albert draped his arm over Kayla's shoulder. "And not only do I like your Kayla, I want to sleep with her too." He moved closer to Kayla. "Dump this bum, will ya. I'll make you a star."

"Sorry." She chuckled and patted his hand.

"Title of my life. Then, how about you and me doin' a sexy scene in workshop?"

"Only with the utmost professionalism, Mr. Cole."

"Only with the utmost professionalism. Ewww, I love how she talks the Queen's English, lookin' like that girl -- what's her name?" Albert snapped his fingers, but no one had an answer. "Hot young singer? You know -- died in a plane crash a few years ago? -- Eye something -- eye -- aye -- aayal? -- eyeyeah?"

"Aaliyah?" Gary offered.

"Yeah!" He pointed at Kayla. "This is her clone! And she

needs to do a sexy scene with me!" Kayla shook her head and snickered in her drink. Albert shook her shoulder. "Huh? No? Oh well. That's show business." Albert turned back to Matt. "Now, kid, listen to this ol' white man's number one rule of show business. Make yourself available for everythin', and work hard when chosen. By the way, of everyone at this table who has the biggest audition in months comin' up tomorrow?" Everyone pointed at Matt. "That's right. It's not every day any of us gets a call for a featured role in a TV mini-series." Albert raised his beer mug and motioned to the others to lift their drinks. "To Matt. And I mean this from the bottom of my heart. Stop bitchin' and break a leg, young black man."

"Thanks, ol' white man," Matt said, touching his cup of soda with Albert's mug.

"Where's the audition?" Jenny asked.

"Universal, Orlando."

"Do you have to stay over?"

"No."

"What's the part?" Gary asked.

"A young black detective."

"Oh yeah. I wanted that role," Albert said. "They wouldn't rewrite it for a middle aged white man though." Albert gulped down the last of his beer, then held his hand up to a passing waitress. "Say, honey, can we get some more beer here?"

The festival lights over Seventh Avenue stayed on, but the bars and restaurants finally closed leaving the avenue empty and threatening.

Outside Carlotta's, Jenny held Albert tightly trying to keep him stable. An alcohol induced glaze coated his eyes.

Matt and Kayla watched with concern as Albert leaned on the little blond.

"Easy does it," Jenny said.

"Are you going to be all right?" Kayla asked.

"Ohhh, I'm okay," Albert said, a wheezing cough seeping through his words.

"We can make it," Jenny said. "I'm driving."

"But what about my SUV?" Albert asked.

"We'll pick it up tomorrow morning."

"Oh yeah."

"He'll be fine," Jenny said. "We'll see you two Thursday."

"Okay," Matt said.

"Don't forget that scene copy," Kayla said.

"I won't. Break a leg tomorrow, Matt."

"Thanks. Take it easy, A-C."

"See ya, young black man," Albert responded. Jenny seemed deceptively strong as he leaned on her. They meandered together down the walk with Albert singing a show tune. "Tonight, tonight -- won't be like any night -- tonight -- la, la, laaa, la la, laaa --"

Matt and Kayla didn't have far to walk. They held hands and walked a block to a century old, brick building with a 1960's antique shop on the first floor. Over it were storage rooms the landlord remodeled as affordable apartments. One of them was their home.

Through an old steel door and up a narrow stairway was a rectangular space barely 800 square feet in area. Drywall covered the brick, and wood frame walls split the space into a living room, bedroom, kitchen, and bathroom. There were only two windows, one in the living room and one in the bedroom.

For a year and a half, Matt and Kayla had struggled in making their little home comfortable. They furnished it well, but owned very little. They rented everything from the living room furniture, to their electric stove. They both knew this place was only temporary until they had enough money for their ultimate goal, Los Angeles.

The next morning, orange sunlight illuminated their bedroom. Matt's eyes opened when he felt the solar heat on his face. He rolled over and saw Kayla sitting on the side of the bed in only a thin nightshirt and panties, meticulously applying nail polish to her toes. She was unaware Matt was watching her.

When Matt saw how the thin fabric of her night shirt cupped around her buns, the dawn's early light flickered brightly in his shorts. He crept up behind her and straddled her, startling Kayla enough to smear some of the polish.

"Hey!"

"Sorry," Matt said. "Did I mess you up?"

"It's all right. Good morning." She stretched her neck to kiss him over her shoulder.

"Morning." Matt held her face and kissed her with increasing depth. His hands roamed and squeezed, massaged and poked. "You're feeling good this morning, gal."

"All right now. You better slow down."

"Can't. I need my morning cinnamon buns."

"Can't you wait a few minutes? I'm almost done."

"I don't know. Mind if I rub on you until you're finished."

"Unbelievable."

Matt rubbed himself against Kayla while she continued

touching up her toe nails. She wiped off an errant drop of polish, and flexed her toes trying to get them fully dry while pretending not to notice the growing mass pushing hungrily on her rear. "What about your sides?"

"I've got my lines. I'm more concerned about your undersides right now. Hurry up with them nails."

She remained composed even with Matt's gentle caresses on the inside of her thighs. She calmly checked her polish as Matt kissed her neck and tongued her ear, but wavered when Matt's gentle hand dipped inside her panties. She paused and took a deep breath as Matt's insistent pelvic thrusts and hand play raised goose bumps on her skin. Kayla hoped the polish was dry, but it didn't matter now. She calmly twisted the top back on the polish bottle, and dropped it on the floor. She rose up and sat more firmly on Matt's bulge, shifting her hips like a lap dancer. She raised her hair up and closed her eyes, her breathing growing more fervent, her lap dance more vigorous. Matt leaned back on the bed, pulling her with him. While continuing to grind on her, he removed her panties, then freed himself from his shorts.

Chapter 2

I need this part. This is the one. Matt's eyes had the determination of an athlete battling for a championship. Thoughts of dreams coming true flashed in his mind as he drove to Orlando. *I can finally quit my job. I want out. I'll have enough credits to go to L-A. Hell, what are my lines? Shit!* Matt turned to the passenger seat and saw a ten-page script on it. He sighed with relief, but thoughts of the morning he had so far intruded on his focused goal. A silly smile crossed his face. *Daaammmnnn that was good. I gotta get back to that.* He glanced down at his lap, feeling an increasing tightness in his jeans. *Down boy, shit. She ain't here. Think of something else. Down boy. Football -- no. Baseball? Shit, that doesn't work. What were those lines? Dammit. Clear your mind. It'll come back to you.* Matt turned to the passenger seat again, then turned his eyes back to the road. "Kayla, get out of my mind."

"Hi, I'm Kayla Ross calling for Passport Credit Customer Service. How are you this morning? -- Good. The reason for my call is we are offering a 30-day free trial membership in our credit protection program – huh? -- Basically, it's a program that will keep your payments current on this or any other credit cards you may have should you lose your job due to injury or illness. -- I'm sorry? -- But we are offering it on free trial basis. You're under no obligation -- hello?"

Kayla shook her head and keyed in the results of the call on her computer. After she entered the data, another call popped up on her computer screen. It was only an answering machine. So were all of the next twenty calls.

She stood up, adjusted her headset, then looked over the fabric covered walls of her cubicle. Here, she was one among four hundred telemarketers canvassing the nation for Passport Credit Services. Here, she was buried in an artist's nightmare, a humdrum job where she felt like an inconsequential rat in a wheel. She was bored, and felt more tired now than earlier in the morning. At least her arms and legs still tingled from the sexual feeding she gave Matt, and that brought out a serene smile on her face.

"What're you smiling about, Kay-R?"

Kayla came out of her brief daydream and turned to her neighbor, a woman about the same cinnamon complexion and age as Kayla, with gold streaked hair wrapped tightly like an extra skin over her scalp.

"Nothing," Kayla said. "I was just thinking about something." Kayla disconnected another answering machine on her computer.

"From that smile, I think somebody got more than just breakfast this morning."

Kayla was speechless, and bashfully shook her head. "Shawnda, I swear. Stop being so nosy."

Shawnda disconnected a call on her computer. "Nosy?

Me? No. Just wishing I could find me something like you got. And hanging with it so long. Y'all gonna get married. I come from Louisiana. I can foresee this."

"You're cracked."

"What? You don't want to?"

"I didn't say that." A call flashed on Kayla's computer. "Hello?" It was just an answering machine. She cleared the call, sighed, then looked at the clock. "Come on time."

Shawnda cleared a call from her computer then bounced a crumpled piece of paper off the monitor. "This file sucks."

"Same here."

Shawnda bent down and picked up the paper. "You still singing with your future husband this weekend?"

"Yeah. Saturday at Cambridge Square."

"I might just drop by for a listen -- see what you got. What time?"

Kayla disconnected another answering machine. "From one to two, unless Matt gets called back for that part."

"I thought he had that audition already?"

"No, it's today -- in about an hour."

"Well, good luck. Maybe I should get into acting. I'd be -- Hello? Mrs. Carson? -- This is Shawnda Tilman calling for Passport Credit Customer Service. How are you?"

A call flashed up on Kayla's computer, but it was another answering machine. "Bloody hell," she whispered.

"Kayla?" A male voice broke in on Kayla's headset startling her. "This is Mark. Watch your mouth."

"Sorry."

"Pause your machine and come up front. I want to go over your performance review."

"Okay." Kayla pressed a button on her keyboard. A red

banner flashed on the screen with the word *Paused* on it. She carefully slipped off her headset, not wanting to get it tangled in her hair.

It was a long walk from the back of the office to the front, and everyone Kayla passed, no matter how busy they were, had to stop and look at her. Some of the men leaned back beyond the fabric walls of their cubicles watching her walk, each having lust-struck looks on their faces.

She felt their stares, but ignored them. It was something she always had to deal with, but still couldn't completely understand. Even Mark, her boss, had that stare when she saw him at his desk.

"Have a seat," he said with his Floridian drawl. Mark rummaged through a pile of papers looking for her file. "You doing all right?"

"Sure."

"Good." He pulled a folder from the bottom of a pile. "Here we go. Let's see. Yep, you are doing all right." He leaned over to her showing the statistical breakdown of her work for the last month. "You made a 115% quota on credit protection, 94% on the legal service program, and a whopping 125% on the auto club. When added up, that comes out above quota on the combined programs, but just off bonus. The legal program hurt you. Work on that."

"Okay."

"You missed two days last month. Bad girl."

"Sorry."

"You'll do better. Sign on the dotted line, ma'am." Mark handed the pen to Kayla, then stared at her smooth hand as she signed the review. "Heard you finally got a gig?"

"Yeah. We're at the Cambridge Square Saturday."

"On Himes?"

"No, Palm -- north of Downtown."

"Oh yeah."

"I'll catch your act one of these days. Just been too busy lately." Mark took the file back from Kayla. "That's it. Thank you, Miss Kayla."

"Thank you."

Mark closed the folder and slipped it back into his drawer. His eyes gravitated to Kayla as she walked away. An unconscious sigh slipped through his mouth, and that caught the attention of a woman supervisor who sat in the next desk. Mark met her disapproving stare with a sheepish shrug. "She had a hot month."

Twenty-eight -- twenty-nine -- thirty. Matt felt blood pumping in his muscles from doing push-ups. He sat up and inspected the amount of cut in his upper arms showing through his shirt. He was on the porch of the bungalow offices of casting director May Stadler, but he wasn't alone. Seven other young black actors had the same idea. It sounded like a steam engine with these guys exhaling on each push-up.

Matt stood, stretched, then walked back into the lobby to stay cool. Inside, there wasn't a place to sit with another twenty black men patiently waiting their turns to read for the director. So, Matt pulled his folded script from a back pocket and stood against a wall.

Being black and actors were the only things these men had in common. Some had light skin. Some were dark. Some were very tall, while others were short. Some were muscular and athletic. Others were fat. Some were drop-dead handsome, while others were dead-drop ugly.

Matt looked around the lobby sizing up his competition. The others did the same. As they were sizing up each other, one question circulated through all their minds. What type of black man were they looking for in this role?

Two actors dressed in sharp suits walked out of back office and quickly exited the lobby. Matt saw how they were dressed and straightened the collar of his casual shirt.

May stepped through the door with a clipboard in her hand. “Ben Kelly! Kush Daddy! And Matthew Redcrop! You’re up next. Come on in.”

Matt was the first to the door catching May’s attention. “Let’s see,” she mumbled, thumbing through the headshots on her clipboard. “Matthew?”

“That’s me.”

“Good. You’re third in the group. Have a seat inside.”

Matt walked into a surprisingly spacious lounge with three blue couches and a plush, gray carpet. He sat in the couch closest to the director’s office.

“You’re Kush, right?” May asked outside.

“Right.”

“Have a seat inside.”

A dark, smooth looking actor with short twisted hair strutted into the lounge and gave Matt a compulsory nod. “S’up, bruh?”

“Hiya doin’?”

Kush took a seat across from Matt, confidently cross his legs, and stuck a toothpick in his mouth. He wore a black suit and a gray silk shirt with an open collar showing a glowing gold chain. After seeing Kush, Matt felt woefully underdressed until --.

"Ben?"

"Yes, ma'am."

"Have a seat inside."

– Until Ben walked into the lounge. He wore only a T-shirt and saggy, baggy jeans, something that must have been hard to find considering his degree of obesity.

"Hey," Ben said, tugging up his pants to keep them from sagging too low.

"S'up?" Matt responded.

Kush only nodded.

"Don't forget to sign in, fellas," May said to the others in the lobby. The door closed, muffling her chatter.

The three men looked at each other with puzzled eyes; the same question crossing their minds.

Matt snickered and shook his head. "Yeah, we came out for the same role."

Kush smiled. "Any negro in a pinch."

"Really," Ben said.

They became silent when May marched back into the lounge.

"Give me a moment, fellas." She placed her clipboard on a small table with a printer. From behind it, she pulled out a digital camera. "First, let's get some stills. Ben, you're first. Step up to the wall and give me your best smile."

Ben did as she asked, expanding his chubby cheeks wide. May snapped the picture, and the printer came to life extruding a small photo.

Kush was next, then Matt. May picked up the pictures and gave them quick inspections.

"All right. Ben's first inside, then Kush, then Matthew. Just relax and listen to the director. Break a leg, fellas." May placed the camera behind the printer, and took the photos and her clipboard into the director's office.

The lounge was almost sound proof. The humming air conditioning system dominating the silence. The three actors waited together without a word or a glance between them. Each actor was alone with his thoughts, eying their scripts, praying internally the director would find him perfect for the role.

Muffled voices behind the director's door pulled Matt's attention from the script. He leaned his head closer to the door to hear better, but the words were too faint. He returned his attention back to the pages on his lap. He mentally tested his emotional buttons looking for choices within words that offered little guidance. It was just an interrogation scene.

After five minutes, the door opened and an actor walked out with a smile on his face. Matt heard laughing inside, but was too shy to look in the doorway.

May leaned through the door.

"Ben?"

Relieved his wait was over, Ben almost leaped off the couch, and hustled into the office. May closed the door behind him.

The silence returned. Each minute seemed an hour, and five of them passed before the door opened again. Ben walked out, looked at Matt and shook his head before leaving. Matt wondered what that meant.

"Kush Daddy?" May called.

Kush stood, tugged on the sleeves of his suit jacket, making sure it hung correctly from his shoulders, then strolled into the office without a look in Matt's direction. May pulled the door shut.

This time the wait was longer, nearly seven minutes. Matt grew jittery, not from fear of the director or the audition. Matt had dozens of auditions like this. A few of them he had won. But in the last year he had a losing streak of eight failures in a row, each eroding his confidence, each feeling like a final chance. He needed a victory on this one.

His palms became damp so he wiped them on his jeans, then lifted the script for closer evaluation. He whispered the words searching for the slightest emotional emphasis. He believed each line was a world of motivations and underlying tensions, but which ones were right for the director's artistic sense?

"Thanks, Kush," May said, holding the door for him. "I'll see you this evening."

"Solid." Kush nodded at Matt as he walked out the door.

"Matthew, we're ready for you."

He took a deep breath and entered a surprisingly small office which only had a table, little more than a card-table, and three metal chairs. Behind the table was a bearded man with a kind face, and a tired looking woman.

May placed her hand on Matt's shoulder. "This gentleman is Matthew Redcrop, SAG-AFTRA-Equity. Matthew, I'd like you to meet Director Andy Shearer and his assistant Lourdes Brown."

"Nice to meet you," Matt said.

"Pleased to meet you too. Is it Matthew or Matt?" Andy asked.

"You can call me Matt."

"Would y'all excuse me?" May asked. "I have to prep the next group."

"Sure," Andy said. May left Matt standing alone before Andy and Lourdes. "So, is Matthew Redcrop your real name?"

"Sure is."

"I had to ask after meeting a guy named Kush Daddy. Is that Indian or something?"

"No. I guess I had an ancestor in Virginia who grew red cabbage or something just after the civil war." Andy and Lourdes chuckled.

"Tell me more about yourself, Matt," Andy said.

Matt rolled his eyes toward a ceiling light. "I'm a native of Youngstown, Ohio -- a graduate of Cleveland State University in Theater Arts. I studied under Colby and Winnstead, and I'm continuing my studies under Shelley Isaacson in a workshop here in Tampa."

"That's fine, but that's on your resume. I want to know about you, Matt. Tell me about you, the person."

Matt tightened his grip on the script. "I'm an actor, another starving artist. I love anything artistic. I have a love/hate relationship with the process of making it in this business. That's an art in itself, you know." Andy nodded in agreement as Matt continued. "I play guitar, sometimes for money. I like sports and travel, and I never do enough of either." Matt paused and smiled broadly. "You know, if we have another hour, I could go on and on."

"Oh no. That's fine. But what brought you to Tampa? I never thought of Tampa as a prime destination for theater majors."

"My girlfriend and I both hated winters. We found

Tampa warmer, and far more affordable than New York. And there's a lot of TV and film work around here too. You're here, right? We figured we could build up some credits, save some money, and maybe move to sunny L-A for more ambitious work."

Andy nodded in agreement. "Sounds like a plan. Now, Matt, what we're planning on doing is a hard-edged, reality based mini-series called *Tropical Knights*. It might become a series one day, who knows. The role you'll be reading for is a rookie detective, Damon Jennings. At best, it's a featured role. You'll be one of a team of assistants supporting the lead character. Did you have a chance to go over the sides?"

"Yeah." Matt held up the script.

"Good. We're starting on page thirty-four. Lourdes will feed you your cues. Be natural. Let's see what you can do. Need a minute?"

"Yeah."

"Take your time."

Matt opened the script to the reading, quickly scanned the first lines. Taking a deep breath, he dropped the script to the floor.

"Ready."

Lourdes smiled, then turned her eyes to the paper. She read coldly with no emphasis or feeling. "I was watching TV on my bed when I heard the first shot. I thought it was a firecracker. But then I heard two more quick shots -- pow-pow. I went to my window and I saw a man on the ground with another man looking over him."

Matt walked closer to Lourdes and gestured with one of his hands, hoping to pull from himself a dramatic power that could carry the reading. "You said the man was white, about 5-7 and 140 pounds?"

"Yeah, and very pale looking too. I didn't get a good look at his face because he wore this black ninja suit with a hood. The man lingered over the body. He almost looked like he was laughing. He looked around for witnesses. That's when I ducked out of my window."

"So, you didn't actually see the shots fired?"

"No."

"Did you see anyone else?" Matt asked.

"No. When I tried to sneak another peek, I saw the man running through the woods toward the golf course."

"What did you do then?"

"I called the cops right away. I swear. Then, I went down to see if I could help the man."

"Did you touch the body at all?"

"No, sir."

"Did you know the Pritchards personally?" Matt asked.

"No. And I'm sorry about that. My business keeps me so busy."

"Thank you, Mr. Adams."

Lourdes looked up from the script and smiled.

Andy nodded, impressed by Matt's preparedness. "Nicely done. I tell you what, Matt. After dinner, we'll be calling back a few of the guys for a second reading. Why don't you hang around too. I want you to think about the character in terms of this being Damon's first interrogation, and it's with someone he greatly admires. I want to see that this evening in your second reading, okay?"

"Yes, sir."

"Be back here by seven."

"Thank you."

"Sure. On the way out, tell May we're ready for the next group."

"Okay. Thanks again."

Matt returned home around 10:30 that evening after performing well for the director again. He ran up the stairs, unlocked the door and rushed inside only to find Kayla asleep on the couch wearing a short denim skirt and a t-shirt.

He picked up the TV remote, turned down the sound then knelt in front of her. Moving some of her hair aside Matt began nibbling on her nose.

Kayla felt the tickling of Matt's lips intruding into a dream, and a smile grew on her face. She raised an arm and draped it around his neck pulling him closer for a sleepy kiss. She blinked her eyes until her vision cleared.

"Hey, sleepy head," he said.

"How did you do?"

"My best audition yet. This one might be it, babe."

Kayla swung her legs around and folded them under her as she sat-up. "Call-backs can't be bad."

"That's for sure. I don't want to get ahead of myself 'cause I'll probably have to do another reading next week. But baby, if I was the director, I would consider myself perfect for the role."

"Now stay level," Kayla counseled.

"I am. It looks good though."

"I hope it is. But stay level."

"I am."

"Level?"

"Level."

"Good. What time is it?" Kayla asked.

"10:30."

"You better get some sleep. Don't you have an overnighter tonight?"

"Yeah. But I'm too keyed up to sleep."

"What did I say?"

"I know -- level."

"Good." Kayla pulled Matt toward her. "Layout here and relax." Matt rested his head on her lap. "You want something to eat?"

"Food? No."

Kayla ran her finger nails over his scalp. She picked up the TV remote and raised the sound of a newscast, then quickly switched to another station. Matt, noticing the sweet lavender fragrance of her thighs, pushed his nose against her skin. He extended his tongue and took a tiny lick. Feeling a tickle, Kayla flinched and looked down.

"I thought you weren't hungry."

"Not for food." Matt turned over and worked the top of his head just under her skirt hem while gently nibbling higher areas of her thigh. "Still want to eat though." Matt immersed his head under her skirt making Kayla drop the remote. She unfurled her legs and closed her eyes. She hunched down and held Matt behind his head, careful not to push herself too hard against his face.

"I hope -- you like – my cooking."

Matt's mind was at rest. With his eyes closed, comfort engulfed him, caressing his body, sending him on his way to a world of dreams.

"Matt?"

Though he needed to, Matt didn't want to listen to the little voice calling his name through an earphone.

"Hey, Matt? Fifteen seconds."

Matt nodded his head without opening his eyes. It was the only part of his body responding. Exhaustion paralyzed his arms and legs.

"Ten seconds."

He wanted to squeeze out these last few seconds of dozing.

"Five – four – three – two – one –"

Matt heard the music coming back from a break. His eyes snapped open. He sat up straight in his chair, and blinked until his vision cleared.

"Go, Matt," the voice in his ear said.

He faced a studio camera and its piercing red light.

"And welcome back to Watch N' Shop. I'm Matt, bringing you the best values in video shopping. Stay with us, because this hour we have that big, 65-inch HD TV, surround sound, by Hiyoshi. Stay with us for that. We also have jewelry including an exquisite ruby and diamond cocktail ring, five carats of genuine stones. Stay with us for that.

"But first, off the top of the hour, we have an 18-karat gold neck-chain, number 505-167. This is a rope link with diamond cut notches making this thing really sparkle. It's twenty inches in length, one quarter inch thick. Its normal retail value is 560 dollars, this morning we are offering it at only 115 dollars and 99 cents. This deal is on for only four minutes so get on your phone and call the number at the bottom of the screen. It's toll free. Or use any app for your devices at WNS.com."

As Matt went on with his pitch, he noticed increasing activity in the vast phone room beyond the camera. Hundreds of operators, scattered over dozens of rows, were talking to customers and taking their orders. His computer monitor showed over a thousand dollars a minute pouring in for that gold chain.

Except for a few commercial breaks, it was push-push-push for Matt all night. Even though it was three o'clock in the morning, he couldn't allow his computer to show anything less than a thousand dollars a minute.

By six o'clock, Matt's show had ended. All he wanted to do was go home and sleep, but he had to wait for the revenue report. He stood by his producer who also waited for the data from the computer.

"Here it comes," she said. A printer quietly pushed out the paper. The producer pulled the copy, folded it, and tore off a copy of the report for Matt. "Good show. Over $187,000 in three hours."

"Thanks, Janice."

"When are you on next?"

"I don't know. Usually the weekend."

"All right. I'll see you later."

"Yeah." Matt waved at some of the phone operators as he walked out of the studio. He wandered through the crowded backstage area receiving little acknowledgment from the production assistants who were too busy scurrying around, searching for products for the next show.

He checked his mailbox in the sales host office. The only thing in there was his schedule for the next seven days. He had three shows to do, all overnighters.

"Shit," he whispered. Those shifts always made him feel more dead than alive, but after every overnighter, a smile grew his face, because nothing could be more beautiful than a Florida dawn. That's what met him as stepped outside the studio. The rising tangerine sun over a mangrove lined bay brought him back to life, and it faced him as he drove east over a long causeway between Clearwater and Tampa. He kept the windows open allowing the briny air to blow through his car.

When Matt came home, Kayla was already up and dressed. They only had time enough for a brief kiss, because she was already running late for her job.

After she left, Matt took a small bowl of corn flakes and milk, and sat next to the living room window, watching the morning traffic pass on Seventh Avenue. The rest of the day belonged to him, but in the sunbathed living room, he soon fell asleep on the couch.

Chapter 3

Two young men sat on the floor of the workshop's stage, both facing Shelley and the hot lights. She paced downstage with her back to them, lecturing to the other actors.

"How can I coach you?" she asked. "I can't coach anyone who doesn't understand this process. I won't coach anyone. Why? Because how can I teach something that'll take years for you to learn or experience, and pack it into a tidy, handy-dandy, one-hour course? It just doesn't work that way." She turned back to the two actors on stage. "Mike, Neil, I need you to work more on this scene. Please -- please, think about your character obligations. And I know it's different from anything you've done before. But you can't just think this through or talk this through. It has to come out through your own life experiences. Use what you have inside. Pull your guts out, men, and spread them on this stage for everyone to see. Got it?"

"Yeah," both actors said.

"Okay, I want you to take a moment. Find what it takes inside to give this scene more life." Shelley hopped off the front edge of the stage and took a seat in the front row.

Matt and Albert sat together among the other actors behind her watching the scene.

Kayla and Jenny were in a quiet dance studio in the back of the theater. They sat in metal chairs facing each other, reading a film script aloud.

Jenny leaned forward.

"T-J, this is me -- your old roomie. Talk to me."

"Why do you have him locked up?" Kayla responded.

"He may be wanted on several federal charges."

"What charges?"

"Kidnapping you for one."

"He saved my life. I love him."

"You love him?" Jenny asked. Kayla nodded in response. Jenny leaned back in her chair and stared at her. "Nothing's definite about the charges. But, you better talk to me. That man may have killed ten terrorists and cured eighteen people of life threatening injuries. The U.S. Government wants to know how he did it. You're the only person known to have been with him. So, how did he do it?"

"I don't know."

"You were shot. How did he heal you?"

"He -- uh. I really don't know."

"T-J! Come on!"

"I SAID I DON'T KNOW!" Kayla responded.

Jenny paused and sighed. "All right. I'm sorry. I don't want you to get upset." Jenny pushed her hair back. "Is he the one?"

"What?"

"You know -- what you were talking about in college. Is he the one?"

Kayla rarely had to look at her script by this time. She locked her eyes on Jenny's face. "You always ridiculed me in college for my beliefs. Why are you so interested now?"

"Because, after what I've seen in this case, I'm almost convinced maybe you might be on to something. Yes or no, is he the one?"

Kayla's eyes shifted and began blinking rapidly. She turned her head downward.

"T-J!" Jenny shouted.

"No," Kayla said softly.

"No? Then who the hell is this guy?"

Kayla looked up and smiled playfully. "He's -- no one."

The women paused. Jenny was the first to drop out of character. She sighed, adjusted her hair again, and smiled. "Kay-Kay!"

Jenny and Kayla high-fived each other.

"Jen-Jen! You were right. That worked perfectly."

"That's all you have to do. Read the script over several times so you'll know the concept. Then improvise your lines. It's always surprising how close your responses are to the script."

"And it forces me to listen better too. Matt was trying to tell me about that technique."

"See how simple it is?" Jenny said.

"Yeah."

"We can try the scene next Tuesday on stage, if you want."

"Sure. I feel great about it now." Kayla checked her watch. "It's almost break-time. Let's go."

The two women walked out of the dance studio in time to hear applause for the two actors on stage. Kayla and Jenny quickly took their seats near Matt and Albert.

"Much better!" Shelley said. "I'll expect even higher quality next Tuesday." The two men on stage rolled their eyes and walked off the stage. Shelley turned out to the other actors, then checked her watch. "Okay, before we take ten. We have some serious news around here. First, I want to acknowledge Matt Redcrop. Yesterday, he auditioned for director Andy Shearer who is putting together a TV mini-series. And Matt got a call-back! Now, I know, through some of my sources, he may be among the final three for a major role in this project. So, he's on the verge. And I'm so proud of him." Shelley began clapping her hands and the others joined her.

Matt was surprised by that little piece of inside information from Shelley.

"Now, that's some news," Kayla said, squeezing his arm.

"Sure is," Matt said.

Albert playfully elbowed Matt. "What did I tell you, kid."

"I haven't got the part yet."

"It's a cinch."

"Keep it up, Matt," Shelley said.

"Thanks."

"Second, Ben Kingsley is coming to town to shoot a film in January. And the production company wants me to help with the principal and extra casting. That means plenty of opportunities available for some of you in here, especially my SAG women. Expect to hear calls from your agent, Jenny." Shelley winked at her. "You too, Sara -- and possibly for you too, Kayla. There may be something for almost everyone. And remember, even if it's only an extra part, it's still a film credit -- with Ben Kingsley no less. Use it. All right, people, take ten and only ten. We still have two scenes left."

Cambridge Square, little more than a warehouse posing as a combination organic food court, coffee shop, and craft market, was especially busy on Saturday afternoon. With so much space to cover, many customers needed a place to rest.

In the middle of the complex was an open square filled with shaded tables and hungry shoppers. There were few unoccupied seats, and that churned Kayla's intestines as she stepped onto the square's little performance stage.

Her eyes scanned the tables and the surrounding bars. When some of the people looked back at her, she turned away from them and toward her comfort, Matt, who was busy checking a little tripod holding his tablet for their recording.

He looked up at her and noticed her nervousness. "You okay?"

"Not really," she whispered, not wanting the microphone to pick up her words.

"We did this before."

"Two times. And in front of our friends."

"You were great. Do what you did before. We'll be all right. I'm rolling video on this."

"Just great." Kayla exhaled forcefully, resigned to the fact she had to go through with this. She slipped off her sandals searching for more comfort. She shook-out her legs like a track star, capturing the attention of some of the male customers at the nearby bars.

Matt sat on a stool at Kayla's side, picked up his acoustic

guitar and strummed a few notes, tuning each string. He then looked up at Kayla who had her eyes closed, releasing tension by rolling her head and blowing out her breath.

"Ready?" Matt asked.

"Does it matter?"

"No."

"Right. Let's get started."

Matt nodded and began fingering the strings of his guitar vigorously. Jazzy cadences resonated from the wooden instrument in his arms. His foot tapped and his head bobbed up and down, keeping the rhythm. Matt's instrumental was compact and competent, but did little to hush the din of the square.

Kayla opened her eyes and saw Shawnda, her co-worker, standing at the edge of the square behind them. Shawnda waved and Kayla waved back. She then closed her eyes again. With her cue coming up, Kayla turned around and put both hands on the microphone, holding it like a shield against prying eyes. She glanced out and saw Albert and Jenny at a side table. Knowing they were there brought out a smile on Kayla's face. She swayed to the music and closed her eyes again.

Matt reached her cue, and paused on a note. When it faded, Kayla brought her lips close to the microphone and allowed her silky voice to flow forth. Without opening her eyes, she sang softly, swaying side-to-side. Soon, it didn't matter who watched her or what they thought. She was in a private world, making love to every note. And Matt loved watching her sing for that very reason.

When Shawnda heard Kayla's voice, her mouth dropped open and she walked around to the front of the stage. Albert and Jenny turned to each other, surprised by Kayla's smooth sound. Even the din of coffee-shop faded for a short period of time. But Kayla didn't notice those things.

When they finished their forty-minute set, the coffee house was full of applauding shoppers and diners. Kayla embraced Matt, relieved about surviving their show. She held him tightly like a baby's blanket, not wanting to let go.

"You were great," Matt whispered. "I'm proud of you." Kayla's whole body felt hot. He felt her forehead. "Feels like you have a fever, babe."

"I'm okay."

"Hey, kids," Albert called.

Matt and Kayla looked out, and saw Albert and Jenny approaching them.

"Hey. Thanks for coming," Matt said.

"Wow! Just wow," Jenny said. She embraced Kayla, then stepped over and hugged Matt. "Both of you were so surprising."

"Thank you," Kayla said.

Albert opened his arms wide and embraced Kayla. "It takes a lot to impress me. But kid, you impressed me." He embraced her again and felt the unusual heat of her body. "You have a fever or something?"

"No. Just nerves."

Albert stepped over and gave Matt a back-slapping embrace. "I didn't see any nerves. I saw a damn good singer, and a damn good guitar player."

"Thanks, that's nice of you," Kayla said.

"Hey, I'm serious. I hold my praises tightly."

"Y'all doing anything the rest of the day?" Jenny asked.

"No, not really," Matt said.

"Good. Want to get a bite and some drinks?"

"I'm buyin'," Albert said.

"Here?"

"No. Ybor."

Matt looked at Kayla, and she shrugged positively while wiping her brow with a napkin. "Sure. We just have to clean up a little," he said. "Meet you outside?"

"We can give you a hand," Albert offered.

"Need help?" Jenny asked.

They had little to carry, just Matt's guitar, amplifiers, cables, and Matt's tablet. There was space to spare inside Matt's car trunk.

When they reached Ybor City, they couldn't agree on a restaurant. So, they settled on carryout Chinese food and a couple of bottles of wine. They drove back to Matt and Kayla's apartment. For most of the rest of the hot afternoon, they sat in cool comfort. One bottle of wine sat empty on the coffee table surrounded by Chinese food cartons and brown paper bags. Kayla knelt on the floor pouring wine into her glass from a second bottle.

Albert waved his glass at her. "Can I get another hit, Kay?"

"Sure."

Albert leaned out from the couch and took the bottle.

"I don't understand. Just Matt, that's all? What's the matter with using your full name?" Jenny asked.

"I didn't want my full name soiled," Matt said. "Redcrop is a noble name. At least to me it is." He took a sip of his wine. "Anyway, I don't want my family name associated with Watch N' Shop."

"No. Just your family face, I guess," Albert said, placing the bottle back on the table.

"Nobody watches overnight."

"Yeah? Somebody's buyin' that shit on your show. You watch, one day when you're famous, somebody will find a tape of you hostin' a fake jewelry show and put it on a TV show sayin' this was how Matthew Redcrop made money ten years ago."

"No last name gives me plausible deniability."

"Yeah, right. Plausible deniability," Kayla said. She sat-up, grabbed Matt's face, and spoke with an announcer-like voice. "Is this television sales host really the movie star Matthew Redcrop? The resemblance is truly remarkable."

Jenny stood and said, "And if he isn't, who is this man known only as Matt? Is it just a coincidence the crash of the fake jewelry market worldwide is associated with this man's disappearance? We may never know." Jenny took the bottle, and sat down next to Kayla.

"The investigation will never cease," Kayla said.

"The truth will be known," Jenny said.

Kayla added, "Tune in next week --"

"You silly girls done yet?" Matt asked.

"Not until the case is solved, Matt-man," Jenny said.

"Jen-Jen. Anyway, it's just until next spring anyway."

"Next spring? What happens then?" Jenny asked.

"L-A," Matt said, Kayla nodding in agreement.

"You set a date?" Albert asked.

"March. The lease is up in March. The lease on the furniture is up in March. By then, between Kayla and me, we'll have a few thousand dollars to carry us for a few months out there. We both have our union cards. We may never have a better chance to make the move."

"Damn," Albert said.

"Damn what?"

"Just damn." Albert took another sip of his wine. "Hope you know what to expect."

"We already have information about apartments out there." Kayla hopped up on her feet, grabbed a tablet off a shelf, and clicked on a website showcasing Los Angeles apartments. "We're zeroing in on Culver City and North Hollywood. There are some pretty good deals in those areas." She handed the tablet to Albert.

Jenny sat next to him and looked at the guide with him. Albert slid his finger over the screen, looking at each deal as it passed his view. "Guides are fine. But have either of you been there before?" he asked.

"No," Matt said.

Albert made a smacking sound with his mouth and shook his head. "The business there is like nothin' you've ever experienced."

"Come on," Matt said.

"I not kiddin'," Albert said. "When are you goin' out there to scout around?"

"I don't know. Maybe a month before we move," Kayla said.

Albert laughed. "Shit. You need a contact. You won't find a good apartment without one. And when I say a good apartment, I mean somethin' that's clean, affordable, close to the action, and not fought over by street gangs."

"So, what do you suggest?" Matt asked.

"Fear not, my children, for I am Albert. I know a contact who's a rental agent at a nice complex in Culver City."

"Who?"

"My old buddy Milo."

"Milo?" Kayla asked. "The guy in *Now You See Me?*"

"Yep."

"I thought you said he was a success story."

"He is. I didn't say he made a million dollars a picture, but he's a workin' actor who just happens to be out of work three hundred days of the year. Now, if you want to make it a go, I can call him and see if he can hook you up in his complex."

"We're months away from even packing," Matt said.

"That's fine. I'll call him next week. Then I'll give you his number, and you'll call him. Don't waste your time on this crap." He tossed the tablet into the couch. "You don't want to be homeless in L-A."

"It can't be that bad," Kayla said.

"Well, maybe I'm a little cautious. Actually, it's not so bad once you know your way around. Bring some good maps though. The traffic's worse than Tampa's. The weather's cooler and dryer. The beaches are not as nice as Florida. But the people -- man, you ain't never seen such a variety of people. Culver City's a good choice. It's a relatively safe, middle class kind of town."

"Sounds good," Matt said. "I don't know about Kayla, but I'm pretty hyped about our chances out there."

"I am too," Kayla said. "I just don't like the idea of a 3,000-mile move."

"We managed the Cleveland to Tampa move smoothly."

"That doesn't mean it wasn't hard."

"Were you two living together in Cleveland?" Jenny asked.

"No," Kayla said. "Matt had a dorm. I commuted."

"But when I said I was moving to Tampa, she discovered she was hooked on my love," Matt added.

"Stop it," Kayla responded.

"The girl couldn't live without me."

"You're cracked."

"She told me Cleveland would be a cold lonely place without me."

"You said that to me," Kayla said.

"She begged me to take her."

"The truth of the matter is he begged me to come with him."

"You were the one begging, babe," Matt said.

"Nope-nope-nope --"

"Yes, you were."

"No, I wasn't."

"I believe Kay," Albert said.

"Why are you believing her?"

"I look at you, then I look at her. Believe me, kid, Kay doesn't look the type to go beggin' for nothin'."

"So, what are trying to say?" Matt said.

Albert finished his wine with one last gulp. "I'm sayin', count your blessins, young black man." Albert held up his empty glass.

Jenny scooted over and snuggled close to Albert, running her fingers through his silver hair. "I know you count your blessings, don't you?" she asked.

"I do, sweetie." Albert pulled Jenny close. "I do." Albert and Jenny kissed briefly.

"Anyway, I'm glad we're both here," Matt said. "Though sometimes I think we should've gone straight to L-A. Remember all that talk about Hollywood coming to Florida little by little?"

"Yeah," Jenny said.

"That was a lie."

"Damn right it was," Albert said. "Hollywood will always be out there. And I understand your ambition. I used to have it myself, but they took it from me."

Jenny continued smoothing some of the silver locks on Albert's head. "You know, I'll have to try Hollywood someday too," she said.

"Of course. Every ambitious actor has to try her. That's fine as long as you remember Hollywood's like a prude with a whore's reputation. She'll lure everyone to her, then slap them all for testin' her warped virtue." Albert looked around, rolling the empty wine glass in his hands. "Anymore Sauvignon, Kay?"

"Sure."

Chapter 4

Monday's lunch traffic packed Seventh Avenue. Revving motors and car horns melded together to form a low rumble echoing off the old buildings, but inside each of them was refreshing silence.

Matt slept peacefully after pulling another overnighter on Watch N' Shop. It would take quite a sound to disturb his rest, a sound like the bugle fanfare ringtone on his phone. The jolting first sound caused him to roll over. The second opened his eyes. The third made him remember about an important call from his agent this week. He sat-up and quickly grabbed his phone.

"Hello?"

"Matt?" a woman's voice answered.

"Yeah."

"Eileen."

"Hey!"

Eileen paused, Matt hearing a pensive swallow on the other end.

"Sorry."

"What? I didn't get it?" he asked.

"No. They canceled the third reading. Shearer decided on that Kush Daddy guy."

"Kush Daddy?"

"Yeah."

"Shit. Shit!"

"Shearer liked you, Matt. He may call you on another project, but on this one, Kush tested higher among the sponsors and consultants."

"You gotta be kidding me."

"It's all right," Eileen said. "We have a couple more things coming up. Stay loose."

"Yeah. That's all I can do."

"And don't doubt yourself. I know your work. I know you can do it."

"Yeah, well -- thanks for the chance, Eileen."

"Sure. By the way, I need updated headshots for your file. You're getting a more mature look."

"I'll send them over."

"Okay. Take it easy, Matt."

"I will, thanks." Matt set his phone on the night stand then violently jerked the sheets off the bed. Everything about his day came to a halt. He couldn't sleep any longer, so he sat on the couch watching TV all day. He rarely moved from that spot, and didn't eat.

When Kayla came home from work, she found him still in his robe and shorts sprawled on the couch watching afternoon reality shows. Matt turned his vacant eyes toward Kayla, and her smile faded. Seeing Matt in this state before, Kayla already knew what troubled him. "You didn't get the part?"

"No."

Kayla sat next to him and pulled him close. She began

rubbing his shoulders, but Matt kept his eyes on the television. "Who got it?"

"This Kush Daddy guy."

"Kush what?"

"Kush --" Matt shook his head. "Shit," he whispered. "I thought I had this one. This was the big one."

"I know, but there'll be others." Kayla sighed disappointedly. A part of his dream was hers as well. She closed her eyes and shook her head. "Damn." She shook her head again, then continued rubbing Matt's shoulders. "Oh well. You coming to workshop tonight?"

"I guess so."

"Jenny and I have a scene."

"I'll be there."

"I want to change things about myself that I can't change. You know, be prettier -- be taller -- have longer legs -- bigger tits, without surgery I mean -- and so on." Jenny sat on a metal chair with her legs crossed at center stage of the workshop. She unconsciously rocked, and spoke through a sweet natural smile. "I need to feel better about myself, I guess. But I also want to be better in other people's eyes. Sometimes it just doesn't matter about how you feel about yourself, you know. If it were up to me, I'd never lose an audition. But I need something more when it comes to how others look at me, especially directors. I want that something. I need to find a way to get it."

"Cut! What do you got against tit implants?" Shelley asked. Laughter broke the silence of the workshop.

"They might leak."

"Awe, they solved that problem. Try saline or soy oil, honey."

"You talk you have some experience with this."

"Discussion closed." The other actors chuckled again. "You have a scene coming up with Kayla?"

"Yeah."

"You're up first after the break. Let's take ten so we can get everything in before ten."

Matt was already outside when Shelley called break. He sat on a low brick wall enclosing small shrubs, and watched a crowd of high school kids gathering at a theater across the street. Many wore strange costumes as if it were a Halloween party. A gust of wind rustled the palm leaves, and whipped up their black capes and shawls.

Feeling a chill, Matt buttoned up his shirt a little higher than normal, and lowered his rolled-up sleeves.

Albert emerged from the building with three other actors. He pulled out a cigarette, placed it in his mouth and lit it. He saw Matt sitting on the nearby wall and walked toward him. "Hey, kid." Matt turned and gave Albert a nod. "You still in a funk?"

"Naw, I'm all right," Matt said. "I just have to gather myself for the next push. Is it break?"

"Yeah." Albert braced one of his legs on the wall and took a drag of his cigarette. He looked across the street at the crowd of teenagers lining up in front of the theater. "Looks like Halloween or somethin'. Is that a Rocky Horror show over there?"

"No, a deathpunk concert."

"Don't those kids have school tomorrow?" Albert took another long drag. "It's Tuesday night."

"You should see Friday and Saturday, when the grown folks come to party all up and down this street."

Albert chuckled and blew out some smoke. "I think Jenny and Kayla are the first ones up for scene study after the break. You comin' back in?"

"Yeah."

Albert took another drag, and allowed the smoke to pour out of his mouth and nose. "Listen, Matt. I know how you wanted that role, but you need to have a tougher hide than this when you go west."

"I'm fine."

"It's not goin' to get any easier."

"Hell, I haven't won an audition in over a year. When you're on a losing streak like mine, you start to have doubts. And I'm just in Tampa."

"Different markets, kid. Lower budget films, lower priority roles. Here, you're just a local -- a non-pro in their eyes. Take your union cards to Hollywood, and you'll have a shot at somethin' special, even starrin' roles. You may not get any of those either, but at least you'll have a higher level of rejection."

Matt turned to Albert and saw him nodding with a slightly deranged look in his eyes. Matt allowed a soft laugh to filter through his lips. "A higher level of rejection?"

"That's right, kid."

"My dream come true. Thanks."

"Think of it," Albert said. "You'll be a rejected star rather than a rejected day player." Albert finished his cigarette, flicked the butt toward a nearby waste basket and missed it. "Come on. Let's get back inside."

Their last lines spoken, Jenny sat on a desk leaning forward toward Kayla who sat in a chair. Each held their characters until the other actors began clapping their approval.

"Cut! Wonderful!" Shelley removed her glasses and clapped with the other actors. "For a first time, that was wonderful, girls." Kayla and Jenny relaxed and smiled. Shelley stood and hopped up on stage. "There were some wonderful subtextual things happening in your faces, especially you, Kayla. You were very surprising to me, and far more in command of your part than before. Now, Jenny, it seems your character brought Kayla's character into for questioning. Is that right?"

"Yeah."

"One thing you might experiment with next time is, what if Kayla was the one coming into the station, demanding the answers at the beginning of the scene. By the end of the scene, you would still have to be in charge, right?"

"Yeah."

"I want you to explore how your character can turn the tables on Kayla by the end of this scene. Try it, and see what you can discover."

"Okay," Jenny said.

"Wonderful work, girls."

"Thank you," they both said. Kayla and Jenny hopped off the front of the stage and went back to their seats.

"Next scene, *True West* -- Kip and James!"

An overnight rain put a shine on Ybor's old streets and sidewalks. Even with the intense sun, it was still unusually chilly for a November morning in Tampa.

Kayla pulled her sweater tighter before walking out the door of her building. As soon as she stepped on the sidewalk, she almost bumped into the shopping cart of a homeless man.

He wore layers of stained old clothes, and was too ashamed to look in her face when he asked, "Would you have any extra change to spare, Miss?"

Kayla caught a whiff of his stench and leaned away, trying not to show her offense. "I'm sorry. I'm a little short myself."

"Okay. God bless you."

"Sorry." The man pushed his cart away and Kayla tightened her sweater again, lowering her nose to the collar checking for any offensive scent from that man.

A young woman decorating the display window of an antique shop saw Kayla and waved at her. Kayla waved back, then strolled down the sidewalk. Her hair caught the cool breeze as she passed Carlotta's restaurant. From there, Kayla saw the old theater building housing Shelley's acting workshop. The building was unusually busy this morning with small groups of attractive young women entering it.

Kayla reached into a pocket of her sweater and fingered a group of folded papers. She checked her watch, then hastened her pace. She arrived at the workshop door at the same time as two other women whom she had never met.

When they went inside, they all had to wait in line to sign in for their auditions. A young assistant of Shelley's, Beth, sat behind a table with three sign-in sheets. Beth immediately recognized Kayla and gave her a smile, then went back to processing the actresses coming through the lobby. "Put your name, union affiliation if any, and call time on the sign-in sheets as you come in. Have a seat in the theater, and wait for your name to be called. We are on schedule."

Kayla stepped up to the table. "Hi, Beth."

"Hey, Kayla. Which part are you in for?"

"The cocktail waitress."

Beth slid one of the sign-in sheets over to her. "This is your sheet. You need sides?"

Kayla pulled the folded two-page script from her pocket and showed Beth. "I have them."

"Good. Break a leg."

"Thanks."

Beth stepped to the middle of the table. "Everybody must sign their name, union affiliation if any, and call time on one of the sign-in sheets. Keep the lobby clear. There are plenty of seats in the theater."

After signing in, Kayla walked into the workshop theater and took a seat near the back. Twenty other women were in the theater. Most looked up when they heard Kayla's footsteps, but they soon went back into their private worlds.

Kayla opened her script and quietly read it. She became like the others, looking up briefly when hearing footsteps. Each time, it was a stranger, possibly going after the same role. She had to put the competition out of her mind and concentrate on what she had to do.

Shelley's voice echoed through the P-A system breaking the serene silence. "Annette Iaccobucci."

A young actress stood and walked to the back of the theater toward the dance studio.

After a half hour of watching other actresses being called in, Kayla had to stand. She removed her sweater revealing a sleeveless yellow top. With her tight jeans and suede ankle boots, Kayla walked out into the aisle and down toward a water fountain near the restroom. Kayla turned plenty of envious eyes in her direction as she quenched her thirst. When finished, she walked to the back of the theater and stood against the wall waiting for her call. As she waited, three other actresses stood, removed a portion of their outer clothing, and walked down to the water fountain for a drink.

"Kayla Ross," Shelley said through the P-A system.

Kayla closed her eyes and sighed. She folded the script again and placed it inside the pocket of her sweater. She then walked quickly to the dance studio. When she entered, all she saw was Shelley, a tiny camcorder, and a large video monitor.

"How are you, Kayla?"

"Fine. And you?"

"Don't ask. And the day's just starting. Lay your sweater in that chair over there, sweetie." Kayla tossed her sweater over to a chair along the wall, then stood in front of the camera.

Shelley struggled in loosening a clamp on her tripod, then lifted the camera a little higher. "Okay. Stand on that little piece of tape on the floor." Kayla took one step forward. "Good. Now let me get you framed up properly." Shelley adjusted the camera's tripod again. She eyed Kayla, then squinted her eyes in puzzlement. "Where are your sides?"

"In my sweater."

"You need them?"

"No."

"Good girl." Shelley turned back to the camera's monitor. "Okay, sweetie. I'm the eyes and ears for the director. I'm going to roll, then I want you to say your name, your union affiliations, and your hometown. I'll ask you some other questions, then we'll do the reading. All right?"

"Okay."

"Now just relax. This is one of those non-demanding principal roles. If you look right, you'll get the part. So be natural."

"Okay."

"Rolling." Shelley pressed a button on the side of her camera, then pointed at Kayla.

"Hi, I'm Kayla Ross -- SAG/AFTRA/Equity. I'm originally from Shaker Heights, Ohio."

"Ms. Ross, tell us about yourself."

"Well, as I mentioned, I'm from Shaker Heights near Cleveland. My mother is English, my late father was Jamaican. I'm a graduate of Cleveland State University and as you can see from my resume, I had done some summer stock theater. I did some extra work in television and film. I'm a singer with some dance training." Kayla bit her lower lip, and smiled with a shrug. "I ran track. I even set a high school record in the four-hundred meter dash. I'm relatively new to Tampa and have grown to hate snowy winters." Kayla shrugged again. "That's about it."

"All right, Ms. Ross. You're reading for the role of the cocktail waitress?"

"Yes."

"Do you need your sides?"

"No."

"Do you need time to prepare?"

"Not really."

"Good." Shelley reached for a script on a nearby table.

Kayla adjusted her hair, making sure it was away from her face, then shook the tension out of her legs.

Shelley looked at the script, then eyed Kayla. "Hey, sweet buns! Aye! Sweet buns! Get over here!"

Kayla focused her eyes on Shelley and gave her a forced smile. "Can I help you, sir?"

"We're waiting for our drinks here."

"I'm sorry. We're a little swamped tonight."

"I don't give a shit. Why don't you trot your sweet ass up to the bar and see what's up."

Kayla's smile faded from her face. "Yes sir." Kayla held her character, careful to not let her eyes wander away from Shelley.

"Cut!" Shelley paused her camera. "Good. Now I'm going to adjust the camera so we can have a full body view of you." She watched the monitor as the camera zoomed out to a wide shot. "Now, do me a favor and give me one of those high-fashion model spins." Shelley started her camera. "And -- action!"

Kayla shifted her weight from one leg to the other, lifted her right hand to her hip, and did a slow 360-degree turn. She then smiled at the camera.

"Thank you very much, Ms. Ross."

"Thank you."

Shelley paused the camera. "Cut! Okay, Kayla. That was nice. What we'll do is send your headshot and resume along with the video to the director in L-A. There won't be any call-backs. He'll just make the choice based on the video. If you get the part, your agent will hear from us. Okay?"

"Sure."

"Okay. I'll see you later."

"Thank you."

"Sure, sweetie."

Kayla collected her sweater and left the dance studio. She walked swiftly through the lobby toward the exit. As she was about to push the door open, Jenny walked in with her head down nearly bumping into to her.

"Oops, I'm sorry." Jenny looked up, then looked again. "Kay?"

"Jen-Jen? Hey. How are you?"

"Fine. I thought your call was in the afternoon."

"Just finished."

"How was it?" Jenny asked.

"Okay, I guess. The director's not here. Shelley's in charge of the whole thing."

"Were you going for the bank teller?"

"No. The waitress," Kayla said.

"Oh. Good."

"Good?"

"I mean, I don't want to compete with you," Jenny said. "Not today that is."

"Okay." Kayla wasn't sure what she meant by that.

"I better check in. See you later?"

"Sure. Break a leg."

"Thanks." Jenny hurried by Kayla, returning her focus to the audition.

Chapter 5

It wasn't Matt and Kayla's intention to overly familiarize themselves with Tampa Bay. It was only their temporary home. Splitting their time between the workshop and their jobs, shopping and housekeeping, auditions and love making, they had little time left for exploring. But at least once a week, mostly on Saturday mornings, they would travel across the bay to the Gulf of Mexico.

On the southern tip of the Pinellas County barrier islands, they had discovered a relatively uncrowded stretch of sand on the edge of a quaint village called Pass-A-Grille. Here, the beach was wide and clean. Here, a sea breeze always buffeted sunbathers' bodies making the sun's stinging rays easier to take. Here, the green Gulf waters were placid, warm, and clear. Here, Matt and Kayla swam like high performance swimmers through the low waves, using bathing buoys as markers for their two-hundred meter laps.

When finished, they emerged hand in hand from the Gulf with water sheeting off their glistening, brown bodies. The workout always left them both with an aerobic high that made them both feel invulnerable to physical and mental stress.

Each time they came here, there was a different group

of people, usually foreign tourists, tanning themselves in the shadows of the grassy dunes. But no matter who they were, their reaction was usually the same when they saw Matt and Kayla. Most of these people paused and stared as if there were some uniqueness, even a risk, to Matt and Kayla's presence on this beach.

Matt and Kayla neither ignored their stares, nor paid much attention to them. They had no time to dwell on the reasons behind the curious looks they drew. This was another of their weekly escapes, and the setting couldn't have been more pleasant. They playfully applied sun screen on each other's bodies, then reclined on their blanket, allowing the sound of the lapping water and the sea breeze to ease their minds.

With few musical assignments on their calendar, lazy weekend afternoons filled Matt and Kayla's time with blissful idleness. Sometimes they practiced a song or two to stay sharp, but most of the time, they lounged around their apartment -- Matt storing up energy for another overnight Watch-N-Shop show, watching videos on his tablet. Kayla reading magazines and watching TV movies.

Their small-talk was scarce, but it didn't have to be abundant. After almost two years of living together, they were comfortable enough with each other not to engage in clever bantering.

"You passed a thousand views," he said.

Kayla lowered her magazine. "What?"

"You passed a thousand views – a long list of thumbs-up." Matt turned the tablet toward Kayla with a video of her singing. She took it and slid her thumb over it.

Kayla smiled as she scrolled through the responses.

A phone's vibration rattled the kitchen counter top as she continued scrolling through their site. "It's yours." The phone repeated its rattling.

"No. That's you," Matt said.

"How do you know?" When Matt pulled a phone from his shirt pocket, Kayla dropped the pad, swung her legs over Matt, and bolted across the living room to the phone on the counter. She snatched it up.

"Hello?" She smiled. "Eileen? Hi. What's up?"

Matt sat-up puzzled by a late Saturday call from their agent.

"What?" Kayla's eyes widened. "Are you kidding? -- NO! I don't believe – YES -- That fast? -- Well, yes. When? -- January 12th? When will you send me the paperwork? -- Good. -- Oh my God, yes! -- You know it! -- Okay. -- And thanks, Eileen. I love you." Kayla kissed her phone and ended the call. She bent low and let out a brief scream startling Matt.

"What the hell, babe?"

"I GOT THE PART!"

"What, the Kingsley film?"

"YES!" Kayla skipped through the living room and leaped into Matt's lap.

"Damn. That's big."

"It's just a few lines, a day of shooting, but it's my first real SAG contract."

"What happened? I mean, that was quick."

"It's looks -- just like Shelley said. I look like a cocktail waitress, I guess."

Matt, torn by a bout of envy, smiled and shook his head.

"Well -- congratulations." He held her tightly and kissed her. "At least you're getting some breaks. When's your shoot?"

"January 12th. The director's renting a warehouse for a soundstage near Brandon."

"Baby, that's great. I'm proud of you."

"That'll be several hundred more dollars for our L-A fund," Kayla said.

"The credit's the important thing. A Ben Kingsley film won't look bad on your resume."

I'm happy for her. I'm supportive. A good man should be supportive of his woman. I hope she doesn't get the big head. She won an audition, why can't I? When is it going to be my turn? I shouldn't worry. We're going to L-A. I know I'll have a better shot there. Just wait. Yeah, I'm happy for her. Hope she doesn't lose faith in me before we go west.

It was a grim night's drive across the bay for Matt. He sat in his car with the radio low, fighting feelings of inadequacy. He dreaded another night of push-N-sell at Watch-N-Shop.

In the sales host office, the producer, Janice, went over the final line-up for the show with Matt. But he was only listening with half an ear while applying cake make-up to his face.

"I pulled a cultured pearl necklace set from the inventory," she said. "It's been hot the last couple of days. If we fall a little behind in the second hour, I'll throw it in, and we'll hammer it."

"The what?"

"The cultured pearl necklace set?"

"Oh yeah. Can we get that in the show?"

"That's what I just said. We can put it in in the second hour if we're behind."

"Great. Can we also have that Hiyoshi TV standing-by?"

"Sorry. I-C's holding it only for the afternoon shows."

"It figures. They raise my quota, then put holds on my hot items. That's been happening too much lately."

"Don't worry. I have you covered. I found those Tiffany style lamps, and a ton of those big gold over silver neck chains you like so much."

"We have what?" Matt asked.

"The Tiffany lamps, and the big gold over silver chains?"

"Oh yeah."

"We have thousands of each," Janice said. "The day-people haven't touched them yet. One hundred and ninety thousand's not out of the question."

"I guess so."

"No problem. Anything else you need?" she asked.

"No. I guess that covers it."

"You seem a little out of it. Anything wrong?"

"Just tired."

"Well, wake-up, man! We have a show to do in ten minutes. I'll see you outside. And try not to sleep so much during the breaks."

"Okay, Janice."

Janice left Matt straightening his tie. He stopped, pulled it apart and tied it again.

~

It was ten minutes before workshop and Shelley was busy mulling over the spreadsheets on her desk. She heard actors gathering outside, a noisy bunch, but didn't let anything break her concentration until she heard Kayla's name called out.

Shelley checked her watch, removed her reading glasses, then walked quickly to the door. She stuck her head out of the office, and saw several actors conversing and joking with each other. She saw Kayla standing with Matt in the center of the group.

"KAYLA!" Shelley called. Everybody paused and turned toward her. She walked swiftly toward Kayla opening her arms wide. Her toothy grin seemed wider than ever. "KAYLA!"

"Hi, Shelley."

Shelley embraced her tightly, almost forcing air from Kayla's lungs. "Kayla, Kayla, Kayla! I am so proud of you. Congratulations."

"Thanks."

"When did they call you?"

"Saturday."

"Wow." Shelley held Kayla's hand and turned out to face the others in the theater. "EVERYBODY! Let me have your attention for a second!" All conversations stopped in the theater. "For those of you who haven't heard yet, Kayla Ross landed a principal role in the upcoming Ben Kingsley film shooting in Tampa after the New Year. Let's wish her congratulations." Shelley led the applause, and the others joined her. "See what hard work can do? We'll get started in five minutes. We have three scenes tonight." She turned back to Kayla and grabbed her hand. "I'm so proud of you. You're on your way. Believe me."

Shelley was about to walk back to her office when Jenny stepped in front of her.

"Excuse me, Shelley. You know if they decided on the bank teller role?"

"Oh yeah. You auditioned for that?"

"Yeah."

"You didn't hear from your agent today?"

"No."

"Well, I'm sorry, dear. If you haven't heard from your agent by now. You probably didn't get the part. Sorry." Shelley checked her watch again. "Let me get to my office. I have too much work sometimes." Shelley walked away leaving Jenny a little stunned.

Albert walked up behind her and gently massaged her shoulders. "What did she say?"

"I probably didn't get it. The calls have already gone out."

"You checked your messages?" he asked.

"Yes."

"Well, there'll be other chances."

Jenny shook Albert's hands off her, and spun to face him. "I'm just not getting enough here. Every audition feels like a last chance."

"There's plenty of work comin' in."

"Promises -- promises." Jenny looked over at Matt and Kayla joking with some of the other actors. "Excuse me for a second." She walked away from Albert over to them, pushing through some of the other actors congratulating Kayla. "Hey, you two."

"Hey, Jen-Jen," Matt reached out for her hand, but Jenny was all business.

"Hi, Jen. Did you hear anything?" Kayla asked.

"Nothing yet. Congratulations by the way."

"Thanks. Maybe you'll hear something tomorrow."

"I doubt it. I was wondering, can you text me those websites for the L-A apartment guides?"

"Yeah, sure," Kayla said. "Going to L-A anytime soon?"

"Yeah. March -- like you. Maybe I can follow y'all out there?" Her eyes switched back and forth between Matt and Kayla. Jenny never looked more determined.

Matt and Kayla glanced at each other. "Follow us?" Matt asked.

"I gotta get out of Florida. Does Milo have any other apartments available?"

"He might. But we had to mail the man a $500 bribe for our arrangements. I don't know how much he'll charge you."

"I don't care. I'm not getting enough work here."

"Are you sure, Jen?" Kayla asked.

Jenny put her hands on her hips and gave Kayla an irritated glare. "Now what do you think?"

Kayla raised both her hands. "Okay -- okay. Sorry for asking."

"Yeah, sure," Matt said. "You can follow us out there. Why not. What about A-C?"

Jenny looked around and saw Albert nearby. He had overheard some of their conversation and turned away, ruffling his silver hair as he entered the theater to take his seat.

Shelley walked out of her office and clapped her hands. "OKAY, EVERYONE! I'M READY TO GET STARTED! LET'S GET INTO THE THEATER!"

"I think I need to stop drinkin'. Makes me wild. But I want to drink sometimes, because it makes me wild. I just like bein' wild! I need to be wild!"

"Get serious, Albert," Shelley said.

"I am, sweetie pie."

"Albert! Jesus Christ."

"Okay -- okay." Albert turned his eyes to the floor and took a breath. "Here's one for you. I need to be twenty-five again. How's that? I want to do some things differently -- the old if I knew then what I know now routine. That's one thing I've been thinkin' about lately."

"Like what?" Shelley asked.

"Huh?"

"What would you do differently if you were twenty-five again?"

"That's personal. Trust me, I know those buttons."

"Albert, goddamit!"

"Well goddamit, Shelley! There are some things I want to keep personal. Some things I need to keep personal. Can I do that?"

"Why does this have to be a constant battle with you?"

"I don't see how all this is goin' to work for me."

"Ohhh, Albert, I'm not asking you to reveal your most intimate secrets. I'm sure you think about those a lot. I'm sure you have many strong buttons inside. But as one of the more experienced and respected actors in here, I do expect you to show some of our younger people how this exercise works. Just give us a taste, a tiny taste, of your motivations. Can I get you to do that?" Albert sighed and shook his head. "Please, Albert? Just a taste?"

He turned his head to the side and shrugged. "All right.

Maybe I would have fewer ex-Mrs. Coles in my life if I didn't have so many compulsions. That's one thing I would change. Children would have been good too. I look back on it -- wish I had been more involved in their lives. They don't want to have anythin' to do with me." Albert eyed the shadowy figures sitting in the theater behind Shelley and took a deep breath. "Hell, for the first time I have less years ahead of me than behind me." A half smile crossed his face. "Shit. I envy you kids. Here you are with me on the same level – strugglin' artist. Only, I'm more than half way through my life, and what have I done? What do I have to show for it? Funny thing is, no matter what, I'll always be doin' this. I can't let it go now. I should have. I should have. But I never grew up. That's what it takes to get out of this profession before it eats you alive, knowin' when to grow up. I-ah -- you -- awe shit." He glared at Shelley. "Don't let me go any further with this."

"Cut," Shelley said softly. She silently nodded her head.

Albert turned and walked off the stage to the back of the theater. He stood by himself in the darkness.

Chapter 6

Thanksgiving passed with little fuss for Matt and Kayla. They spent it together, calling their mothers up north, watching football games, and having a light turkey dinner. But the day after Thanksgiving was the busiest shopping day of the year, and they were again at Cambridge Square preparing for a performance.

Maybe it was the experience of performing here last month. Maybe it was the excitement of the Christmas season. Maybe it was a new-found confidence she had gained from winning a film role. Whatever it was, Kayla was different. She still removed her shoes, rolled her head, and shook out her legs to relieve her nervousness, but she did so while facing the audience – smiling at them – greeting them.

When she sang, Kayla no longer grabbed the microphone stand with both hands. She took the mic off the stand and stepped from behind her comforting shield. She fearlessly opened her eyes and let them roam from table to table, watching the people who watched her.

When Kayla sang, her voice ranged from soft and smooth, to rough and raspy. She improvised, trampolined, and emoted on every song.

Matt didn't have to lead her with his guitar. He had

to keep up with her. To him, it no longer felt like a forced performance. It felt like a jam session. Energy flow from her to him and back, and at such levels that Matt no longer could sit.

He was off the stool moving his body with the guitar. He bent low, sliding his left hand back and forth on the fingerboard forcing out a harder edge to the cords. Matt played like he had never played before, and played for Kayla who answered with her melodious vocals.

She swayed elegantly at his side, singing as much to Matt as to the audience. The threshold of a locked-in performance engulfed them, clouding their eyes. It didn't matter that people walked in and out of the square during their show. It didn't matter that the applause was no more enthusiastic than the last time they played here. Nothing mattered while Matt played for Kayla, and Kayla sang for Matt.

When finished, they embraced on stage. This time both their bodies were hot – sweat glazing both their faces. They pulled back and stared deeply into each other's eyes.

"Let's get out of here," she whispered.

They quickly packed their equipment and drove across town to Ybor. As they had hoped, the heat of their performance stayed with them. When they arrived home, Matt hardly had time to close the door behind him. Kayla penned him against the wall, pushing her hand inside his zipper sorting out fabric from the skin. She frantically rubbed her pelvis against his hip, sparking him to reach under her skirt and pull her panties to one side.

They slowly sank to the floor grappling, squeezing,

panting, moaning, but without a word, because they rarely needed clever small talk.

Tuesday evening, Shelley stood on her stage finishing out another workshop session. She paced at the edge, clapping her hands to make issues stick in the minds of her actors. "Commitment! Commitment! Commitment! If you don't have it, then as an actor you won't have it. You're defeated before you even reach your audition. Most of you in here have it. But there are a few – ohhh, I can just wring your necks sometimes. I'm not going to mention any names. You probably know who you are already. The vast majority of you – I've just enjoyed working with. I know some of you will have to leave us. I'll miss you, and hope what you experienced in this workshop carries not only through your acting careers, but through your lives as well. Let's face it, even with commitment there are no guarantees. You think I'd be doing workshops if I could make twenty-million dollars per film? So, remember what I told you.

"Now, the workshop is closed for a month because of the holidays. I'm going to Jersey to visit my mommy so don't call me for nothing. Happy holidays! Now, go home. I'll see you next year, those of you who are staying."

All the actors stood and applauded Shelley as she walked off stage. Matt tried standing, but felt a hitch in his back. Kayla helped him get out of his chair. Jenny, sitting on the other side of Matt, also grabbed his arm to help.

"Are you all right?" Jenny asked.

Matt glanced at Kayla, then turned back to Jenny. "Yeah. Just overdid my workouts over the weekend."

"You have to be careful."

"I'm fine." Matt began clapping as Shelley walked by them. Shelley smiled and gave Kayla's hand a squeeze, then walked back to her office. "Anybody up for pizza?" Matt asked.

"Sure," Kayla said.

"Mind if I join you?" Jenny asked.

"Yeah, sure. Come on."

"And what about me?" Albert came up behind Matt, slapping him firmly on his stiff back. "I want to celebrate with some good friends."

"Celebrate what?" Kayla asked.

"Celebrate a momentous decision I've made." Albert looked at Jenny with tender eyes. "I've decided I'm goin' back to Hollywood."

"Really?" Matt said.

Albert gave Matt's shoulder a squeeze. "I'm goin' back – give it another try – commit myself like Shelley says."

"You said you hated it out there," Kayla said.

"What about all the work you get here?" Matt asked.

"I'll still hate it out there, but maybe I'll get bigger paying commercials. If not, I still have a little money. I'll make it." Albert focused his eyes on Jenny, projecting apologies and shame over issues unknown to everyone except them. "One thing's for sure, Tampa will be a cold lonely place without my little Jen-Jen." She hesitated, then leaned into Albert's arms. Albert smoothed Jenny's blond hair with deep long strokes. Albert blinked his eyes rapidly, then looked up at Matt and Kayla. "Mind if I tag along with this merry little band? I have a big ol' SUV for our stuff. We can follow you."

Kayla smiled broadly and nodded her head. "Safety in numbers."

"It's a long drive," Matt said.

"Might be fun," Jenny said.

"Someone has to be your guide out there, right?" Albert said.

"Right," Kayla agreed.

"You'd all get lost inside a day without me."

Matt checked his watch as he walked into the Watch-N-Shop studios. This place was just as busy at 4:40 AM as any other time of the day. He navigated through the backstage area where dozens of production assistants pushed, carried, and stacked merchandise of all kinds. No one greeted him. With shows broadcasting on two different networks at the same time, no one had the time.

Matt didn't linger in the commotion. He walked into the quiet sales hosts room and prepared himself for a rare daytime opportunity, a 6 AM to 9 AM show. He set his suit coat down on a chair, then checked his mailbox where he found a list of products available for his show. A little hand-written note fell to the floor. Matt picked it up and unfolded it.

Matt,

See me after your show this morning.

My office.

Brad

Matt pocketed the note from his boss, then walked over to his desk, sat and studied the list. He noticed his quota was $220,000.

"What?" *Oh yeah. More people might be watching this time spot. Maybe it's do-able.* "Right. Right." He sat at the desk for almost an hour, watching a little television, listening to music on a radio, and studying his list. Many people passed the open door, but no one came in or even said hello to him. With a red marker he crossed off the products he believed wouldn't work on his show. He had finally completed his line-up, but his producer was still absent.

The minutes dragged. It was too quiet for him. There was nothing to do. It was easy for Matt's mind to wander, especially with all his California dreams. *What if the apartment's crap? Six month lease -- good thing. Need an agent. Eileen? Connections? Maybe. What about Shelley? She must have some. A-C? What about Milo? They know some people. Yeah. We're good there. Cars. Mini-vans are better. We'll just give up our cars and buy one. Hope it can carry all our stuff. Money -- money -- money. Sixteen hundred dollars a month -- utilities not included. Furniture -- oh shit. Wait. Our rental company must have an office out there. We'll get the same deal or something. Yeah, we'll be fine. No problem. God, get us through this.*

At 8:30 that morning, the Passport Credit Services phone room was almost empty and blissfully quiet. Kayla was one of the few showing up early to her shift. She sat at her desk, opened a cup of coffee and took a sip. She slouched in her chair staring at a blank computer screen.

"Another day of this," she whispered. She turned her eyes to the ceiling and leaned back. She heard cowboy boots thumping the floor from the back of the room and turned her head toward the sound. Mark, her boss, was passing out memos on each desk. He smiled as he approached her.

"How are you, Miss Kayla?"

"Not bad. Another memo?"

"Yes, indeedee."

"Oh, I just love memos."

Mark saw the coffee cup on her desk. "Well then, you'll really love this one." He handed her one of the sheets.

She read the two lines, then looked at her coffee cup. "Oh." She smiled at Mark. "Sorry." She picked up her cup.

"We had two people spill theirs. Nearly shorted out the equipment."

"Breakroom?"

"Anywhere but your desk."

"Sorry."

"Forget it. Go, and sin no more."

Kayla took her coffee into the breakroom which seemed a mile away in the vast facility. Inside, it didn't take many of her co-workers to fill all the seats of the eight large tables. They gabbed among themselves until Kayla entered, then their conversations quieted down noticeably. Kayla felt their stares, but acted as if she didn't. She walked over to the sink, tore off a paper towel from a roller and wrapped it around her coffee cup. In her peripheral vision, Kayla saw some of her co-workers leaning close together, casting scornful looks in her direction. Their muted words were not loud enough for Kayla's ears.

"Hello." A friendly male voice caught Kayla off guard.

She flinched almost spilling her cup. A tall young man with a pleasant, reddish brown face strutted toward her with one hand in his pocket. He flashed a charming smile, and stared deeply in her eyes.

"Oh. Hi," Kayla responded.

"I'm Jay. I work in card services. You?"

"Me too. I'm Kayla."

Jay extended his hand and shook Kayla's, holding it gently after the greeting. "Listen. This might seem a little forward. I just couldn't help but to notice you over thc past few days. I noticed you didn't have a ring or anything. You married, single, or otherwise occupied?"

Kayla rolled her eyes to the side and withdrew her hand. "Ahhh, you're right. You are forward. I'm otherwise occupied. Sorry."

"That's all right. I'm depressed, but optimistic."

"Why?"

"Because you're not married – we work together – and I'm a good friend. I hope you don't mind if I talk to you every now and then -- as a friend of course."

Kayla cleared her throat. "Sure. As a friend of course."

"Good. Of course, if your man slips up, it's a friend's duty to be there for you. That's just the kind of friend I am."

"Really?"

"Really."

"I'll keep that in mind," Kayla said.

"Good, good." Jay ran out of things to say. He glanced at a table filled mostly with young men who snickered among themselves while looking at Jay and Kayla. Jay winked in their direction.

Kayla took a sip of her coffee and shifted her eyes in the

same direction, noticing the other young men. A giddy little chill ran up her spine and made her smile behind her coffee cup. *This is so cute.*

Jay cleared his throat, and rubbed the stubble of his left side-burn. "So, friend, when did you start work here?"

"Six months ago," Kayla said.

"Really? This is my second month. But this is just something that pays the bills. I'm taking some night classes at the community college."

"What are you majoring in?"

"Business."

"Nice."

"Yeah. I'll probably go to USF next year."

"It's a good school," Kayla said.

Jay didn't know what to say next. He rubbed the stubble of his side-burn again. "You in college?"

"No."

"So, where you from? You sound English or something."

"Shaker Heights."

"Is that in England?"

"No, Ohio – near Cleveland."

"Cool. Lebron fan?"

"Always."

"Yeah." Jay lost his train of thought when Kayla's smile broadened. "So – uh, you thinking about going to college?"

"No, I had enough."

"You seem bright enough to go to college."

"I mean, I'm a graduate from Cleveland State," Kayla said.

"Graduate?"

"Almost two years ago."

"Cleveland State?"

"Yeah. And so did my boyfriend." Kayla sipped her coffee, looking Jay in his eyes.

Jay nodded his head. "Whatcha you doing here then?"

"Like you, it's extra money. I'm an actress."

Jay cracked a half smile. "I figured. You kinda look special, you know -- like a star or something."

"Thank you."

"Damn, I'm honored. I can say I knew you when. Where do you act, local theater or something?"

"Something like that. Sometimes film. Sometimes TV." Kayla took another sip of her coffee.

Jay heard her words and, in his mind, they added up to a woman who may be a little beyond his reach. He swallowed hard, his eyes shifting nervously. "That's great." He had never talked to this level of a young woman -- form, polish, confidence, and education all wrapped up in this one telemarketer. He had to balance the scales. "You know, I thought about getting back into that too."

"You were an actor?"

"Oh yeah."

"Equity?" she asked.

"Yeah, this and that. I was thinking Hollywood though. I didn't know you could do that here."

"It's not Hollywood. But there's work out there."

Jay shifted his stance. His hands began sweating. Two of the young men at the table stood up to dispose of their napkins and cups in a garbage can near the sink. When they came close, Jay grew brave again.

"Good, good. Say, Kayla, I gotta get out to my desk. But I want you to remember, my name is Jay. And if your man slips up, I have some pretty nice shoulders to lean on, all right?" Kayla laughed softly at him. "I'm serious, lady."

She patronized him with a nod of her head. "Thank you, Jay. I'll keep that in mind."

"See you outside." The two young men walked out of the break-room ahead of Jay, and he hurried after them.

Kayla leaned back against the sink, crossed an arm over her stomach, and snickered softly while sipping the rest of her coffee.

Two hundred and ten thousand dollars was short of quota, but Matt was satisfied with getting close to it.

After his show, he folded the revenue report and put it in the inside pocket of his jacket. He was ready to rush home, but remembered the little meeting with his boss. He walked quickly out of the studio building and crossed the broad parking lot to a corporate building.

It was a humid, sunny morning with distant rain clouds deflating themselves along the Gulf beaches. Matt took his handkerchief and dried his brow before entering the building. The reception area was empty, but he knew where to go. He walked up one flight of stairs and just across from the stairwell was Brad's office. He tried the door with a knock.

"Come in."

His boss was at his desk, looking busy. "Morning, Brad."

Brad stood and loosened his tie. His voice was pleasant, but his face remained serious. "Good morning, Matt. How are you?"

"Fine."

"Good. How was that time slot this morning."

"Not bad. I can get used to it. Got 93 percent."

"Fine. Listen, have a seat for a minute. I'll be back." Brad walked out of the office.

Matt sat in a chair in front of the desk, took out his handkerchief and dabbed his brow again. Small traces of cake make-up left over from his show stained the small cloth. There wasn't a window or much else to divert Matt's attention. He sat there trying to read the upside-down writing of some documents on Brad's desk, mainly inventory reports and requisitions. He thought his wait would be longer, but Brad came back three minutes later accompanied by a miserly looking black man.

"Matt, this is Charley Mims from personnel."

"Nice to meet you." Matt reached out to shake his hand, but Mims only nodded.

"Would you shut the door, Charley?" Brad asked. Charley closed the door behind him, then sat next to Matt. Brad sat behind his desk, leaned forward and folded his hands. "Matt, we have to let you go."

"What?"

"The reasons are straight forward. You're not looking polished on the air. You're not running pricing games as well as the other show hosts. In running down your performance over the last six weeks, you've made quota only 77% of the time. We need at least 80%."

"You've been raising the quota on me for every show. It's hard to adjust."

"No one else is having that problem."

"This is bullshit. And you know it. You wanted me out of here for a while."

"Matt, I think --"

"Hold on. You said your piece. Now, it's my turn. You fucked around with my schedule. When others could rely on having certain days off every week, you kept me guessing. Sometimes I worked long stints without a break and didn't complain. Other times you barely scheduled me. Then you raised my quotas and prevented me from having full access to the inventory. So, how can I have a reasonable chance of making it? How does it look, Brad? How does it look?"

"Mr. Redcrop, we must try to remain calm here," Charley said. "Brad had these concerns --"

"Oh, I'm calm. This shit ain't worth fighting over, but this stuff Brad's saying is bullshit! And I'm gonna have my say! Did you see any of my sales figures before November?" Mims shook his head while Brad tapped his pencil on the desk. "I didn't think so. Then you need to listen up, bruh man."

"Matt, your attitude is also under consideration here," Brad said. "I've had reports from many people who worked with you."

"Oh really? What did they say?"

"They said you were constantly argumentative, and had a disrespect for procedures and company policy."

"Who said that?"

"Herb Strotter."

"Herb? The production manager? I never worked with the man. In fact, I've only seen the guy three times since I've been here. That's just more bullshit."

"There were other complaints."

"Yeah? What else you got?"

"That's not important now. Anyway, it's confidential."

"Confidential my ass. Shit, just give me my damn check so I can get the hell of here. I gotta get some breakfast."

Brad pulled out a file with Matt's check in it, but Brad wouldn't give it to him unless he signed some exit interview forms. After initially refusing, Matt signed them, but Brad and Mims just didn't notice Matt signed the name Daffy Duck.

Slamming the door behind him, Matt left those two in the office hoping, in some way, he made their day a bad one. He drove home searching himself for any sadness over the loss of his job. *I have none. My body is quiet. I actually feel relieved. No more embarrassment about pushing that shitty stuff on television. I'll miss the money though. I can sleep nights -- every night -- all night. Three and a half months until LA. Gotta find something to bring in a little money at least. What will Kayla think?*

After work, Kayla stood just inside the door with her eyes wide and her mouth open. "Why?"

"They trumped up some shit on me, like I wasn't polished enough on the air and didn't make enough quotas."

Kayla placed her bag on the kitchen counter. "I'm sorry."

"Nothing to be sorry about. I'm all right about it. No more embarrassment."

She sat on the couch next to Matt. "You know, I never liked being alone on those nights you had to work."

"You have me every night now."

"I am worried about our budget though?"

"We're fine," Matt said. "I figure even if I can't find a

job, we'll be out west with ten to twelve-thousand between us. I'll find something temporary. Don't worry."

"Christmas may not be so festive this year," Kayla said.

"I'm not worried about that."

Kayla nodded and rubbed Matt's hand. "How 'bout going out to dinner tonight? I'll buy."

"Where?"

"We could go to the Colombia down the street."

"The Colombia? Gal, I just lost my job."

Kayla stood and pulled Matt up to his feet. "I said, I'm buying. Besides, I always wanted to go there. Let's celebrate a little and not be so bloody well bent on saving money."

"We'll need every cent for L-A."

"I know, but we're not there yet. And you'll make it up when --" Kayla had a sudden idea. "Wait a minute. Passport Credit's hiring another hundred people. How about that?"

"Telemarketing?"

"It's a job."

"It's sales again."

"It's a job, Matt. We can work the same shift, commute together, be home at the same time together, have weekends off together. Think about it."

Matt shrugged his shoulders. "I don't know. I'm taking off until after Christmas though. I need a break."

"Sure, but apply tomorrow if you want to work for Passport. I don't know how long the application period will last. The next training class isn't until after New Year's anyway."

Chapter 7

"Mr. Cole, have a seat. Thank you for stopping by this morning. I'm Ralph Porter."

"Nice to meet you." Albert shook hands with Ralph then sat on a chair at a small round conference table where two other smiling people were waiting to greet him.

"Thank you. I'd like you to meet Missy Larchmont, creative director for Adams/Jorgensen."

Albert leaned forward confidently in his chair, smiled with a nod and shook her soft hand. "Nice to meet you, ma'am."

"Me too, Mr. Cole."

"And you know our director, George Cameron."

"Good to see you again, Georgie."

"You too, Al."

Ralph sat between Missy and George at the conference table. "In fact, it was George who recommended you for this regional spot," he said.

"I guess I owe him one, huh?"

"You bet," George said.

"Mr. Cole, tell us a little something about yourself," Ralph said.

Albert thoughtfully puckered his mouth, then leaned

forward. "What's to tell? I'm a Yale drama graduate. I've been in several commercials, several plays, and several marriages. I have several children, several hobbies, and several home towns."

"You've packed a lot in your life."

"Yeah, I guess. I still have several more things to do."

Ralph chuckled. "I hope so. One of the reasons why you're here is because we've seen several of your spokesperson spots, and we're hoping you'll do the same for our client Bay Bank."

"Well, if it doesn't have anythin' to do with home improvement products or chicken restaurants, I'm there."

"Bill consolidation loans usually are not directly associated with things like that," Ralph said. "So, I guess we'll have no conflicts there. How about availability? We're shooting two days in the second week of January."

"I'm free."

"Good. That's easy. We'll send your agent the contract and script as soon as they're ready." Ralph stood and walked up to Albert. "And I guess we'll see you on the set."

Albert stood and shook Ralph's hand again. "Thank you very much, Mr. Porter. I won't let you down."

"Sure, sure. We're very pleased to have you on board."

"Thank you. Take it slow there, Georgie."

"I'll call you, Al."

Albert nodded to Missy. "Ms. Larchmont, nice to meet you."

"We'll see you, Albert."

"Jennifer Rappaport, huh?" a director asked.

"Yes, ma'am."

"What do you prefer, Jennifer or Jenny?"

"Jenny's fine."

"What can you tell us about yourself?"

"I studied drama and literature at the University of South Florida. I could have gone away to college, but I wanted to stay close to home." Jenny shifted her weight from one leg to the other. "I'm a fan of the classics -- Shakespeare, Oscar Wilde, Lillian Hellman. I love jazz dancing, and bass fishing. I would do both, but I think the boat would shake." Jenny laughed softly, but the director and her assistant didn't even crack a smile. Jenny cleared her throat. "I'm a beach lover, and an ocean swimmer. And I -- I-ah -- am also a fan of your -- of your product."

"We're pleased to hear that, Jenny. What I want now is high energy. We need all you can give since this will be a fast-paced spot. Do you need a minute?"

Jenny's lips flapped when she forced out a breath. She shook her shoulders, and flexed her legs. She hopped a couple of times, then pushed the hair away from her face.

"Okay," Jenny said.

"Anytime you're ready. Just go ahead."

Jenny blew out another breath. She stood motionless with her head turned toward her shoulder. Suddenly, she snapped her head to the front, her hair swinging wildly, and her eyes wide with pleasant shock. "WOW! WHAT A TASTE!" Jenny ended her line with a brilliant smile.

"Okay. Try it again. This time I want more of your body involved."

"Sure." Jenny straightened her hair and turned her head toward the shoulder again. This time, she snapped her head around, bent her knees, and flung her arms wide. "WOW! WHAT A TASTE!" Jenny kept her brilliant smile, and held her position.

"Okay, Jenny." The director picked up Jenny's head shot and turned it over. "Your agent is Sunscreen Associates?"

"Yes."

"All right. You'll hear from us. Thanks for coming out."

Jenny nodded, her smile fading from her face. "Yeah, sure. Thank you."

"Hope you had a good holiday. Welcome to the phone floor. I'm Mark Kyle, your supervisor for the card services division. Personnel brought you out on the floor for your last day of training. I'm gonna place you with some of our more experienced callers and you'll just listen to their pitches this morning. Watch how the system works. When you think you're ready, we'll get you on the phones by this afternoon. As for me, I'm an easygoing guy. If you're good, I'm good. If your bad, I'll fire you." Mark smiled and held up his right hand. "Just joking, but don't do bad." The three trainees smiled. Mark picked up a file, then looked at the only woman in the group. "Erleen?"

"Yes."

"I'm placing you with Claire. She's the woman in the red blouse, fourth seat in the third row."

"Okay." Erleen picked up her bag and walked into the sea of telemarketers in Mark's section.

"Juan?"

"Yeah?"

"You're going with Bobby -- 12th seat, row four."

"Thanks."

"Knock 'em dead. Matt?"

"Yeah?"

"Let's see. I have you with one of our hot newcomers, Jay Oliver -- ninth seat, seventh row. Go get 'em, kid."

"Thanks."

Matt walked into the rows, drawing curious stares from the dozens of busy telemarketers. The women looked, and while on a call, many of them looked again with smiles sprouting on their faces. The men glanced at him, then immediately turned back to their business. Matt gazed out over the tops of the cubicles hoping to see Kayla, but she was down in her seat taking calls. He wasn't sure where she sat.

He walked up behind Jay, who was busy with a call, and quietly stood behind him listening.

"-- 6-7-4, Inverness, that's I-N-V-E-R-N-E-S-S, Road; Almont, Michigan, 4-8-0-0-3. Is that correct? -- Good. Now in seven to ten days you'll receive the package for Passport's Legal Services Plan. Remember, the first sixty days are free – Huh? -- Sure. You can use any of the services and benefits available during that time. If, for any reason, you're not completely satisfied with the program, you can call our toll-free number to cancel your membership. If you like it, just keep it. After the sixty-day trial period, we'll bill your Passport Card fifteen dollars per month for as long as you are a member. Okay? -- Great. Mrs. Grant, I want to thank you so much for your time this morning. -- I will. Bye-bye." Jay press a button on his computer disconnecting the call and clapped his hands. "That's three."

Another young man in the next booth stood and leaned over the wall. "Three already?"

"Yep. One more for quota." Before Jay entered the information on his computer, he noticed Matt out the corner of his eye. He turned back to him. "You the trainee?"

"Yeah. Matt Redcrop." Matt and Jay clasped hands.

"Jay Oliver. Why don't you grab that empty seat over there and pull it up." Matt did as Jay said and sat just behind him. Jay looked up at his buddy in the next booth and gestured in his direction. "This is Mao-Mao Garrett by the way. He started with me."

"What's up," Matt greeted.

"Good luck, bruh. You'll do all right."

"Yeah. It's just like what you learned from the training classes," Jay said. "Just follow the script on the screen, it seems to work best when you put your own personal spin to it."

"Adlib?"

"Within reason. They won't scorch you if you're truthful."

"Right."

"Hey, Jay," Mao-Mao called, staring at something across the room. "She's up."

Jay sprang to his feet and looked in the same direction. "Awe yeah. That always makes my day." Jay slapped hands with Mao-Mao as they both stared with hungry eyes across the room.

Matt was curious, so he stood and looked across the room too. They were staring at Kayla who was at her station having a conversation with her co-worker Shawnda.

"Why you even keep trying?" Mao-Mao asked.

"I'm wearing her down, kid. That's the classiest lady in here."

"Hey, now, wait," Matt said. He looked at these guys wanting to say more, but thought better of it.

"Wait for what?" Jay asked.

Matt smiled sheepishly. "Which girl you're talking about?"

"What is you, blind or something? Which one you think?"

Matt looked out again at Kayla. "That girl is something, huh?"

"Damn skippy," Mao-Mao said.

"That's the ass of asses, my man," Jay said.

Matt ground his teeth together. "You get anywhere with her yet?"

"A little. But she has some punk in her life interfering with my plans."

Kayla turned in their direction and noticed the three men watching her. She smiled warmly and waved at Matt. Jay waved believing her greeting was for him. He didn't see Matt waving at her too.

During the morning, Matt listened to Jay's pitches, and endured the occasional turbid comments about his Kayla. When lunch came around, Matt followed Jay and Mao-Mao to the breakroom for a bite. Kayla was already there, using a microwave to heat up a chicken sandwich.

Jay walked up quietly behind her and tapped her on the shoulder. Kayla turned and saw the three men. She made eye contact with Matt for a split second. At that moment, they understood each other. She then smiled at Jay.

"Oh, hi."

"How's your morning so far, Kay?"

"Not bad. I have four on the auto club." Kayla heard

the beeping of the oven, turned and removed her sandwich. "How are you doing?"

"Easy day on legal. I might double."

"I-I have two so far," Mao-Mao said.

"Good." Kayla placed her sandwich on a napkin and turned back, looking at Matt. "So, who's your friend?"

"He's a trainee. Matt. What was your last name?"

"Redcrop."

"Yeah, that's it. This is Kayla."

"Pleased to meet you," Matt said, raising a mischievous eyebrow. "Heard a lot about you."

"Oh, really?"

"Yeah, Jay seems to know a lot about you."

"Does he now," she said, turning to Jay.

"I wouldn't say all that, shhhiii," Jay said.

"Did Jay tell you how much I love men with the word 'red' in their name?"

"No," Matt answered.

"It drives me crazy." Kayla then sauntered closer to Matt and put her hands on his belt. She swayed her pelvis close to his, pulling him tight against her. At first, she gently tasted his lips, then devoured them shifting her head from side to side.

Matt's hands roamed from her shoulders to her butt, squeezing, messaging, their full body contact bringing a halt to all activity in the breakroom. Only soft whistles from some of their co-workers broke the silence. Jay and Mao-Mao stood there dumb-founded by the sight.

Kayla ended her kiss, and caressed Matt's face with the tips of her finger nails. "I want you tonight," she said softly.

Kayla grabbed her sandwich and left the breakroom without another word.

The three men, and most everyone else in the room, watched Kayla's sexy strides as she exited.

"You two know each other?" Jay asked.

Matt turned to Jay with a firm smile on his lipstick stained lips. "Yeah, I'm the punk who's interfering with your plans."

Mao-Mao bent low covering his mouth as he laughed. "Daaamn, Jay. How you like your Nikes, fried or roasted?"

Chapter 8

The smell of freshly cut wood filled the air inside and around a little used Brandon warehouse. To those passing it, nothing seemed unusual about the large metal and concrete structure, but inside, set designers and carpenters had, within two days, turned this empty space into a motion picture sound stage containing a cruise ship's casino lounge. Blackjack and roulette tables covered the floor. Slot machines lined the walls on raised steps surrounding the floor. Dozens of extras and crew members spent much of their time waiting for the director to organize his thoughts.

Shelley stood behind the cameras picking lent off the shoulders of a male extra. She gave him one last brush off, then adjusted the lapels of his sports coat. "You're all set. Where are you supposed to be?"

"On a slot machine," the extra answered.

"Get on up there."

Kayla stood on the lowest floor of the set wearing a strapless black mini-dress that conformed perfectly with her form. Her worries about wardrobe malfunctions were constant, but not about the dress. Her fish-net stockings seemed a size or two too big. Every couple of minutes she had to reach down to smooth them out, then check her boob-line making sure the dress didn't reveal too much, then push her fluffed up hair off her face. It became a nervous ritual for her as she waited for her scene -- first her stockings, then her boob-line, then her hair -- stockings, then boob-line, then hair -- stockings, boobs, hair.

Finally, an assistant director finished reviewing the scene with three elderly actors sitting at a blackjack table. He then walked over to Kayla.

"Okay, remember your blocking. Marty wants you to be between the third and second actors at the blackjack table when you say your second line. Leave the scene at a forty-five degree angle. All right?"

"Right," Kayla responded.

"We're shooting this at three angles, and we'll be pretty quick so don't wander too far between the shots."

"I won't, Gordon."

Gordon gave Kayla a second look, noticing her legs. "You're still having troubles with those stockings?"

Kayla looked down and sighed. Stockings -- boobs -- hair. "It's all right. They'll hold up."

"Good girl. Take your first position."

Kayla picked up her tray and drinks, and stepped off to the side of the camera. She felt a loosening of her stockings again, but ignored it. It was showtime.

Gordon walked a circular path on the floor. "EVERYBODY! TAKE YOUR FIRST POSITIONS! LET'S QUIET DOWN, AND TAKE YOUR FIRST POSITIONS!" Three tones sounded on the set. Gordon walked back toward the director who sat in chair surrounded by three monitors. "All set, Marty."

"Thank you, Gordy. Ready, Alf?" The cinematographer

and focus operator both turned back and nodded. Marty raised a blow-horn to his mouth. “Extras, when I call background, I want conversations -- not too loud -- but I want to hear voices. If you were given an assignment of movement, do it smoothly and naturally. Stand-by.” Marty leaned over checking the script.

Kayla positioned the tray on her left hand, and exhaled nervously. She took a glance back at Shelley who motioned for her to smile. Kayla did, then rolled her head releasing more tension.

“Okay, everybody,” Marty said on the horn. “Roll ’em, Alf.”

“Speed!” Alf responded.

One of Alf’s assistants leaned in front of the camera with a clapboard. “Scene 87, shot A, take one.” He clapped the board, then moved out of camera range. Kayla giggled quietly, feeling a shiver climbing her spine.

“BACKGROUND,” Marty yelled. All the extras began conversing and gambling. Marty lowered the horn and pointed to the actors at the Blackjack table. “ACTION!”

The dealer drew a card and placed it in front of the first old man. “Twenty-three. Bust.” He turned to the second old man. “Sir? Eleven showing.”

“Hit.”

The dealer flipped another card out on the table. “Seventeen.”

“You’re doing this on purpose, aren’t you,” the second old man said.

“Would you like another card, sir?” The second old man made a slicing motion with his hand. The dealer turned to the third old man.” And you, sir? Twelve showing.”

The third old man tapped the table with his finger. "Hit."

The dealer laid a card in front of the third old man. "Nineteen."

The third old man waved his hand over his cards.

The dealer had a two showing, then flipped over his one card. "Dealer adds a nine -- eleven showing." The dealer drew another card and flipped it over. "Another nine. Twenty. Dealer wins."

"Awe -- for crying out --" All three old men bobbed their heads in disappointment as the dealer swept up their chips.

"I told y'all not to gamble on the seas," the third old man said.

"Ante-up?" the dealer asked.

"Not me, pal. I'm finished here," the third old man said.

Kayla began her walk-through. "Yeah, me too," the second old man said, then noticed Kayla's character. "Hey, sweet buns!" He raised his hand. "Hey! Sweet buns! Get over here."

"Can I help you, sir?" Kayla asked.

"We're waiting for our drinks here."

"I'm sorry. We're a little swamped tonight."

"I don't give a shit. Why don't trot your sweet ass up to the bar and see what's up."

"Yes sir." Kayla walked away from them.

The old men kept their eyes on her. The second old man put a cigar in his mouth and smiled.

"A young girl like that can kill old men like us."

"What a way to go," the third old man said.

"Blackjack!" the dealer called. The first old man had

stayed at the table and won. The other two turned toward him and held their positions.

"CUT!" Marty yelled. That tone sounded again. Everyone froze and became quiet. "That was a good one, but let's do it again, Gordy."

"Right." Gordon walked out on the floor. "BACK TO FIRST POSITIONS! BACK TO FIRST POSITIONS! WE'RE DOING IT AGAIN!"

Kayla walked back to her position off camera, then stockings – boobs -- hair.

After four hours, Marty had all the angles he needed for the scene. Kayla's day was over. She sat on the steps of small motor home that was one of three women's dressing rooms. She no longer worried about her sagging stockings. She only waited for Marty to release her and the other day players.

Shelley walked up to her and patted her on the head. "I'm so proud of you. You handled yourself like a pro out there. I wouldn't be a bit surprised if they call you again for something. How do you feel?"

"Wonderful, but I'm a little disappointed I didn't get to see Ben Kingsley."

"He's coming to town later in the week. He'll only be here a week or so."

"All right." Kayla removed her stilettos and massaged her feet.

"Listen, maybe I can get you on the set when he's here," Shelley added.

A big smile bloomed on Kayla's face. "Really?"

"Sure."

"Great."

Gordon walked back toward Kayla and Shelley. "Kayla?"

"Yeah?"

"Marty says you're all set," Gordon said. "Thank you very much. You did a nice job."

"Thank you. I enjoyed it. When will the film be released?"

"Marty's shooting for late August, early September."

"Okay. Thanks for your help, Gordon," Kayla said.

"No problem. Shell? Marty wants to talk with you."

"Okay," Shelley responded. Gordon walked swiftly away from them. Shelley then squeezed Kayla's arm. "Get dressed. Go home. I'll call you."

"Okay. Thanks again, Shelley."

"You did it, honey. I did very little."

Kayla stood and her stockings fell to her ankles.

"Hello? Mrs. Day? -- Hi, I'm Matt Redcrop calling for Passport Credit services. How are you today?" Matt heard a hard click on his headset. He popped a key on his computer ending the call, then balled his fists tightly. *I hate this shit. What am I doing here? I feel like I'm in* -- A call flashed on his screen. "Hell-o? Is this Ollie Hancock? -- Hi. I'm Matt Redcrop calling for Passport Credit Services – huh? -- Yesterday? -- Yes sir, I'll remove your name from our system."

Matt popped a key on the computer erasing the file. He then slouched down in his chair, looking up at a distant clock. It was two minutes before noon. He leaned forward and paused his machine. He removed his headset, dropping it carelessly on his desk, then stood. Dozens of telemarketers were already migrating to the break-rooms.

Mao-Mao and Jay paused their machines too, Jay turning back to Matt. "Lunch."

"About time," Matt said.

"Hard time this morning?" Mao-Mao asked.

"Shutout, so far."

"You'll get 'em this afternoon. You coming?"

"Yeah," Matt answered.

Matt, Jay, and Mao-Mao walked together down one of the long aisles toward the break-rooms.

"Where's Kayla?" Jay asked. "I didn't see her this morning."

"She had a shoot."

"Model shoot?"

"Movie."

"Get out of here," Mao- Mao said.

"Which movie?" Jay asked.

"Something called *White Caps*."

"She's an extra?"

"Day player. She actually has some lines."

"Weeew. Then she's on her way up."

"Yeah."

Jay put his hand on Matt's shoulder. "You better be moving up too, bruh. When she's a star, she ain't gonna want to hang around no telemarketer."

"It's handled," Matt responded.

"It's handled, huh?"

"It's handled."

"All right now."

Actors were on their backs, covering Shelley's workshop stage. They all had their eyes closed, but not because of the bright lights. They were dim. Under Shelley's guidance, they each sank into their personal inner worlds, connecting with subtle sensations and emotions.

Shelley tip-toed around their bodies watching their faces, punctuating the silence with soothing words. "Allow your minds to drift to a beautiful place -- a place where you'll feel safe, and warm, and loved." She stepped close to Kayla's body and noticed Matt had his head propped on her belly.

Many images swirled in his mind, but the one that gave him most comfort was of pole vaulting. It wasn't a skill he had any experience with, but just an imagined feeling of flying after the pole-plant – lifting off, inverting his body, reaching for the bar with his legs. He saw himself flipping over, thrusting his hips high, releasing the pole and feeling the bar just brush his stomach as he passed over it. He felt suspended in space, falling backwards through the air, but never reaching the ground.

"Can you hear the sounds of your body?" Shelley asked. "Your heartbeat? Your breathing? Feel the blood pulsing through every part of your body."

Kayla was very aware of her breathing. She felt the weight of Matt's head on her stomach as it rose and fell. Under her closed eyes she saw a pulsing vein that seemed to glow in the darkness. She counted the pulses trying to estimate her heart rate. To her, it seemed a little slower than normal. Kayla heard Shelley tip-toe to the side of the stage and lost count.

Shelley sat on a table and quietly yawned. Albert caught

her eye by reaching up and scratching his nose. "Don't be so quick to destroy a sensation on your skin," she said. "Let it linger. Appreciate its feel. Figure out its cause."

Before he destroyed the itch, Albert stopped scratching and allowed its survival so he could study it. The more he concentrated on the itch, the less it seemed a bother. It soon faded away, and Albert began noticing a warmth along his left arm.

Jenny was near Albert's left side -- motionless, almost like a corpse. She saw nothing but darkness, a numbing, opaque cover setting her apart from the world. She felt none of her limbs. She wasn't aware of her breathing or heartbeat. She was just blank, only awaiting the stimulus of Shelley's voice announcing the end of the exercise.

"Take a deep breath and blow it out." All the actors did what Shelley said, raising a breeze in the theater. "Now, I want you to rise -- slowly rise at your own pace -- slowly rise in your own way to your feet. Uncoil your bodies one vertebra at a time and stretch."

In the darkness of the stage, human figures rose like sprouting plants from dark soil. Some lifted their arms, stretching for the lights. Others stayed low, lifting themselves to their hands and knees before rising to their feet. A few like Albert stayed motionless on the stage floor, until Shelley began brightening the lights. Albert then popped up on his feet.

"Very good," Shelley said. "Shake it out." Shelley began flicking her hands and rolling her head. The actors did the same, loosening their bodies.

Shelley stood and clapped her hands. "Okay, people, clear the stage. We're going to run through at least five scenes tonight. Up first, we have Kayla and Jenny with *Forever Man*. Then we have May and Gloria with *Agnes of God*."

The actors hopped off the front of the stage, leaving Kayla and Jenny up there scrambling around, setting up their props.

At the end of that night's workshop, the actors were slow to leave. Matt, Kayla, Albert, and Jenny had gathered around Shelley's office door.

Shelley stood just outside, nodding her head thoughtfully. "Yeah, you're ready. All four of you." She turned to Albert. "Yeah. So, when are you going?"

"March," he said.

"We're going together," Matt said. "Got our apartments all set-up through Milo."

"Stankavich?" Shelley asked. Matt and Albert nodded. "Really? How much did you have to bribe him?"

"The boy made a thousand dollars off us," Albert said.

"Same ol' Milo. That creep. So, Albert's trying it again, huh?"

"Nothin' better to do, hun."

"Keep my kids from getting lost, will ya?"

"Yeah."

"And do the same for yourself."

"I'll try."

Shelley gave Albert a playful tap on his face, then eyed the others. "So, what do you need from me?"

"You know anyone out there we can contact for representation?" Matt asked.

"Did you check with your agents?" Shelley asked.

"None of them have any West Coast offices or contacts."

"What about your old agent, Albert?"

"I don't think they'll be much help," he said. "They probably hate me anyway."

"We thought, with your background, maybe there's somebody you may be acquainted with," Kayla added.

Shelley sighed and rubbed her second chin. She held up one finger, then quickly walked inside her office. Thirty seconds later she came back to the door holding up a small business card.

"Don't lose this. This is my only card from this guy. My copy machine is out. So, make copies and return this to me tomorrow night. This is Oscar Gold, an agent in Century City. He's not big like International Artists Agency, but he wants it that way. He's not only an agent, he's also a manager of some fairly big clients. You just can't walk into his office. He only takes referrals. After you move there, call me. I'll set something up for all four of you." Shelley handed the card to Kayla.

"Thanks," she said.

"We can use all the help we can get," Jenny said.

"No problem. I'm sure he can do something with you guys. Be nice to him. If I refer you to him, you had better be nice. He's the best agent I know in Hollywood."

"We'll be nice," Albert said.

Shelley grabbed Albert's hand. "Oh God, Albert please don't screw this up again." She shook his hand emphasizing every word.

"Shelley, what are you --"

"I'm pulling for you. You're too talented."

"Okay. Damn."

Shelley turned to Jenny. "Will you watch him, sweetie?"

"I will."

"Please -- please, keep him out of trouble."

"Okay."

"Damn, what happened out there?" Matt asked.

"I don't know what's she's talkin' about," Albert said.

"Ohhh, Albert, you're such a shit," Shelley said. "You are such a shit, but I love you. Just keep an eye on him, okay kids? And be careful yourselves."

"Okay," they said.

"Good. Now go home. And bring that card back, Kayla."

"Yes, ma'am."

Chapter 9

It was late Friday afternoon, one of those winter days when fifty degrees in Tampa felt colder than twenty degrees in Cleveland. Brooding gray clouds, flowing from west to east, obscured the bright sun and whipped up damp winds. Anyone walking outside had to pull their jacket snugly to their neck. Cars filled Seventh Avenue, but the chill kept the old sidewalks almost empty. Only a few basket people wandered unnoticed among the store fronts and bars, adding more urgency to their meanderings as they searched for shelter before dark.

In the cramped parking lot behind their Ybor apartment building, Kayla shivered under her heavy coat standing outside a sparkling blue, pre-owned Chrysler Town & Country. Matt was inside the side door on his stomach under one of the back seats, exploring its connecting bolts.

"Found anything?" Kayla asked.

"It's like I thought. No problem with the back and middle benches. They'll tilt down. I just don't want to fool with removing the middle one."

"So, what do we do?"

Matt pulled himself out of the mini-van. "I still like the space. It should be enough."

"I'm still concerned about when we get out there. We may both have to work."

"I don't see any problem with getting a little runabout when we get there."

"Great. Can we go in now?" Kayla's teeth chattered. When a gust of wind cut through Matt's jacket, she didn't have to ask again.

Saturday afternoon was warmer, almost seventy degrees and sunny. Matt and Kayla couldn't wait any longer to take their mini-van on its first long drive. Matt took the wheel, and Kayla jumped into the passenger seat carrying a bag of CD's.

Matt was cautious with his driving, having been used to sub-compact cars until now. As he turned on Seventh Avenue, the street seemed far narrower to him. When they passed the acting workshop, they saw a group of children going in.

Matt turned on Nuccio Parkway toward the crystalline towers of downtown Tampa. Passing through its heart on Kennedy Boulevard, they crossed the Hillsborough River and drove through the shadows of the Indo-Persian minarets dominating the University of Tampa.

Kayla popped the forward button on their CD player repeatedly, searching for her favorite songs. On each song, she kept adjusting the knobs searching for the right level of base tones and speaker balance. She turned the base knob one way, and the thumping beats of her music shook the dash board.

Kayla nodded her head to the beat. Matt bopped his head too, feeling the beat through the steering wheel.

"How's that?" she asked.

"Huh?"

"How's that? The base!"

"Maybe you need to turn it down a bit. I can't hear you."

Kayla nodded and turned the knob in the other direction making the base softer. "Now, what did you say?" Matt asked.

"You answered me already."

"Oh."

Just west of the river, Matt turned south and entered Hyde Park Village a small sample of upscale urbanism along the bay shore. Rome Avenue, at the village center, was a tighter squeeze for their van than Seventh Avenue. Matt drove slowly as pedestrians felt free enough to cross the street outside the cross-walks. When they cleared the village center, the road was wider and traffic free.

Matt made a right, then a left onto a half concrete, half cobblestone avenue called SoHo. Tampa Bay's blue water sparkled at the end of it, its view partially blocked by a cluster of high-rise condos.

Matt turned into the parking lot of one of those buildings, pulling into a visitor's space. He didn't turn off the van. Instead, Kayla thumbed her phone.

"Hey. -- Yeah. We're in the parking lot. Wanna see? -- Okay. Bye." She ended the call. "They're on their way down."

Matt stepped out of the minivan and thought he saw a flaw inside the front door hinge. He stooped down for a closer look, and only saw old grease clumps on the hinges. It wasn't anything he could reach.

"What's the matter?" Kayla asked.

"Just dirt."

Albert and Jenny emerged from a side entrance. "Heeeyyy! Not bad," Albert said.

"It's beautiful," Jenny said.

"Thanks," Matt said. "Our vessel to fame and fortune."

"How old is it?"

"Three years old," Kayla said. "With our two old cars as trade-ins, we got this for two, fully loaded."

"Two thousand dollars?"

"That's right."

Matt walked around to the passenger side, and opened the sliding door for Jenny and Kayla.

Albert stuck his head inside the driver's side and whistled. "Tinted windows. Good for security. Maybe you can get a black curtain or somethin' to go behind the front seats to keep anyone from lookin' in through the front." Albert gestured toward the middle bench. "Can you take those out?"

"I don't think we need to," Matt said. "Both benches fold down."

"Only 29,000 miles on it," Albert said. "This wasn't a storm car from Houston or Miami was it?"

"I don't think so. I checked the vehicle history webs."

"Y'all heading somewhere?" Jenny asked.

"We were going to Pass-A-Grille."

"A little chilly for the beach ain't it?" Albert asked.

"We're just joy riding," Kayla said. "I have a bag of CD's. And there are a couple nice restaurants in the village center. Care to join us?"

"Hmmm. Whatcha say there, Jen Jen?" Albert asked. "Have anythin' pressin' this afternoon?"

"Not really."

"Okay, sounds good. Give me a minute to make sure the house is situated." Albert jogged back to the building.

"Bring my wallet, will ya?" Jenny said.

"Yeah."

The sun had gone red and floated lower through distant clouds, staining the sky with tangerine streaks. The Gulf waters were more placid than usual and though the evening was chilly, those who took in this sunset felt blessed just being there.

At an outdoor bar on the third floor of the Storm Tide Restaurant, dozens of people faced west bidding the sun good-bye for another day. It was like some ancient sun worshiping ritual, with soft music accompanying their quiet stares.

Matt propped his feet up on the rail, holding hands with Kayla as they sipped their drinks. Albert leaned forward, resting his head on his left fist. Small beads of sweat dangled just under his hair line. Jenny gently scratched his back with the tips of her nails. Five empty glasses were on the rail between them.

"Al?" Kayla called.

"Yeah, sweetie."

"Are the sunsets like this in California?"

"They're not bad. Not bad at all."

Jenny sighed and moved her hand up to Albert's neck. "I'm still going to miss this."

When the sun touched the horizon, a tubular bell sounded in the rear of the beach pavilion. Matt looked down there and saw a group of people surrounding a little girl pulling the bell's string. He pointed in the direction of the bell so the others could see it too. "A Pass-A-Grille ritual. They do that almost every day at sunset."

The sun melded into the horizon faster than anyone expected, leaving only tangerine streaks in the distant clouds. As its brilliant edge vanished, some of the people felt moved enough to applaud the sun for yet another fiery performance.

Ice cubes clanked in Albert's glass as he downed the last gulp of his drink. "Another round? On me."

"I don't know," Matt said. "I'm driving."

Kayla sat forward on her stool. "Excuse me? Who's driving?"

Matt jokingly slapped his hand on his chest as if he were enforcing his masculine will. "I am."

"I don't think so, dear. It's my turn."

"Ah --"

"Ah, nothing. You've been driving the van all day. It's my van too. And besides, I only had one drink today."

Matt threw up his hands. "Oh, so now I'm drunk, huh?"

"I don't care if you're drunk or not. I'm driving. That's it. Case closed. I've got to get used to the van too."

"Damn, gal. I guess you're driving then."

"Right." Kayla then gave Albert and Jenny a sweet smile.

"All I just wanted to know is who's in the next round," Albert said.

Matt looked at his nearly empty glass. "Might as well count me in on the next round. I'll take another V and T."

"You got it, kid. Kay?"

"Just a Seven-Up."

"Jen Jen?"

"I'll take the same as Kayla."

Albert spotted a waitress delivering drinks at a nearby table. He waved at her and the young woman came over with a smile.

"Yes, sir."

"Sweetie, can you get us two Seven-Ups, a Scotch-rocks, and a vodka-tonic?"

"Sure. Any particular brands on the Scotch and Vodka?"

"Surprise us. But only with good stuff."

"Okay." She walked away.

Albert rubbed and squeezed Jenny's thigh. "I think this might be the last round this evenin'. It's been a good day, huh Jen Jen?" She nodded in agreement.

Matt finished his old drink and crunched an ice cube in his mouth. He closed his eyes and rubbed the skin on his scalp. "Hey, A-C."

"Yeah?"

"What happened to you out there, man?"

"Where?"

Matt faced Albert. "Hollywood."

Kayla turned in Albert's direction. Jenny shook the hair away from her face, and looked at Albert too. Albert laughed softly, turned his eyes away from them, and shook his head. "Just some mistakes. Nothin' to talk about now."

"It sounded pretty serious, whatever it was."

"It was nothin'. Someday, maybe I'll tell you, but right now I'm feelin' too good, kids. Next month is Hollywood time! Right? Hollywood time!" Albert slapped his hand on the rail and laughed.

Jenny smiled nervously and turned toward Matt and

Kayla, wanting to change the subject. "So, uh, were you two planning on working until just before we leave?"

"Not really," Kayla said.

"We might put in our notice next week," Matt added.

"They won't take notice," Kayla said. "If you tell them you're quitting at a certain time, they'll just find someone to fill your seat and fire you within a day."

"A corporation that doesn't take two-week notices?" Albert asked.

"That's Passport for you," Kayla answered. "We'd be better off just walking out. What about you two?"

"I had already quit," Jenny said. "Albert and I are almost ready."

"Yeah. I have a cousin coming down from Atlanta who wants to rent my place," Albert said. "He's been dyin' to move here. Hey!" Albert's eyes widened, and so did his smile. "I've got another reason why we should take the northern rout west."

"Why?" Matt asked.

"My Aunt Libby. She lives in Gold Plume, Colorado, right in the mountains. That'll be a great place to stop for a couple of days. It's free, nice and safe, and you can't beat the scenery."

"But that could add a couple of days to the trip."

"So? How many times do we have the chance to see the Rockies. You'll love it, and nobody's better than my Aunt Libby."

"I-10's a straight shot, A-C."

"Yeah, I know. I just thought it was a little dull.

Come-on, kid." Albert shook Matt's arm. "Live a little. I'll show you the rout when we get back to my place."

"All we have to do is take I-75 to Atlanta. Pick up I-24 there and take it to Illinois and I-57. Go west on I-64 into St. Louis. Swing around to I-70, take it all the way through Denver. It passes close to Gold Plume. We rest up a couple of days, then get back on 70. Take it all the way to I-15 in Utah. And I-15 takes us to I-10 just outside L-A. See? It's not that bad."

Matt, Kayla, and Jenny sat at Albert's dining table in the spacious great room of his condo. They went over the rout Albert mapped out on his road atlas, then Matt and Kayla looked up at him with great concerns about his sanity. Jenny just shrugged and sipped on her cup of coffee.

"Look at this again, A-C." Matt took a pen out of his pocket and marked another rout. "I-75 out of Tampa to I-10 in North Florida -- straight shot to L-A. Four days max. Can you see this?"

Albert raised a cup of coffee to his lips and nodded. "But what would you see?"

"New Orleans, Houston, San Antonio, the Mexican Border, Phoenix," Matt said.

"The mountains aren't as pretty down there. Besides, my Aunt Libby can give us two nights of rest at her place. It's two free nights away from motels, kid."

"Aunt Libby again?" Kayla said.

"She's like my mother. I haven't seen her in a few years. I really should see her before goin' back out there. That'll be nice for her. Yeah, that'll be nice." Albert became very pensive as he sipped on his coffee. He sat down at the head of the table and pulled over the atlas.

"The drive's so long," Jenny said. "Two days away from the road wouldn't be bad, the way I figure it."

"No, I guess not," Kayla said.

"I kind of want to get settled as quickly as possible," Matt said. "I need to make some contacts and win some roles."

"Will a couple of days make that much of a difference?" Jenny asked.

"Maybe. We had already arranged for the rental furniture company to deliver our furniture on the 16th. With the delay, we won't be there until the 18th."

"Milo will let them in," Jenny said.

"Yeah, I guess he could." Kayla began nodding in agreement. "Matt?"

"Of course, it's no problem if you want to go your own way," Albert said. "We'll still meet up with you a couple of days later."

Matt leaned back in the chair shaking his head.

"Matt, you can't just zip across the country like you're commuting to a job," Jenny said. "You have to pack it with some memories."

"Two days in the Rockies, kid," Albert added.

Matt turned to Kayla who only shrugged her shoulders, but in her eyes he saw a spirit of adventure, and knew she wouldn't mind a two day side trip. He took a sigh and glanced at the map again. "I guess, if Kayla doesn't mind, we can go see Aunt Libby in the Rockies."

Albert clapped his hands. "Deal! You'll like it up there, kid."

"And it'll be a lot more fun with all of us traveling together," Jenny said.

"I think so too," Kayla said.

Matt reached over and pulled the atlas back from Albert. "Let me study this crazy rout again."

Chapter 10

Kayla kept one eye on the clock. It was 4 o'clock, the end of another work day. She disconnected another answering machine, then removed her headset. She stood and stretched, turning her head toward Shawnda who was still wrapping up a call. It was then it hit her. She wouldn't be coming back here next week.

Jay Oliver strolled down the aisle toward Kayla with a smile on his face. "Kay, how'd you do?"

"Not so hot."

Jay leaned on the wall between Shawnda and Kayla, and looked at Kayla's computer. "Two? On auto?"

"Yeah."

"That's struggling." Jay looked over the wall at Shawnda who was still on that same call. She looked up at him, and held up her index finger requesting his patience. Jay whispered to her, "It's quitting time."

Shawnda nodded, then, deciding this call was not productive, disconnected it. "Hey," she greeted.

"Let's go, lady," Jay said. "Mao-Mao and Benita are going to Stinsons."

"And that's where we're going too, I take it?" Shawnda said.

"You take it right."

Shawnda packed her notebook and pens in her purse, then looked up. Seeing Kayla leaning over the top, sadness lengthened Shawnda's face. She stood, walked around Jay and embraced Kayla. "I'm gonna miss you," she whispered.

Kayla closed her eyes tightly. "I'll miss you too. You made it fun for me here."

"Good luck to the both of you out there. I know you're gonna make it."

"Thanks." Kayla wiped a small bit of moisture from the corner of her left eye.

"This is your last day?" Jay asked. Kayla nodded. "Oh, hey. Good luck out there. Hollywood, right?" Kayla nodded. Jay hugged Kayla briefly and politely. "Y'all will do all right." Jay saw Matt walking up the aisle, and walked down to meet him. "Hey, I didn't know this was your last day." He offered his hand, and Matt took it with a slap, their grips changing on every shake. "Take care out there."

"We will, thanks."

Jay pulled his hand away with a snap of his fingers. "Hollywood's swingin', bruh. You'll like it."

"I think so."

Jay leaned in close to Matt. "Handle your business with your girl." Matt shook his head skeptically in response to Jay. "I'm serious, man. Out there, the shit's for real. I know. I've seen those reality shows."

Shawnda walked up and embraced Matt. "Nice knowing you, and take care of my girl out there."

"I will."

Jay and Shawnda gave Matt and Kayla a last nod and wave before leaving.

Matt walked up to Kayla's desk where she was busy filling out a report. With a final tap of her pen, she punctuated her last sentence, then folded the report and gave Matt a nervous smile.

Matt raised his eyebrows and said, "T-minus three weeks and counting."

Matt pulled a military style foot locker from a closet, plopped it on the floor of their living room. He opened it, and found only magazines and some college mementos inside.

From the bedroom, Kayla dragged out another chest and opened it. It was virtually empty. "There's room here," she said.

"Same here, but we may have to get two more like them."

"Can four fit in the van?"

"No problem."

They didn't have a lot of dishes and glasses, but they wrapped each item carefully in newspaper and stored them in a chest. Their pots and pans, eating utensils, and miscellaneous knickknacks topped off the first chest.

They pulled books from their shelves, dusting them before packing them inside the second chest.

Matt and Kayla then purchased two more storage chests and used them for their portable stereo system, CD's, a couple notebook computers, and clothes. Not all their clothes could fit in the chests so they used plastic bags for the rest.

Matt and Kayla didn't rush their packing. They did a little bit every day, but they were still too quick. A week and half before their departure, Matt and Kayla had to unpack some of their clothes and dishes to make it through those last few days.

Their furniture remained, but the apartment looked barren without books and dishes. There were no clothes hanging off door knobs or over the backs of chairs. There were only sheets and blankets on the bed, simple blinds on the windows, and, in the closet, three sets of clothes for each of them.

With nothing to do, those last days dragged for Matt and Kayla. They just drove around Tampa Bay, taking last looks at their favorite places -- Pass-A-Grille Beach, Cambridge Square, Bayshore Boulevard, and Ybor City.

Though they had technically withdrawn from the workshop, they still visited on some evenings and watched scene studies.

From time to time, they went out with Jenny and Albert on casual dinners, and made endless plans about their futures in L-A. Jenny and Matt had fearless dreams. Kayla had cautious optimism. Albert, however, remained vague, covering his insecurities with a confident attitude of having been there before, of having been seasoned heavily by Hollywood's various spices.

Eileen, Matt and Kayla's agent, still called them for auditions forgetting they were leaving town. Their agent even had an audition for a big part in a low budget movie for Matt. It pained him to turn it down, but he and Kayla were too focused on making it across the country safely.

It was before sunrise on a chilly Monday morning in March. A sodium light high on the back of the building was the only source of illumination for the dark parking lot.

Matt felt vulnerable loading the only things they owned in the world in the back of the minivan. Every movement behind the nearby fences, every strange sound coming from the street caught Matt's suspicious attention.

He didn't waste any time, straining to lift the final chest into the back. Matt stacked them two on two leaving the middle bench clear for their bags of clothes, towels, and blankets.

He gently placed his guitar case in an open slot just behind the driver's seat, then stood guard while Kayla ran in and out of the apartment with smaller bags and luggage. The last thing Kayla brought down was a little cooler and a thermos.

"That's it," she said. Kayla placed the cooler and thermos in a space between the two front seats.

"Did you check all the shelves, the kitchen, the bathroom?" Matt asked.

"Of course. Everything's clear."

"The door's locked?"

"Yep. And I put the keys in Murphy's box with a nice note."

Matt searched for something else to check, but after running over his mental check list there was nothing. A nervous chill surged through his body as he looked at the old brick building that was their Ybor home. "I hope we're doing the right thing," he said softly.

Kayla held his hand. "Don't go soft on me now. You brought us both to this point."

Matt smiled and kissed her hand. "Let's get in and stay warm until they get here." Matt and Kayla entered the van and waited quietly.

It was ten to six, and the morning sky was reddening from the pre-dawn sunlight. Kayla closed the dark blue shower curtains behind the front seats, and their spacious van suddenly felt like a sub-compact car.

By a quarter after six, the sound of a single chirping cricket seeped into the van, and so did the morning's chill, fogging the windows. The sky's brightening glow back-lit the old Ybor buildings. Kayla sighed and glanced at her watch. Her stomach purred softly, but in the quiet of the minivan it sounded like a lawn mower.

"Was that you?" Matt asked.

Kayla had an embarrassed smile. "Sorry."

"Hungry?"

"Yeah. Wish they'd hurry up."

"Maybe we'll stop at a B-K or Mickey D's for breakfast."

"Fine by me." Suddenly she remembered something. "Change of address. Did we do that?"

"For the fourth time, yes."

"And you're sure there's no problem with the banks."

"It's a nationwide bank," Matt said. "Our accounts are the same out there. Relax."

Kayla sat back and tapped her fingers on her thighs, then adjusted herself in the seat. "I can't. I always feel like I'm forgetting something."

"Just relax."

Her mind continued running down a mental check list until the bright lights of a car flashed in the entry of their parking lot. Matt and Kayla turned in its direction. A huge SUV pulled up behind their minivan and stopped.

"Finally," Matt said. He hopped out and walked up to the passenger window with his arms out wide. "It's about time."

"Well good morning to you too, Mr. Redcrop," Jenny said through her half open window. She saw Kayla stepping out of the minivan. "Hey, Kay Kay."

Kayla waved back.

"Ready to go?" Albert asked.

"Hecky yeah." Matt looked back into their cargo area where storage chests and luggage filled every bit of space. "Looks like you're hauling more stuff than us."

Albert jiggled a little plastic earphone in his right ear. "Everyone have a Blue-Tooth headphone?"

"Yeah." Matt pulled the neck ring device from under his collar and plugged an earbud into his right ear. Kayla lifted her hair off one ear showing she had hers already plugged in.

"The drivers should keep it on, so if there's a move we have to make, there won't be any surprises," Albert said.

"We'll switch drivers every two hours," Jenny said.

"Right, let's go," Matt commanded.

Albert pulled his SUV forward allowing Matt to back the minivan out of its space. He drove down to the parking lot entry, and waited for Albert to turn his SUV around. When Albert pulled up behind, Matt entered the street and led them around to Seventh Avenue. The two vehicles were the only ones on the street, except for two homeless men on bicycles.

As rush hour peaked, they were on I-75 heading north into Florida's horse country. By the time the men's two-hour driving shift had ended, there was no trace of Tampa Bay's urban sprawl, just rolling pastures and extravagant ranches. Billboards along the highway bragged about former Kentucky Derby, Preakness, and Belmont winners who were put out to stud on some of these ranches.

Kayla and Jenny were on their driving shifts. Albert was sound asleep in the SUV. In the van, Matt leaned toward the window staring out at the passing countryside. He noticed distant clouds boiling to the sky, signs of developing storms, but didn't worry about them. He only turned back to the front and closed his eyes, resting up for his next driving shift.

Kayla adjusted her sunglasses, and was one with the wheel, holding it with two hands until the radio station faded out leaving only static. She pushed the scan button, but almost every stop on FM was static or a country-western station.

"Matt?"

He answered without opening his eyes. "Yeah."

"Is the bag of CD's near your feet?"

Matt felt around with his foot and heard the crinkle of a plastic bag. He reached down and picked it up. "What do you need?"

"John Legend."

"Okay." Matt rummaged through more than twenty discs in the bag. He pulled them out one at a time reading each label.

Kayla heard a beep on her earpiece and pressed its button. "Hello?"

"Kay Kay?" Jenny answered.

"Jen Jen."

"Turn your radio to 101 FM."

Kayla reached down and turned the dial to that frequency. There was a clear signal, but an old song. Kayla listened, but wasn't sure of its significance. "I have it. And?"

"You never heard this before?" Jenny asked.

"It sounds familiar."

"What are we listening to?" Matt asked.

"I don't know."

When the song reached its chorus, Kayla and Matt both recognized it immediately.

Jenny began singing with the music in Kayla's ear. "California dreamin' on such a winter's day -- like we're doin' --," she said without breaking the melody.

"Got it." Kayla smiled. "The Mamas and The Papas." Kayla began singing softly. Matt hummed along because he wasn't sure of the words until the chorus.

"California dreamin' on such a winter's day," they all sang. "California dreamin' on such a winter's day-ayyyy-ayyy-ayyy-ayyy-ayyyy-ay."

"Good God. I hope the brothers can't hear us," Matt said softly.

Kayla broke out with a lip flapping chortle.

They crossed the Georgia border by 10 AM, and made the passage from there to Atlanta in four and a half hours. With Matt and Albert taking their driving shifts, Kayla and Jenny had their cameras out capturing images of the city's skyscrapers.

"No live tube, please," Matt said.

"Why not?" Kayla asked. "We're going to have a ton of video."

"We'll edit it, and maybe package it later. I don't want to be in performance mode the entire trip."

"Smile."

'Matt turned and found Kayla aiming her phone at him. He pulled his lips wide, but returned his concentration to the road.

Just outside the city, they drove up into the Appalachian Mountains and continued northwest on I-24 for the rest of the day until they reached Nashville where they stopped for the evening at an inexpensive motel in the northern suburbs. They made it a point to obtain two rooms on the first floor, and parked their vehicles just outside the front doors for security.

Even with their van three steps from their door, Matt had difficulty relaxing that evening. Every half hour or so, he would walk to the window and check on it. He wasn't comfortable with idea that everything they owned in the world was inside a vehicle thieves might find attractive.

Albert was no different. While reclining on the bed, he always kept an eye on the SUV's shadow showing by the light of a street lamp through the drapes. A bump outside, or the sound of a passing car would have Albert up on his feet and at the window.

Even with those worries on their minds, the two men eventually fell asleep. Kayla and Jenny then became the worriers.

Morning snowflakes hung in the air like feathers from a pillow fight, but didn't stick to the ground. Matt and Kayla had just loaded their overnight bags in the van, then waited for their travel partners. Matt inhaled deeply the pre-dawn air, savoring its flavor. It had been two years since he had taken a whiff of air like this which held the fresh, but threatening, fragrance of snow.

Kayla reached over to him, and zipped his jacket higher, then leaned into the passenger side for a duffel bag just behind the curtain in the cargo area. From inside, she pulled pairs of fluffy white mittens and black leather gloves.

"Here." She handed the gloves to Matt who quickly slipped them on.

"Thanks." They both looked toward Albert and Jenny's door. "Hope they're up."

"We told them the time."

Matt checked his watch then motioned for Kayla to follow him. They walked up to the door and knocked softly. They heard nothing, so Matt knocked again. They heard a muffled male voice.

"Just a minute."

Kayla and Matt waited for a few seconds until Albert opened the door. He was fully dressed and ready to go.

"Hey, kids. Come-on in."

"Ready?" Matt asked.

"Yeah, just waitin' for Jen Jen."

"No, you're not." Jenny came out of the bathroom with a travel bag over her shoulder. She blew her nose in a tissue, then balled it up and threw it in a trash can. "I'm ready."

"We could get a quick breakfast," Matt said.

"If we do, let's find a place on the road," Albert said. "I'm ready to get going." Albert hoisted his bag on his shoulder and headed toward the door. When he stepped outside, the frigid air stung his face causing him to hop. "Holy shit!"

Jenny stepped out and pulled her jacket tighter. She sniffed, her nose turning red almost instantly.

"Did you get enough sleep last night?" Kayla asked.

"Yeah," Jenny said.

"Yeah, we managed, when we weren't slappin' skin," Albert said.

Matt barked out a short chuckle. Kayla's mouth dropped open. Jenny's eyes narrowed from embarrassment.

"It was good, wasn't it, honey?" Albert added.

"Shut-up. Sometimes – I swear." Jenny passed Albert on her way to their SUV. As she passed, Albert gave Jenny a playful slap on the butt.

"I know," he said. "Motel rooms do that to me."

Jenny climbed up into the SUV and slammed the door.

"Oh, come on, honey," Albert continued, extending his arms wide. "We're all adults here." Albert waved at Kayla and Matt, then entered the driver's side of the SUV.

Overcast skies held the night's darkness a little longer, so all vehicles on the highway had their lights on hours after sunrise. Thin veils of snow floated across the road's surface riding the wakes of cars.

Albert's SUV took the lead which was problematic because Albert had a heavy foot. Without noticing, their speeds had reached ninety miles per hour several times during their first shift.

In Kentucky, during a driver change and fuel stop, they discovered their jackets weren't enough. Matt and Kayla both added heavy sweaters under their jackets.

Albert had on a heavy parka, and held an unlit cigarette in his mouth while pumping gas. Jenny opened the door and pulled her coat tighter.

Albert noticed her flushed face. "Look at you."

"I'll make it." She sniffed and wiped her nose with a balled up piece of tissue. She saw the large gift shop next to the gas station. "You think they have some cold medicine in there?"

"Maybe, but you're drivin'," Albert said.

"They might have the non-drowsy kind." She hopped out of the SUV.

"Let me go get it," Albert said.

"I can do it. The fresh air will help clear my nose."

"Go get Kayla then."

"Yeah." She sniffed and walked back to the other gas pump where Matt was finishing filling his tank.

"How're those sniffles, Jen Jen?" Matt asked.

"I'm making it."

Kayla lowered her window. "You look red." Kayla stepped out of the van, took off one of her mittens, and felt Jenny's forehead. "I guess you don't have a fever yet, but we better watch this."

"I know. Maybe the gift shop will have some cold medicine."

"Good idea." She nodded at Matt. "We'll be back."

"Okay."

Kayla and Jenny walked hurriedly through the cold winds and into the shop. Matt finished gassing up the van, took the credit receipt from the pump, and walked over to Albert was still pumping gas into the SUV. He looked up with that cigarette hanging out of his mouth and nodded a greeting to Matt. "What's the damage for you?"

"Forty-two dollars."

"Not bad. But I'll beat you again by ten dollars." Albert looked at the jacket Matt wore and shook his head. "I hope you have somethin' warmer than that. We'll be in the Rockies tomorrow afternoon."

"Actually, this feels good. It's the layering."

"If you say so, but the way it is here I wouldn't be a bit surprise if we see some heavy snow up there."

"Sounds good. Haven't seen a good snowfall in a while."

The gas pump clicked off, and Albert pumped a few more cents in the tank just to even out the price, then grabbed his credit receipt. "Fifty-three dollars."

"I-10 straight to L-A would have saved us."

Albert stepped to the other side of his SUV and flicked a lighter on his cigarette, then waited with Matt for the women.

Kayla and Jenny came out of the shop wearing simple stocking caps and ear-muffs. Jenny carried a bag with cold medicine in it. Kayla carried another pair of ear-muffs and another stocking cap, and handed them both to Matt.

"What's this?" Matt asked.

"I figure we'll need these."

Albert checked Jenny's bag, and pulled out a little box of no-drowsiness cold pills. "Good." He nodded his head. "Girls on the wheels. Let's go."

Albert and Matt were the passengers on this shift. The women crossed the Ohio River near Paducah, Kentucky and made good time in Illinois where the skies cleared, and the winter sun brightened the rural land. Bands of stark, leafless forests crisscrossed the rolling farmlands. Dirt fields with the long dead remains of last year's crops filled the spaces between them.

Near Mt. Vernon, Matt and Albert had the wheels and exited I-24 onto I-64 on the way to St. Louis, Missouri. By one o'clock, they were passing through a sea of recovering urban desolation, with highway construction, vacant land that used to be vibrant neighborhoods, and old brick public housing blocks. Looming optimistically ahead, hundreds of feet above it all, was the silver Gateway Arch.

Again, Kayla and Jenny had their phones out taking aim on the landmark as they passed over the Mississippi River. They quickly passed through downtown St. Louis and, after a half hour, were out of its metropolitan area.

The weather had held steady through Missouri until Kansas City. There, a heavy snow flurry forced them into a motel for the evening.

Chapter 11

Western Kansas had little scenery to relieve Matt's eyes of its monotony. He grew tired, but had to continue because Kayla had just finished a driving shift and was already asleep.

Grasslands had taken the place of forest bands, leaving stretches of tens of miles where there were no trees at all. Skyscraper-like grain towers were the only things breaking up the flat horizon. Simple farm houses somehow survived against the onslaught of corporate farms covering thousands of acres. Matt opened his window slightly, and the cold air roared through, smacking the left side of his face.

Kayla opened her eyes when she felt the breeze and sat up, looking at Matt as if he were insane. "What the -- Baby, it's getting cold in here."

Matt nodded his head. "It's keeping me awake."

"Are you tired? I can take over."

"Just rest. I'll finish my shift. It's just a dull drive. Look at it out there."

Kayla looked forward, and saw treeless grasslands that stretched to an almost perfectly flat horizon. The highway ran flat and straight, except for artificial bends in the road -- the only things helping tired drivers like Matt stay alert.

"I thought Florida was flat." She zipped her jacket higher, slipped on her mittens, then settled back for more nap time.

Rocky ridges, a few hundred feet high, broke the flat plains up into progressively higher prairies. Each one lifted the road higher, raising it close to four thousand feet above sea level at Colorado's border.

At a gas stop, the thinning air was far less noticeable than the cold. In the corners of the gas station's lot were piles of old snow. Impulsively, Jenny strolled over to one of the piles and scooped out a hand full of it. She then walked up quietly behind Kayla, who stood next to Matt as he pumped gas. Jenny suddenly flung the crumbling snowball at her shoulder.

Kayla flinched from the impact, her mouth falling open in indignant shock. She slowly turned toward Jenny. "Girl, you must be out of your bloody mind."

Jenny stuck her tongue out and nodded.

Kayla wiped some of the snow off her jacket, eying Jenny angrily. Suddenly, she sprinted to the nearby snow pile, and scooped up an even bigger mass of snow. Like little school girls they squealed, and chased each other around the snow pile pelting each other, drawing the attention of other customers at the gas station.

Albert walked out of the gift shop, peeling off the top of another pack of cigarettes when he heard the laughter and squeals. His steps slowed when he saw the snowball fight. He popped a cigarette in his mouth, and walked up to Matt. "What's this?"

"Girls and snow," Matt said.

Albert took the cigarette out of his mouth and whistled

loudly, gaining their attention. "Okay, children. Recess is over."

Kayla and Jenny paused with snowballs in their hands. They looked at each other, then walked slowly toward the men with devilish smiles on their faces.

Albert put the unlit cigarette back in his mouth. "Don't even think about it."

"Any attack would require us to take our vengeance," Matt added.

"And revenge is somethin' I take seriously," Albert said.

Kayla and Jenny kept coming forward.

"It may not be now. But could be at any time," Matt added.

"You won't see it comin', girls," Albert said.

Jenny and Kayla stopped only ten feet away from them. Kayla bobbing her snow filled hand up and down threateningly.

"You wouldn't want me to take vengeance on someone I love." Matt smiled shyly, like the first time he met Kayla. "Would you?"

Kayla bit her lip, then sighed. "Bloody hell. You're no fun." She dropped the snowball and walked up to Matt, caressing his face with her wet mittens, kissing him softly.

Jenny still stood there with her weight shifted on her right leg.

Albert smiled sweetly at her. "I don't want to do that either, Jen Jen." He held his arms wide, but Jenny took one step forward and threw the snowball. Albert bent low, but didn't have to because Jenny's toss was well over his head, almost hitting a passing car.

"A warning shot across your bow, Mr. Cole," she said.

Only Albert was familiar with this land. To the others it was almost foreign. Rolling grasslands swept by their windows with the only evidence of urban civilization being billboards at the side of the highway. Herds of cattle and antelope huddled around some of their bases, shielding themselves from the frigid winds. Patches of old snow remained in the gullies, becoming sources of temporary creeks and ponds.

In the SUV, Albert resisted his smoking urges, but couldn't take it any longer. With Jenny's approval, he cracked open his window and lit one up. He became more relaxed at the wheel, the driving less a chore.

Jenny popped two pills in her mouth, and washed them down with a swig of bottled water. She sniffed and wiped her nose with an old tissue.

In the van, Kayla nibbled on an egg salad sandwich while quietly watching the passing scenery. The sandwich was almost two days old, but held up in the fresh ice of their cooler. At least it tasted good to her.

Matt concentrated on keeping up with Albert's occasional speeding. He searched the horizon, hoping to spot a distant mountain peak, but all he saw were grasslands and teasing undulations in the horizon.

The clouds broke up, and the setting winter sun tortured their western facing eyes. Night was closing in, and they hadn't reached Denver. Driving in the Rockies at night was becoming a real worry for Matt. He tapped his earpiece. "A-C?"

"Yeah," Albert answered.

"Sunset's in about a half hour or so. Want to stop?"

"No. We'll make it."

"Where's this town?" Matt asked.

"Thirty miles west of Denver, in the mountains -- about a ninety-minute ETA."

"What about rush hour? We'll be catching the end of it."

"Make that about two hours. We can't stop here though. We can make it."

Matt resigned himself to following Albert into the mountains at night. He sighed. "All right. Lead the way." Matt tapped his earpiece.

"Are we going on?" Kayla asked.

"Yeah."

Kayla shook her head defiantly. "I'm not driving in the mountains at night."

"I'll take it in. Albert says we're two hours away."

Dusk was short. As the cityscape of Denver opened up before them, the eastern wall of the Rocky Mountains appeared, looming like a jagged black and blue wave against the fading light of the setting sun. The drive wasn't so monotonous now.

Thousands of headlights and tail lights stung their eyes. Yet, they coasted through the heavy Denver traffic with few delays. Albert and Matt worked together on lane changes. Whenever Matt spotted an opportunity to pass, he slid over into the next lane, allowing Albert to squeeze in ahead of him. Within a half hour, they were out of the city and climbing up into the mountains. The city's traffic thinned out, and the surrounding land descended into a profound blackness.

In their headlight beams, they saw stone ridges

encroaching the sides of the highway and snowflakes hovering in the air. Some of the exit signs showed the direction to towns like Golden, Idaho Springs, and Black Hawk. A few signs even had digital messages with the word 'OPEN' as the most prominent message.

"Open? What's open?" Kayla asked.

"The roads."

"The roads? When are they closed?"

"When there's an avalanche threat."

Kayla sat up in her seat. "What?"

"Avalanche. When the snow gives way --"

"I know what a bloody avalanche is." She looked out at the stone slopes lit by the lights of passing cars, but only saw darkness beyond it. "Right," she whispered.

Matt heard a beep on his earpiece and tapped it. "Hello?" He only heard a brief burst of Albert's voice then nothing. "Hello? You kicked out. Can you hear me?" He looked up ahead, and noticed Albert had turned on his hazard lights. Matt flashed his bright lights. "You okay, A-C?" He tapped off his earpiece.

"He's slowing down," Kayla said.

Albert now had his turn-light on. They were approaching an exit ramp into an unlit valley. Matt's earpiece beeped again. "Hello?"

"Hey, Matt." Albert greeted. "Can you hear me now?"

"Yeah. I thought there was trouble."

"No. Stay with me, though. This is our exit, and the road's pretty tight."

"Okay."

The terror of a night's drive through Rockies soon opened the pores on Matt's brow. They made a steep climb up a narrow two-lane road. On the left side of the road was a snow frosted wall of sheer rock. On the right was a cliff of unknown depth. The shoulder guard on the cliff's edge was little more than three cables held by short steel posts. It didn't look strong enough to restrain a car from going over the edge.

Streaks of slush on the road caused brief tire spins, but neither vehicle fish-tailed. As he followed Albert, Matt rarely blinked his eyes, fearing a mistake of life threatening proportions.

Kayla scooted away her door, staring at the void just to her right. She turned to Matt with wide, fear filled eyes. He tried keeping a calm face, but she noticed beads of sweat on his forehead. She took a paper towel, folded it, then gently dabbed the moisture from his face without blocking his eyes.

When the road finally leveled, and a rocky ridge filled the void on the right side of the road, they both felt tremendous relief.

There were snow fields on the nearby slopes standing out from the night by the lights of passing cars. The depth of the snow was almost two feet on the edge of the road. Water from daytime melt had frozen on the side and in the middle of the pavement. With icy conditions like this, Albert had to slow down.

They drove around a bend, and down a slope into a valley. The lights of a small town covered its floor, a wooden sign beckoning a welcome to Gold Plume.

They turned onto a cozy side street that sloped upward toward a black wilderness. On either side, warm glows filled the windows of tall old houses, each with lamp posts half buried by snow piles.

Albert turned up into the neatly plowed driveway of one of those houses. Matt felt his tires slip briefly as he pulled the minivan up behind Albert's SUV.

Everyone stepped out and stretched. They had just finished their longest day of driving, and standing felt wonderful. Matt and Kayla pulled out their travel bags from behind the front seats. Albert and Jenny already had theirs and were waiting for Matt and Kayla. Jenny suddenly sneezed, her hair falling forward. Her sneeze jolted the silence, echoing faintly in the still air.

Albert trudged toward the front of the house with the other three following. The snow crunched under their boots, but the air didn't feel as cold as it did back on the Great Plains.

Matt noticed a threshold where the stars and clouds of the night sky met the featureless blackness of nearby mountain peaks. Impressed by its height, Matt whistled softly. "Can't wait to see what this place looks like in the daylight," he said. "Look at that ridge."

Kayla looked up too, but was more concerned about her breathing. She exhaled big puffs of steamy air from her open mouth, but couldn't catch her breath. Jenny had the same discomfort. They both composed themselves when the front door opened, and a woman in her sixties and a couple in their thirties met them.

"Howdy, strangers," Albert called.

"Dumpy!" the woman greeted.

"We made it." Albert leaped up the front steps and into the woman's arms.

"How are you?" she asked.

"Great, Aunt Libby."

"Dumpaaay!" The younger man reached out and grabbed Albert's hand.

"How's it goin', Freddy?"

"Goin' good, man. Goin' real good."

"You look great," said the younger woman.

Albert hugged her. "You're a sight for sore eyes."

Jenny walked into the front light. Aunt Libby saw her and smiled. But when Matt and Kayla walked up behind her, Aunt Libby's smile decayed slightly.

"So-ahhh. So, who are your friends here?" she asked.

"Oh yeah. These are my Florida friends, Matt Redcrop, Kayla Ross, and this is the famous Jennifer Rappaport. Kids? This my favorite aunt in all history, Aunt Libby. And this is her baby boy Fred Cole and his wife Clara."

"Pleased to meet all of you," Aunt Libby said.

"Nice to meet you, too," Matt said, Kayla and Jenny nodding in agreement.

"Please, come in. We kept your dinners warm. You can leave your boots on the mat at the side."

Kayla stepped inside, dropped her bag, then bent over, putting her hands on her knees. Her back rose up and down from her heavy breathing. She looked around at the others. Jenny's face turned red from her difficulty in taking in oxygen. Matt was breathing through his mouth, and found removing his boots was more of a chore than normal.

"Are we that much out of shape?" Kayla asked.

"Welcome to the sky, young lady," Libby said. "We're

83-hundred feet above sea level. It'll take a while before you low-landers get used to it. Just take your time."

In Aunt Libby's living room, Kayla and Jenny sat shoulder to shoulder on a couch. Matt squeezed himself in at Kayla's side, draping his arm over her shoulder. Albert did the same on Jenny's side.

"Everybody comfy?" Libby asked.

"Fine," Albert said.

Libby looked through Kayla's phone, then pulled it away from her eyes. She wasn't sure how to use it. "Is the flash on?" she asked.

"Do you see a little light bulb?" Kayla asked.

"Where?"

"On the upper left of the screen."

Libby examined the screen on the back of the camera. "Oh, I see it. Everyone say cheese."

"Cheeeeezzzee."

Libby snapped the picture, then handed the camera back to Kayla.

Jenny sneezed hard.

"Bless you," Libby said.

Kayla leaned away from Jenny. She and Matt made a discreet exit from that lounge and sat in another closer to a low burning fireplace.

Jenny blew on her cup of steaming tea, sipped it and swallowed hard. "I know it won't be easy. It hasn't been easy so far. But it's like an addiction, you know?"

"Oh, I know," Libby said. "I used to work in summer stock in New England. I never went to L-A though." She looked at Matt and Kayla. "And you two -- going to college right in the middle of Play House Square. You know that's the second largest theater district behind Broadway?"

"I know," Kayla said. "They reminded us of that again, and again, and again."

"I guess if our interests were in theater, we probably would have stayed," Matt said.

Kayla nodded, then blew steam off her cup of tea. "It just seems like we'll have a better future in films. There're not as many opportunities on the stage." She took a quick sip and still found it too hot.

"Why Florida?" Freddy asked.

"Seemed a good idea at the time," Matt said.

"They heard Hollywood was movin' to Florida little by little," Albert said. "There are some film studios there, but the boom kind of fizzled."

"It wasn't a total loss," Kayla added. "We had some pretty good opportunities."

"Aunt Libby, that young woman over there had a part in a Ben Kingsley film that's comin' out later this year," Albert said.

"Really? Ben Kingsley? Nice. I'll look forward to seeing that."

"It was just a little part," Kayla said.

Libby chuckled. "You know what they say. There are no little parts." Everyone joined Libby when she said, "Only little actors." They shared a laugh. "Anyone need more tea?"

"None for us, Ma." Freddy stood and stretched. "Clara and me better work our way back. How long you here for, Dump?"

"We're here all day tomorrow. But we'll have to go first thing Friday."

"That's cool, cuz. I'll see you tomorrow evenin' then." Freddy and Albert shook hands. "And nice to meet all of you."

"I'm excited for you," Clara said. "We'll see you tomorrow."

"Nice to meet you," Matt said.

"We'll see you," Jenny said.

"Bye," Kayla said.

Freddy and Clara left Libby's house. Libby rose out of her chair, and used a poker on the charred logs in her fireplace, making the flames a little brighter. She then turned back and sighed pensively. "Well now. About the sleeping arrangements."

"Aunt Libby," Albert moaned.

"Just a minute. I know my generation started the sexual revolution, but this is my house. My guest rooms have two beds each. The girls get one room, and the boys get the other."

"I'm a forty-year old man."

"Forty-four, and unmarried."

Albert pointed to Matt and Kayla. "And these two are all but married."

"All except married. I don't need to hear any strange noises through my walls. Know what I mean?"

"When did you become a prude?"

"Prude my butt. Boy, come help me with the dishes." She looked at the others. "Anything you want, just help yourselves. My home is your home."

"Thank you, Mrs. Cole," Kayla said.

"Thanks," Matt said.

Albert picked up the cups and saucers. He leaned over to the others and whispered, "Sorry."

"Dumpy!"

"Yes, Auntie."

Matt and Kayla laughed softly.

"Dumpy?" Matt whispered with a shrug.

Jenny's laugh ended with another sneeze.

"Bless you," Kayla said. "That's not sounding good."

"I don't feel bad. But it's not going away either."

"Keep drinking that tea."

"Yeah."

Matt pulled Kayla close and put his mouth to her ear. "Can you get along without me tonight without losing your mind?"

She smiled bashfully. "How about you?"

In the kitchen, Albert brought some plates over to the sink and dropped them into hot, sudsy water. Libby began soaping down the dishes while Albert dried his hands.

"She's pretty young," Libby suddenly said.

"Yeah, I know."

"Twenty-two, twenty-three?"

"Twenty-six."

Libby shook her head. "You need a stable, older girl."

"I need, Jenny. She's stable. And she has one thing I can't resist in a woman."

"What's that?"

"She actually likes me, even with my baggage."

"And that's another thing." Libby stopped washing and looked Albert in his eyes. "Why are you going back?"

"Jenny was goin'." Albert lowered his head. "I probably wouldn't have seen her again."

"Dumpy, I thought we wouldn't have to worry about you going to Hollywood again. I'm scared for you."

"Don't be. I'm older. I'll handle it better. Besides, those kids out there need an old Hollywood vet like me to show 'em the ropes."

Libby lovingly tapped Albert's cheek with one of her soapy hands. "If things go wrong out there again, you know where to come."

"Yes, ma'am." Albert gently kissed Libby on her forehead and started walking toward the kitchen door. He paused, turned and walked back toward Libby. "By the way. Did you notice two of my friends are black?"

Libby calmly shrugged her shoulders. "Things change. I can change with them."

"I'm so proud of you."

Libby smiled as Albert walked out of the kitchen. When the door closed, she rolled her eyes.

After a good night's sleep, Matt was first up and dressed. Curiosity drew him to the window, and its tantalizing views lured him outside. Wearing a sweater and jacket, he stepped out on the front landing of Libby's house and found himself in an alpine wonderland.

He put on his sunglasses and looked down the street. There was a panoramic view of the little town at the bottom of the valley where old brownstone buildings jutted up above the pine trees. Behind the town on the other side of the valley was a snow-covered ridge sitting like a great wall hiding this high-altitude secret. The air was so clear he could make out individual rocks on its treeless upper slopes. The snow made the morning's sunlight even more brilliant. With no wind, the cold air felt wonderful.

Matt walked down the driveway to check the van and the SUV. They were both undisturbed. He then turned back to the house and saw what was behind it. Libby's house was at the foot of a mountain -- its slopes covered by a forest of dark green fir trees. Just over the tops of the trees, he saw its snowy summit. It seemed so close and inviting that Matt had a brief flirtation with the idea of a morning hike to its summit. He instead climbed the mountain only with his eyes while slowly walking back to the house.

Libby was in the foyer straightening some boots along the wall. She grabbed a broom, walked out to her landing and began sweeping the snow away from her door. She saw Matt walking up her driveway. "Good morning," she greeted.

"Good morning. How are you?"

"Fine. Pretty morning, huh?"

"I've never seen anything like it," Matt said. "This has got to be one of the prettiest places on Earth."

"I thought the same thing when my husband and I first visited here."

"This place has a lot of potential. It could be another Aspen or Vail."

"Oh God, no," Libby said. "We don't want those hassles around here. We like it just the way it is." She quickly brushed the snow off her landing, then leaned pensively on her broom looking at Matt. "I was wondering. How long have you known Dumpy?"

"About a year and a half, but I didn't know he had a nickname like Dumpy."

"Well, that's not enough time to know everything about a person."

"Yeah."

"I'm concerned about him going back to Hollywood, Matt."

Matt took off his sunglasses. "Why?"

"I don't know if he told you, but he had some troubles out there the first time around."

"He mentioned something about it."

"He didn't tell you everything?" Libby asked.

"No. Only that he really didn't want to go back. We didn't press him about why. He seemed pretty disturbed about it."

Libby began sweeping again. She sighed and shook her head. "Dumpy was close to being a star. He had the starring part in a big film all lined up. Then he fell in with the wrong crowd and blew everything." She stopped sweeping. "All you young folks will face those temptations I guess, but it nearly destroyed Dumpy. All I can tell you is, he needs good friends out there -- good drug-free friends, which is what I hope you all are."

"We are, Mrs. Cole. We studied long and hard to be professionals at this. It's tough enough without distracting problems like that."

"I know. Dumpy studied long and hard too -- at Yale no less." She resumed her sweeping, but did it slowly. "He's like my son. Oh, I know he's up in age, but he can still be such a child sometimes. If you're all going to be together out there, I hope you keep an eye on him, like he wants to watch over you."

"Yeah. Sure."

She stopped sweeping. "I'm telling you this because you're a man. He doesn't respect women as much as men. That's why he has so many ex-wives."

Matt smiled and nodded. He looked down to the snow at his feet, then a question surfaced in his mind. "He had a drug problem or something?"

Libby nodded. "Among other things."

"Like what? I mean, he didn't kill anybody did he?" Matt smiled again.

Libby went back to sweeping the landing. "He's a fragile, gentle man. And I'll let him tell you in his own time. There are some things, I'm sure, he wouldn't want the world to know. But if there's any kind of problem with him, take down my phone number and call me."

Matt nodded, but he now had more questions than ever about the real Albert Cole. He felt he had to do something at that moment. "Can I help you with that?"

"Oh no. You just relax. Breakfast will be coming up in an hour."

Chapter 12

An old gold and silver mill, with thick red brick walls, was the biggest building in the town. Matt and Kayla read the plaque in the iron fence surrounding its lot. The mill had closed long ago, becoming a seasonal museum open during the summer months. So, with nothing to see here, they continued their late morning stroll through the town center and its quaint shops.

The main street was not only clear of snow, but also clear of traffic. In a town this small, no one needed to drive. They could just walk down the middle of the streets.

There were few opportunities for quality shopping, only a grocery store and a pharmacy. Most of the rest of the shops were more hobbies than businesses. Artistic trinkets, paintings, and sports clothes dominated the display windows. Kayla and Matt paused for quick looks, and even walked inside a couple of the shops, but other than post cards and some supplies for their cooler, they didn't buy anything.

After an hour of strolling, the thin cold air had taxed their lungs and penetrated their jackets, sweaters, and gloves. They had to get back to Libby's house or freeze.

It was an uphill walk all the way and with every step,

Kayla felt more stiff and tired. She kept her head low hoping to shield her face from the cold. "I'm definitely a tropical girl." She slipped on an ice patch and Matt grabbed her arm keeping her from falling. "See? I can't even walk."

Their boots crunched through ice and snow on the sidewalk. A soft gust of wind blew a dusting of snow across their path, and Kayla turned her back to it to blunt its sting. She stomped her feet and bounced. She also needed to catch her breath.

"Let's pause a little bit," she said through chattering teeth. She and Matt stopped, lowered their bags, and rested on a street corner for a couple of minutes. They both were breathless, Kayla bending low resting her hands on her knees. "You know, I always thought Albert seemed slightly off." She blew air out of her mouth. "He does drink too much sometimes."

"Yeah, but Libby made it sound like he did something worse."

Kayla's breathing calmed a little. She pushed her hair back and adjusted her stocking cap to keep it off her face. "He's not a murderer or something?"

"I don't think so – although." Matt laughed. "Now that would be something."

"What?"

"If A-C was the zodiac killer or something."

"That's funny?"

"Or if he's the guy who killed Nicole Simpson."

"Stop it," Kayla said.

"Then O-J would be innocent, right?"

Kayla shook her head. "He's your friend."

"Yeah. I shouldn't think like that." They picked up their

bags and began walking again. They turned off the main street and headed toward the mountain peak in the direction of Libby's house. "You remember the name of the street?"

"Valley Vista, wasn't it?" Kayla asked.

"Sounds right. It's not too far from here." They walked another block silently, until another question crossed Matt's mind. "Have you seen that 'most-wanted' TV show lately?" Kayla shook her head, then playfully shoved Matt in the shoulder causing him to almost slip on the ice and drop their bag. "What's that for?"

"Now you've got me thinking about that too," she said.

"Think Jenny knows?"

At Libby's house, Jenny sat on the couch still fighting off the sniffles. She still had on her pajamas and robe while sipping on another cup of hot tea.

Across from her, Albert sat in an easy chair reading a newspaper. He adjusted his reading glasses and turned the page. An article immediately caught his eye, and he chuckled.

"What?" Jenny asked.

"Remember that stupid remake of that Orson Wells classic?"

"Yeah."

"It bombed in its openin' weekend. Only three-million dollars. Must have cost them eighty-million to make it. Serves 'em right."

"Why do they keep doing old stuff again?"

"They say it's a sure-fire way to make money. I just think creativity is dead out there."

Jenny sniffed and took a sip of her tea. "I don't know. It

might be fun to redo some of the old films. I always loved *The Heiress.* That's an old part I'd like to do. You?"

"Me?"

"Is there an old part you'd like to do?" she asked.

"Never thought about it." He lowered the paper and looked up to the ceiling. "Yeah. Anything by Hitchcock -- *The Man Who Knew Too Much, The Wrong Man, North by Northwest* -- films like that. They'll never be able to do those films again like ol' Alfred." Albert went back to reading the paper.

Libby came in from the kitchen, grabbed a part of the newspaper off the ottoman and sat in another easy chair. Jenny curled herself up tighter on the lounge and looked out the window.

"It's so pretty here, Mrs. Cole. Wish I could go out there."

"Now you just stay right where you are, young lady. You don't want that cold to turn into pneumonia."

"I really appreciate your hospitality."

"That's all right. That's all right. Dumpy, I need a couple things from Bauer's for dinner tonight. I should've asked your friends to get them while they were out."

"No problem. I thought I'd take a stroll down there around lunch anyway."

"I appreciate it."

"Sure."

A simple lazy day in the Rockies could pass too quickly. Night fell, and dinner time had passed. If Matt, Kayla, Albert, and Jenny wanted to leave before dawn, then bedtime was approaching rapidly. Freddy and Clara stopped by and lounged around the living room with the others.

Jenny, dressed in jeans and a T-shirt, wanted to show Libby a workshop exercise. She sat in the middle of the floor with her eyes closed. "I need -- a tissue for my running nose." Freddy and Clara laughed. "I want -- I want -- this scratchiness in my throat to go away. I need -- I need to not be scared of the future. I want -- I want to -- be there now." She opened her eyes. "And it can go on and on, and get kind of personal. There was this one girl in the workshop who even opened-up in front of us about sexual abuse by her father. That was scary."

"I remember that," Kayla said. "But didn't she blossom as an actress after that?"

"She sure did. She's in New York last I heard, and getting a lot of work too."

"I don't care what you say, that's still Lee Strasberg type of stuff," Libby said. "Seems like we did that when I was with the Actor's Studio last century."

"Maybe so." Jenny jumped to her feet and sat on the couch next to Albert.

"Shelley incorporates later teachers like Eric Morris and Susan Batson," Matt said.

"Maybe new slants on old ones," Libby said. "But I remember that one. I remember all of them."

"With your background, why did you quit acting?" Kayla asked.

"Honey, I married Dumpy's late uncle, a good old fashion country doctor who lavished comfort on me. Comfort is the biggest enemy of an artist sometimes. Yet it's all we dream about."

"You can say that again," Albert said.

"Twenty-million dollars a film," Matt said, "That's comfort enough for me."

"I'd settle for just a million a film," Jenny said. "I don't need much to be comfortable."

"Just a million?" Libby asked.

"That's all." Jenny, mocking a glamor girl's moves, shook her hair back and seductively crossed her legs.

"Confidence is good," Libby said. "Confidence is good. Just remember, you'll never hear about starving accountants."

"True." Matt smiled and nodded.

"They're comfortable too," Libby added.

"Yep, yep. But they have no chance of getting twenty million dollars per spreadsheet," Matt responded.

Libby chuckled and shifted her position in the chair. "You got me there."

"I hope those apartments are comfortable," Freddy said.

"They're fine," Albert said.

"How do you know?"

Albert turned his eyes toward Freddy. "Because, I trust my friend."

"You trust your friend?"

"Yeah."

"I heard that somewhere before." Freddy shook his head critically, a sarcastic half smile on his face. "Payin' for apartments, sight unseen."

"Listen, don't start with me again. I've had enough tonight."

"I'm not startin' anything. I just don't want to see you make any more mistakes."

"Hey, Freddy, who the hell are you? I'm thirteen fuckin' years older than you -- you little shit."

"DUMPY!" Libby stared angrily at Albert.

Jenny grabbed Albert's arm, but he shook his arm away from her grip. "Shit," he muttered.

"We have guests here." She turned her angry eyes toward her son. "Freddy?"

"Sorry, Ma." Freddy blew some air out of his mouth. "Sorry, Dump."

Albert waved at him, then leaned forward, staring at the carpet. Jenny gently rubbed his neck.

"Dumpy?" Libby called.

Albert tilted his head to the side. "Sorry too."

Clara cleared her throat and uncrossed her legs. Matt and Kayla remained uncomfortably motionless, trying to ignore the little tiff.

Kayla's eyes met Libby's and they exchanged uneasy smiles. "Ummm -- we really appreciate you letting us stay here, Mrs. Cole," she said. "This is an experience I'll never forget."

"Well, I hope you enjoyed yourselves."

"Oh, we did. Maybe we'll come back some day for a visit."

"Please do. There's plenty of room. More refreshments, anyone?"

"None for me, Ma. Clara and me should be gettin' back." Freddy stood with his wife. He walked over to Albert and cautiously offered his hand. Albert looked up at Freddy and shook it. "Good luck, cuz."

"Thanks."

"Everybody gets a second chance, I guess. Stay focused this time, Dump."

"Yeah."

"It was good to see you again," Clara said. She bent down and gave Albert a kiss on his cheek. A dim smile grew on his face.

"Jenny, Kayla, Matt -- I look forward to seein' all of you on the silver screen one day," Freddy said.

"Take care," Matt said.

Clara, Kayla, and Jenny exchanged waves. Freddy squeezed Libby's shoulder as he walked out of the living room. "See ya, Ma."

"Okay."

As the front door closed, everyone sat silently, avoiding eye contact. Albert reached out for the TV remote control on the coffee table and clicked on the TV. "Any good movies tonight?"

Chapter 13

Before dawn, the four actors stepped out of the house. Libby had hugs and small bags of sandwiches for everyone. She reserved her warmest hug for Albert who was like a little boy in her arms. He held her tight as she whispered, "Keep out of trouble, will ya?"

"I'll do my best."

"Call me when you get there."

"Okay."

She stepped away from Albert, blinking her eyes rapidly. She smiled and waved to the others. "Y'all be careful out there, ya hear?"

"Yes, ma'am," they said together.

"Matt? Don't forget." Libby gave him an extra special wave.

"I won't."

"Don't forget what?" Albert asked.

"She wants postcards. I promised." Matt and Kayla loaded their bags and were the first to back out of the driveway.

Albert backed his SUV out, then led them back down the mountain ridge to I-70 west.

The men took the first two-hour driving shift while

the women slept. They saw the fiery orange light of the rising sun illuminating the snowy peaks of the Rockies. They passed through the lengthy Eisenhower Tunnel and emerged into even more spectacular scenery, a new world of deeply cut river valleys and jagged mountain ranges rising on both sides of the highway. Pristine forests of enormous fir trees made portions of this land the greenest since Florida, even with snow.

Just before her shift, Kayla was busy thumbing her phone. Matt glanced at her then returned his eyes to the road. "Texting Shawnda again?"

"No."

He took another quick look at her, always amazed at her speed in manipulating her phone. "You're surfing the net?"

"I'm thinking there has to be something about Albert's problems on the web. I found his filmography. It's pretty impressive, but not a bloody thing about his troubles."

"Better start wrapping it up. We're switching in five minutes."

A half hour into the women's two-hour shift, the high mountains gave way to wider, flatter mesa lands scarred by spectacular canyons. The highway descended into one of them where the mountains encroached it and the river so tightly, that highway had nowhere to go except into the side of a mountain. Kayla's heart sank as the mountains close in on them. To her relief, a tunnel provided an escape from the trap.

Matt found amusement in Kayla's locked open eyes and nervous two-handed grip of the wheel. He saw small drops of moisture building up on her brow, and wiped them off with his hand.

"You never told me about these slopes and canyons," she said.

"They're just like that drop on Rockside Road in Cleveland. Relax."

"Don't give me that. And I hated Rockside Road too." Brilliant light briefly stung her eyes when they emerged from the tunnel. Another view of tight mountain walls filled their windows. "Bloody hell. When are we getting out of these mountains?"

"When we get into our apartment tomorrow. It's all mountains from here on. I bet Jenny's not having any problems."

In the SUV, Jenny's knuckles were white, and her eyes were just as wide as Kayla's. Next to her, Albert was on his phone finishing up a call.

"I'd say between 11 AM and 2 o'clock tomorrow. -- Yeah. -- Hey that's great. -- Yeah. -- I know, we owe you another favor. -- I know. -- No. -- No. -- No more money, Milo. -- Just a favor. -- What? -- Say again. -- I'm losin' you. -- Yeah. -- Hey, I'm goin' out of range, man. We'll see you tomorrow. Thanks again. Bye." Albert closed that call, then dialed up Matt's phone. "Matt? -- Hey, I just spoke with Milo. The rental company had delivered your furniture yesterday. Milo has our keys. And he'll be waitin' for us at the rental office. -- Good. Talk to you later." Albert slipped his phone in a shirt pocket, clicked off his headphone and sat back with a satisfied smile on his face. He then reached forward to reduce the heat in the car.

In the last hour of the women's driving shift, they approached the town of Grand Junction where mountains no longer encroached on the highway, and valleys didn't seem as deep. The town was on an inviting plateau surrounded by dry lands crossed by ranges of flat-top mountains.

As they approached Utah, multilayer cakes of stone ridges dazzled their eyes with color. No stone layer had the same hue as the next. Gas stations were scarce here. Highway signs warned drivers of the distances between them, thirty to fifty miles. The exits on I-70 were onto roads leading to small towns and villages twenty-five to thirty miles away. Sometimes those roads didn't go anywhere. Their exit signs only had a route number with no destination.

During the men's driving shift, they approached the Wasatch Mountains, and the end of the Rockies. The highway took them south along its spine to a spot in the western foothills where I-70 met I-15.

On one side of I-15 were inviting alpine forests and snow frosted peaks. On the other, the land sloped downward to rolling hills and orange/yellow valleys barren of trees.

Matt reached out and turned down the heat, then noticed the time. The men's shift had ended and, with gas tanks only a quarter full, their next stop had to be a gas station.

Albert led them off to a road with only a log cabin gift-shop, and a gas station/diner. They all emerged from their vehicles in sweaters and winter jackets. When Albert felt the seventy-degree air, he snatched his jacket off, rolled it up and flipped it behind the driver's seat. "It feels good out here."

The others heard him, and did the same with their sweaters and jackets.

"This is better," Kayla said, stretching her arms and legs.

Jenny stretched, closed her eyes and rolled her head.

When she opened her eyes, she noticed a cluster of palm shrubs at the base of the service station's sign.

By six that evening, they had crossed a corner of Arizona and into the southern Nevada desert. The men had the wheels again and were racing down I-15 toward Las Vegas in the fading daylight.

Vegas was their planned stop for the evening, but the weekend traffic grew heavier with every mile. They couldn't change lanes for passing, and couldn't go any faster than the traffic surrounding them. It was like rush hour traffic in a city of five million people, but there was no city in sight, only glitzy billboards hinting of what was ahead of them.

They came around a rise of barren hills and descended a gentle slope into a vast valley covered by a galaxy of lights. Clusters of skyscrapers stretched from one end of the valley to the other.

"Wow," Kayla said.

Matt couldn't appreciate the dazzling sight as much as Kayla. He was too busy navigating the frantic traffic going into the valley. "We might be too late to get a room around here."

"Sure looks that way," Kayla said.

Matt pushed the button on his earpiece, but heard a warning beep. "Shit. Babe, my battery's low. Ring-up A-C on yours and put him on speaker."

"Okay." Kayla stopped her web surfing and hit the quick dial.

"Kay Kay, what's up," Albert answered.

"Hi, Albert. Matt's running out of battery. Here he is."

"A-C?"

"What can I do for you, young black man?"

"I think we're going to have a hard time finding a place to stay tonight."

"There are some smaller motels just off the highway behind the Strip. You didn't think we were stayin' at the MGM Grand, did you?"

"Wouldn't mind it."

"Forget it. Those type of hotels are either packed or too expensive."

"We could go all the way to L-A tonight too," Matt offered.

"I don't want to drive at night through the desert. We'll see what's in those motels. If they're full, we'll go from there."

"Okay."

"Let's work together to get through this shit, kid."

"Roger that."

Kayla and Jenny waited for Matt and Albert outside their two vehicles in the parking lot of a roadside motel. Neither were facing the motel lobby where the two men were inquiring about rooms. Instead, they faced the direction of the highway and the man-made mountain range on the other side.

Enormous hotel/casinos, glittering buildings of almost all shapes, glowing with all the colors of the rainbow, made the night more dazzling than desert daylight. Their glows bathed the women's faces, and lassoed their hearts.

"I have to go there," Jenny said.

Kayla sighed. "We have a long day tomorrow."

"When are we ever getting back here again?"

"Anytime. We'll only be four hours away." Kayla rubbed Jenny's head like a little sister. Just behind them, Matt and Albert emerged from the lobby each holding two card keys. Kayla and Jenny turned to them.

"Well?" Kayla asked.

Matt held up his card-keys. "We were just in time."

"Last two rooms in the complex," Albert said. "Only we're not together. We're stayin' in the B-wing on the third floor."

"We're in A-wing on the second floor." Matt handed one of the cards to Kayla.

"What about our vans?" she asked.

"I hope we can get a space within view of our window. That's all we can do."

"Ahhh, they'll be fine," Albert said. "The people around here are too busy lookin' for the slot machine of their dreams to worry about our vans. Speakin' of which, anyone up for a trip to the Luxor, the MGM Grand, or New York, New York, later on? It's all just over there."

"Yeah," Jenny said, bouncing on her toes like a little girl.

Matt looked at Kayla and read a negative look on her face. "You two go ahead," he said. "We're both a little tired."

"Oh sure. Two nights away from each other has got your nature up. You can't fool ol' Albert."

Matt and Kayla smiled. "We're just tired," Matt said. "But you two have a good time and don't lose all your money."

"Solid, kid." Albert slapped Matt on the back and

grabbed Jenny's hand. "Come on, Jen Jen. Let's get our room situated."

"Are we walking?"

"We'll catch a shuttle bus or somethin'."

Albert and Jenny entered their SUV and went to their wing of the complex.

Matt and Kayla drove their van around to the A-wing and their room. Just before getting out of their vehicle Kayla turned to Matt. "I thought you promised Mrs. Cole to keep an eye on Albert."

"I can't keep an eye on him 24-seven. He's a grown man. Besides, I rather keep my eye on you."

Matt lifted her hand up and kissed its palm. His right hand began caressing her thigh, moving higher until his pinkie finger brushed against the warm area where her thighs met.

"You know, I suddenly don't feel so tired," she said.

Kayla sat motionless staring into Matt's eyes. Devilish smiles grew on both their faces. Suddenly, they frantically grabbed their bags and jumped out of the minivan. They ran through the door and into the motel.

Chapter 14

Kayla stood on their hotel balcony enjoying the dry morning air. It wasn't cold, but goose bumps covered her sleeveless arms. She rubbed them trying to fend off a gust of desert wind. Her view from the balcony wasn't as majestic in the golden daylight as it was at night. The Strip looked more like a family amusement park with World's Fair style pavilions.

Matt came out on the balcony, his shirt unbuttoned, and embraced Kayla from behind, resting his chin on her lavender scented shoulder. He kissed her there gently, and squeezed her tighter against him.

"Ready?" he asked.

She caressed his arms. "I guess so. You?"

"Can't wait. We'll be there this afternoon."

"Yeah."

Matt heard a lingering doubt in her voice, and turned her around to face him. "Regrets?"

"No," she said weakly.

"What's the matter?"

Kayla smiled and shook her head. "Really. I have no regrets. Maybe -- sometimes I fear change. And then someone like my father when I was a little girl, or someone like you now, would prod me forward. I think I have to start doing that for myself or I'll never have a chance out there."

"You're strong. You just have to have confidence in your talent. I do. I only like to hang around really talented, strong people."

Kayla shook her head and lowered her eyes. "And there are so many pretty girls out there."

Matt chuckled, then lifted her chin. "Really? Are you kidding me? Babe, they're pretty girls everywhere, and when I look at them, I compare them to you. And there's no comparison to you. You're transcendency in the flesh, gal. Hell, you're the reason why I even know that word." Kayla and Matt shared a laugh. "Baby, I'd proudly parade you up and down Rodeo Drive, the Sunset Strip, Venice Beach. I know all the men would envy me for being with you."

Kayla smiled again, and rested her head on Matt's shoulder. "Are we leaving now?"

"In about a half hour. A-C's still recovering from last night."

Kayla lifted her head. "How much did he lose?"

"Two -- three hundred dollars, and most of the contents of his stomach after all the drinks he had. Jenny had to call a cab to bring them back."

"I told you we should've kept an eye on him."

A wet rag covered Albert's eyes as he sat quietly in the passenger seat. Jenny had the wheel and followed Kayla and Matt into the desert.

The traffic had dissipated. The last of the Las Vegas subdivisions abruptly vanished. There were no more casinos and hotels, no more condos and residential subdivisions, only barren land of yellow/orange dust occupied only by clumps of brush.

Near the California border, there was a last blast of Neveda, an amusement park-like cluster of gaudy casinos and resorts standing out in the dull desolation. But after that, on the other side of some low mountains, was the most hostile land in the United States, yellow and flat, reaching to distant mountains that never seemed to grow any closer. Sand, tumble weeds, rocky crags, and long dead river valleys were the drivers' only diversions. Even the highway signs showed the way to regions with hostile and thirsty names, the Soda Mountains, the Devil's Playground, Death Valley.

Kayla lifted a bottle of water to her lips and gulped down half of it before putting it back on the dashboard tray. She adjusted the air conditioning to a higher level and checked the engine temperature. It was normal. She glanced over to Matt who was comfortably asleep. She checked her watch. She still had a half hour left in her driving shift.

In the SUV, Jenny flexed her shoulders and adjusted her sunglasses. Her lips were a little dry so she licked them. Hearing Albert moan softly, she took a quick look at him as he lifted the rag off his eyes and looked back at her.

His voice was hoarse. "Where are we?"

"Approaching Barstow," she said. "How do you feel?"

"I'm fine now."

"I swear, you need to stop overdoing things," Jenny scolded.

"What did I do?"

"Last night. Remember?"

Albert's slightly deranged eyes squinted down in a

moment of intense thought. "Oh yeah." Albert smiled. "Did you have a good time?"

Jenny made a smacking sound with her lips and returned her concentration to the road without an answer. "Can you drive? Your shift's coming up."

"Yeah." Albert sat up and stretched his arms. "Yeah, I can make it."

He reached around Jenny's seat and pulled two bottles of water from their cooler. He handed one to Jenny and they both drained their bottles quickly.

The men took over the driving at Barstow in the Mojave Desert. It was over ninety degrees outside, but comfortable inside the vehicles. They passed through a flat desert plain with peculiar, square shaped communities of inviting, tree shaded streets. Sprouting right out of the barren ground outside these towns, were abundant crops on circular farms. Pipes sitting high on spindly stands gushed fountains of water over vegetables and fruit. With the growing number of farms and desert communities, the desert became less intimidating.

By 11:30 that morning, they approached the San Gabriel Mountains, a soothing break from the desolation. Some of the higher peaks still had a dusting of snow, but that wasn't what made Matt and Albert excited about these mountains. They knew what was on the other side, the Los Angeles metropolitan area.

They sped through a pass in the mountain range, descended into a broad valley in the suburbs of San Bernardino, and exited onto I-10. From there, they faced a solid mass of urban sprawl.

The valley was greener than they expected with clusters

of tall broad leaf trees and ample green lawns. Palm trees jutted high from the neighborhoods and business districts of the countless suburbs along the highway. It almost looked like Florida, except for the mountains.

They picked a good time to enter the city, Saturday at midday. Traffic was thick but not at a stand-still. Matt always kept his eyes on the horizon ahead, looking for the towers of downtown L-A, but they weren't in sight, even after forty-five minutes of speeding through this dense urban sprawl.

Finally, at the top of a plateau east of the city, he saw the distant towers. "There it is," Matt said softly.

Kayla removed her sunglasses and sat-up.

At the wheel of his SUV Albert said, "Finally."

They descended into the L-A basin and circled around downtown looking for the Santa Monica Freeway. Both Kayla and Jenny had their cameras out, staring with reverence at the skyline.

Matt couldn't enjoy the sight. He was stuck in a bad lane, and the Santa Monica Freeway was coming up fast. There were few breaks in the traffic for him to make a smooth move. When a huge truck veered over from the outer lane behind him, Matt made a jolting two-lane change, just making the exit. Kayla fell against him, screaming. Some of the cargo shifted in the back and the minivan wavered, but Matt kept it under control.

"Bloody H. Hell, Matt!"

"Sorry."

Albert somehow managed to stay with him. He tapped his earpiece.

Matt answered quickly. "Sorry about that."

"I think I should take the lead from here," Albert said.

"I think you're right." Matt yielded to Albert as they continued onward.

The highway gently sloped up and down, accommodating city street overpasses, then passed into some low hills just west of downtown. The traffic was still heavy and fast moving. Exit after exit passed. Kayla then saw a Culver City sign, Washington Boulevard.

"That's our turn, isn't it?" Kayla asked.

"No. We're looking for Venice Boulevard." He then saw an exit sign for that street just after the Washington exit. "Shit! They don't give you much warning."

Matt and Albert made another jarring lane change, went down the exit ramp, and stopped at a red light at the end. Matt looked one way toward a hospital on the other side of road. He then followed Albert as he made a left under a highway overpass and continued until reaching Le Cienega Avenue where he took another left.

Matt continued following Albert as they took a right on Washington Boulevard. When they reached the intersection of Washington and National boulevard they encountered a long lasting red light. Kayla's phone vibrated. She saw it was Albert and popped it, placing him on the speaker. "Hello?"

"Kay, put me on speaker."

"You're on."

"I wanna give you guys the ten-cent tour of the real Hollywood, if this fricken red light ever changes."

"Okay."

"I think somewhere in this intersection was the location of the old Hal Roach Studio," Albert said.

"Where?" Matt asked.

The light finally changed. Kayla looked around as they passed through the intersection, but only saw a vacant lot, an apartment complex, and a railroad bridge. She shrugged her shoulders. "Hal Roach?"

"Hal Roach," Albert repeated. "You know, *The Little Rascals, Laurel and Hardy* – Hal Roach."

"Oh." She still wasn't sure who he was and looked at Matt. He only nodded his head as if he knew.

"Comin' up on a real studio on the left, kids," Albert said.

Kayla stretched her neck and ignored the large older buildings on the right. All she saw was a low cluster of structures, looking more like a complex of condos than a film factory, dominating a corner of an intersection.

"That's the Culver City Studios," Albert continued.

"Can't see much," Matt said.

"Not from here. Most of it is away from this street. Used to be the Selznick Studios. *Gone with the Wind, King Kong, Citizen Kane,* the Desi and Lucy TV shows. That's a big deal there, kids. I did a couple things there."

Kayla took off her sunglasses and looked back, but their trunks blocked her view. She checked the passenger side rear-view mirror, but the studio was out of range.

A couple of blocks later, they passed a large office building shaped like two staircases with a huge atrium between them.

"We're now passin' what I used to call the stairway to heaven," Albert said.

"Another studio?" Kayla asked.

"Only the crown jewel, Kay Kay. That's ol' MGM, now the Sony Studios headquarters, at least it used to be when I was last here. The studio lot is a across the street. There's a thin rainbow over there in the middle of the trees. You can barely see it."

"Oh yeah," Kayla said.

"I see the soundstages down further," Matt said.

"Yep," Albert said. "Big ones. Did a few things here too." Another red light stopped them. While he waited, Albert searched his pockets for a small piece of paper, but couldn't find it. He pointed to the glove compartment. "Sweetie, pull that envelope out of there." Jenny reached in and handed the envelope to Albert. The light turned green. "Hey Matt, what street are we lookin' for, La Roche?"

"Yeah."

"We should be gettin' close."

"Yeah. Big time stuff around here," Matt said.

"Culver City's the real Hollywood, kid. I told you we're in the middle of the action." Albert's sharp eyes caught the name on a street sign. "Oh, here's La Roche. We're takin' a left. Just follow me." Albert clicked off his headphone.

Matt followed Albert onto a side street lined on both sides by brick and wood apartments buildings, none were more than three stories. The street was immaculate with tidy lawns, and sharply trimmed shrubs. The cleanly pruned trees looked like props on the back-lot of a film studio.

Albert slowed down, unfolded one of the papers in his hand, and looked over each address as he passed it. He was looking for 4008 La Roche, the Roundtree Apartments.

"Here it is." He flipped on his turn-light, then pulled through an open gate. Matt followed him in. They parked side by side in front of the rental office.

Matt reach over Kayla, popped open the glove

compartment and pulled out an envelope containing their rental agreement and receipts.

Kayla and Jenny stayed with the vehicles while Matt and Albert went inside. They threw their arms wide and embraced, sharing their feelings of relief over the completion of their journey.

"Now, it begins," Jenny said. She kept her arm around Kayla's waist while Kayla kept hers draped over Jenny's shoulders. They both scanned the apartment's surprisingly spacious grounds.

Five buildings surrounded a plaza of manicured lawns and parking lots. An inviting swimming pool was at the side of the rental office, but no one was using it. Instead, some of the residents sat on blankets in the soft grass lawns. A few hung around the landings of their buildings in small groups.

The sound of a guitar caught Kayla's ear. She turned and saw a young man sitting under a tree, strumming an unknown song on an acoustic guitar.

"Hey girls?" Albert's voice drew their attention back to the rental office. They saw Albert and Matt approaching with a short, bearded man holding a silly grin on his face. "We're all set. And this is the famous Milo Stankavitch, star of *Now You See Me*."

Milo bowed to them like performer on stage. "Kayla," Milo shook her hand. "Jenny, pleased to meet you both."

"Thanks for your help," Kayla said.

"Yeah. You made it a lot easier for us," Jenny said.

"It's the least I can do considering the money you paid, aye." He nudged Albert and slapped Matt on the shoulder.

"This feels like an artist colony or something," Jenny said.

"Well, it is, kind of. It became that way in the last few years. We have actors, musicians, writers, directors -- everyone a wannabee by the way. So, you should feel right at home." Milo slapped Matt on the shoulder again. "I'm going to lunch now. You have your keys?" Matt and Albert held them up. "You know your buildings and units?"

They both nodded.

"Unit 125, building B," Matt said.

Jenny pulled the key tag from Albert. "Hmmm, 216, building D. My lucky number," she said.

"All right. If you have any questions or need anything, just come on down. I'll be here until five."

"Thanks, man." Albert and Milo gave each other a manly, back slapping hug.

"Y'all take care now." Milo gave Matt another firm slap on his shoulder before walking away.

"Okay," Matt said, flexing his shoulder.

The four of them stood between their vehicles staring at each other.

"Well?" Matt shrugged his shoulders.

"Well?" Jenny repeated.

Albert nodded his head joyously. "Well nothin'." He grabbed both women and pulled Matt into the group embrace. The young man playing his guitar saw the four new residents embracing in the parking lot, and chuckled to himself.

Chapter 15

Wearing a low cut yellow sweater, denim mini-skirt, and low-heeled pumps, Kayla walked into the office of talent agent Oscar Gold. The receptionist had just disconnected a call and greeted Kayla with a polite smile.

"Can I help you?"

"Yes. I have a 2:30 appointment with Mr. Gold."

The receptionist glanced down at an appointment book in front of her. "Your name?"

"Kayla Ross."

"Oh yes. Have a seat. I'll let Mr. Gold know you're here."

"Thank you."

The receptionist immediately went back on the phone. Kayla sat on a plush blue couch and rested her small attaché case on her lap. She looked around the room, expecting to see pictures of Gold's famous clients. But there were only dull paintings designed to blend in with the office's conventional decor.

She crossed her legs and put her case on the floor. She didn't want to stare at the receptionist, but she was the most interesting thing in the room -- a middle aged, human phone system taking call after call, disposing each of them in seconds. The receptionist looked up at Kayla and smiled, then went back on the phone again.

Kayla waited twenty minutes before the inner office door opened. A balding man in his low thirties, wearing a slightly wrinkled shirt, jeans, and deck shoes, came out of the office. He looked at some notes on the receptionist's desk, then noticed Kayla. Oscar looked at his watch, then rubbed his forehead.

"Shit, I forgot." He walked over toward Kayla with his hands out wide. "You're Kayla?"

She stood and smiled. "Yes."

"I'm Oscar Gold." He shook her hand. "I'm sorry for the wait. It's been some day so far. Why don't you go in my office and have a seat. I'll be there in a moment."

"Thank you."

Oscar's office was huge with burgundy carpeting covering the floor. A massive cherry wood desk sat in front of a back wall full of matching shelves packed with old video tapes, disc's and books. On the other side, a pine and leather couch with a matching pair of chairs surrounded a glass coffee table with a dozen newspapers hanging on its edges. A loaded bar filled the empty space on the wall behind it.

There were two office chairs in front of Oscar's desk and Kayla sat in one of them. She placed her case on the floor and crossed her legs. Kayla took a deep quivering breath and stretched her arms. She heard the door behind her close and looked over her shoulder. Oscar came in holding a file folder.

"So, how are you today?" he asked.

"Fine. And you?"

"I could complain, but why?"

He sat behind his desk and opened the file. Inside was

Kayla's headshot and letter. He quietly looked over the resume on the back of the photo.

Kayla scooted to the front of her chair trying to see what he was reading.

Oscar looked up at Kayla. "Would you like a refreshment or something?"

"Oh, I'm fine. Thank you." Kayla leaned back in her chair.

"I have wine, soda, coffee -- water?"

"No, thank you."

"So, are you from England?"

"My mother was. I'm from Cleveland. I guess my accent comes from her."

"Don't lose it. How long have you been in L-A?"

"About a month."

"Good. Enjoying it so far?"

"It's something out here."

"That's for sure." He went back to reading her resume, spinning his chair to the side. "Oh. Weren't you supposed to bring me a recording of your singing?"

"I have it." Kayla reached down to her case and pulled out a little player. "It's cued, but it's probably not the best quality recording." She handed it to him.

Oscar took the player, briefly examined it, then pushed the play button. He closed his eyes and concentrated on the sound. Unconsciously, he began nodding. Seconds after he started the player, he turned it off and handed it back to Kayla. She was a little stunned at the small amount of attention he paid to her singing.

Oscar leaned back in his chair and folded his hands over

his stomach. He stared at Kayla as if he were wavering on a major decision. "Would you mind standing up?"

"No." Kayla put her case down and stood.

"Walk over there, spin around, and come back."

Kayla did as Oscar asked, walking over toward the lounge area of the office. She made a full, elegant spin then walked back to the desk holding a smile on her face.

"Okay. That's fine." Oscar sighed and looked at her headshot on the desk. Kayla sat in the chair again. "Shelley had a lot of good things to say about you, and your friends too." Oscar leaned forward and rested his arms on his desk. "Kayla, I can't represent everyone. I work with a select few who I believe have the best chance for success in this town. Keeping my list small helps me give my full attention to my clients. Do you understand?"

"Yes." Kayla's smile began decaying.

Oscar sat back in his chair and eyed Kayla again. "Allow me to represent you."

"Huh?"

"Allow me to represent you. I can't make you any promises except that you'll get a hundred percent effort from me. I'm impressed by your potential, your look, your experience. Hell, you even have decent singing voice. Let's see what we can do together."

Kayla's eyes brightened from the excitement welling up inside her. She fumbled for a response. "Well -- yes. What do you need me to do?"

Oscar pulled from Kayla's file a small contract. "Just sign this and we're in business. It's a standard contract. I get ten percent. We both have the option of terminating the contract on two months written notice -- you know, the standard fare. You can take it home and read it over if you like."

"Can I?"

"Sure."

"I don't think there'll be any problem."

"That's fine. Just fax it back to me, or mail it, or bring it with you." Oscar stood and checked his watch. "Crap. Kayla, I have to make a call in a few. Listen, I look forward to working with you. I might have a couple of things brewing for you in the next few weeks. So, hurry up and get that paper back to me."

"Yes sir, Mr. Gold."

They shook hands. "Call me Oscar, will you? Remember, I work for you."

Kayla's smile grew wider. She swallowed hard and nodded. "Sure. And thank you, Oscar."

In twenty-four hours Kayla had Matt, Albert, and Jenny look over the one paragraph contract. None of them saw anything wrong with it. She signed it the next day, kept a copy and mailed the original back to Oscar.

By now, the other three were beginning to wonder why they hadn't heard from Oscar Gold. Matt received his answer in the mail a week after Kayla's interview.

He pulled a large envelope from their mailbox and saw a return address for Oscar Gold Associates. He sat on the curb at the base of the mail boxes and opened the letter. Inside, he found his headshot, resume, and a simple note.

Dear Matt,

After a careful review of your resume, which we found very impressive, I am sorry to say we will not be able to offer you representation at this time.

Good luck in your career.

Cordially,
Oscar Gold

Matt sat still on the curb, a look of pained frustration crossing his face. He crumpled the little note in his hand, then changed his mind and opened it again. He sighed, looked up and saw a young couple jogging by him. They nodded a greeting to him. Matt nodded back to them.

It was the same story for Albert and Jenny, both receiving the same note as Matt.

Albert sat on a bus stop bench with four other people, but when the bus came, he was the only one who remained.

It was half past noon. He took a puff of a cigarette and allowed the smoke to slowly pour out of his nose and mouth. His eyes gravitated back to the main entry of a nearby black-glass office building, the Beverly Hills headquarters of Saxby International Management.

Albert had been sitting on that bench since 10:30 only a block away from one of the most envied shopping and dining districts on Earth. The well dressed and well connected strolled or drove by, but Albert only had eyes for the entry of the SIM building. He carefully examined every face coming out the doors.

Two strolling police officers took notice of his loitering and lingered nearby, hoping to deter this strange man from causing trouble. Albert was aware of the police officers' attention, but was on a mission.

A steady trickle of people exited the building. Every face was a stranger to Albert, but finally he saw a familiar one, a short, gray-bearded man wearing a blue suit and brown shoes.

Albert crushed out his latest cigarette on the bench, tossed the butt into a nearby trash can, and jogged slowly toward the man. The two cops watching him reacted, walking quickly in the same direction.

"TOBIN," Albert called. The man heard his name called, but wasn't sure what direction to look. Albert waved at him. "Tobin!"

Tobin turned back and saw Albert jogging up to him. He squinted his eyes to have a clearer look at this man. "Who are you?"

"Come on, man. Look at me." Albert folded his arms across his chest and gave Tobin a deranged glare.

Suddenly, Tobin recognized him. "Albert? Albert Cole." Tobin laughed and shook Albert's hand as the two cops walked up behind them.

"How are you, Mr. Theobold?" one of them asked.

"Fine -- just fine."

"Is everything all right?" the officer asked.

"Oh sure. Thanks," Tobin answered.

"Yes, everything's fine, officer. Thanks for askin'," Albert said.

The two cops glared at Albert with smirks on their faces. One of them nodded at Albert as a warning not to cross him. They then went on with their rounds.

"So, Albert, how are you?"

"Not bad. I just got back into town about six weeks ago."

"Really? Are you visiting?"

"No. I'm stayin'. That's why I was tryin' to call you."

Tobin chuckled and patted Albert on his shoulder. "Come on. Walk with me a little bit." They strolled toward Rodeo Drive, walking slowly among those hurrying to their lunch appointments. Tobin smoothed his beard. "I received your messages. Sorry I couldn't get back to you -- pretty busy time. I guess you're still acting?"

"Yeah. I was makin' a pretty good livin' in commercials in Florida. I was averagin' between 100 and 150-thousand dollars a year in residuals. I figured if I move out here, and if we hook up again, maybe you and me can really get somethin' going."

Tobin had a melancholy smile on his face and gave Albert another gentle pat on his shoulder. "Fifteen years ago, you were on your way to big things -- the next Nicholas Cage -- Kevin Costner. That was fifteen years ago though."

"I know things have changed, but I think I'm still a good character actor at least. Dress me up and shove me out in front of a camera. You'll always get my best. You know it too. Remember?" Albert's pleading eyes burned the side of Tobin's head.

Tobin's face grew longer as he stopped and faced Albert.

"Yeah, I remember. I also remember the trouble. I had you all set-up to break out as a star, and you blew it."

"Yeah, I know. But that's behind me now."

"Albert, you not only blew it for yourself, you blew it for a lot of people. You blew my commissions. You almost tarnished my rep. That film had to be re-cast. The delay was so bad, that the studio finally shelved the project. A lot of people were counting on that job, and this town has a hard time forgetting something like that."

"It was an accident, Tobin. I paid for it. How long do I have to keep payin'?"

"I don't know." Tobin looked at the ground and smoothed his beard again.

Albert's face lost color. "Then you can't take me on again?"

"No. Sorry. I've always been straight with you."

"What about the money I'm makin' in commercials in Florida alone."

"It's more than the money, Albert. It's a question of reputation, my firm's world-wide reputation. That's what I'm up against." Tobin looked up ahead and patted his stomach. "Look, you want to have lunch or something? I'm going up to Soraya's of Rodeo."

Albert smiled sadly. He gave Tobin a pat on the arm. "No." Albert shook his head. "No -- uh, you go ahead. I got some other people to see this afternoon anyway. Hey, thanks for talkin' to me at least."

"I'm really sorry, Albert."

"I know."

"Take care of yourself, and good luck."

"Thanks, man." Albert spun around and nearly walked

into a young woman. He meandered through the crowds back toward the SIM building.

"Jenny, I don't represent anyone unless I am absolutely sure they have what it takes to make it. Young lady, you are going to be a star! Based on that monologue, and your background, you can be assured that I will put the full power of my firm behind your career."

"Thank you, Mr. Getz."

"And call me Sammy. Right now, I have six roles on my desk," Sammy rubbed his hand over a stack of files. "You're absolutely perfect for all of them. These are not little roles. These are starring roles in independent romantic films. You do romance, don't you?"

"Yes, it's my favorite kind," Jenny answered.

"Good. I don't send my gals out on projects where they bang twenty-five actors at a time." Jenny laughed. "On these projects you'll bang three men at the most -- one, maybe two, at a time. By the way, you any problem with girl-on-girl action?"

Shock lit her eyes after hearing that. Jenny ran out the entry of the street corner agency. Sammy was right behind her and leaned out the door. "FINE! HAVE IT YOUR WAY! PORN'S YOUR BEST CHANCE AT STARDOM! YOU'LL KNOW IT SOON ENOUGH!" He ducked back into the building, slamming the door.

Jenny tore Sammy's card into tiny pieces and angrily tossed them into the wind.

Kayla came running into apartment 125 excited over a manila envelope in the mail for Matt.

Matt was at the kitchen counter languishing over some bills when she slipped the envelope in front of him. Matt laid down the electric bill and picked up the large letter. He felt it and flexed it. When he noticed the stiffness of its contents, he knew what it was and shook his head at Kayla. He opened it anyway and confirmed it. Another agent had returned his headshot with a short note.

> *Dear Actor/Actress,*
>
> *We're sorry to inform you that our*
> *client list is far too large for us*
> *to take on any new talent at this time.*
> *Thank you for considering Mutual Talent*
> *Agency. Good luck in your career.*

Matt showed Kayla the note. "The least they could do is address me by name."

Kayla sat next to him and offered some comfort, but Matt went back to the bills muting his frustration.

"Jenny, we women have to stick together in this town. We are gaining more power, but the boys club still tries to exploit us."

"I know. But there's still not a lot of diversity in the parts coming my way," Jenny said.

"It's changing, and I'd like to think it's agencies like

mine helping to expedite this change. Allow us to represent you, Jenny."

"This is legit?"

"Totally."

Jenny scooted forward in her chair and spoke softly. "No porn films?"

"Believe me, we'll only send you out on legitimate projects. You won't have to do anything against your conscious."

Jenny sat back in her chair. "Okay, what do I need to do?"

The agent pulled out a five-page contract and handed it to Jenny. "Simply sign this contract. Of course, we get 10 percent with a two-year commitment. If you want to terminate the contract, you must give us two months written notice. The processing fee is nominal, and will be credited to you upon the completion of your first job."

"Processing fee?"

"Yes."

"How much is that?"

"Just $950."

Jenny walked out immediately. Outside, she sat on a bus bench feeling dejected. She held her phone in one hand while trying not to cry. She didn't want the passing people to notice her despair.

Her emotions soon settled, and she tried sending a text. She then looked up at the walls of the old Culver City Studios across the street. Traffic was light that morning, but a red Porsche and a classic Roll Royce followed each other toward the gates of the studios. They were like two carrots on a stick to Jenny, inspiring her to keep planning her next move. *Why not me?*

After a satisfying lunch, a brunette woman in her upper twenties walked into a simple two-story office building. On the second floor, she entered a cramped office lobby and noticed a middle-aged man with silver hair and faintly deranged eyes sitting on a couch.

Without a word, she picked up her messages from the receptionist's desk. The receptionist whispered to her, and pointed toward the man.

He looked up, quickly undressed the young woman mentally, then went back to reading a magazine.

The woman checked her watch, then walked over to the man. "Mr. Cole?"

Albert looked up, his eyebrows rising high from surprise. "Yeah, that's me."

"I'm Shannon Hape."

Albert placed the magazine down and stood. "You're Shannon?"

They shook hands. "Yes I am. Would you like to come into my office?"

"Ahhh, yeah -- sure."

Shannon held the door open for Albert. "Make yourself at home."

"I don't think you want me to do that."

"I don't, huh?"

"Naw. I'd feel funny lyin' around your office in my shorts." Albert sat in a chair in front of her desk.

Shannon followed him with a big smile on her face. "I

have some calls to make this afternoon, so I want to keep this short." She sat at her desk and leaned forward. "First, I'm willing represent you. I've seen some of your work when I was in Florida recently. I'm impressed. I also know about your troubles, so my agency contract will have a stipulation that I can terminate our relationship at any time for any reason. Stay clean, Mr. Cole -- please. My agency is new, but I'm not desperate for clients. Understand?"

Albert gave her a military salute. "Yes, ma'am."

Shannon softened up, her eyes filling with empathy. "Call me Shannon, please."

Albert's face never changed expressions. He only held it straight, but his voice became thick, cracking and quivering. "Shannon, call me whatever you want. I'll never forget this. You're a goddess to me at this moment." Albert offered his hand, and Shannon took it. Albert pulled her hand to his face and kissed it.

Shannon looked at her hand and chuckled. "Well. Albert. I haven't done anything yet."

"I'm just grateful for havin' somebody believe in me again."

"Many actors have been forgiven for past sins. Why not you?" She pulled a contract from her desk drawer and slid it over to his side of the desk. "It's standard. The usual 10 percent for my services, standard termination options for both of us, except for what I already specified. You can take it home if you like."

Albert pulled a pen from his pocket, clicked it, and quickly signed his name to it. "Can I get a copy?"

"Yeah. Sure."

Matt leaned forward and signed his name on a short contract. He then turned the paper around to the older man sitting behind the desk who looked it over before signing his name on it too. He then pressed an intercom.

"Beth? Can you come in here?"

"Sure, Roger."

The two men stood, extended their arms and shook hands. "Well, that was easy," Roger said.

"Yes, it was." Matt was relieved. He had finally found an agent.

Beth entered the cramped office.

Roger handed her the contract. "We'll need a copy."

"Sure." Beth exited.

Matt looked around the office admiring some of the movie posters on the wall. "Mind if I ask why you left William Morris, Mr. Doctorow?"

"Call me Roger. Lucy and I wanted to call our own shots."

"Lucy?"

"Lucy Sapirstein, the S in D-S Management Group."

"Oh."

"There's always a lot of new talent to go around. Some will do well, others will disappear. Same with agencies too. We hope we'll do fine. And we have great hopes for you too. Roger shrugged his shoulders. "So, stay loose for the next couple of weeks. We have some projects coming up that might be right for you."

"I'm ready for anything."

"That's the right attitude."

Beth walked in, and handed the copy and the original to Roger. "Here you go."

"Thanks," Roger said.

The young woman gave Matt a smile as she left the office. Roger handed Matt a copy of their contract. "We're in business, my man." He shook Matt's hand again.

"Thanks a lot, Roger. I'll look forward to hearing from you."

"You will. Definitely."

Matt glanced at the copy, then folded it up as he walked out of Roger's office. He tapped Beth's desk. She was on the phone at the time and could only wave at him.

As he stood in the hall waiting for an elevator, Matt unfolded the copy and read it. It was a simple one paragraph contract, just like the one Kayla signed. The down-light flashed on, and Matt folded the little paper, slipping it into his shirt pocket.

When the door slid open, only one person was inside. To Matt's surprise it was, "Jenny?"

She looked up, and her eyes grew wide. "Matt? Hey! What are you doing here?" She stepped out of the elevator.

Matt held open the door and pulled out his little folded piece of paper. "I'm newly signed by the D-S Management Group."

"Really? That's who I'm seeing."

"Roger Doctorow?"

"No. Sapirstein -- Lucy Sapirstein." She looked down the hall and leaned toward Matt. "How are they?"

"They seem professional enough."

"They don't deal in porn do they?"

"I don't know." Matt chuckled. "I guess if it made them a buck, they might. I don't think they'd force you in it though."

Jenny sighed and tugged on her blouse making sure it hung neatly over her belt line. "How do I look?"

"Fine."

"Wish me luck."

"You're in. They don't set aside time for people they don't want to deal with. You want me to wait?"

"No. I-ah, I have some errands to run after this. Where's Kayla by the way?"

"That's why I asked if I could wait. She's up in Burbank with the van, and I needed a lift."

Jenny checked her watch, then bit her lower lip unsure about giving Matt a lift. "Okay. Wait for me downstairs in the lobby."

"Sure. Thanks."

Jenny hurried down the hall, looking like a little girl trying to make it to class on time. Matt released the elevator door and took it down to the lobby.

A bookish male casting director escorted Kayla into a bungalow office at the Warner Brothers Studio complex. Inside, she stood in front of a long leather couch that held a balding white man with baggy jeans, a young black man with a gleaming bald head, and a black woman with afro-authentic dreadlocks that held unnatural splashes of red color.

"This is Kayla Ross," the casting director said. He then left her standing there.

The three people on the couch looked at each other for clues on their initial impression of Kayla. The white man whispered in the young black man's ear. The young man nodded and stood, forcing a nervous smile from Kayla.

"Ms. Ross, I'm Russ Brown, director of *Tug and War.*" Russ pointed to the older man. "This is Edgar Braun, our producer. And this is Fulani Ayakimtomi the author and screenwriter for this film."

"Pleased to meet you all," Kayla said.

The others nodded, and Russ sat back on the couch. He picked up her headshot and read the back of it. "You're one of Oscar Gold's girls, huh?"

"Yes."

"How come I haven't heard of you before?"

"I'm new to town -- three months."

Russ nodded as he continued looking over her resume. "Are you from England or something?"

"My mother is, but my hometown's Cleveland -- Shaker Heights."

"That's wild. Halle Berry's from Cleveland too. You know her?"

"Not personally."

"You will if you get this part." Russ laid her headshot back on the coffee table. "You're playing the baby sister of Halle Berry's character. You're a graduate student, the youngest of a group of five black woman struggling to cope with life and men." Russ smiled and scratched his nose. "I don't know how you're going to get around the accent problem. Everyone's southern on this project." He looked at Edgar. "I'm a little surprised at Oscar. Anyway, Fulani will feed you the lines. Let's see what you can do."

"Okay."

"You need some time?"

Kayla loosened her shoulders and rolled her head around a couple of times. She blew out her breath, shook her hair around, then dropped the script on the floor. "I'm ready."

Russ turned to Fulani who lifted her script and read aloud with no emotional emphasis. "I thought maybe you wanted to come back home with me for Christmas. That's all. It's no big deal."

"Well ah cayan't," Kayla said, trying to cover her accent with as much of a southern accent as she could stand. "Thayat's no big deayal. I have to spend time with my family too."

"I just wanted to return the favor after the nice time I had with your family last year. What's the matter with you? You've been acting like this for weeks."

Kayla focused her angry stare at Fulani, but her accent faded the more emotional she became. "Nothin'. Ain't nothin's the matter with me."

"I'm finding it harder to reach you. What's going on?"

"Look. Why are you on me like this?" Kayla responded.

"Did I do something wrong?"

"No."

"Tell me. I want to know."

"Everything's fine!" Kayla responded sharply.

"Bullshit. You seein' someone else?"

"Goddammit, Lamont!"

"Just answer me. I'm calm. Are you seeing someone else?"

"I don't have to answer to you. Ain't no ring here."

"I thought you were my girl."

"I'm nobody's girl! Let's get that straight right now. We had an understanding."

"Understanding? Hold up a minute. What the hell's an understanding?"

"Look, I don't have time. You think about it." Kayla took a step toward the door, stopped, then looked at her arm. "Boy, you better let my arm go. Now!" She snatched her arm downward, breaking an imaginary grip, then walked toward the door. She stopped and turned back to Russ, Edgar, and Fulani.

Russ scratched his chin, and nodded his head. Edgar looked surprised. Fulani had no emotion on her face.

"Very nice," Russ said. "But I still had the feeling you wanted to say 'bloody' something toward the end. I want you to try it again. This time find a comfortable accent you can hold on to longer than the first few lines."

"Okay."

Jenny had finished her interview and gained an agent, but Matt was a little confused about her subdued mood. He sat passively as Jenny drove the SUV down Melrose. She took a left on Gower, passing the walls of Paramount Studios.

At the northern edge of the studio complex was another wall worthy of a film studio, but behind it were no massive sound stages, only monuments to the dead.

Jenny drove through the open gate of the Hollywood Forever Cemetery. On either side of the narrow road were rolling greens and towering palms. Dense clusters of flamboyant tombs, some soaring higher than the walls, paid immortal tributes to long forgotten stars.

"Why are we here?" Matt asked.

"I have to pick up Albert."

"What's he doing here, digging up graves?"

"No."

Matt looked around at the rows of grave markers, reflecting pools, neo-classical temples and obelisks. There were mausoleums large enough to house two or three families of living people, and in between were the resting places of more modest people. Matt saw Albert sitting on the grass in front of one of them, a simple white slab.

Jenny stopped the SUV and pulled the emergency brake. Matt was about to get out of the vehicle when Jenny grabbed his arm. "Please, try to understand. He wanted to tell you in his own time."

Matt wasn't completely sure what she was talking about, but he suspected it had something to do with his past troubles. "Come on," he said.

When Matt hopped out of the SUV, Albert saw him, then turned back toward the grave. He closed his eyes tightly and lowered his head.

Jenny timidly followed Matt up to where Albert sat. "Hi," she said.

"What's up, A-C?"

Albert took a deep breath and gave Jenny a disappointed stare. "Well, this is a surprise."

"Jenny was just giving me a lift. I didn't know she was coming here."

Jenny sat down next to Albert, and rubbed the back of his head.

Matt walked up to the marker which had a dozen fresh roses leaning on it. He read the inscription. "Debra

Kastraki?" He looked at the dates. "Only eight years old. You knew her?"

Albert only shook his head.

Jenny gave his arm a supportive squeeze. "It's all right," she whispered.

Albert looked up at Matt. "I didn't know her. But I killed her."

Matt's mouth went dry. His eyes narrowed. Questions collided in his mind and seeped out of his mouth with a half whispered, "What?"

"It was an accident. I was strung out on coke and gin, cruisin' in broad daylight in North Hollywood, havin' a good time behind my third wife's back. The woman was a dealer -- had a purse loaded with stuff. We were snortin' in my car." Albert lowered his eyes to the ground and began pulling up blades of grass. "I didn't see the little girl -- just didn't see her. It was like slow motion -- the thud -- my brakes -- she didn't even scream. She never made any sound. Then, there was noise everywhere -- people all over the place, some of them cursin' me. Her mother's screams. I'll never forget her screams." Albert's eyes shifted from side to side. He looked up at Matt and chuckled bitterly. "My woman ran from the scene. I thought I would too. Don't know what made me stay." Matt lowered himself to the grass and sat in front of Albert. "So, what do you think of the great Albert Cole now?"

"That was some time ago," Matt said. "I'm sure you paid a price for that."

"Eighteen months jail time, plus six months rehab, and five years probation. My wife and son left me." Albert's eyes wandered to the Hollywood sign on the side of the distant hills. “I lost a chance at stardom too. I deserved everything I got.” He looked at Matt and gave him a sad smile. “So that’s the story, kid.”

Matt, fishing for anything empathetic to say, only came up with, “It’s all right.”

“Naw, kid. She’d be twenty-three today. Ain’t a day goes by without me thinkin’ about what her life would be like.”

Matt’s eyes gravitated back to the marker and the flowers. “You put the flowers there?”

Albert nodded. “I started comin’ here every so often after I found out where she was buried.”

Matt, Albert, and Jenny sat silently in the grass near the grave for another five minutes. The sound of the rustling the palms soothed them. Matt and Jenny temporarily forgot their individual career pressures. Their problems didn’t seem so important anymore.

Albert stood, stretched his legs, then blew a kiss to the grave marker. “Come on.”

They spent the rest of the afternoon lounging around Matt’s apartment. They didn’t say much to each other there either. They didn’t have to. Albert always held his depressed moods tightly, fearing a high amount of conversation would cause him anger. Jenny knew it. Matt knew it too. So, their only effort in bolstering his spirit was just being there.

Matt draped his leg over an arm of his lounge chair while reading the classified ads of a newspaper. Jenny sat on the floor with her back against the couch, watching an early evening newscast. Albert was half reclining on the couch, keeping his feet off the couch while watching TV too.

A commercial came on and Jenny rose up on her knees. “You have any orange juice or something?”

"Help yourself," Matt said.

Jenny walked into the small, tidy kitchen and pulled out a carton of orange juice. She then pulled a paper cup from a dispenser on the wall.

"Anyone else want some?" she asked.

"No. Thanks, sweetie," Albert said.

"Matt?"

"No thanks, Jen Jen."

Jenny brought her little cup back into the living room, and sat at the base of the couch. She turned to Matt, took a sip of her orange juice, and noticed his newspaper. "Looking for a job?"

Matt lowered the newspaper and looked over the top. "Huh?"

"Are you looking for a job?"

"Kind of."

"What happened to the nest egg y'all brought out here."

"It's cracking."

Jenny smiled, and took another sip on her juice.

"If you ever need any help, you know where you can come," Albert said.

"Thanks, but we're not hurting yet. I just figured by now one of us would've had a job."

"Same here," Jenny said. "It's no better than Florida so far."

"It takes time," Albert said. "The more people you meet the more jobs you'll have a chance for."

"How did we meet so many people in Florida?" Jenny asked.

"That's your home for one thing," Albert said.

Matt lowered the newspaper to his lap. "Yeah, for me it

was Shelley's workshop. Kayla and I didn't know anyone in Florida before we joined."

"So, why not join a workshop here?" Jenny shrugged her shoulders.

"Yeah, right." Albert rubbed his eyes. "You two go and join a workshop. I don't want to go through that again."

Jenny turned her head to Matt. "What do you say? Want to join one with me?"

"Another bill?" He sighed and lifted the newspaper back up to his eyes. "Check with me after I get a job."

Jenny finished her cup of orange juice and crumpled the paper cup. She settled back on the floor, watching the TV news.

The room became quiet again until Kayla's key tickled the outside lock. She opened the door, came in with a big smile on her face. "Hey." She was so full of energy, but the response she received from the others was only slightly friendlier than a murmured grunt. She closed the door. "What's the matter with the three of you?"

Matt folded his newspaper. "Nothing, babe. How'd it go?"

Kayla lean over Matt and kissed him briefly. "They called me back, and I might have to come in next week for a third reading." Kayla posed like a glamorous star. "Just think, I could be Halle Berry's baby sister." Kayla kicked her shoes off and smoothed her hair. "So, did you see the agent?"

"Yeah. I'm all set," Matt said. "Jen Jen's with them too."

"Really? Fantastic! Congratulations!"

"Thanks," Matt and Jenny said together.

"There's a letter on the counter for you," Matt said.

"Thanks." Kayla was still confused by their lack of joy.

She walked up to the kitchen counter, sat on a stool, and opened the letter. Kayla glanced at the TV, and only saw a sportscaster delivering highlights on the Dodgers' game. She quickly read the letter. Her eyes grew wide. "Oh my God!"

"What?" Matt asked.

"The world premiere of *White Caps*. It's September 21st at the El Capitan Theater. And we're invited."

"All of us?" Jenny asked.

"Me and one guest. Matt of course." It was quite a day for Kayla. She looked at each them. Not even Matt seemed all that excited about it. They all kept their eyes on the TV. Kayla turned serious and tossed the letter aside. "Okay, you want to let Ms. Ross in on the gloom. I feel a little left out here. Somebody die or something?"

Albert turned his eyes toward Kayla.

Chapter 16

At Venice Beach, a troop of aerobic exercise women used the red morning sun as the back-drop for their video. Wearing uniforms consisting yellow spandex shorts, sports bras, and sneakers, they had just finished their routine and were warming down. Three camera people surrounded them. One had a steady-cam, and walked closer to the leader. He lowered the camera toward the ground tilting the lens upward, and the leader faced it while stretching her legs. "How's that feeling? Now hold -- two, three, four, five six, seven, eight. Shift over to the left leg and stretch." Behind the mobile production van, dozens of bystanders watched the show.

A herd of young rollerbladers rattled down the nearby Ocean Front Walk. Most of them were unsteady on their wheels, and some stumbled when buzzed by an elderly black man on old fashion quad skates. Though old, the man was like a teenager, bouncing rhythmically, kicking, and crossing his skates. He spun and adjusted his earphones, then threw his dreds back, blew a kiss to the others and sped away, his loud laughter drawing the attention of the fitness women as he passed.

Across the walk from them, micro-business people

opened their stalls. Gusts from the chilly sea breeze inflated their tarpaulins and banners as they stretched them out. They meticulously arranged their products so beach walkers could have a clear look at their most profitable items.

A Mexican herbalist lit incense sticks -- the breeze carrying the exotic fragrances far from his stall. Hearing distant guitar music, he then turned out toward its source further out on the beach.

It was Matt, fingering his guitar lightly, sliding his left hand back and forth on its neck to reach each note. He wore a light sweater and jeans, and sat barefooted on a large blanket with Kayla who was dressed similarly to Matt, her sweater hanging off one of her shoulders.

Jenny and Albert were with them on a separate blanket, quietly listening to Matt's jazzy melody. Kayla gave them a serene smile, then closed her eyes.

When Matt finished his solo, he looked at Kayla and gave her a wink. She knew her cue and began singing softly, sounding so much more polished, so much more confident. Slowly, her eyes opened and her radiant smile never faded as she sang. When she sang of someone coming into her life, she reached over and ran her fingers over Matt's scalp. She gazed at him lustfully as she sang of surrendering to her desires. When singing of having her life turned around, her voice coursed with emotion from deep within her body. Her song was hypnotic, and chased the morning's chill away. Whatever else was going on around them, Albert and Jenny were, for those few minutes, wrapped up in Kayla's world.

She finished with a soft, drawn out note that never wavered, Matt adding a short instrumental finish at the end.

He winked at her, then noticed applause from some of the nearby beach-walkers surrounding them.

Kayla was surprised by the appreciation others showed for her singing. She then tentatively waved at them. "Thanks. Thank you." She turned back to Matt with a bashful smile. "I'm so embarrassed."

"Hey, people expect a show out here," Albert said.

"That was beautiful. What's that called?" Jenny asked.

"*Tonight I give in* -- an old Angela Bofill song."

"I don't know her."

"My mother was big fan," Kayla said as Matt continued fingering his guitar.

"You need to take that act out around town and get paid," Albert said.

"Been thinking about it," Matt said. "But the unions are pretty strong. We can't even get into the coffee houses."

"Cut a tape and send it to a record company."

"I don't know."

"Can't hurt."

Matt strummed his guitar forcefully. "Shit."

"What's the matter?" Jenny asked.

"Just thinking about getting a damn job," Matt said.

Albert smiled and stretched his upper back. "Be a star and you won't need a job, young black man."

Matt chuckled and laid his guitar down on the sand.

Kayla looked down shyly, fingering some nearby sand. "Maybe I should look for one too."

"What are you talking about?" Matt asked. "Gal, you are up for a big role."

"You're getting a lot more action than we are, that's for sure," Jenny said.

“That’s what we’re out here for -- acting,” Matt said.

“Oh!” Jenny lifted herself to her knees. “Speaking of acting. I found an acting workshop right in downtown Culver City.”

“How much is it?” Matt asked.

“Not as expensive as I thought.”

“How much?”

“Hundred and fifty a month. It’s run by this guy in a wheelchair, Roland DeCosta.”

“Never heard of him.”

“He’s one the best teachers in the country. I’ve already talked to him.”

“Why didn’t you sign up?” Matt asked.

“I did, but I was kinda hoping one of you would join me too?” Jenny pleaded with Kayla through her blue eyes.

“Jen, we’re a little tight on money right now,” Kayla said. “I have to wait and see what happens with this film.”

“And my job search,” Matt added. “We may check it out, but not right now.”

“Let us know how it is,” Kayla said.

“Okay.”

First thing Monday, Matt walked into the personnel office of a home improvement company. After filling out an application, he handed it to the secretary. She looked it over as Matt stood in front of her.

“Watch-N-Shop?” she asked.

“Yeah.”

“What did you do there?”

“I was in sales.”

"Oh." She placed the application down on her desk and handed Matt a laminated card. "I want you to read that out loud."

Matt thought her request was a little strange, but he did it. "Fusion-bond texture coating -- a revolutionary new surfacing for concrete block homes. Helps to protect against moisture and mold, and keeps your home looking brand new for years." Matt handed the card back to the secretary. "What's that for?"

"To see if you can read."

"I graduated from college."

"Doesn't matter. I know some so-called college graduates who can't even read their names smoothly. That can be a big problem in telemarketing. Okay, have a seat. Jimmy will see you in a few minutes."

"Thanks."

At home, Kayla was on the lounge watching a TV show when her phone vibrated near a newspaper on the coffee table. She wasted no time in answering it. "Hello?"

"Kayla?" a male voice on the other end answered.

"Yeah."

"Oscar."

"Hey. Any news?"

"I wish I had some good news."

Kayla wilted. "I didn't get it?"

"No."

"I thought the director was going to call me back for a third reading."

"Oh, he was. Russ really liked you, but the writer,

whatever her name was, she had her reservations, and veto power on the cast."

Kayla rubbed her brow. "Bloody hell."

"Hey, don't worry. A big-time director and producer met you. You'll have other chances. And I have some other ideas brewing. In fact, what are you doing this Friday night?"

"Nothing right now."

"Good, why don't you and some of your friends come on down to Olivia's at the Center. It'll cheer you up."

"Olivia's?"

"A nightclub near L-A Live, around the Staples Center. I'm part owner of it. Come on down and have a good time."

"Well -- sure. Are you going to be there?"

"Maybe. It doesn't matter. I'll put your name on the list. Check with the doormen so they'll let you in."

"Can I bring Matt?"

"Sure. Bring anybody you want. Just don't bring the whole damn town. We have to make some money."

"Okay. Sounds great."

"Good. I'll text you the directions. And don't worry about this rejection. It wasn't bad for a first audition."

"Thanks, Oscar."

"No problem. See ya."

He hung up, but Kayla lingered on the phone. She saw the newspaper on the coffee table and separated its various sections until she reached the employment ads.

Chapter 17

"I need to be more assertive, I guess. I want to lose my fear of pushing too hard." Jenny sat on a single chair in the middle of a small stage surrounded by three rows of bleachers. She couldn't see the faces of those who watched her because of the lights. "I want more respect too. I'm serious about what I do. I've studied for years. But it doesn't matter what your education is, or the accolades you've won. I'm tired about how some people who have the right look just seem to coast along with all the attention of the big shots, you know? But people like me?" Jenny shook her head. "I need that too. I want -- I want -- to ah -- I want to coast along too sometimes. Why not me? I need -- I need --"

"Thank you, Jenny," a voice said from off the stage. A soft squeak from a wheelchair drew Jenny's eyes in the direction of the voice. Emerging from the darkness, Roland DeCosta gave her an approving smile. He rolled up to her side and scratched his beard.

"That certain look is a very important thing to most people in this town. But I never thought I'd ever hear a blond, blue-eyed cutie like you complain about not having the right look." A soft murmur of laughter flowed from the other actors in the workshop. "Even those with the right look must have the talent to keep working in this business, or else they'll be back to crashing parties for attention. Don't fret over your looks though. Think of Sandra Bullock. She's not doing too bad for a fellow cutie pie." Roland spun his chair around to face the other actors. "Where's Tory?"

"Here."

"I need; I want, Tory. Thank you, Jenny."

"Thank you."

Jenny jogged off the bright stage. The rest of the evening she watched from a bleacher bench while numerous actors took their turns doing exercises and scene studies. She sat apart from the rest, still too shy about meeting them.

When the night's session ended, she gathered her bag and sweater, planning to be among the first out the door, but Roland rolled toward her. "Jenny?" he called.

She turned back. "Yes?"

"I just wanted to say, there's nothing to be intimidated about in this town. Your fellow actors are just like you. A lot of us put on airs of invulnerability. Lord knows I once did that too. It's lot harder for me to do that now, as you can see."

"Are you kidding? You scare me the most. All acting teachers scare me. I don't know what it is. Maybe it's not having enough work on my resume, or maybe it's that damn Hollywood sign on that hill. I feel a little overwhelmed sometimes."

"Well, stop feeling that way. And for crying out loud, don't be scared of me. Always know that I want to see all my students find some measure of success. Especially you. I'm here to help keep you sharp and ready for your next break."

Jenny looked down shyly and bit her lower lip. "Mind if I ask?" She gestured to his wheelchair.

"Car accident. Five years ago. It took me out of the rat race and made me a sage."

"I'm sorry."

Roland shook his head and waved his hand at her. "I'm adjusting." He sighed and looked up at her. "Well -- anyway. You hang on in there. Find any way you can to act. Any way you can. Make your own little breaks if you can't get the big breaks. That's the important thing."

"Yeah, you're right." Jenny looked at her watch. "Look, I have to run. I'll see you Wednesday, okay?"

"Sure. And start looking for scenes. There are a lot of people looking for scene-study partners."

"Okay." Jenny turned and walked away.

Roland lingered between the bleachers watching her walk out the door.

It was day for night. The sun had already set hours ago, but the lights around the L.A. Live complex were so bright no one noticed. The traffic passing Olivia's had to slow down because of the cars pausing in front of the nightclub. Couples and groups emerged from each car, but they couldn't just walk right into the club. There were already dozens of people waiting in line in the mild night.

Five huge doormen stood in front of the main entrance, each had physiques that would make the steroid producers of America reconsider the dosages of their products. Their mere presence forced out a higher sense of patience from the dressy people in line.

Albert's SUV pulled up to the front of the club, and Matt hopped out of the back seat to hold the doors open for the ladies. Kayla scooted out the back seat wearing a one-shoulder, red blouse with an asymmetric hem flaring out from under a black belt over her skin tight black denim slacks. Black, cut-out high heels covered her feet. Jenny cautiously emerged from the front seat wearing a form fitting, sleeveless black mini-dress with an aqua matador jacket, and black stilettos that made her almost as tall as Kayla.

Matt closed the back door and leaned in the front. "Why don't you let the valet people park it?"

"Hell no," Albert snapped. "I wouldn't them park a tricycle around here. Wait up for me."

"Okay." Matt shut the door, and stood with the women in front of the main entry. "He's parking it." Matt eyed both Jenny and Kayla admiring how good they looked. He draped his arms over both women. "Damn, I'm with some good-looking girls." The way some of the women in line stared at Matt, he stood out in his own way. He wore a black muscle-fitting shirt with blue paisley print, black jeans, and casual denim-blue shoes.

"Hey! You folks are going to have to get in line or move along!"

They turned back after hearing that threatening voice and saw one of the massive doormen walking toward them. Matt swallowed hard, knowing a nervy display of manly honor would be risky against this guy.

"We're guests of Oscar Gold," Kayla said. "We were just waiting for the fourth member of our party."

"Oscar Gold, huh?" Kayla nodded, but the guard turned back to the others. "Henry?"

"Yeah."

"Bring that list out here, will ya?" A shorter side of beef brought a clipboard out to the others. The taller guy took the board and flipped through a couple of pages. "What's your name, red?"

"Kayla Ross."

"Kayla Ross. R-O-S-S?"

"Yes." Kayla nervously glanced at Matt.

The big man flipped another page over, running his rough looking index finger down the list. "Kayla Ross." He tapped his finger on the spot on the list where he saw her name. "You're in. How many in your party, Ms. Ross?"

"Three others with me. We're waiting for the other member of our party."

"Sure. Anytime you're ready, just walk right in. Henry, these people are okay. Let the others know."

"Okay, Patrick."

"You folks enjoy yourselves tonight."

"Thank you," they all said at once.

All three watched the big man walk back toward the door. The spread of his upper back muscles, and the thickness of his thighs, were unlike anything they had ever seen before. Matt glanced at Jenny, and then at Kayla. Both looked like they were under hypnosis.

Matt waved his hand in front of Kayla's face and she began blinking her eyes. "You want me to look like that?" he asked.

"Oh no, babe. You're more than enough man for me." Kayla giggled and cleared her throat. Jenny looked at Kayla, and playfully bit a knuckle on her hand. They both laughed like two silly school girls.

"All right now. I wonder what the girls are like up in here." He tugged on his belt buckle and stepped out in front of the girls toward the entry.

"Ohhh?" Kayla tugged Matt's arm, pulling him back towards her.

"Okay, kids." Albert walked up behind Jenny and pulled her against him. "We're all set. How much of a wait do we have?"

"None," Kayla said. "Just follow me." Kayla sauntered up toward the main entry with the others following. She walked with such confidence that those stuck in line wandered if she were a celebrity. All their eyes were on the lady with the red one-shoulder blouse.

When Kayla reached the entry, Henry stepped to the side, and offered Kayla and her friends the right of passage. "You and your party have a nice time, Ms. Ross."

"Thank you."

They walked through a conventionally lit, barrel-vaulted hall with forest murals around them. They heard the thumping music seeping through the walls. Few people passed them going or coming, until they reached a curve in the hall where it was darker, and the music clearer. When they turned a corner, a recessed space, thousands of square feet in area, glowing in predominantly blue light, opened up before them. Hundreds of people covered the vast dance floor, each moving in their own way, each caught-up in the music's driving rhythms. Lightning flashes of red, green, yellow, and white burst forth adding an electric edge to the misty atmosphere.

Crowded lounge balconies and smaller bars were on the mezzanine around the theater-like interior. Toward the back was a second dance floor equally as crowded, but more like a circus with aerial artists swinging to and fro through pillars of multi-colored spotlights.

Kayla led her friends down a gentle ramp that was so thick with people it was almost impossible for them to avoid having a hand or a body part brush-up on them. Jenny felt a pinch on her butt. She jumped and looked around believing at first it was Albert, but it was on the side away from him.

"What?" Albert asked.

Jenny looked around him, but the pincher had blended into the crowd. She shook her head at Albert.

Kayla gingerly squeezed through a group of people near the dance floor. She held Matt's hand, pulling him through too. They all walked up to a wooden rail, looking for a place to sit, but there were no empty stools or tables around the dance floor.

Jenny looked a little hassled by the crowd and the noise. Her angry eyes relaxed when she put her hands on the rail. Albert adjusted his sports-coat and stepped up beside her.

Matt stared at a group of tall women on the floor who danced together. Three of them were sensually grinding front to back on each other, rather than making an effort at dancing. They eyed Matt with their riveting stares -- their lips slightly parted, like they were venting heat through their teeth. One of them inserted a finger in her mouth, pulling it in and out, then swallowed suggestively while eying him. "Shit," he whispered. He then turned his eyes in another direction.

Kayla was caught up in the music, and began moving

her hips and hands. Her smile grew wider. When the music changed, the floor cleared enough for new dancers. Kayla grabbed Matt's hand. "Come on, baby." She pulled him through an opening in the railing and claimed a spot on the floor. She lifted her arms high and swayed her hips, freely expressing with her movements the passionate power of the music. Matt leaned from side to side, hooking each arm around her waist allowing Kayla to brush her hips against him.

Within seconds, the dance floor filled up again. They felt constricted by the sweaty people surrounding them. Yet, Kayla still gestured for Jenny and Albert to come join them.

Jenny looked up at Albert. "You want to dance?"

"Not right now. I have to get warmed up first. You want a drink or somethin'?"

"Yes. A Margarita?"

"Come on. I'll walk you to the bar."

Jenny hesitated looking back at Matt and Kayla working out on the dance floor; the music stirring her youthful energy. "You mind if I go out and join them?"

"Huh?"

"I just want to dance with Matt and Kayla. You mind?"

Albert was a little surprised. He glanced out to Kayla and Matt dancing so vigorously within the thick crowd. Everyone out there was young like Jenny. "Well, no. I guess not."

Jenny gave Albert a kiss on the cheek, then pulled her hand from his. Somehow, she managed to squeeze her way through the crowd to where Kayla and Matt danced, and joined them.

Albert watched her out there on the floor and

remembered the differences in their ages. At that moment, he wondered about having a relationship with a woman so young. Doubts crossed his mind, but he fought them. It wasn't anything new to him. He turned toward the nearest bar and walked toward it.

Perspiration shimmered on Matt's forehead as he tried keeping up with Kayla's energetic moves. She still looked cool and in her element. Somehow, she moved effortlessly in the narrow space.

Jenny danced, but not without inhibitions. She watched Kayla's moves and tried imitating them with little success. Suddenly, a young man in a sweaty tank-top dropped to the floor near her feet, and pushed his pelvis in her direction before spinning upright again. Even in the blue light, Jenny's face became red.

The man leaned in to Jenny. "What's your name?"

"What?"

"Your name! What is it?"

Jenny coolly continued dancing, and quickly evaluated this man's intentions. "Hillary Rodham!"

Kayla laughed when she heard Jenny's response.

"Hillary? You dance nice, Hillary! I'm Manuel!"

"Good to meet you."

"Stick around, Hillary! I can pop something for you like you ain't never seen." Manuel flexed his shoulders and arms, and snaked his body through a series of pelvic thrusts. He then spun to the floor and back to his feet before dancing back into the crowd. Kayla and Matt both laughed. Jenny turned to them with a sour look on her face.

"What the hell," Matt said.

"Hillary Rodham?" Kayla asked.

Jenny shrugged her shoulders and kept dancing. "I guess it didn't ring a bell with him."

Kayla shook her head, then closed her eyes when she felt Matt's hands dancing on her body. The music slowed and the lights darkened. Slowly revolving spots of yellow lights covered the walls and a cool mist flowed out on the floor. Matt and Kayla pulled each other closer. She embraced his right thigh with both of hers and swayed her hips like they were making love. Matt's hand went under her blouse hem, gently massaging her buns.

Jenny made discreet exit from the floor and went back to the spot where she left Albert. He wasn't back yet, so she leaned on the rail and watched the few couples on the floor slow dancing.

"Want to slide on out there?" a smooth Latin laced voice said.

Jenny turned back to the voice and found another young man. This one wore a white, custom-made suit. He held out his hand and smiled with a charm that must have conquered dozens of women. Jenny smiled politely. "No thank you."

"Why not? We can have a nice time together."

"Because the lady is with somebody, kid," Albert said, walking up with two drinks.

"Yeah? Who's she with? You?"

"Yeah. So, if you will excuse us, young man." Albert handed Jenny her drink.

"I'll excuse you all right, pops." The young man walked away with an arrogant smirk.

Jenny sipped on the straw of her drink. "Thank you."

"No problem."

They both continued watching Kayla and Matt in

each other's arms, dancing nose to nose, grinding to the music's slow rhythm. She rested her head on his shoulder and glanced up to the mezzanine where someone's waving caught her eye. She lifted her head and squinted her eyes. A man leaned over the edge, vigorously waving at her. It was Oscar. Kayla paused her grind with Matt and waved back at him.

Jenny and Albert looked up, but couldn't see the person who caught Kayla's attention.

"There's Oscar." Kayla pointed, directing Matt's attention. Oscar motioned for them to join him. Kayla nodded and waved. "Come on. I want you to meet him." Kayla took Matt by the hand and walked off the dance floor to where Jenny and Albert stood. "Oscar Gold's up in one of the lounges. Come on."

Jenny and Albert held their drinks, and followed Matt and Kayla through the thick crowd around the dance floor.

The music changed again, becoming quick and hopped-up. The crowd parted in front of Kayla as she passed. Most male eyes followed her. Many females stared too.

Kayla stopped near a bar, and looked around at the walls. She wasn't sure where to go. "You see any stairs around here?" she asked.

Matt shook his head.

"Wait a minute." Albert walked over to the bar and flagged down one of the tenders. She whispered in his ear and pointed toward the restrooms. Albert nodded, took a sip of his drink, and walked back to the group. "There's a private elevator near the restrooms."

Albert led them to it and pushed the up button. It was an unexpectedly long wait. Matt used a napkin to wipe the sweat off his brow. Kayla jostled her blouse to get cooler air on her skin.

"Weeew." She glanced at Matt. "Glad you came?"

He nodded with that dimpled smile. "Yeah, I am."

Kayla turned to Jenny and Albert. "How about you?"

Jenny looked back at the lights of the dance floor. "This is something else. Now if I can only get ol' Dumpy here out on the dance floor."

"Don't worry about me, sweetie." He held up his drink. "Two more of these and I'll dance you under the floor."

The elevator door slid open and another of Olivia's big bouncers met them. "Can I help you?"

"I'm Kayla Ross. We're guests of Oscar Gold. Is this the way up?"

"Yeah. Come on in."

The bouncer rode up with them. The elevator wasn't that big, and the bouncer took up a substantial portion of it. He stared at them through eyes recessed under thick eyebrows.

The others struggled not to stare back at him. To their relief, it was only a few seconds before the door slid open again. The big man stepped outside and they followed.

"What's your name again?" the bouncer asked.

"Kayla Ross and party."

"Wait here."

They waited in a small lobby with a beautiful Persian-style rug in the middle. Small palm trees lined the walls. In the barrel-vaulted opening ahead, they saw the blue glow of the dance floor.

Matt reached over and felt one of the leaves of a nearby palm tree. "This is real."

Albert looked up at the ceiling and whistled softly. "Your agent and his buddies sunk a pretty penny in this place."

A couple minutes later the bouncer came back to the lobby. "You're in."

Kayla led the others through vaulted opening and into a cocktail lounge area overlooking the dance floor. Men in formal evening suits, and women in outfits accessorizing and/or displaying tastefully, areas of their bodies they were most proud of, mingled in small groups between plush couches and chairs.

Oscar emerged from the middle of the lounge with his arms wide, and a big smile on his face. "KAYLA! KAYLA-KAYLA-KAYLA!" His greeting caught the attention of most of the people in the lounge. Oscar grabbed her by the shoulders and kissed both her cheeks.

"How are you, Oscar?" Kayla greeted.

"I'm fine. Ahhh, look at you." He pulled back from Kayla, letting his eyes scan her body. "You are sharp, girl. How long have you been here?"

"We've been here about a half hour."

"Good. I'm glad you came. Who are your friends?"

"Oh. This is my boyfriend, Matt Redcrop. He's an actor, and the guitarist on my recording."

Oscar shook his hand. "From Tampa, right?"

"Yes, sir."

"Pleased to meet you."

"Nice to meet you too."

"This is Jenny Rappaport, an actress."

"No kidding." Oscar shook her hand and continued holding it. "Pleased to meet you."

"Nice to meet you too -- finally."

"Finally?"

"I sent you my headshots a few months ago."

Oscar smiled and patted her hand. "Well, what can I say, young lady. I know you have an agent by now, as pretty as you are."

"Well, yeah." She blushed faintly.

"Good-good." Oscar looked over at Albert. "I bet you're an actor too, huh?"

Albert gave Oscar a sugary smile and nodded. He offered his hand. "Albert Cole."

"Albert Cole?" Oscar nodded his head. "That name has a ring to it. Nice to meet you. Hey, enjoy yourselves. I had just closed a big deal for one of my clients and we're celebrating. The bar is free, and we have lots of hors d'oeuvres. Matt, mind if I borrow Kayla for a few minutes?"

"No, go right ahead. What are you drinking, babe?"

"A rum and Coke?"

"Okay."

"We'll be over there," Oscar said. He took Kayla by the hand and led her away to a lounge near the edge of the mezzanine. "I want you to meet some of my other clients." He snapped his fingers. "Delbert? Hey Delbert!"

A tall, skinny white man with bushy hair pulled himself away from a model looking woman. He had an expensive looking digital camera strapped over his shoulder.

"Yes, Mr. Gold?"

"I need some photos over here."

"Sure." Delbert followed Oscar and Kayla toward a black leather, circular couch that had a panoramic view of the dance floor. The four women on the couch were enjoying the attention of a dozen men. "Patty -- Raven -- Constance -- Ann

Marie?" When they heard Oscar calling them, they immediately cut-off their conversations with the surrounding men, stood and walked toward him.

Kayla recognized two of the women from films she had seen in the past. Her eyes widened and her smile faded.

"Girls, I want you to meet a new client of mine. Ms. Kayla Ross. Kayla, this is Patty Hargrove, Raven, Constance Poe, and Ann Marie Grant, the young lady we're celebrating tonight."

"Nice to meet you all," Kayla said, controlling her thrill over meeting recognizable stars.

"Nice to meet you too," Ann Marie said.

"Are you British?" Raven asked.

Kayla widened her smile. "I'm a Clevelander by way of Tampa."

"Tampa? Really?"

"Hey, Mr. Gold, let me get this shot," Delbert said.

Oscar nodded his head and walked into the middle of the women. "What do you want me to do?" he asked.

Delbert thought for a moment, then saw the couch. "Let's clear that couch, and put you on it. And have the girls stand over you from behind it."

"Good idea." Oscar walked over to the couch asked the few people sitting on it to move. They did as Oscar asked, and stood behind Delbert.

"Sit right in the middle, Mr. Gold." Oscar did as Delbert directed. "Now the girls. I want you to stand behind the couch over Mr. Gold." Kayla lingered not sure if she should be in this. Delbert saw her and waved at her. "You too, doll."

Oscar gestured for Kayla to join them. She jogged around the couch and stood next to Patty.

Delbert looked through his lens, then lowered his camera.

"Ann Marie, why don't you stand in the middle, right over Mr. Gold."

"Okay," she answered.

She and Raven traded places. Delbert raised his camera.

"All right. WHO LOVES MONEY!"

"MEEEEEEEE," they all responded.

The flashbulb lit lounge.

Matt worked his way back to Kayla holding two drinks. A laughing woman bumped him, spilling a little of the drinks.

"Oh, I'm sorry." The woman placed her hand on Matt's chest and pulled her heavily colored lips wide in a sympathetic smile. "Are you all right?" She sensually rubbed her hand on his chest.

"No Problem," Matt said. He spun away from her, but noticed her inviting smile and eyes as he continued weaving through clusters of Oscar's friends. When he found Kayla, he saw her sitting on the couch conversing with Ann Marie and three men standing around them. Matt walked around the back of the couch and presented the drink to Kayla over her shoulder.

"Huh? Oh. Thanks, babe. Hey, Matt, you know who this is?"

Kayla pointed to Ann Marie. Matt took a sip of his drink, and squinted his eyes. He bent lower to get a better look, then began nodding his head. "Yeah. You're uhhh -- Ann-uhhh -- Ann Marie." Matt slapped his head. "Damn, I can't remember your last name."

"Grant," Ann Marie said, offering her hand.

"Yeah. Nice to meet you."

"Matt's the guy I was telling you about." Kayla reached up and caressed his face. Matt lowered his head to her bare shoulder. "He's my sweetie, and an actor too."

"Really? You should be getting a lot of work with your looks." She tapped Kayla's arm. "Weeew."

"I'm okay," he said.

"Good. Oh, these gentlemen by the way are Pete, Jacob, and Dumont. They're my sweeties."

Matt looked up at the three men standing in front of them. They smiled and nodded their greetings to him.

"Kayla?"

She heard her name called, and looked around the three men in front of her. "Kayla? Over here." Oscar was near another large couch with three other people, waving at her.

"Excuse me, Ann. Duty calls."

"He will keep you busy."

Kayla handed her drink to Matt, and left him there with Ann and her three men. Matt kept his eyes on Kayla as she jogged over to Oscar. The three men in front them turned back and stared at Ann Marie and Matt. Matt's eyes shifted back to Ann Marie. Turning toward Matt, she smiled, slipped off her shoes, and pulled her smooth legs onto the couch. She began twirling a lock of her red hair. "So, Matt, how's Hollywood treating you?"

Matt took a nervous sip of his drink.

Kayla walked up to Oscar's side, and he hooked his hand around one of her arms. "Kayla? I'd like you to meet a very important person." Oscar held his hand out to a casually dressed older black man who stood between two younger black men wearing business suits that made them look like security twins. “This is Howard Rowe, the chief executive and producer for NTA records. Howard? Kayla Ross.”

Howard smiled warmly through his silver goatee. “How are you, young lady?”

“Fine, thank you.” Kayla still wasn’t sure why this guy was so important to her.

“I was just telling Howard about you.” Oscar pointed at Kayla, and looked back at him. “See? A dynamite look, an actress with dance training, and even has a decent singing voice.”

“Where are you from?” Howard asked.

“Cleveland.”

“Cleveland?” Howard began laughing. “What’s up with that accent?”

“My mother’s English. Just genetics, I guess. But I’m a Clevelander though. Go Browns.”

“For real?” Howard had an impressed look on his face as he gave her a second look. “I see what you mean, O-G. But that’s still a couple of months away at least.”

“Well, keep her in mind.”

“We’ll see. Right now, I’m gonna raid that little bar over there. You want something?”

“I’m too hydrated, my friend. Enjoy. Enjoy.”

“Very nice to meet you, young lady.”

“Nice to meet you too,” Kayla responded.

The two young men with Howard followed him to the bar. Oscar put his hand on Kayla’s shoulder anticipating her questions. “Howard’s has a long history in the industry, from Motown to Sony Music. He’s working on some project, but he’s not letting anyone in on it. All I know is what he told me. In the near future, he wants to see some attractive women of color with singing and dancing ability. You were the first person I thought of."

"You have no idea what it is?"

"None."

"A video maybe?"

"No. Not the way he's being so hush-hush."

"A film?"

"Don't know. As soon as I hear anything I'll let you know. In the meantime, go have some fun. Where's that man of yours?"

She looked back at the couch where she left him, and saw Ann Marie and Matt deep in conversation. "I'd better get back to him," she said.

"Okay."

"Thanks, Oscar."

"Hey, it's my job. I work for you."

Kayla smiled, then hurried back to Matt.

Albert and Jenny sat on stools at the bar, nursing drinks. Jenny looked sleepy. Albert looked bored. Three empty glasses were in front of them. "So, this is glamor and glitz?" she asked.

Albert burped, then yawned. "Yep. This is the life." He gulped down another mouthful of pretzels.

Chapter 18

"Hello? Mrs. Menendez? -- Hi, I'm Matt Redcrop calling for Carpenter's Square Home Improvements. How are you? -- No Español. English? – Sorry. -- Okay."

Matt terminated the call on his computer and leaned back in his chair. His eyes roamed a room filled with telemarketers, each of them busy with calls. It wasn't a cavernous, full acre facility like the one in Florida, but it was comfortable and had a professional feel.

Another call flashed on his monitor, but all he heard on his earphones was an answering machine. He popped a key on his computer, then sighed.

"Gentlemen, this is Albert Cole," a casting director said. She then left Albert standing alone in front of three producers.

One stood and held his arms wide. "Albert!"

A big smile grew on Albert's face. "Benny?" The two men embraced. "Son of a bitch. You're behind this?"

"I'm the man. And you're looking good after all these years. I couldn't believe my luck when I called your agent and she sent me your headshot. So, how are you?"

"I'm hangin' in there. I didn't think anyone wanted to see me again."

"How long have you been in town?"

"Going on six months now," Albert said.

"You haven't been getting any nibbles?"

Albert shook his head. "My first call since I got back."

"Awe hell, man. Don't worry about it now. Those troubles are behind you." Benny turned to the other two men sitting on the couch in the office. "Albert, I want you to meet Lawson Reynolds, and Cap Epstein. They're the co-writers and producers of the television pilot we're planning."

"Nice to meet you fellows."

"Good to meet you too," Cap said. Lawson only smiled.

"Guys, this is one incredible actor here. We go back a long way together, aye Al?" Albert nodded. Benny draped an arm over his shoulder. "Now, I want you two to think in terms of that crusty old bartender's role. Can you see it?"

Cap nodded his head, but Lawson squinted his eyes.

"He looks too young," Lawson said. "I'm still thinking about Brian Dennehy types."

"Brian Dennehy looks too classy for the role," Cap said. "With a little make-up, I can definitely see this guy in the part."

Albert's smile faded a little.

"I don't know." Lawson sighed.

"Look at him," Cap said. "Even without the make-up he looks like a punch-drunk ex-boxer."

Albert raised his eyebrows.

"And there's no way he'll clash with Topper Jamison," Benny said.

"Yeah. Topper never could stand working with other good-looking men," Lawson said.

"No worries here," Cap added.

"Benny, do I have to put up with this?" Albert asked.

"See?" Benny cupped his hand under Albert's chin. "He's a perfect side-kick." Benny slapped Albert on the back.

"Mind doing a reading, Albert?" Lawson asked.

"I guess. If I'm not too punch-drunk today."

Kayla was alone in her apartment listening to soft music on a TV music channel. She sat on a stool at her kitchen counter, picking through a small salad. She pierced a small tomato and placed it in her mouth, chewing it slowly, savoring the taste of the oil and vinegar dressing. She found a patch of dry skin on her hand and rubbed her fingers over it. It was nothing a little hand cream couldn't cure.

She raised a leaf of lettuce to her mouth and chewed it just as slowly as the tomato. She tried, but couldn't resist a look. Her eyes slowly shifted to her right and there it was, silent and inert, tethered to the wall by its charge cord – her phone.

Ring dammit! Ring! Matt and Kayla hadn't had any calls for three weeks, none from their agents, none from even their families. Matt had grown accustomed to the phone not ringing for him, but Kayla was getting irritated. *What the hell is Oscar doing?*

Suddenly, it vibrated, startling Kayla. She dropped her fork and some of the salad on the floor. She hopped over to the phone nearly kicking over the other stool. She stopped and waited for a couple more vibrations, taking a calming breath.

"Hello?" Her eyes closed, muting her disappointment. "No, this is not Valley Mortgage. They don't have this number."

Kayla ended her call, sat on the stool, then contemplated cleaning up her little mess on the carpet.

"How can I stop now?" Jenny kept her eyes locked open on the darkness beyond the stage lights, staring at a face that was only in her mind. "You know I can't. For ten years -- for ten long years, I've been chasing you, this ghost -- this delusion built up in my mind." Her lower lip quivered. Her eyes turned glassy. "I always believed you were real. Now I see my insanity. I've given up so much -- my career, my family, my soul just for you -- this unreachable man." She paused with angry eyes. "Who are you? Why do you have this hold on me?"

Jenny held her stare, then lowered her head, rubbing her eyes. Clapping began and grew into a smattering of applause from the other workshop actors.

"Oh my. Oh my." Roland DeCosta rolled out onto the stage to Jenny's side. He reached out and held her hand. "Yeah. Very nice. The emotion was right on, and done so effortlessly."

"Thanks."

"Jenny, I need to see you in some scenes. If you're having trouble finding challenging material, I have a library full of scripts. See me after class, okay?"

"Okay."

Roland held her hand and gave it a jiggle. "Nicely done. Who's next?"

After the long workshop session, Roland wheeled himself along some low selves filled with file folders in his office. Jenny sat on his desk patiently watching and listening to him.

"Sure, I thought about it," he said. "Every now and then, I receive a script or two some producer wants me to direct. But it's usually low-grade material, what they used to call B-movies. I never did movies like that when I was acting, and I certainly don't want to direct anything like that." He stopped and reached for a file. "Here it is." He pulled it out and held it up for Jenny. "*Postcards from the Edge*, Meryl Streep and Shirley Maclaine -- a wonderful film." He handed it to Jenny who immediately thumbed through it. "It involves a drug abusing actress, and her over-bearing, superstar mother. Leigh Perlman is looking for a scene study partner. Why don't you two team up and do this one?"

"Yeah. I'll check with her tomorrow." She quickly looked over the dialog. "This looks good." She didn't notice Roland's consuming stare. He was embracing her with his eyes -- embracing this new student who seemed to capture more of his attention each time he saw her. He then checked himself, forcing his eyes to look in another direction.

Jenny lowered the script on her lap, and gave him a smile that made his heart skip.

"Well," Roland sighed.

"Well." Jenny responded with a shrug. "I guess I better get home."

"Yeah, me too. If you ever need more material, it's all in the shelf here."

"Thanks, Roland."

Jenny hopped off his desk and gave him a gentle squeeze on his shoulder as she left his office. The door closed behind her. Roland stayed still in his wheelchair, staring at the spot where she sat on his desk. He rolled up to it and put his hand on this warm remnant of her body. He lowered his head on the area, inhaling deeply, exhaling slowly, whispering, "Oh God," just before his exhalation ended.

Jenny came home, and found Albert asleep on the couch. The TV was on with the eleven o'clock news. She placed her keys on a hook near the kitchen sink, then slipped off her shoes.

She opened the refrigerator, searching for a snack. The sound of two jars clanging inside caused Albert to stir. He turned and saw Jenny's butt sticking out from behind the refrigerator door.

"Hey, Jen Jen."

"Hey." She continued searching the refrigerator, but nothing peaked her appetite.

Albert saw the clock, then checked his watch. "You just now getting in?"

"Yeah." She stood up straight in front of the refrigerator and smacked her lips. "I'm hungry, but there's nothing I want in here."

"My agent called tonight."

Jenny turned out to Albert, closed the door and walked to the edge of the kitchen. "Well?"

Albert sat up on the couch, a smile slowly growing on his face. "I got it."

Jenny screamed and jumped in his arms. "Oh my God! OH MY GOD! You did it! Why didn't you call me?"

"Surprise. It's only a pilot. It may not ever see the light of day. But it's a job and baby, I needed that."

"Oh baby." Jenny pulled his face close and kissed him deeply. "Dumpy's back in business."

"Dumpy's back in business," Albert repeated.

"How much are you getting?"

"They're still negotiatin', but I'm looking at 20-K for the shoot, and 15-K each time the pilot show airs. And if it goes to series, and if my character is on a particular show – who knows."

Jenny whistled and said, "That can add up."

"It's not big money, but it's work." Albert playfully buried his face in Jenny's bosom, and she slowly massaged the back of his head.

When Milo heard Albert got a part in a television pilot he gathered the Tampa group together at Joe Blue's Bar and Grill near downtown Culver City for a celebration. Calling this bar a hole-in-a wall would have been a compliment, but Milo had a soft spot for places like this.

Tar paper looking walls and floors dominated this place. The tables were old enough to be antiques, but had too much graffiti carved on them to be valuable. The walls had glamorous headshots of total unknowns who had eaten there over the years.

The Tampa group sat around a large table in a corner under one of the headshot filled walls, laughing and talking about their lives here and in Florida. A surly looking waitress interrupted their conversations when she brought a tray full of French fries, juicy hamburgers, and a second round of drinks. "What else you want?"

"Just keep them drinks on my tab, Liza," Milo said.

"Right."

Milo squeezed the hand of his trophy-gal date, then picked up his beer and raised it to Albert.

"Here's to my old buddy Albert Cole. Heee's back. Let's keep it going forever."

"Here-here," Matt said.

Everyone touched glasses and sipped their drinks. Milo remained standing, shrugged his shoulders, then turned to his blond showgirl. "I don't know, Steffi. Maybe these people hadn't heard yet." She only smiled at him.

"Heard what?" Albert asked.

"I kind of expected to get a toast too, you know," Milo answered. "I guess nobody told y'all." Milo nodded to Steffi, who only giggled.

"What?" Kayla asked.

"Seems like someone should tell them -- like my publicity person here." Milo tapped his date's shoulder. "Hello?"

"Huh? Oh, yeah." Steffi stood and cleared her throat. She pulled a folded piece of paper from the back pocket of her jeans. She giggled again, then composed herself. "This just in this afternoon, Milo Stankavich, star of the blockbuster film *Now You See me*, has been signed to another major motion picture -- a science fiction classic called *The Beast Without*. Filming starts in November in Vancouver, British Columbia. Milo has a four-day contract."

Milo leaned over, looking at the paper in her hands.

"That part about the four days -- you could've cut that," he said.

"Just being thorough," Steffi responded

"Congratulations," Kayla said.

"We have a double celebration," Jenny said.

"That's all right, man." Matt reached over and shook Milo's hand.

Albert swallowed a mouthful of his beer, then slapped the table. "Goddammit, Milo! Congratulations!" He stood up and raised his mug. "Here's to our human passport to Hollywood. Continued success."

"Oh, you shouldn't have," Milo said. "But thanks." Everyone touched glasses again. Milo sat and took a big bite of his hamburger never bothering to swallow before talking. "Yeah. Shelley's old students are doing well out here."

"We're hangin' in there," Albert said.

"It's fun ain't it." Milo looked at the others. "Right?" Matt, Kayla, and Jenny quietly ate their burgers unable to add to Milo and Albert's stories of success.

Steffi looked across the table and saw a ketchup bottle near Kayla. "Excuse me. I'm sorry. What's your name again?"

"Kayla."

"Kayla. That's right. Could you pass the ketchup please."

"Sure." Kayla handed the bottle to Steffi.

"So, are you up for any roles?" Steffi asked.

Kayla chewed and swallowed a couple of fries, then shook her head. "No, not really. Just some flirtations here and there, but nothing serious."

Steffi turned to Jenny. "How about you?"

Jenny shook her head. "I'm just like Kayla."

Steffi looked at Matt.

"Don't even ask," he said. "The silence is deadly on my end. Maybe I need another agent."

"Sometimes it goes like that," Milo said. "This town has 1.2 million actors in it, and you're doing better than almost all of them just by having your union cards."

Albert finished the last of his beer and tapped the glass on the table looking for that waitress. When he saw her, he raised his hand and snapped his fingers. The waitress turned with a perturbed look on her face.

"Can I get another round?" Albert asked.

The waitress pointed the eraser of her pencil at his nose. "Just snap those fingers again, and I'll see how quickly they can break. You hear what I'm sayin'."

"Whoa!" Albert leaned back in his chair and hid his hands under the table. "I'm sorry, okay? -- Ma'am? -- Majesty?" Albert bowed his head repeatedly.

She cracked a half smile. "Majesty. I like that. Just remember that."

"Yes, Majesty."

"I'll get that round, peasant." The waitress popped Albert on his shoulder with her pencil, then walked toward the bar.

Albert looked at Milo with shocked eyes. "Holy shit. She scared me." He began laughing.

"What did I tell you," Milo said.

"Whips and chains kind of girl, huh?"

"This is a good place to eat though. The burgers are good."

Jenny swallowed a bite of her burger, and sipped on her soda. She looked up at Kayla and Matt. "I still think y'all need to stay sharp while waiting. At least come and check it out tomorrow night."

"Check what out?" Milo asked.

"The Pro-Performers Workshop," Jenny said.

"Oh, DeCosta's place."

"Yeah."

"Y'all members there?" Milo asked.

"No. Just me," Jenny said, "but I was hoping some other people would join me." Jenny looked at all her friends.

Albert concentrated on his burger and shook his head negatively. "Not me."

"Why not?" Milo asked

"I had over ten years of that shit. That's enough."

Milo looked at Matt and Kayla. He shrugged and tilted his head slightly. "A workshop can't hurt. I mean if you're getting regular work that's one thing. But if there's nothing -- like blondie says, find a way to stay sharp."

Matt and Kayla glanced at each other, then turned toward Jenny.

"It does strip you bare," Roland said, while wheeling himself to the center-stage of his studio. "So, in a sense acting dredges out your darkest demons and lusts, your cobwebs and skeletons, your fantasies and desires. If you're truly honest with yourself, the performance you give on stage, or on the screen, will always be some facet of yourself.

"I never want you to –," Roland raise two fingers on his right hand as if they were quotation marks, "—act. Here, I want you to use as many of your personal experiences to become the character. Make me believe you. Make your audience believe you." Roland turned and saw Kayla and Matt sitting next to Jenny. He pointed to them. "You two, come out here, please." They stood and walked out to middle of the stage with Roland. "I'm sorry. What're your names?"

"Matt."

"Kayla."

"That's right. Matt and Kayla are new here, but I understand they're experienced professionals. You two have a very close relationship, don't you?" They both nodded. "You actually live together?" They nodded again. Roland wheeled his chair toward the side of the stage. "Do me a favor. In front of this class, I want you to kiss each other passionately, without regard to the eyes that are on you. Feel free to allow your hands to roam. Do whatever you feel, except strip."

Kayla's eyes narrowed a little as she looked at Roland. Matt didn't hesitate. He grabbed her hand and nodded his head.

"It's all right," he whispered. "I know what he's doing."

He brought his face close and tasted her lips. Kayla's eyes fixed on Matt's lips and she tasted him back. They voraciously sucked each other's lips, shifting their heads from side to side, their bodies gently, rhythmically bumping. Audible exhalations through their nostrils became more forceful. Their hands began roaming.

Some of the actors vented their arousal with soft whistles and hoots, but Kayla and Matt didn't hear them. She was almost off her feet, her head falling back as Matt began kissing her cleavage."

"All right," Roland said. But they kept going. Kayla sighed audibly. "CUT!" Roland barked.

Matt paused and looked up at Kayla. She opened her eyes, remembering their surroundings. She calmly adjusted her hair and caught her breath. Matt wiped off his lipstick stained lips.

Roland rolled back to center-stage. "Good. You know, one of the hardest things in acting is to be a sexually active couple playing a sexually active couple on a project. Elizabeth Taylor and Richard Burton, Tom Cruise and Nicole Kidman, Will Smith and Jada Pinkett all had to wrestle with the fear they were cracking open the doors to their bedrooms whenever they worked together. But that's life in Hollywood. Kayla, would you sit down for a moment?"

Kayla nodded and walked back to her spot next to Jenny. Roland glanced at Kayla, then looked around the room. His eyes fixed on a sexy redheaded white woman. "Tatiana, would you come on stage?"

"Awe shit," one of the other actors said ominously.

Tatiana walked up to Matt's side. Roland rolled to the side of the stage and spun his chair to face them.

"Matt, I want you to kiss Tatiana with as much, if not more passion, as you kissed Kayla." This time Matt's eyes narrowed. He looked at Kayla who sat there uncomfortably with her mouth slightly open. "Never mind Kayla. At this moment you're on my stage, and I'm the director. Tatiana is your lover. Make me believe it. Go."

Matt looked at this stranger. She was certainly attractive -- fine feminine body, waist, ass and tits. Tatiana wasn't shy about having those attributes. She turned her back to him, lifted her hair and gave him a jiggle. Matt's eyes gravitated to her ass, and the lack of a panty line showing through her tight white slacks.

She turned back to Matt, reached up and, with the tips of her fingernails, stroked his cheek. She came closer to his face. Matt felt the heat of her chewing gum breath. With the hand outside of Kayla's direct sight, Matt grabbed her waist. Tatiana lifted her head and made contact with his lips. Like a starved lover, she engulfed his head in her arms, probing her tongue deeper into his mouth. She pressed her pelvis against his, feeding his arousal. By now, Matt had both his arms around her, holding her tight against him.

The whistles and hoots were even louder this time. Kayla held her face still, fearful of exposing a corrosive jealousy she felt at that moment.

Tatiana lowered one of her hands to Matt's waist, then continued moving it toward his penis. Matt felt her fingers between his legs, and his eyes popped open. Roland saw this too. "CUT!"

Instantly, Tatiana stopped. Matt stumbled forward and sighed wearily. Tatiana held his hand and helped straighten his stance. "Nice meeting you, Matt," she whispered.

"Yeah. Sure. Me too."

"Very good." Roland rolled to center-stage. "Thank you, Tatiana. Thank you, Matt. You can both sit."

Matt walked stiffly off stage and sat next to Kayla. She glanced at him -- anger briefly shooting through her eyes. Matt didn't know what to say. He just wiped his lips, and shook his head.

"Kayla?" She turned back to the stage. "Your turn." Matt's breathing paused. His eyes narrowed again. A smile crossed Kayla's lips as she took center-stage. Roland looked up at her, then looked around at the other actors. His eyes stopped on a well-built Italian. "Geno!" Geno clapped his hands and rubbed them together as he walked to the stage. "Kayla, I want you to kiss this man with as much passion, or more, as you did with Matt." Geno kept his eyes on Kayla while Roland talked. Roland rolled to the side of the stage and turned back. "Go!"

Kayla didn't have time to even catch her breath. Geno grabbed her in a heavy embrace and began kissing her neck. Her instincts were to resist such a heavy hand, but she relaxed. Geno pulled his head away from her shoulders and chest. He looked Kayla in her eyes. Just before their lips met, Kayla smelled tobacco breath. She closed her eyes, and when Geno tried slipping her his tongue, she squinted and tightened her lips.

Roland saw they looked uncomfortable together. Rather than prolonging this, he cut it short. "All right, all right," Roland said. Kayla pulled away on his command, but Geno reached out for more as Roland rolled up to them. "Cut – Cut." Geno finally stopped. "If you were working together, I'm sure you would have more time to work on the chemistry. Take your seats. Thank you."

Kayla walked back and sat next to Matt who stared at her silently. She looked back at him with a disgusted look.

"It's very hard watching a lover of yours making love to someone else on stage or in film," Roland said. "Especially, if they show more passion or kinkiness in the bed scenes than what you were already getting."

The class murmured with chuckles.

"You had more fun," Kayla whispered to Matt. "I need a shower."

"I need something too, but it ain't no shower."

"You better wash that other girl away first."

When the workshop ended that evening, Matt and Kayla waited near the exit for Jenny. Tatiana walked up to them, took Matt's arm and turned to Kayla. "I hope I didn't offend you."

"No, not at all," Kayla responded. "We're all professionals, right?"

"Sure. This is a gorgeous man." She looked up at Matt and pulled his arm into her breast. "I hope we have a chance to work together again. There are plenty of scenes I need a good partner for."

"Yeah, sure. I'll see you."

Tatiana gave Kayla a smile and walked out the door. Lucky for her, Kayla's eyes weren't guns. She turned her hard eyes to Matt and caught him watching her walk away.

Matt turned back and met Kayla's stern gaze. "What?"

Kayla shook her head and turned away.

"Nice meeting you," Geno said as he walked by them.

Kayla waved at him. Matt jokingly put his hands on his waist in a feminine matter and puffed in mock jealously at Kayla.

"Oh stop," she said.

Matt threw his head back and shook it as if he were shaking hair off his face. "Well," he sighed.

They saw Jenny coming their way. She came close and talked as if she didn't want others to hear her. "Y'all go 'head. I have to stay a little later."

"What's up?" Matt asked.

"It's nothing. Roland needs a little help cleaning up the place. And he can't get anyone to stay."

"You want us to wait?" Kayla asked.

"No. I'll be fine. Roland can drive me home."

"Okay."

"That was sexy tonight, you two. See ya."

"Yeah."

Jenny walked back toward the workshop offices and a small group of loitering actors. Matt took Kayla's hand and they went home.

Chapter 19

"Thanks for forgivin' me." Albert stared down at the little girl's grave marker, his eyes twinkling in the dawning sunlight. He stooped down and laid a dozen red roses at the base of the marker. "My first day on the set. It's kind of nerve rackin' you know. Maybe if you can see your way clear, you might stop over there and ah, I don't know, keep me calm or somethin'." Albert sniffed and chuckled. "I don't think the guards will hassle you." Albert sat in the dew moistened grass and leaned back on his hands. "Did you ever want to be an actor? I know I thought about it a lot at your age. Couldn't think of anything else I wanted to do. Everyone thought it was beneath me." Albert sighed and glanced at the distant Hollywood sign. "Maybe I could've done more with my life. Acting was a selfish choice, but it feels good when I'm pretendin' to be someone else. I enjoy the attention too. And you can't beat the money and the women," Albert checked himself. This was a little girl here. "Well anyway, that's what it is out here. I this and I that -- I -- I -- I -- everything in acting starts with I -- my personal gratification. That's how I got in trouble. And it cost your life." Albert blinked back the moisture building up in his eyes. "I'll be different this time. I swear. I got you to think about now. I'll keep my wits about me." Albert sat forward and scratched his hand. He heard a distant bell sounding off in the direction of the old Paramount Studios. He turned back and stared at its water tower. "Sometimes I just want to hug this town. Then other times –." Albert took a deep breath. "I have to run, Debbie. I don't want to be late for my call. I'll see you next week."

An electronic tone sounded within Stage Six at S and G Studios. A hundred and fifty people sat in bleachers overlooking a four-room set for the TV pilot *Top This*.

The director had to cut a scene short because, for some reason, the star, Topper Jamison, couldn't stop laughing. It was just another of his many streaks of silliness. His squeaky, wheezy chortle was infectious, and had dozens of people in the audience laughing with him.

"I'm sorry," Topper said. He stumbled away from his chair at a table. The woman sitting across from him, and most of the extras, just watched him stumble around the barroom set.

The director's voice boomed out on the intercom. "Take your time, Topper. We'll go when you're ready."

Albert stood at the bar with his face covered with thick make-up and small patches of silicon that made him look twenty years older. He felt a little sweaty, so he gestured to a nearby make-up artist to come over and check him.

The young woman walked up with her little repair kit in hand.

"I feel a little warm. Am I all right?" he asked.

The young woman lifted Albert's chin, then lowered it,

searching all parts of his face for any problems. She pulled out a brush and swept some of the cake make-up over small shiny areas on his forehead and nose.

"You're fine, Mr. Cole."

"Thanks, sweetie."

Albert saw his friend Benny standing along the wall at the base of the audience gallery. Benny made eye contact with Albert and shook his head, perturbed by Topper's silly delays.

Topper walked past the third cameraman and slapped him on the butt. He held up his hand and concentrated on calming his laughter. Slowly, his humorous convulsions eased. He looked up to the glass enclosed control room. "Okay-okay. Hey, Cap?"

Lawson and Cap ended their conversation up there, Cap leaning over to a microphone. "Yeah, Top."

"Sorry, man. I guess I have the giggles today."

"Really? Hadn't noticed."

Topper swallowed back another laugh, his face finally becoming serious. "So where do you want to pick it up?"

"Just a second."

Topper walked back to his position at a bar table. The young make-up artist hurried over to check Topper's head and face. She only adjusted his hair.

After consulting with Lawson, Cap leaned over to the microphone. "Let's pick it up with the line before Chanelle slaps you."

"Awe, man. She really hits people hard too." The audience laughed.

"I'm ready, Cap," Chanelle said, glaring at Topper while smacking her right fist in her left hand.

"All right," Cap said. "Stand-by." Three electronic tones sounded in the studio. A floor director scooted between the cameras.

"Stand-by." The floor director raised his hand. "We're rolling. Aaaannnddd -- action."

"So, what's your answer, woman?" Topper asked. "I ain't got all night."

Chanelle's smile became sinister. She leaned back and suddenly smacked Topper in the jaw. The audience ooohhhed at the sound of the impact. Chanelle stood, grabbed her bag, and marched toward the door. Everyone in the bar looked at them.

Topper rubbed his jaw, then tried guarding his male ego in front all these people. "Yeah, okay. I'll see you tomorrow then, sweetie buns." While still holding his jaw, he picked up his nearly empty beer mug and walked toward the bar. He set it down in front of Albert. "What say you, Lefty."

Albert shook his head in pity, then took the mug to refill it. "What say me? -- Nothing. I was just admirin' your way with women. You've been slapped more times than a fly on a horse's ass." The audience laughed on cue.

"I must be in a slump. Just when I think I have them figured out, they throw another curve. I don't even know how the game's played anymore."

"What game, Topper?"

"The sex game."

"Awe that should be easy for you by now. But let me start in the beginnin'."

"Lefty."

"You see it's like when the bees fly to a flower and they snuggled up in the middle of it --"

"Lefty."

"And they get all that yellow stuff on them --"

"Lefty!"

"Huh?"

"I know sex."

"Ohhhh."

"What I mean is, I don't know women -- what makes them tick."

"Well, let me tell you somethin'. I been on this planet for 64 years and you know what I learned about women?"

"What?"

"NOTHIN'!" The audience laughed on cue. "Sixty-four friken years, and I still don't know nothin' about women. And let me tell you somethin'. Nothin's a great education."

Albert and Topper held their positions staring at each other.

"Cut," the floor director said.

That tone sounded again. The audience applauded politely. Topper and Albert shook hands.

"That's a print," Cap said on the intercom. "We're setting up for scene 14-A on set C. Talent, take fifteen."

Shimmering golden lights formed the phrases World Premiere, *White Caps*, and Ben Kingsley on the El Capitan Theater marquee. On the sidewalks in front of the theater, a line of people stood quietly, waiting to enter the theater's splendid lobby, but the festiveness of the occasion was moderate by Hollywood standards. There were no screaming film fanatics, and no oscillating spotlights shining up to the stars. And where was the film's star? This world premiere was no more glamorous than the opening of a new exhibit at an art museum.

This was a Hollywood premiere and for such an occasion, few actually dressed for it. Kayla and Matt couldn't afford to dress like the big stars, but they were among the few who made the effort. She wore a blue mini-dress suit, and styled her hair so it would hang over her right shoulder. Matt wore a simple, but stylish black suit with a gold and onyx collar link on his white shirt.

Kayla felt a chill, and leaned closer to Matt who held her around the waist. They watched some of the more prominent actors in the cast walk down the red carpet to polite applause and scattered flashes of photographers' cameras.

"Kayla?"

Hearing her name, Kayla looked out to the red carpeted walkway and saw a familiar male face emerging from a small group of mingling VIP's. She knew him from the film, but couldn't remember what did he did. "Hello," she said softly.

He smiled at her. "You don't remember me, do you?"

Kayla squinted her eyes and held her smile. "I'm sorry. I'm bad with names. You were on the film. I know that."

"Gordon. Gordon Van Keller?"

Kayla tilted her head back and took a deep breath when the memory hit her. "Ohhh, yeah. Gordy, I'm sorry." She reached out and held his hand. "Matt, this is the Assistant Director of the film."

Matt reached out and shook his hand. "Nice to meet you."

"Good to see you too."

"I'm so embarrassed," Kayla said.

"Don't be. Few people remember the assistant director."

Gordon raised his fist and playfully gritted his teeth. "But one of these days --. So, Kayla, why are you over here? The cast and crew are up front taking pictures."

"Well, I didn't know if I was supposed to --"

"Of course, you are."

"It was just a little part."

Some of the people around them turned toward Kayla, struggling to see her face. Gordon unhooked one of the big velvet cordons, and held his arm out in the direction he wanted Kayla to go. "Lady, get with the scene."

Kayla and Matt stepped through onto the red carpet.

"Hey!" A security man hurried over to Gordon. "Hook that back on the pole!"

"It's all right. She's a member of the cast. There was a mix-up."

The security man nodded, his face looking like a loaded fist. "Just hook it back on there."

"Okay, okay." Gordon re-attached the cordon, then led Kayla and Matt into the glow of the theater's main entry within the base of this six-story, art-deco cube.

No one was sure who they were, but the eyes of those behind the ropes followed Kayla, Matt, and Gordon as they walked up the red carpet. A couple of children even waved at Kayla. She smiled and waved back.

"So, where's Ben Kingsley?" She asked. "These people want to see a star."

"I don't know. Maybe he doesn't go to many premieres. We need more actors like you to show up and give a show."

Kayla and Matt looked ahead, and saw actors and actresses posing for group pictures in front of the theater's marquee. They joked, laughed and mugged for the cameras.

Gordon squeezed Kayla's arm. "You need to be up there." He leaned over to Matt. "I'm sorry, what was your name again?"

"Matt."

"Matt? You mind if I borrow Kayla for a moment? She should be in some of these pictures too."

"Naw, go ahead."

Gordon almost didn't wait for Matt's answer. He took Kayla by the hand and pulled her away from him. Kayla smiled apologetically before the crowd of actors and VIP's absorbed her. He watched her mingle with these people like old friends, having fun with the cameras, having the hands of unknown men around her waist, being kissed, being acknowledged.

Matt turned back to the line of outsiders waiting to enter. Did he belong there? He then turned back to Kayla, who was smiling, mingling, and posing like a star. Is that where he belongs?

Sometimes she looks like a completely different woman, like the ones I see on TV, and wished I could be with. But I am with her, and yet it feels more and more like I'm reaching through a lens just to touch her.

Matt looked at his watch and sighed. The night air suddenly had more of a chill. It was only Thursday night, and tomorrow he had find another way to wrangle four more home improvement appointments at his telemarketing job.

The sun was barely up for the morning. Matt didn't sleep that well last night. Wearing only a pair of slacks, he sat in a lounge chair, softly strumming his guitar. Matt's lilting and random melodies drew Kayla out of their bedroom. Wearing only a T-shirt and panties, she hopped on the couch and pulled her feet under her. She had always caught his eye, but his time he didn't look up from the vibrating strings of his instrument.

She looked down at herself then back at Matt, forcing out a smile. "Did you have a good time last night?"

"Yeah." Matt didn't interrupt his guitar strumming, and said nothing more.

Kayla pulled a scrunchy from her hair and shook her head allowing her hair to fall free. "Did I tell you mom left a message?"

"Your mom?"

"Yeah."

"She's talking about coming out here for Thanksgiving." Matt nodded and kept on playing. "We'll see if she follows through this time."

Matt jumped from song to song as if he were changing stations on a radio. He hit on a song that Kayla loved singing to and she began humming it, but when he heard her voice, Matt changed to another song. Kayla ended her humming. She was unsure about the reason he was so quiet and inattentive toward her.

"Did you want to rehearse or something?" she asked.

"Not now. Have to go to work."

Kayla sighed and reclined on the couch. She picked up the remote and clicked on the TV. The Weather Channel was on, showing a satellite photo of the Gulf of Mexico. A round cloud mass sat off the coast of Western Florida. Kayla turned it up and heard the meteorologist mentioning about a tropical storm threatening Tampa. Kayla sat up on the couch again.

"Did you hear that?" she asked. Matt glanced up at the TV. "Tropical storm near Tampa."

Matt nodded his head, said nothing, and went back to playing his guitar.

Kayla lowered her feet to the floor, and turned down the TV. She then scooted down the couch closer to Matt. "Can I ask you something?"

"Shoot."

"Did I do something wrong?"

Matt stopped playing his guitar, and finally looked at her. An issue was at the tip of his tongue, but he thought about it and shook his head. "No. You're fine, babe."

"Then what's wrong?"

Matt set the guitar down at the side of the chair. "I don't know."

"Is there something I can do for you?"

"Naw," Matt said softly.

"Anything, baby. You know it."

"Naw, it's nothing." Matt chuckled. "Just hire me when you're a star."

"Huh?"

"Shit, the way you're going, you'll be able to hire me soon."

"The way I'm going?"

"The way you're going."

"Honey, I only had one good audition since we moved here."

"But the attention you're getting sometimes." He shook his head. "And I'm getting absolutely nothing." Matt rubbed his head. “Shit, I’m just in a mood. It’s only me. You’re doing great. And I’m proud of you. I just need some of that too. I don’t want to lose your respect.”

Kayla rolled off the couch and sat on Matt’s lap. “My God. You know I love you. I’ll never lose respect for you. I’d do anything for you.”

Matt rubbed her hands, and tilted his head toward the sunlit window. “I’m just in a mood, babe. It’s going to be hard to shake it today.”

“Call that agent of yours and get something going. He’s supposed to be working for you, remember? You’re the most talented man I know, and he needs to do more for you.”

Matt nodded his head, then ran his fingers through her hair. “What’s on your agenda today?”

“The usual nothing. What do you want to do this weekend?”

“I don’t know. You?”

“I don’t know.”

Chapter 20

Jenny teetered toward doubt, and away from a loyalty made up of thinning strands of love for Albert. Each day it grew harder for her to hide that someone else was slowly penetrating a place in her heart reserved only for troubled men. It had been that way since she first entered Roland's workshop.

For Roland? At first, he couldn't tell if Jenny's attention toward him was motivated by pity, love, or just butt-kissmanship, then it didn't matter anymore. All he knew was how he felt about her.

Albert just had no idea. Until now, he never noticed Jenny's silent stares across the breakfast table. A newspaper held more of his attention as he sipped his coffee. He put the cup down, spilling some on the saucer under it. He then lowered the newspaper and poured the spillage back into the cup. It was then he noticed one of her contemplative stares. "What?" he asked.

She just shook her head, and turned her eyes down to a half-eaten bacon and egg sandwich. She picked it up, took another bite, chewed slowly, then turned her eyes back to Albert.

For the first time, he sensed there was something behind

her silent stares and lowered the paper to his lap. “You know how I hate being stared at. What’s up, sweetie?” He wiped his nose. “I have booger or somethin’?”

Jenny smiled and shook her head. “It’s nothing I guess. So, what are you doing today?”

“I have a first read-through of the second show. They’re just going on like the show’s already sold. And what’s ‘nothing I guess?’ Is there a problem?”

“Nothing. It’s just a girl thing.”

“Oh, a girl thing.” Albert nodded his head in mock understanding, then raised the newspaper back up to his eyes. “That explains everything.”

An answering machine played in his headphones, another of the dozens Matt had this morning. He popped the enter button on his computer releasing the call and the data, then looked up on the tally board. He only had one lead near his name while others had three or four.

Another call flashed on his screen. It was just another answering machine. So, he released it and checked the clock.

“LUNCH,” a supervisor called.

Matt stood, stretched, then hurried toward an exit leading into an outside hallway. He pulled out his phone and frantically check his messages. There was only one -- a good one.

“Matt? This is Roger Doctorow from D-S Talent. Give me call. It’s urgent. I’m in my office until three. Bye.” He clicked back on the number and listened for the ring. His hands began sweating as he waited for an answer.

"D-S Talent Management," a voice on the other end answered.

"Hi, this is Matt Redcrop returning a call from Roger."

"Oh, hi. Just a second let me check and see if he left for lunch already."

Matt waited, closing his eyes and grinding his teeth together. He whispered, "Be there. Be there." He then heard a click on the other end.

"Matt?"

"Yeah?"

"Thanks for calling back. Listen, I've got you a big-time audition tomorrow. Hope you're free."

"No problem."

"Good."

"It's for one of the lead roles in a sensitive romantic comedy with a bit of urban edge set in the early 90's. It's called *Gonna Get That Ass*."

Matt snickered. "Gonna get what?"

"That ass. Written and directed by some old-time hip-hop star, I forgot his name."

"You're kidding, right?"

"No, I'm not. You're auditioning for a character called Tough Act, a hustler trying to go legit as an actor. I have the sides in my office. My secretary's here until six. They want to see you tomorrow at two at the Blue City Bungalow at Sony Pictures. You want it?"

"Wha -- yeah. I mean --"

"Good. You know where the Sony Studios are?"

"Yeah. I live a couple of blocks away from it."

"Good. Come get these sides, and knock them dead tomorrow. I gotta run. Bye."

Matt heard the phone click. *Gonna Get That Ass? What the hell kind of film is that? Shit, it's an audition. It's for a lead. I need to try it. Gonna Get That Ass?*

"Where my piece? Shiiiit! I'ma fuck 'em up!" Matt stormed around the living room in front of Kayla.

She just sat there on the couch with a script in her hands. "Act, wait," she said.

"Wait nothing! If they can't respect me, they can -- they can --" Matt slapped his head. "Line?"

"They can taste dirt," Kayla said.

"That's right. Damn." Matt noticed a smile on her face. He dropped totally out of character. "What?"

Kayla shook her head and squinted. "It's funny seeing you doing this."

"It's a job."

"I thought you said these kinds of films were something you would never do."

"I know what I said. Now feed me the damn lines. Take it from the top."

Kayla took a breath. "Baby! Baby, what's wrong?"

"Nothing!"

"But why --"

"I SAID, NOTHING!" Matt went back to pacing the living room. "Where's my piece? Shiiit! --"

The next day, Matt didn't shave his face but made sure his scalp was clean. He wrapped a blue bandanna around his head, wore some old work jeans that fell below his hips, and an oversized blue shirt. He walked in front of Kayla like a model showing off the latest in retro-urban thuggery. "What do you think?"

"I guess you look like a street hustler."

"That's not a ringing endorsement."

"I just hope you won't meet any real thugs on the way to the studio."

"Babe, thugs are running the show." Matt leaned over and kissed her. "Wish me luck."

"Break a leg."

Matt walked out the door. Kayla closed it behind him, then walked to the window where she saw him climb into the minivan and depart.

She sat on the couch, and picked up the remote to see what was on television. Just as she settled in, her phone vibrated on the kitchen counter. She muted the sound and hurried to answer it before the third vibration. "Hello?"

"Kayla?"

"Yes?"

"Oscar Gold."

"Oh, hi. How are you?"

"Great. I have something for you to consider. Remember that record exec you met at Olivia's a couple of months ago?"

"Yes?"

"Howard Rowe?"

"Yeah."

"He's wants to put together a musical act, and has put out the audition call. He doesn't necessarily want pros or divas. He's looking for women of color on the margins of the industry with marketable looks, dancing skills, and reasonable voices. He wants girls like you, Kayla. He called me and specifically asked if you would audition for him."

"Singing?"

"Yep."

"Is this a group or something?"

"Might be. All I know is, Howard asked for you. In my book when someone like Howard asks for you in this town, you go."

"But I'm an actor."

"Success in music makes it easier to be an actor. Look at Jennifer, Tupac, Brandi -- I could go on. Say you'll go, and I'll get on this phone right now and tell Howard."

"Where are the auditions?"

"NTA's offices in Santa Monica."

"When?"

"Next week. You in?"

"Well, yeah. It'll be different. Singing?"

"You'll do fine. Oh. Do you have sheet music?"

"Yeah."

"Bring it with you. They'll have their own piano player."

"But what about --"

"Listen, let me call Howard. I'll call you back with all the details. You stay near that phone, okay?"

"Sure." The phone clicked in her ear. She slowly set it down on the counter. Her eyes wandered to a box of sheet music on the floor under the TV.

An hour after he left for his audition, Matt returned home. He parked the van and opened the door. He paused just outside, rubbing his head. When he thought about his performance, he closed his eyes and grimaced. They had laughed at him, calling him 'a brother with no soul' to his face. They belittled his years of study and training. Their laughing faces taunted his mind. It was his most humiliating failure, but he didn't want Kayla to know it. So, he took a deep breath and buried his disappointment under his usually optimistic face.

He walked up the stairs to the door and opened it. Sheet music was all over the living room floor. He saw Kayla down there in the middle of it. "Hey," he greeted.

Her face blossomed with happy energy. "How'd it go?"

"Not bad. I don't know if it's my cup of tea. We'll see though. What's all this?"

"You won't believe this."

"Nothing surprises me, gal."

"Oscar called. Remember that record executive we met at Olivia's a couple of months ago?"

"What record executive?"

"The one Oscar introduced us to?"

"I never met him."

"Anyway, he wants to audition me for a musical act."

Life returned to Matt's red eyes. "A musical act? What kind?"

"I don't know, but the audition is next Tuesday at 10 AM in Santa Monica."

"Musical act? That means you'll need me to play for you."

"Huh?"

"Maybe he'll need some musicians too."

"But --"

"Maybe we can work together on this. Hey, this IS a big break."

"Matt, they'll have a pianist there for the singers."

"A pianist?" Kayla nodded. Matt took his bandanna

off and fiddled with it in his right hand. "Yeah, that's right. Sure. That ah -- That works better. What am I talking about?"

"It's just for girl singers."

"Yeah? Well, hey, I'm happy for you. You'll do fine, babe. Which song were you thinking about doing?"

"*Tonight I give in*. But I can't find one of the pages."

"Let me shower up. We'll find it, then we'll rehearse it."

"Okay."

Chapter 21

The morning of her audition, Kayla drove Matt to his job at a small office building in the Fox Hills area. He kissed her, got out of the van, then took another look at her. She was looking extra special -- perfect make-up, her hair cascading away from her face, simple yellow tank-top, tight black jeans, and her lucky ankle boots.

"Break a leg, babe."

"Thanks. I'll call you."

"Okay."

He shut the door, and she drove rapidly out of the parking lot. Matt turned toward the entry of the building, already hearing that monotonous sales pitch in his head. *Hello? Mr. or Mrs. so-and-so? I'm Matt Redcrop of Carpenter's Square Home Improvements. The reason for my call, we're offering a 15% discount on all of our exterior products.*

"If you are here to audition, please sign in on the lists in front of me. Put your name, call time, and union affiliations, if any, on the sheet." A short white woman with unnaturally red hair waved her hands to gain the attention of the dozens of stunning, but noisy young singers standing around her. “HEY!” They quieted down a little. “I SAID, SIGN-IN SHEETS ARE HERE! IF YOU HAVEN’T SIGNED IN, THIS IS THE PLACE TO COME!”

Kayla had already signed the sheet at the table, and stood against a side wall with several other women who couldn’t find seats. Adding to the general commotion were the noises some of the woman made in warming-up their voices.

“HOOO! HA-HA-HA!” a woman puffed in one corner.

“EEEOOOWWWOOOOEEEEE!” another howled again and again while pacing.

“Hmmmmmm-ha-hahaha-haha,” yet another warbled in an operatic style.

Kayla was amused, but couldn’t laugh. She had made similar sounds in the van on the drive here. She was ready, but still had a wait ahead of her.

From a back office, a middle aged black woman emerged with two large men in business suits. For her age, she still had a youthful figure, and a gracefully aging face that still retained the box office appeal of a beautiful younger woman. The two men followed her over to the sign-in table where she whispered something to the short white woman who immediately began waving her hands again.

“CAN I HAVE EVERYONE’S ATTENTION! ATTENTION PLEASE!” The singers became silent, and turned toward the two women. “The lady to my left is Gale Lindsey, our director for production and management. Gale?”

“Good morning, ladies.”

“Good morning,” everyone said.

"We are entering phase one of the auditions. Would everyone please stand?"

Everyone did as she asked. The little white woman picked up the sign-in sheets, and followed Gale through the crowd of singers. Gale eyed each girl carefully looking at their style of clothing, the condition of their hair, the features of their faces, their shoes, even their hands.

She stopped at one girl. "What's your name, dear?"

"Keisha Lynn."

Gale nodded, pulling her mouth tight in a moment of intense thought.

The little white woman ran her pen down her list until she found Keisha's name, then checked it. "Got it," she said.

"Step over to the sign-in desk, would you please?" Gale asked.

"Sure." Keisha did as Gale asked.

Gale wandered around the reception area like a sergeant inspecting new recruits. She pulled more girls from the crowd, and had them stand near the sign-in table.

She passed Kayla at least three times, but gave her little more than a glance. Kayla was beginning to wonder what was happening here. She felt every bit as attractive as the girls Gale selected. She was ready to sing, and was confident about it, but wondered if she would get the chance.

Gale stood in the middle of the reception area and slowly spun around taking one last look at the girls she hadn't selected. Half of the fifty women in the group stood around the sign-in table. The other half stood around the chairs and couches, all holding sheet music in their hands, and increasingly worried looks on their faces. "That's it,"

Gale said. She turned to the girls standing around the sign-in table. "Thank you very much for coming. I'm sorry."

"What?" Keisha shouted.

"I'm sorry," Gale repeated.

"We're out?"

"Walk this way please," one of the big men said.

Most of the women filed out quietly. But Keisha hesitated. "Hold-up! What the hell kind of shit is this?"

"It's showbiz shit," the big man said. "Now, would you please leave?"

Keisha turned defiantly to the big man and faced his belly. With a greater appreciation for the man's massiveness, she thought better about picking a fight at that moment and walked toward the exit.

"This is still bullshit," she muttered. "Y'all don't know what you're missin'."

When the door slammed shut, there was utter silence. This was not a game. All the remaining girls had their eyes on Gale, fearing her next move.

She smiled and walked closer to them, pacing in front of them as she talked. "There's a certain look we're looking for on this project. You girls have it. It's a look of vibrant youth, with mature sophistication. It's a look of women who enjoy being real women, and not little hoochies or gang mamas. We're looking for women who men will fawn over, but not be threatening to other women. We're looking for role models with talent. You all have the look. Now we'll see if you have the talent. Mr. Rowe and I will be inside. You'll be called in one at a time to perform a single song. Have your music ready. If we stop you before you're finished, don't think anything about it. We rarely let people sing an entire song. We just don't have enough time. Any questions?" Most of the girls shook their heads. "Good luck to you all." Gale walked back toward the office with the little woman following her. Gale put a hand on her shoulder. "Give us a couple of minutes, then call the first girl in."

"Yes, ma'am."

Gale walked into the back office with the two big men following her. When the door closed, the little woman walked over to the sign-in table, and took her seat. She looked down her list, and marked little numbers beside the names of the girls who survived the first cut. She put a three next to Kayla's name, then noticed the silence. She looked up at the girls and found herself the object of all their stares. "Would you please relax. They're not monsters."

Kayla's steps were the only sounds as she walked into the small recording studio. There was an upright piano along the side wall, and a video camera at the side of a table in front.

Gale and Howard were at that table looking over a list. When Kayla walked up to the microphone stand, they stopped talking and looked at her.

"Just a second, dear," Gale said. She whispered something else to Howard, and he nodded his head.

The pianist and videographer just stared at her. The videographer smiled and gave her a wink. Kayla smiled back, then looked down at her sheet music.

"Pete?" Howard pointed to the camera.

"Yes, sir," Pete said, returning his attention back to the camera.

Gale turned out toward Kayla. "What was your name again?" Gale asked.

"Kayla Ross."

"Kayla, as you can see, we'll be rolling video on this. So just relax and be yourself. Is that your music?"

"Yes."

"Hand it to Hal." The pianist walked out to her. Kayla had written directions at the top of the sheets and pointed them out before handing them to him. He nodded his head and walked to the piano. "Now, when we roll the video," Gale continued, "I want you to tell me your name, nicknames or pseudonyms if you have them, where you're from, and a little about yourself."

"Okay."

"Are we ready?" Pete gave Gale a thumbs-up. "Roll-it."

The small red light on the camera glowed. Pete looked out from his eye piece, and gave Kayla a nod.

"Hi, I'm Kayla Ross, my friends call me Kay or Kay Kay, sometimes Kay-R. I was born in Cleveland, where I graduated from Cleveland State. I lived a couple of years in Tampa where I managed to get a part in the recently released film *White Caps* starring Ben Kingsley. We moved to Los Angeles in March and I'm currently living in Culver City." She jokingly inhaled deeply after saying all that.

"You're a bit of a traveler aren't you?" Gale asked.

"A bit."

"Are you married?"

"No. But I'm in a relationship right now."

"A lucky man."

"Thank you."

Kayla and Gale exchanged smiles.

"Okay, Kayla. You know why you're here. What song are you going to do for us?"

"*Tonight I give in.*"

"Angie Bofill? Okay. Anytime you're ready."

Kayla shook out her arms, then nodded in the direction of the pianist. Hal began with full, classical chords that caught Kayla by surprise.

"Wow." She looked back at Gale and said softly, "He's good."

Gale nodded in agreement.

Kayla slipped the microphone out of its stand and walked forward. When Hal ended his big sounding introduction, Kayla began, her voice floating over the Hal's playing like a silky mist over a serene lake. She sang with confidence and ease, keeping a smile on her face the entire time. She never closed her eyes or contorted her face to squeeze out a note. She sang not for Gale and Howard, but to them and for herself. She sang to the camera, and even sang to Hal on certain lyrics where her voice and his playing meshed perfectly.

Gale and Howard listened to her and lost track of the time. By the time they remembered they didn't have to listen to the whole song, Kayla had finished. Hal struck his last note, and began clapping. Pete the cameraman did the same. Gale stood up with a smile her face. And Howard didn't look displeased.

Kayla bowed her head, and curtsied with a little dip.

"That was very nice, Kayla. Could you wait just a second?"

"Sure."

"Cut the camera, Pete."

"Yes, ma'am."

Gale leaned over to Howard, and they whispered to each other. Kayla could almost hear their words in the sound proof room, but couldn't understand them.

Gale turned back to Kayla. "Howard said you're a dancer too?"

"Yes, ma'am. I studied some dance in college, and performed a little in summer stock."

"Good. Can you be back here by four this afternoon? We want a demonstration of your dancing ability."

"Yeah, sure."

"Good. Thank you very much, Kayla. That was nice. We'll see you this afternoon, okay?"

Kayla's smile became more excited. She even bounced a little on her toes. "Yes. And thank you."

"Let my secretary know we're ready for the next girl."

"Yes, ma'am."

Kayla's call-back made it impossible for her to pick up Matt at his job. She called him, and he understood.

Matt stepped off a bus at Washington and La Roche. He wiped some sweat from his forehead, then walked two blocks to their apartment complex.

He opened the door and closed it behind him. Inside was quiet and, with the window shades down, dark. He always had the impulse to check his phone for messages, but remembering he had done that on the bus, he tossed it on the bed and walked off to the shower.

Chapter 22

A workman at the Hollywood Forever Cemetery pushed a wheelbarrow over the paved trails between flamboyant memorials. He looked down at the simple marble marker of Debra Kastraki, a bunch of dried roses littering its base.

The workman lifted a pole with a grasping claw at one end and a hand trigger on the other. He used it to pick up the dead flowers, dropping them into his wheelbarrow with other dead tributes. Without stepping on the grave itself, the workman used a broom to sweep the dried petal crumbs off the marker. He then dropped the broom into his wheelbarrow and rolled on to the next cluttered area of the cemetery.

Albert drove his SUV calmly up a narrow mountain road north of the city. He and Jenny were together, but she was quiet. She had her attention on the passing homes, some looking like small, walled-off kingdoms in the sparsely populated highlands.

A rough stone wall along the road seemed to confine an unusual forest behind it. It was an anomaly of tall pines, cypress, and palm trees among these mountains of brown grass, short trees, and rocks. An arching gate of black metal dominated the next bend in the road.

When he saw it, Albert slowed down and checked the address. "This is it." He pulled up to it, reached out to an intercom box in the wall and pushed the button.

"Yes?" a male voice said.

"Albert Cole and Jenny Rappaport. We're here for the party?"

"Yes, Mr. Cole." Quietly, the gate swung open and they discovered this was no wild forest. A red cobblestone driveway curved out in front of them into a beautiful rolling green lawn covering the top of the entire hill. Every part of it had tall pines and palms. With its cypress and willow lined ponds, this property looked more like a Florida arboretum than a California garden.

Albert and Jenny couldn't see the house from the gate. So, they drove on slowly, careful to not hit any of the lamp posts that were very close to the sides of the driveway.

Jenny looked to her right and saw a uniformed guard walking a German Shepherd. The guard stopped and watched them as they passed. Jenny's heart began pumping a little faster, anticipating a vision of wealth she had never seen. She didn't have long to wait.

"Over there," Albert said, pointing off to his left.

Jenny looked in that direction and saw an enormous green tiled roof rising from a hollow in the side of the hill.

They were still a few hundred feet away from it when another uniformed guard stepped in front of them. He walked up to Albert's side of the SUV. Albert rolled down his window.

“You may want to park over here by the fountain,” the guard said, pointing to a paved area with a rocky water fountain just off its edge. “The spots closer to the house are taken.”

“Okay.” Albert did as the guard suggested. They were the first to park there. When they stepped out of their vehicle, he and Jenny felt the cool air blowing through the trees. Albert looked up into the clear blue sky. “This is nice.”

He took Jenny by the hand and led her out of the parking area. Another car pulled in as they were leaving. The driver beeped at Albert and he waved back.

As they descended the driveway, more of the house came in view. It was a mini-Versailles -- four stories tall, stone walls and classical pillars, sculpted designs, and golden trimmings on the corners and around the edges of the roof. Around it were two pools, small fountains, and gardens of flowers and orange trees surrounding patios with small assemblages of people socializing among themselves. Beyond the house was a wide valley with scattered neighborhoods of homes that were equally as impressive as this one.

“Oh – my -- God,” Jenny said, goose bumps covering her arms.

“It’s good to be the king, ain’t it?” Albert said.

“My God,” was all she could say.

They passed dozens of parked cars flanking the driveway leading up to the house. Whenever they encountered party guests, some of them waved, others held up their glasses in salute.

Shannon Hape and two other guests were at an arching floral gate leading to the largest patio just outside the main house. They were sipping on glasses of wine and engaging in pleasant conversations when Shannon saw Albert approaching them. She immediately interrupted her conversation, shouldered her business case, and jogged toward him. "Albert?" She gingerly stepped on a narrow garden path in her business pumps. "Albert!"

He saw the frantic young woman bounding through a low bush almost getting her skirt caught in it. "Shannon?"

She breathlessly grabbed Albert's hand for balance, then shook her hair back. "How are you?"

"Great. What are you doin' here?" he asked.

"Benny called me this morning. He wanted to change some of the terms of your contract. We both want to go over them with you. I think you're in for a nice surprise." Shannon turned her eyes to Jenny.

"Oh, Shannon, this is Jenny Rappaport, an actress. Jen Jen, this is my agent Shannon Hape."

"Pleased to meet you." Shannon reached out and held her hand as well.

"Nice to meet you too," Jenny said.

Shannon shook Jenny's hand. "Mind if I borrow Albert for a few, Jenny? We have some business to take care of. I promise he'll be back in a jiffy."

Jenny looked up at Albert nervously. "Uh -- no. Go ahead."

"Where are the nearest hors d'oeuvres and drinks?" Albert asked.

"Just inside the gate to this patio," Shannon said. "There's a bar in there."

"I'll meet you there, Jen Jen."

"We shouldn't be long," Shannon added, shaking Jenny's hand just before releasing it.

Jenny nodded, and walked toward the gate. She turned back and saw Shannon take Albert by his arm, quickly leading him to a side entry of the house. She continued walking through the floral gate and onto a large patio. A three-piece jazz band played softly while dozens of people stood around the rose bushes and topiaries drinking and conversing.

She didn't know a soul. They looked at her and smiled. She smiled back, but no one said anything to her. She didn't know where to stand or where to look. She admired the flowers, but how long can you watch a flower. She felt lost without Albert.

"Can I get you something to drink, Miss?"

Jenny turned around and found herself near the bar. A young Mexican man tossed a napkin on a spot on the bar top and pointed at her.

"Yes, please," Jenny said with relief. "A Margarita."

"Coming right up."

In Benny's spacious study, Albert sat in front of a mahogany desk, in one of two oak chairs. Shannon was next to Albert in the other, while Benny leaned on the edge of his desk.

"I'm a fair man," Benny said. "And you're an old friend. I'm gonna let you in on a little secret. You tested almost as high as Topper among the 18 to 35 demographic. I don't know why, but hell, I'm not questioning it.

"Fox bought 48 episodes of *Top This* on the condition that you make an appearance on each show. That's why we're tearing up your old contract. While our offer is not big money by network standards, considering our limitations, and some of the baggage in your background, we think our offer is very attractive. It's guaranteed over two years -- 30,000 per shoot, 20,000 per network airing, 15,000 per airing in syndication. And, on top of that, we're offering a five-hundred thousand dollar signing bonus." Benny reached back, picked a multi-page document, and held it in front of Albert. "Put your John Hancock on this piece of paper, Albert, and you're a millionaire again."

Albert's collar felt a little tight. He tugged at it, then turned to Shannon. Her locked open eyes told him everything he needed to know about her feelings, but he asked anyway. "You like this?"

She nodded her head once and began shifting her crossed legs back and forth. "It's not bad for a come-back, Al."

Benny pulled out a pen and offered it to Albert. "Deal?" Benny asked.

Albert took it and the document, then signed his name on three of the pages. Minutes later, he impulsively danced a waltz with his agent out of the side door of the house. He picked her up and spun her around drawing a squealing laugh from her. He set her down and kissed her on the mouth very hard, then held her by her shoulders. "THANK YOU -- THANK YOU!" His screams caught the attention of some nearby guests.

"You did the work. All I did was make the deal."

"Come on. I'll buy you some drinks to celebrate."

"Can't right now. I was supposed to visit my mother this weekend. But send the roses and stuff to my office, okay?"

"You got it, sweetie." Albert grabbed her again in a big embrace. "I love you."

"Oh, Albert?" Shannon became serious and pointed at his face. "You be careful, all right?"

"Yeah. I understand."

She blew him a kiss, and walked swiftly down the driveway.

Albert clapped his hands and bent low. He spun around looking for the patio where he left Jenny, then sprinted like a teenager toward it.

At the bar, Jenny was nursing her second margarita and was a little more relaxed. She was having a nice conversation with a woman seated next to her, and the bartender who was also a struggling actor.

"-- But in three months of doing this, I couldn't have made as many contacts at any other job," the bartender said. "Be a bartender if you can. And get those private party gigs. It can work."

"It looks like a lot of fun that's for sure," Jenny said.

"Hell yeah."

"I don't know," the other woman said. "Might be good for a man, but those bosses are some horny old bastards, always on the lookout for young starlets like you." She turned to the bartender. "And maybe you too." The woman pushed her empty glass toward the bartender. "May I have another, señor up and comer?"

"Certainly."

Albert leaped out of a nearby crowd of people and grabbed Jenny from behind, pinching her ribs. She jumped, and so did the woman next to her. "Dumpy! You shit."

"Shhhhh." He put his finger over her mouth. "You'll never guess what happened."

"What?"

"Well, they just --" Albert noticed the bartender and the other woman were also waiting to hear Albert's news. "Excuse us." He pulled Jenny to the side of the bar and between two hibiscus shrubs.

The woman continued watching them while the bartender finished pouring her drink. Suddenly, Jenny screamed and jumped into Albert's arms. Half the people on the verandah turned toward Jenny's screams.

"Two years -- guaranteed," Albert said.

"Wow." Jenny's initial joy faded a little. "You're really back."

"Not all the way. But I'm on my way. Remember about that extra space you wanted?"

"Yeah."

"We can get a big condo. Or one of those little villas up in the Hills."

Jenny held a smile on her face, but this was happening a little too fast for her taste. "A villa?"

"Just you and me, babe."

"Albert?" a male voice called. Cap Epstein walked around a couple of guests, trying to hold his drink steady.

Albert saw him and opened his arms wide. "Cappy!" The two men embraced, slapping each other's back.

"Benny told me about some new deal with you."

"It's done."

"Really?"

"Yeah. A few minutes ago," Albert said.

"Congratulations. I'm really happy for you. You're going to be very important to this show." Cap's eyes shifted to the cute young blond at Albert's side. "Who's this here?"

"Oh. Cap Epstein, this is my friend Jenny Rappaport -- an

actress, represented by D-S Talent Management. So, give her a job, will ya?"

Cap chuckled and Jenny smiled with some embarrassment as they shook hands. "Good to meet you," Cap said.

"Same here."

"Hey Albert, let me borrow you a minute." Cap squeezed Jenny's hand. "You mind?" Jenny shook her head, resigning herself to another period of loneliness at a party.

"I'll be back," Albert said.

"Lawson and I believe that in the future shows, we can refine some of the mannerism --" Cap and Albert walked toward one of the trails going off the patio. Jenny turned back toward the bar where the other woman and the bartender were still talking. As she stepped up to her spot, the bartender automatically freshened her drink.

"Well, that looked like a happy occasion," the other woman said.

"Yeah, it was. Albert has a new contract with *Top This*."

"Albert?"

"Yeah."

"Cole?"

"Yeah."

"So that's Albert Cole." The woman took a sip of her drink. "I didn't recognize him without the make-up. He's going to be good. Your man?"

"Yeah."

"Nice, but be careful. Success is better than Viagra for some of these old men."

"He's not old."

"I know, dear. I used to say that about Benny."

Jenny stirred her drink with the little straw, then took a sip. That name hung in her head. "Benny?"

"Benny Arnold?" The woman expected Jenny to know that name. But Jenny only shrugged. "The man who owns this place, and put that show together with your man in it."

"Oh, Benny. Yeah I know him."

"Know who I am?"

"No."

"I'm Rachel Campbell-Genevese-Arnold, the soon to be third ex-Mrs. Arnold."

Jenny laughed and took a sip of her drink, glancing at the bartender who nodded his head affirming Rachel's story. Jenny's smile faded. "You're kidding."

Rachel shook her head and finished her drink.

Jenny turned toward Rachel. "You're so young. I mean --"

"Well, thank you. But I'm not so young."

"You're divorcing?"

"We're working out the paperwork even today. There's just a little thing in the way about a buyout price for my share of Benny's company."

"You're still on friendly terms?"

"Why not? Life goes on. We had four years together. Two of them were even good. But when his company started taking off, psteeeuuu, so did Benny -- with every starlet out there. I halfway expected it."

"When my mother and father divorced they dragged each other back in court for years after the final settlement," Jenny said. "They halfway wanted to kill each other."

Rachel smiled. "So, what's your name, dear?"

"I'm sorry. Jenny Rappaport."

Jenny offered her hand, and Rachel took it. "I bet you're an actress."

"Guilty."

"You have a cute look. You should be working a lot."

"Not yet," Jenny said. "But I'm hoping."

"Let me give you some advice. Don't sacrifice your career dreams for any man. No matter how successful. And just be patient."

"Can I freshen your drink, Mrs. Arnold," the bartender asked.

"No thanks, Marty. Let me have a club soda instead." A phone rang in Rachel's little purse. She pulled it out and clicked it. "Hello? Why are you calling me?" Rachel looked back toward the house. "Damn, Benny. You can't just walk out here and talk to me, for Christ's sake. I'll be there in a minute." Rachel deactivated her phone, took a gulp of her club soda, then stood. "That's a lazy son of a bitch. He could have walked fifty yards to this spot. Nice meeting you, Jenny."

"Same here, Mrs. Arnold."

Rachel walked off across the patio fielding greetings from many of the guests she passed.

Marty the bartender rested his arms on the top of the bar and watched her with Jenny. "Nice lady," he said.

"Yeah," Jenny responded.

"She may start her own production company after the divorce."

"Yeah?"

"Think she has a card?" Marty asked.

Jenny's eyes widened. *I didn't think of that -- not a bad*

idea. Jenny put her drink down splashing some on the bar and hurried after Rachel. "Thanks," Jenny said.

Marty took a napkin and began wiping up the little mess. "No problem."

Albert had been away from Jenny for more than a few minutes. So, after getting Rachel's card, Jenny went searching for him. She couldn't find him on any of the patios or bars. He wasn't listening to the bands.

She asked a servant to check the house, but no guests could go inside without a personal invitation from Benny. So, she walked around the lush grounds of the estate checking every cluster of guests among the shade trees and walking paths.

She finally found a group of about six men and women standing in the rear of a Japanese style guest house near the estate's front wall. Cap was there. She figured Albert had to be there too.

She walked toward them quietly, not wanting to interrupt their conversations. They laughed among themselves, and that brought out a smile on Jenny's face. She was close enough to almost hear what they were talking about, but they hadn't noticed her yet.

A woman stuck out her ample tongue toward Cap, and he seemed impressed by its upturned tip. "My-my," he said. "That's too good for just tasting food." The woman sauntered closer to Cap, grabbing his belt.

Jenny squinted her eyes when she saw Cap raise a tiny eye dropper to her tongue. He placed one drop of a clear fluid on it, and she consumed it with a satisfying moan.

Cap turned toward a man sitting on tree stump and held the dropper out to him. It was Albert.

"You do gibbies?" Cap asked. Albert shook his head. "It's safe. Better than coke."

Albert shook his head again. "I don't know about that."

Jenny stopped, her eyes locked open in shock.

"Anyone for a gibby?" Cap asked. Two of the three other people surrounding them stepped forward, and Cap placed a drop on each of their tongues. Cap's eyes briefly shifted in Jenny's direction. He then looked again and smiled. "Oh, hey," Cap greeted. "Want a gibby?"

Albert looked in the same direction. The shock on Jenny's face pierced Albert's heart. "Jen Jen?" Before he could say anything else, Jenny ran off across the grounds. "JENNY!" Albert ran after her. She dashed by a fountain and over a grassy knoll, running toward the rock fountain near the parking lot. "JENNY! WAIT A MINUTE!" She was fast. It took Albert every bit of his middle-aged strength to keep her in sight. She finally stopped near the fountain. Her eyes were red with the anger brewing inside her. "Jenny?" Albert grabbed her shoulder, but she slapped his hand away. "What's the matter?" he asked.

"You know damn well what's the matter."

"No. I don't."

"Gibbies? Did you take any of that?" Jenny asked.

"No."

"DID YOU?"

"No, goddammit. NO!" Albert said.

"Then why are you hanging around people who take that shit?"

"I can't avoid it. They're my bosses."

"So what!"

"Hey, those people gave me another chance. I can't be rude to them. It's bad for business."

"Those kind of people messed you up before."

"Yeah, but I'm clean now!"

"For how long?" she asked. "You were weak before!"

"That was before. I'm not a druggie anymore. Just because I'm clean doesn't mean the rest of the world is too. I have to deal with them. And sooner or later you'll have to deal with them too. So, grow up, Dorothy. This ain't Kansas." Albert wiped some moisture from his upper lip and caught his breath.

Jenny's face was red. She looked down at Albert's feet. "I want to go home."

"I'm not finished with --"

"Now!"

Albert was now the one feeling anger boiling in his chest. He blew out a heavy sigh. "We'll leave soon, but I won't be rude to these people. I'll say my good-byes and be back here in a few minutes. Want to wait here?"

Jenny folded her arms, then nodded her head. Albert unlocked the SUV. Jenny climbed in the passenger side and opened the window.

"I'll be back in a couple minutes, all right?" He tapped on the door, then walked off toward the guest houses.

Jenny sat there with her eyes turned down to a delicate ring on a finger of her right hand. She turned it back and forth watching a multi-color sparkle glow bright then fade out with each turn.

Chapter 23

"Hello?" Matt cleared his throat and sniffed. "Hi Tory. This is Matt Redcrop. I don't think I'll be able to make it in to work today." He forced phlegm over his vocal cords to make his voice sound hoarse. "Yeah, I don't know what it is. I thought I was over this a couple of weeks ago. Yeah. Thanks. I think I can make it in tomorrow. See you then." Matt ended his call, then rolled over in bed, cuddling Kayla from behind.

"What time's your call?" she asked.

"Eleven."

Kayla opened her eyes and began chuckling softly. He heard her laughing breaths, and felt her humorous body quakes.

"What's so funny?" Matt asked.

"Titanic Jones. Who thought that up?"

"Morris Brothers Productions?"

"The Morris Brothers? It figures with their films."

"Come on, gal. It's a romantic comedy about a cruise ship disaster in the Caribbean with --"

"With an urban slant? I know."

"It's a major part, though."

"Okay, if you say so." Kayla chuckled again, then became still in Matt's arms.

"I say so." He gently rubbed himself on her, reaching his hand under her night shirt. "I need a little of your luck to rub off on me, right now."

She began shifting her hips to his rhythmic thrusts. "It's not luck," she responded. "Just skill, baby."

"Yeah?"

"Oh yeah." She hooked her leg over his and raised her night shirt above her waist. "I'll give you taste." She took his hand and directed it in small rounded caresses slowly passing her navel descending through her pelvis. With her hand on top of his, Matt continued his circular stokes, savoring the softness her skin at the edge of her feminine wilderness. Together they went deep into its steamy center, caressing -- messaging -- exploring. "Rub it." She put her both hand on his. "Rub it – harder -- please."

Matt drove home from yet another disaster of an audition. His ordeal only lasted fifteen minutes, but had a toll on him like eight hours of back-breaking labor. His eyes showed the depth of his defeat with bags under them, and redness in them.

He wheeled the minivan into the apartment complex and to his parking space. Matt was so immersed in self-pity he didn't notice Albert waving at him from the post boxes.

Albert grabbed his letters and jogged across the parking lot, catching up to Matt before he exited his minivan. "Hey, young black man."

Matt opened the door and saw Albert standing there

with a smirk on his face. Matt forced out a half smile. "Aye, old white man. Where you been?"

"Shooting the show. They've been keeping us busy. Man, if it is at all possible, you actually look pale. What is the matter with you?"

Matt scooted out the minivan, stretched, then shook his head. "The losing streak continues."

"Another audition?" Matt nodded to him. "At least you're gettin' calls finally."

"Not the right ones."

"What was this one?" Albert asked.

"A Morris Brothers film."

"And?"

"I wasn't black enough."

Albert stared at him with those slightly deranged eyes. One eyebrow rose, and suddenly Albert started laughing. "That's great." Albert rubbed his forehead. "Unbelievable."

"What?"

"I was turned down for a few roles because I looked too ethnic. And you're getting rejected because you don't look ethnic enough. This is new to me."

"Yeah, well."

"Maybe you should grow some dreds or somethin'," Albert said.

"You're joking, but I'm starting to think about that." Matt looked off toward Albert's building. "So, what's Jen Jen up to these days?"

Albert's laughter calmed down to a nervous smile. He looked back to the building too. "She's ahhh -- she's fine. Between her new job and that workshop, I don't see her a lot. I thought you were in that workshop with her."

"We don't go that often. You still thinking about moving?"

"Not thinkin' about it. We already picked out this nice little place in the Hills, off Mulholland. We might close the deal next week, and be moved-in the week after."

Matt looked up to his apartment window then checked his watch. "That's great. Kay's inside. You want to come up for a drink or something?"

"Yeah, sure." Albert followed Matt to the stairs. "How's she doin' with that music thing?"

"Still waiting. They put her through some shit though."

"It'll be great if she gets that."

"Yeah."

"It'll include you, won't it?" Albert asked.

"Believe me, I've thought about that a lot lately." Matt paused at the top of the stairs. "You want to call Jen Jen over?"

"She's not home."

Matt fumbled through his keys. "Kayla's mother canceled out on us for Thanksgiving again. You two want to come over and feast with us?"

"Yeah. Sure. Thanks." They walked inside.

It was still five hours before workshop that evening, but Jenny was already there. The closed blinds of Roland's office only allowed in thin slivers of sunlight. Within the darkness and old furnishings was movement, the silence disturbed by the sounds of excited breaths. Near Roland's desk was Jenny without her blouse and bra. Her bare legs parted over Roland's lap. He sat passively as she slowly lowered her glistening breasts on his face. Suddenly, he all but devoured them, voraciously manipulating them, using his mouth and face like a third hand.

Chapter 24

The morning after Thanksgiving, Kayla was back in the Santa Monica offices of NTA Records where she sat silently with three other young women in the reception area. Like the others, she had her legs crossed and was avoiding prolonged eye contact with anyone.

She shook her foot nervously, and sometimes looked up, taking mental snap-shots of the other women -- her competition. She looked directly across from her and saw a high-yellow woman with short smooth hair, big brown eyes, and a beauty mark just under her lips. Everything about her seemed a mixture of toughness and beauty. But she also seemed very young and even scared.

The second girl was shorter, but blessed with a figure most women envied. She looked at Kayla and gave her an easy smile. Her face was so pleasant, it seemed a natural environment for a smile. Her skin was milk-chocolate smooth. And she wore her hair in long black swirls that hung to her shoulder blades.

The third girl had a cinnamon complexion like Kayla. And like Kayla, there was also something exotic about her. Her hair was long, straight, and pure black. Her eyes, framed by dense eyebrows, were virtually black. Her wide mouth, full shapely lips, and gleaming teeth all came together in a harmony indicating English was not her only native language. She also had a gifted figure, but seemed a little shy about it, wearing jeans and a loose sweater.

Without offending the others, each woman discreetly sized up the others, wandering what Gale and Howard were looking for in a woman for this secretive project.

The door to the little studio opened and the little white woman who helped Gale coordinate the auditions stepped into the reception area. "They're ready to see all of you now," she said. "Go right in."

She stepped to the side as the four women walked by her. She then closed the door and remained outside.

Howard and Gale were the only people inside. Howard sat on a table and Gale leaned against it next to him. They had set up four chairs in the middle of the studio and the four women walked up to them.

"Good morning, ladies," Gale said.

"Good Morning," they responded.

Howard hopped to his feet and straightened his tie. "Have a seat -- please," he said, and the four of them sat. "Congratulations, the auditions are over. You four have made it." The four women looked at each other not sure whether to smile or not. Howard saw the questions in their eyes. "You might be asking yourselves, made what? Well, I'll tell you. You're forming a singing group that will be backed by the combined resources of my company, and the international record distributor Unique Spin Records, USR. You're going to be the core of what we hope will be a money-making empire that will make us all very rich."

"Excuse me." The woman with beauty mark held up her hand.

"Yeah, Tasha?"

"A singing group? I don't know any of these girls' names. And I'm sure they don't know me. How are we going to be a group?"

Howard nodded and scratched his silver goatee. "We'll start with the introductions." Howard walked up to the women and stood in front of Kayla. "This young lady's Kayla Ross -- a Clevelander with a touch of Europe about her, a singer/dancer/actress. She traveled thousands of miles just to be with us today. Like almost everything else about her, her voice and dance moves are silky smooth." Howard walked over to the girl with the beauty mark. "This is Tasha Garcia of Miami, Florida -- another traveler -- Cuban heritage, but has yet to learn Spanish. She's a flamboyant dancer, blessed with a charismatic singing voice, filled with a fun-loving energy that can make so many people smile." He walked over to the young woman with the pleasant face. "This is Janice Watkins, just a plain ol' Compton girl as she puts it. I disagree. She's very special just like the rest of you. She has a soulful voice fired in the cistern of a Baptist choir, and raw but talented dance moves." He walked over to the girl with the pure black hair and eyes. "And this is Vesta Dhar, an American with roots in the heart India. She opened my eyes to Bollywood talent with her sultry voice and gifted dancing skills."

Howard walked back toward the table. "You all are different from each other. But you have three things in common. You're all nice people. You're all talented. And we want to work with you to form a formidable girl group. This is the opportunity of a lifetime, ladies. I believe that within six months, you'll be the hot new act in pop music. It'll take work. You'll be spending long hours together getting to know each other. There'll be endless rehearsals, and tedious recording sessions. But I want you to know that all our resources will be made available to you. We want you to be comfortable." Howard leaned against the table and folded his arms. "Now, is there anyone here who wants out?" Howard's eyes shifted from woman to woman.

The women looked at each other.

"I'm in," Tasha said. She looked at Vesta. "You?"

"Sure." She looked at Janice. "And you?"

"Yeah." Janice nodded her head and turned to Kayla. "You?"

Kayla smiled. "Count me in. So, what do we do now?"

"Pack," Howard said.

"Huh?"

"Pack a week's worth of clothes. I'm putting all of you on retreat starting Sunday, just the four of you. You'll be staying at my beach house in Malibu. The only thing I want you to do now is to get to know each other, without trashing up my house. If there are any personality conflicts, I want to know about them early so we can deal with them. You'll be all alone except for Gale here, who'll be there with you as a mentor. Listen to her. She's been there before, girls.

"By the time you're ready to debut, you're gonna be sisters. You're gonna be smooth in the studio and on stage. And if we play our cards right, people are gonna talk about you even before they see your work."

"Is there a name for our group, Howard?" Vesta asked with a slight Indian lilt in her voice.

Howard smiled and scratched his goatee. "You'll decide on that. I could give you a name, but you'd probably hate it."

"Is this a reality show or something?" Janice asked.

"No," Howard answered. "This is FOR real! No B-S."

For the first time since moving here, Matt and Kayla felt free enough to splurge on a nice evening away from their increasingly cramped apartment. Within a restaurant courtyard in Santa Monica, a soft candle at the center of an intimate table warmed their faces with a golden glow. They were in a corner among blossoming shrubs and flower beds. Serene ponds with trickling water provided a soothing melody no musician could ever recreate.

Spaghettini and grilled fish covered both their plates, but they waited until a waiter finished pouring their wine. He placed the bottle on a side push tray. "Will there be anything else?"

"Not right now. Thanks," Matt said.

"You're welcome. Enjoy."

Matt picked up his wine glass and lifted it to Kayla. "To you, and your success. I'm proud of you."

She lifted her glass and touched his. "Thank you."

They sipped their wine, and its dryness caught Matt by surprise. He swallowed hard without losing the smile on his face. "Must be good wine," he said. "Dryness is good, right?"

"Maybe," she said, swallowing hard herself.

He cut a slice of his fish and consumed it. Kayla sampled her Spaghettini. She dabbed her mouth with a napkin after each forkful of food. Both were at a loss for words, their eyes meeting regularly, but immediately turning back to their plates.

Kayla sipped her wine and stared into the glass. She swirled the clear, golden fluid around and took another quick sip. "I might have withdrawal pains," she said.

"How do you think I feel? At least you're with three other women. I'm going to be by myself for a week."

"Yeah."

Matt took a sip of his wine and shrugged his shoulders. "Hell, we knew it was going to happen sooner or later. One of us, or both of us, would make it. We would be away from each other for months at a time shooting movies or TV series. Wasn't that the plan?" Kayla nodded to him. "We had discussed this a million times, and I thought we were ready in case things started happening."

"I was ready," Kayla said, watching him picking over his meal with a lost look on his face. "But you weren't?"

Matt shook his head.

Kayla placed her fork down and dabbed her mouth with the napkin again. She reached out and held one of his hands. "Baby, your time is coming too. I was just lucky."

"No. It wasn't luck," Matt said. "I always told you, you're good. You're just discovering that." Matt sighed. "It's just -- I kinda -- you know -- thought that I would be --"

"You will --"

"I just uh -- just set myself up to think -- that I would be the one going somewhere to shoot a film for a few weeks, then come back. And you'll be there for me. It's silly -- a man thing I guess." Matt leaned back in his chair still holding Kayla's hand. "It's not going to be an easy week for me. And when you go on tours and shit – whew."

Kayla looked down at the candle and took a breath. She turned her eyes back toward Matt. "So, what are trying to say?"

Matt leaned forward, staring into the exquisite face across from him. He saw Kayla's eyes wide open and unblinking, as if she were bracing herself for the biggest question of her life.

"I don't know," he said. "Maybe I'm saying, I'm scared of losing you. I'm not exactly a successful man right now."

"Right now --"

"Out there on the road." He began shaking his head. "You never know. You just never know." Matt paused, just staring at her. A quiet chuckle seeped through his lips. "Hell." Matt sighed and shook his head again.

Kayla released his hand and leaned back in her chair, knowing he wasn't going to ask the right question.

"Right," she began. "First of all, I still believe in you. You're going to make it. It just takes time. You think I'd stay with you all these years if you were a loser? Come on. Second, I won't know what's happening back here while I'm away, right? So, if we keep the feelings we have for one another, maybe we'll both behave." Kayla raised her wine glass. "Shall we toast to good behavior?"

Matt's face eased into a smile. He nodded and lifted his glass. "Here-here, my lady."

After Kayla took her sip of wine, she reached for his hand again. "And Matt? I do love you."

Matt sat there holding his mouth tight. He knew what she wanted to hear back from him, but hesitated until he thought of her being away from him. Then it forced its way through his lips. "I love you too."

When he said those words, Kayla's mind became clouded. She turned back to her plate and took another forkful of Spaghettini. Before placing it in her mouth she said, "You know, I could still back out of this."

"Hecky naw, gal! I won't let you. You'll hate my guts forever. You'll be labeled in this town. You won't find work. You'll be working the cash register at a grocery store, and get depress and stay home and eat cinnamon buns and blow up to 300 pounds. And then when I'm a star, I'd have to drag your fat ass into the Academy Awards ceremony and have to blow kisses to you after winning my Oscar. They'd be saying why is he with her? Poor man. Oh no. Hell no. You're staying with that group. In fact," Matt reached across and pulled her plate away from her, "I think there's too many calories here."

"Boy, you better push that bloody plate back, right now."

Matt slid the plate back toward her. "All right. But we're walking it off around the pier tonight. I ain't playing about them 300 pounds, gal."

Chapter 25

Memorizing lines had always been easy for Albert, but it now gave him headaches. The right side of his head felt like it was about to split apart at a skull joint as he walked up the stairs to his apartment.

It was the end of another long day on the set of *Top This*. The sun had already set, and the evening was turning chilly. All Albert wanted to do was go inside and stretch out on the couch.

He carried four letters and pages of mailbox advertisements as he walked into the apartment. He turned toward the couch, stubbing his shoe on one of the many moving boxes on the floor. He slid it over with his foot, then kicked off his shoes, hopped onto the couch, and clicked on the TV set. There was nothing he wanted to see. He just wanted some background noise. Jenny was still at her workshop and wouldn't be back for a while.

He tossed the junk mail on top of a nearby box, then flipped through the letters. There was an electric bill, a pre-approved credit card offer, a letter from Roundtree Apartment Management, and his bank statement.

The Roundtree letter caught his eye. They had rarely

received letters from them, so that was the first one he opened. Inside was a simple typed letter addressed to Jenny.

"Oops," he said. He turned the envelope over. It only had her name on it. He began folding the letter and was about to slip it back into the envelope when a big question flashed in his head. *Why is Roundtree Management sending a letter only to Jenny if the apartment is in both our names?*

He pulled the letter out again and unfolded it.

> *Dear Ms. Rappaport,*
>
> *We are delighted that you are staying with us. Please remember that the terms of your most recent lease still apply, even in month to month arrangements. Should you decide to sign a new lease, the new rates will be $1490 per month (6 months) and $1250 per month (12 months). Again, under the month to month option, your rent is $1600 per month. If you have any question please feel free to call us.*
>
> *Sincerely,*
> *Roundtree Apartment Management*

Albert sat up on the couch and read the letter again. His stomach twisted nervously. He pulled out his phone and raised it to his ear. He heard it purr four times before Jenny's voicemail answered. He ended the call before the tone sounded.

He wasn't completely sure what the letter meant. He

couldn't do anything about it until Jenny came home. So, he held the letter in his hand, and spent the better part of the night pacing the living room and smoking cigarettes.

Tobacco smoke hung in the air when Jenny entered their apartment at 11:30 that evening. She squinted her eyes, slightly repelled by the odor, and saw Albert sitting on the couch. He looked awful, with bags under his eyes, and his hair stringy and pushed forward over his forehead. "God, Dumpy. What's the matter with you?"

He kept his locked open eyes on her as he rose from the couch. He stepped forward and handed her the letter.

Jenny took it and unfolded it. After the first sentence, she knew what it was and why Albert looked so awful. Her hand with the letter in it to fell to her hip. She walked slowly to a bar stool and sat, mentally sorting through strategies on how to tell him.

"Must be a mistake," he said. "Right?"

She turned her eyes to the floor. "I can't move with you."

"Would you care to tell me why?"

She took a deep breath. "I was going to tell you."

"Tell me what?"

"I just couldn't figure out how."

"Try your mouth," he said.

"You did so much for me. And I hope I did the same for you." Jenny looked at him and shook her head negatively with unspoken words hanging on her tongue.

Albert read her eyes and guessed her unspoken words. "You're leavin' me?"

"I have to. It wouldn't be fair to maintain this. I never wanted to hurt you."

"Hurt me? How could you hurt me?" Albert watched

as Jenny turned her eyes toward the floor. "Unless --" His Adam's apple bounced in his throat from a jolting swallow. "Unless, there's somebody else." Jenny still couldn't look at him. "Are you seein' someone else?"

She looked up and nervously shifted her knees. "Only in recent days." Albert stepped back to the couch wanting to sit, but didn't. "Albert, please understand. I know it was wrong, but it just happened. I don't know, maybe I was just --"

"MOTHER FUCK!" Suddenly Albert viciously kicked one of the moving boxes, shattering some of the dishes inside. Jenny screamed, jumping from the stool and running to back of the kitchen. He stomped on the box repeatedly, grunting with each strike, until everything inside was little more than chunks. He then looked at Jenny in the back of the kitchen. His deranged eyes brought chills to her hands as he walked in her direction. She quickly looked for anything that could be a weapon. Nothing was within her reach. Albert was getting closer, but then he stopped just inside the kitchen.

She noticed moisture under his eyes. "Albert -- please."

"I don't understand this." His voice quivered. "I just don't understand this. Why? Especially now -- when so many of our dreams were comin' true!"

Jenny wasn't sure of the answer herself. She shook her head. "So many of your dreams, Albert."

His eyes dimmed. He looked down at the floor and his shoes. *This ain't worth it.* "I've been through this shit too many times." He adjusted his hair. "I don't want to know why. I don't even want to know who!" He stood tall and pointed his finger to her. "Monday, I'm comin' back here to get my stuff. Hope you got a car. Hope you got money to pay for this apartment, because you ain't gettin' shit from me anymore! I thought maybe we can do somethin' together. I was actually thinkin' in terms of a future with you. Albert Cole, a bitch's fool again!"

He yanked his keys out of a pocket and bolted out of the apartment, slamming the door so hard that it bounced open. Jenny heard his heavy footfalls going down the stairs, the faint slam of the SUV's door, then a racing motor with peeling tires.

Jenny slowly shut the door. She thought this was the scary part, but the scary part was trying to figure out how she was going to get along without Albert and his ample residual checks.

She pulled her phone out. Her hand shook as she dialed a number and waited for an answer. "Hello, Roland? --Yeah uhhh -- could you come pick me up? I don't want to be alone tonight. -- I told him. -- Yeah. -- He just took off. I don't know if he's coming back or not. But I'd feel safer with you. -- Okay. -- On La Roche, the Roundtree complex. -- I'll be in front of building four. -- Okay." She ended the call, then ran off to the bedroom to pack some clothes.

It was early Sunday morning, and one of the residents of the Roundtree walked her tiny dog along the edge of the grass around building number two. The little pup had a little boo-boo near a tree and according to the complex's rules the dog's owner had to clean up the mess.

Using a newspaper, she did and as she placed the balled-up mass inside a nearby garbage can, she noticed a black limousine pulling up to the back of the building. It blocked three parking spaces.

The driver sounded his horn, which on a quiet Sunday morning was just as startling as exploding a stick of dynamite. The drapes over most of the building's windows shook as newly awakened people peered out to see origin of the jarring noise.

The driver's side door opened, and the car's trunk popped open too. A small Indian looking man stepped out of the vehicle and walked around to the passenger's side.

Matt led Kayla down the stairs carrying a duffel bag. Kayla looked her casual best and had a garment bag over her shoulder. The little man took the bags and loaded them in the trunk.

Matt and Kayla then turned to each other and embraced. They kissed briefly. Kayla rubbed the lipstick off his lips. "I'll call you when I get there."

"Okay. And be careful."

"You too."

Matt wanted to hold the door for her, but the driver was already there waiting for her. Kayla entered the car and gave Matt a wave. The driver then shut the door.

"Drive carefully now," Matt said.

"Yes, sir," the little man said.

Matt stayed there and watched the big car back away from him. It turned and exited the complex. It then became quiet again. The woman with the little dog walked up to him.

"Was that an actress?"

Matt shook his head. "A singer."

"Really? Who?"

"Kayla."

"Kayla?"

Matt chuckled. "You mean you haven't heard of her?"

"No."

"You will."

Matt felt the little dog muzzling his foot. He reached down to give it a pet, but the little mop with legs ran around to the back of its owner.

It took an hour for Kayla to reach her destination. Through the limo's windows, she watched urban L-A fade away, replaced by empty mountains of yellow, brown, and green on one side, and the turbulent Pacific Ocean on the other. Blowing mist from the waves made everything seem like a landscape from an alien world. It was to Kayla. She hadn't been out of L-A since arriving here. During this drive, she often wondered why not.

The limo turned off the Pacific Coast Highway and onto a short, two lane road descending down a gently graded ridge. Kayla looked ahead and saw enormous homes among grassy dunes with little protection from the ocean should it become angry. Most were tall, some on pillars. Others were low, the owners risking their enormous investments on the mercy of the sea.

A gate blocked the road, and a guard stuck his head out of the hut. He must have known the car, because he lifted the gate before the limo reached it. He waved it on without having the car to come to a stop.

A gusty wind pushed at the sides of the limo. It was so blustery that Kayla began wondering why she didn't wear a jacket or a heavier sweater. She unbuckled her belt and scooted toward the ocean side window admiring the various designs of the houses. She then heard the turn-signal from the front.

"Here we go, ma'am," the driver said.

Kayla looked up front. The driver entered a cul-de-sac with an open gate in the middle. A driveway curved through grounds that were basically beds of white stones with odd clusters of cacti, ferns, and scruffy little palms. The house was every bit as large as the others, but shaped like an off-balanced stack of children's blocks with walls of mirrored glass.

The driver pulled up to the front of a wide flight of stairs leading to double doors. When he stopped, Kayla didn't wait for him to open the door. She stepped out of the car bracing herself for stinging cold. It wasn't. The air was cool, but humid -- comfortable enough for Kayla to forget her sweater. She inhaled deeply, savoring the briny aroma of the Pacific. It compelled her to reach her arms up and stretch her body. Unconsciously, she smiled.

"Kayla!"

She looked up the stairs and saw Gale coming out with Vesta and Janice. Kayla ran up there, and her two group-mates greeted her with embraces.

Gale was the last to embrace her. "You ready to go to work?" she asked.

"Yes."

"Good. Tasha will be here in a few. Go on in. There's breakfast inside if you're hungry."

"Breakfast sounds fine."

"Come on," Janice said, taking Kayla by one arm. Vesta took the other. "You should see this place."

"I could get used to this," Vesta said. The two women led Kayla inside.

Gale turned back to the limo driver. "Herman?"

"Yes, ma'am?"

"Set those bags just inside the door, would you please?"

"Sure."

Chapter 26

With the Rams in a bye week, Matt had no football team to cheer for that Sunday. He clicked the TV remote control. There was a Pittsburgh/Philadelphia game, but it was in the last minutes of the fourth quarter. He clicked to another channel. There was a New Orleans/Seattle game just starting.

He propped up his feet, settling in for a quiet day with no challenges. He could just slouch around the apartment. To him, there was something very liberating about having the place to himself for a whole week. Yet, the day still dragged on. It was hour after hour of freedom, quiet, and boredom.

Matt had fallen asleep, yet the vibration of his telephone could still roust him. He felt it in his pocket. His eyes snapped open. Thinking it was Kayla, he muted the TV's sound and quickly pulled it out. "Hello?"

"Matt?"

To his disappointment was a man's voice. "Yeah?"

"This is A-C."

"Hey, ol' white man. Didn't recognize your voice. What's going on?"

"A lot of shit."

"What's up?"

"Long story, kid. Did Kayla go to that thing?"

"Yeah."

"You doin' anything?" Albert asked.

"Watching a game."

"You wanna have a drink or somethin'? The bar in the Omni lobby has some TV's on the wall."

"The Omni?"

"Yeah."

"Downtown?"

"Yeah."

"Why there?" Matt asked.

"I've been livin' here since Friday night."

Matt chuckled. "What, Jen Jen kicked you out or something?" Matt heard no response. His smiling face became serious. "Dump?"

"Look -- I said, it's a long story. You comin' or not?"

"Yeah. Okay."

"Meet me in the lobby bar."

"The Omni Hotel Downtown?" Matt asked.

"Yeah."

"Give me an hour or so. I know the building. I'm just not sure of my way around down there."

"Okay. I'll see you."

Matt heard the phone go dead. "Hello?" He listened but heard no response. He went into the bedroom to dress.

Albert sipped on a frosty mug of beer and licked his lips. A young woman caught his eye as she passed. She smiled, and he nodded a greeting to her.

"See? It's in the eyes." Albert took another sip, then set

his beer down on a little table between him and Matt. "I have these eyes, these strange lookin' eyes. They almost took me to the top my first go-round out here. That starrin' role before the accident? It was for a mass murderer. Would've made my career, at least my agent thought that before I actually became a murderer. My problem is, women love these eyes for some reason. All ages, all races, all social economic classes -- woman love my eyes. They drew Jenny to me -- a young girl like that, interested in a middle-aged burn-out like me." Albert shook his head and picked up his beer again.

"You have any idea who she's seeing?"

"Don't care." He took a sip and smacked his lips. "Well, maybe I do. Shit, I don't know. Might be someone in that workshop of hers. She also has that customer service job. Could be someone there." He sipped his beer again, then rubbed his eyes. "Women have been doin' this to me for decades. I can't even be mad anymore. I should've expected it."

"Maybe you should've," Matt said.

"What?"

"Jenny was coming out here on her own. Remember? You were the one who tagged along."

"I thought we had somethin' going. That's all. Now I'm stuck out here."

"With a starring role in a TV series, and money coming in from everywhere. Sounds like maybe you owe her a little thank you."

"Well, that's an opinion." Albert took another sip.

Matt picked up his vodka and tonic and took a couple

of sips. "Your Aunt Libby told me to look after you while you're out here."

"Really?"

"Yep. So, you know you can always call me if you want to talk."

"Thanks. But I wonder how come no one ever asks me to keep an eye on anyone?" Albert took another gulp of his beer. His mug was almost empty, so he looked around for a nearby waitress. "Did you hear from Kayla yet?"

"No. I bet she's just enjoying the good life out there."

"COME ON! I'M AN OLD LADY, AND YOU CAN'T YOU KEEP UP WITH ME?" Gale, looking fresh and youthful, ran ahead of the four young women as they jogged on the beach together. The girls were covered with sweat and gasping for air, struggling to complete a two-mile run. "JUST A HUNDRED MORE YARDS!" Gale sprinted out ahead of them toward the back gate of Howard's beach house. She opened the gate, then turned back to this group of attractive, but out of shape young women.

Kayla and Tasha looked up at the steep flight of stairs still ahead of them and collapsed on the sand. Vesta and Janice did the same forming a sweaty pile of women at Gale's feet. They coughed and wheezed, their chests expanding and contracting with each labored breath.

"That's pretty sad, you know." Gale turned and leaned against the gate post, stretching her calf muscles. "I still run three miles a day. It takes that kind of conditioning to perform on those long tours. Believe me I know."

Tasha rolled over to her hands and knees, still short of

breath, but managed to ask, "How would you know? Were you a singer?"

Gale stopped her warm-down and turned toward the girls. "Tasha dear, I was once part of another Howard Rowe project, a group called 'Catwalk' back about hmmm-hmmm years ago." All the girls slowly sat up when they heard that name.

"Catwalk?" Janice asked.

"Oh yeah."

"Nooo – Really? I thought you looked familiar. You're G-Cup!"

"You got it, girl."

"Get out of here," Tasha said.

"You know, I always thought your stage name was a slight exaggeration," Kayla said, cupping her hand at her breast line.

"Whatever, smarty. Now you know, that I know what it takes to win in this business. That's why Howard put me with you. I'm gonna get you all in shape physically, mentally, and vocally. I'm going to map out a strategic plan to get you girls ready to debut in a matter of three months. I'm gonna get you to think in terms of a new way of living. And it's all good, girls, believe me. So, for now, just call me Sergeant Mom."

"Mommy," Vesta called with a child-like voice. "Can we go inside and shower this funkiness off us?"

The other women rose in agreement, jumping up and down like little girls. "Yeah, can we please, Mommy. Please--please--pleeeaaasssse! We promise to be good."

"Well, you are getting a little fragrant. Get in there."

The women walked through the gate and up the stairs as quickly as they could on their sore legs. "Dinner's at 5:30!"

Vesta turned back. "How many years ago was that again?"

"Hmmm-hmmm. Now, g'on-get, girl." Gale chuckled as Vesta hurried after the others.

After freshening up and having dinner, the women had some free time. Vesta lounged on the back patio, enjoying the setting sun and soothing sounds of the ocean. She had a book, but it sat ignored on her belly.

Tasha wasn't far away, sitting at the bottom of the steps leading to the beach. With her feet, she mindlessly shifted around the sand into small piles -- a peaceful smile growing on her face as she scrolled through images on her phone.

Inside, Kayla and Janice walked quietly down a back hallway that was, in theory, off-limits to them. It was the only area of the house they hadn't explored.

They saw a guest bedroom just off the back patio and glanced inside, but there was nothing interesting about it. It was just a normal master suite with one of Gale's suitcases on the floor and some of her clothes carefully piled on the bed.

They softly walked on to the next door which was at the end of the hall. Janice tried the door and opened it. Inside, a wall sized window allowed in the fading red light of the setting sun, illuminating a study. Books filled its shelves, but a simple desk was vacant except for a blotter, and rolled up computer cables dangling at its side. On a diagonal wall opposite the window was a stone and metal fireplace, blackened by soot on the inside, but pristine on the outside. On the mantle were pictures of several children and a portrait of Howard Rowe with two women, one older and one more his age.

Kayla's eyes gravitated to a beat up old silver goblet that was in the middle of the mantle. There was something about it that Kayla found charming. She reached up, tilted it, and looked inside. There were a couple of dead insects at the bottom. "You see this?"

Janice walked over, looked at it and saw nothing special about it. "Probably an old bowling trophy?"

"There's no writing on it," Kayla said.

Janice shrugged her shoulders. "Well. Any place we haven't seen yet?"

"The patio rooms?"

"Yeah."

Kayla placed the goblet back in its place, then walked toward the door. Janice followed her, but they were both met at the door by Gale who stood there with her hands on her hips.

"Uh oh," Janice said with an apologetic smile.

"I thought I told you this area was off-limits," Gale said.

"We got lost?" Kayla said. Gale shook her head. "We're sorry?" Gale shook her head again. "We're sorry, Mum?" Gale smiled.

"We didn't take anything," Janice said. "We were just looking around. I never been in a house like this before."

"If you want to be invited to houses like this in the future, then you better follow the house rules. Now come on. We have a bull session coming up."

"Sergeant Mum?"

"Yeah, Kayla?"

"What's with that silver cup?"

"What silver cup?"

Kayla pointed it out to Gale. "The one on the mantle."

"Oh that. That's Howard's so-called family treasure. He says it's a communion chalice that goes back to a minister ancestor of his around the slave days."

"Really? Fantastic. I love stuff like that. Wish we had treasures like that in my family."

"Yeah, well -- come on. Out with you both. The other two are waiting."

Chapter 27

"Monument Gold Card, this is Jennifer. May I have your account number please?" Jennifer punched in the numbers on her keyboard. "-- Zero – four – one – four – eight? -- Mr. Paez? -- Can I have the last four digits of your social security number? -- And your mother's maiden name? -- Thank you. How can I help you today?"

At the end of a long day, Jenny walked out of the office tired and depressed, circles under her eyes, stringy hair, clothes dark and plain. She was not a camera ready aspiring actress. She walked with a bit of hunch to her posture out to the edge of the parking lot, and stood with a bunch of her co-workers at a bus station.

After a forty-minute ride, she arrived at Washington and La Roche. She walked the short distance to the Roundtree Apartments, but when she reached her building, she noticed Albert's SUV in a parking space.

She cautiously ascended the stairs to her unit. The door was already open, and she heard voices. She looked inside and saw Matt lifting a box onto the counter.

Matt turned to the door and saw her at the entry. "Jen Jen? Hey."

"Hi, Matt. Is Albert here?"

He nodded just as Albert came out of the bedroom with a box. Albert saw her and calmly placed the box on the counter.

"Hi," he greeted.

"Hi."

Albert rubbed a hand on his sweatshirt. "Don't worry. Everything that's yours is still here. All I'm takin' are my clothes and knickknacks."

"You doing okay?" she asked.

"Awe shit. I'm fine. I got a new house to fill, so I'm arrangin' to ship my stuff in from Tampa next month. Uhhh --yeah. I'm fine." Albert rubbed his hand on his shirt again, then glanced at Matt. "Uhhh, Matt? Would you uh --load that box in the car, please?" Albert gave him a special nod, indicating he wanted to talk with Jenny alone.

Matt unfolded his arms. "Oh yeah. Sure." He lifted one of the boxes and walked out the open door.

Jenny turned and closed it. Facing Albert, she bit her lower lip and took a deep breath. "I'm sorry. I'm so sorry."

"Well, you should be." Albert shook his head. "I really cared for you, and I guess I'll always care for you, only not as much." Albert chuckled which brought out a grudging smile from Jenny. "It's been a while since I seen you smile. I must have done some things to cause that smile to disappear over the past few months."

"Well, if it's any consolation, I'll always care about you too. And this was my fault. It wasn't you. Remember that."

Albert nodded, looking around at some of the

apartment's furnishings. "Oh." He remembered a little document folding up in his back pocket. He pulled it out, and unfolded the two copies. "Here." He handed them to Jenny. "I need you to sign these. You can keep a copy."

"What's this?" She read the document carefully.

"My new lawyers. They're not really trustin' of these break-up things." Albert watched Jenny's indignation grow with every word she read. "And with my risin' position in Hollywood, they thought it would be wise to have this release freein' me of all financial obligations to you."

"You have got to be shitting me," she said.

"Hey, I'm sorry. It's not my idea. That's California. They just want to make sure you're not, and these are their words, 'some money hungry vixen lookin' for quick money by takin' advantage of a silly old man.'"

"Ahhhh." Jenny stood there with her mouth wide open. "I--you--son of a --"

"Hey, I know. I'm no silly old man."

Jenny reached a level of offense she'd never experienced. Her mouth remained open in silent shock, the anger so painful she had to relieve it. She yanked a pen out of her pants pocket and scribbled her name on both papers, pressing so hard that the pen strokes gashed the documents. She then balled up both copies and threw them at Albert's face. "Now get your shit, and get out of here!"

Albert picked his copy off the floor. He calmly smoothed it out on the counter, then folded it into his pocket. He took his apartment key and laid it on the counter, then picked up the other box.

"I have five more boxes," he said. Jenny didn't say anything. She just sat on the couch, folded her arms and crossed legs. Albert walked toward the door, opened it and turned back. "I'll send Matt up for the rest. Merry Christmas, sweetie. Say hello to the new little man." Albert turned back to the door and walked out of the apartment.

Janice handed out pieces of paper with hand written lyrics on each one.

"Okay, everybody knows how the song goes?"

"We need some work, don't we?" Vesta asked.

"Of course, we do," Kayla said, taking her lyric sheet. "Gale just wants to see what we can do together."

"So, what are we waiting for?" Tasha asked. "Call Mom out."

Janice gave one last look at her sheet. "Sergeant Mom!" she called.

"You ready?" Gale asked from a nearby room.

"Yeah!" They heard Gale's footsteps coming down the hall. "Don't forget. It's Kayla on the first lead. The rest of us come in under her solo starting with the underlined words. Got it? And don't out-sing each other during the solo, okay?"

The others nodded in agreement as Gale entered the family room. She sat on a couch in front of them, crossed her legs and extended her arms across the back of the couch. "Okay, girls. Dazzle me."

The women looked at each other nervously.

"We're doing *Who's Lovin' You*," Janice said. Gale nodded her head to them. Janice turned to Kayla, who stood at the opposite end of their semi-circle. Kayla cleared her throat, then began nodding her head to a silent count.

Kayla waited for the right count, then sang the first word, drawing it out in a perfect pitch.

Gale's eyes widen when she heard Kayla's beginning solo, but when the other girls joined Kayla in perfect harmony, her initial surprise became astonishment. She didn't show it on her face, but her heart was racing and her palms began sweating. N-T-A had hit the jackpot.

The girls demonstrated their individual strengths -- Kayla's silk, Tasha's edge, Janice's emotion, and Vesta's smoldering sensuality. When they sang harmony, they weren't individuals. They were one organism with four voice boxes, each one with a slightly different tone, all melding together to form one superlative sound.

The girls knew it too. Their power grew with their confidence, and smiles bloomed on their faces. Gale wasn't smiling, but they didn't notice her. They sang to each other, enjoying the birth of their dreams.

The girls ended the song with their arms around each other's waists. They laughed and embraced, then noticed the silence surrounding them. They turned to Gale who still sat there in that same position, with that same look on her face.

"How about it, Mom?" Tasha asked.

Gale slowly nodded her head and lowered her arms. "I wish I had a video of this. Howard's gonna go nuts over you four. I am." Gale clutched her chest. "Girls, you take me back. Here's what I want to do. Remember what you did here, and practice it a little more. I want to lay this down as a studio track next week. Maybe we can get you some publicity as part of a movie sound track or something. That was wonderful. You're definitely a group, but have you got a name yet?"

The girls looked at each other.

"I've got one," Janice said. "How about Love Times Four."

Kayla shook her head.

"No," Tasha said.

"Well that's my idea. How about you coming up with one."

"Okay. The Four Toplesses," Tasha said.

"What!" Vesta responded.

Tasha danced around the others shaking her shoulders and breast. "Yeah. We'll all be topless on stage --"

"No," Vesta scolded.

"We do the shimmy and --"

"No!" Kayla, Janice, and Vesta said together.

"Why not? We all have nice tits."

"Are there more sensible ideas?" Gale asked.

"That was a sensible idea," Tasha said.

"How about Four Silly Girls," Vesta said.

"The G-Cups," Kayla said.

"Cinnamon, Spice, and Everything Naughty?" Tasha said.

Gale held her finger up as if that idea struck a chord with her. She then waved her hand and shook her head. "Next."

"Oh, I got one." Kayla held her hand out to Janice. "Remember that old silver cup on the mantle?"

"Yeah," Janice answered.

"What did Gale call it?"

"A family treasure?"

"No. I mean, what the cup was."

"A communion chalice?" Gale said.

"Right."

"What? You want us to be The Communion Chalices?" Tasha asked.

"No, just Chalice." Kayla looked at the faces of each of the other girls. Her idea did have them thinking.

"Chalice?" Janice had an approving nod. "I kind of like that."

"Ohhh, it's great!" Vesta said.

Tasha stood there with her arms folded. "It's aight, I guess."

"Then it's Chalice." Kayla draped her arms over Janice and Tasha's shoulders. "We're Chalice, Gale." Vesta jumped in and laid her head on Tasha's shoulder.

"Chalice," Gale repeated. "Catchy. Might work." She slapped her knees. "So be it. Of course, my choice was the G-Cups. If you ever change your minds --"

"We don't need to exaggerate, Mum," Kayla said. "We are Chalice."

Chapter 28

"-- That's 4604 Roseway Drive, Inglewood?" Matt asked, adjusting his headphones. "Between Hawthorn and the Avenue of the Champs, west of the race track. -- Right. -- Great. And your number is 310-674-0 --? Right, that's what I have. Okay, Mrs. Waverly, you're all set for next Tuesday at 3 PM. A representative will give you that estimate on the roof. He'll be in a well-marked company truck and will have an identification badge. Please feel free to ask about our other products too, okay? -- Yes, ma'am. Thank you very much for your time this morning. -- Bye-bye."

Matt popped a key on his computer disconnecting the call and completed the information on his screen. He glanced up at the clock. It was only seconds before lunch so he pressed an F-key that performed a function even his supervisors didn't know about, blocking other calls.

"LUNCH," one of the supervisors finally called.

Matt flung off his headset and dashed out to the hall for another message check. He checked his texts, nothing -- his voicemail, nothing. Nothing from his agent. Nothing from Kayla. Nothing from friends or family. He slowly slipped his phone in a pocket, then walked toward the lunchroom.

He didn't bring his lunch, so he scanned the selections

in the food machines and found some lemon cookies. He slid in his coins for two packages of them. He then found a seat at a mostly empty table near the window.

For the first time, it looked like winter. Fluffy gray clouds blocked the sun, and a whistling wind, sounding off softly somewhere above the lunchroom's ceiling, made the day seem even chillier.

Matt just ate cookies, and admired the moody day. He didn't feel like being sociable, but someone decided to intrude on his quiet time anyway.

"Hi."

Matt had half a cookie sticking out of his mouth when he turned around. "Hmmm?"

"I said, hi." A petite black woman with a chestnut complexion, and short black hair took a seat at his table. She wasn't at Kayla's level of physical beauty, but she was eye-catching, and cute enough to have Matt concerned about her impression of him.

He shoved the rest of the cookie in his mouth, swallowed, and wiped his mouth with a napkin. "Um -- hi."

"Nutritious lunch there," she said.

"Nothing like lemon cookies for good health." He took a bite out of another.

"I'm Terri, by the way."

"Matt." He reached across and shook her hand, then went back to eating cookies.

"The way you rush out to check your phone all the time makes me think you're an actor or something."

"Yeah." Matt popped another cookie in his mouth.

Terri pulled out a rather large BLT sandwich from her bag. Matt caught its aroma, and watched her as she took her first bite. She felt a little mayonnaise on the side of her mouth and licked it, then grabbed a napkin to wipe her mouth. Through a hard swallow she said, “Well?”.

“Well what?” Matt responded.

“Are you an actor?”

“I’m working a bit in that industry. You?”

“Me? No. I take night classes at UCLA.”

“Acting classes?”

“No. Education. I’m trying to get my masters.”

“Pretty good.” Matt ate another cookie.

Terri took another large bite of her sandwich. She hoped to keep the conversation going, but Matt was not being cooperative. “So, are you from around here?” she asked.

“No.”

“Where are you from?”

“Ohio.”

Terri paused before taking another bite of her sandwich. “Really? Where?”

“I was born in Youngstown.”

“You’re kidding.” Terri smiled, and laid her sandwich on a napkin. “I’m from Warren.”

“Warren, Ohio?”

“Yeah.”

“How about that,” Matt responded.

“Yeah.”

“And you came all the way out here not to be an actress?”

“Yes, just to be a school counselor. In case you didn’t notice there are people in this town who just want to be normal. There’s nothing wrong with that. So, do you get back home often?”

“Not really.”

"Yeah. It's hard when you're 3,000 miles away. Any family out here?" Terri raised the sandwich to her mouth.

"No. Just friends." Matt finished his last cookie. "What are you calling?"

"I'm only doing the painting. You?"

"Roofing, siding, and texture coating."

"Get anything?"

"I have three. Not bad this morning."

"I'm at three too."

The Chalice girls, running through the mist of Malibu Beach, were doing better at keeping up with Gale on her daily runs. In their sneakers and warm-ups, the girls still broke a sweat in the chilly air. But when they reached the back gate of the beach house, they didn't collapse. They remained standing, their labored breathing calming down within a couple of minutes.

Their week-long retreat was nearing an end, but Chalice's journey was just beginning. On Friday, Howard sent a fashion consultant, four cosmetologists, and a professional photographer to the beach house to capture the first images of Chalice as a group.

They tended to them like supermodels, giving each of them a different look. From a smooth Anglo-Clevelander, the consultant and cosmetologists made Kayla into a goddess of the sun by intensifying the reddish tint of her brown hair, and using darker shades of lipstick and eye make-up. They dressed her in silks with Australian aboriginal designs that clung closely to her body shape, but had streamers that would look like flames when caught in a breeze.

Each girl took almost two hours to dress, but when finished, Kayla, the sun goddess, was joined by Vesta, goddess of the seas, Tasha, goddess of the sky, and Janice, goddess of the Earth. Seeing each other in costume for the first time jolted them to belly cramping laughs.

The photographer walked them outside onto the misty beach and posed them with various backdrops. The photographer's favorite location was a small rocky crag at the end of the beach. He and the girls struggled to the top of it just so he could get a few shots of them with the moody, gray Pacific in the background. He allowed them to pose themselves, if they kept to their individual themes.

Two hours later, the girls ran back into the house, wet and cold. Gale already had a fire going in the living room fireplace, and they all huddled in front of it. As she draped blankets over her girls, Gale noticed a nasty scrape on Tasha's foot. She later applied a bandage and an ointment to the injury.

"There you go." She smoothed the bandage. "Keep an eye that."

"Okay."

Gale then stood up over them with her hands on her hips. "All right. Now, good news. Howard's not wasting any time with you. Next Wednesday, we're going into the studio in Santa Monica to lay down your track of *Who's Lovin' You*. By Thursday, we'll have a band ready to accompany you on your studio recordings. Ike Jeffries is the music director of the band which will likely be going with you on tour." Kayla lifted her hand out her blanket. "Now, the Monday before Christmas --"

"Excuse me, Mum.

"Yeah, Kay?"

"I thought there would be auditions for the band. My boyfriend is a guitarist."

"No. Hell no." Tasha shook her head. "If one of us can have a boyfriend on tour, all us of us should have ours too."

"But Matt's a musician."

"My Torian is a pianist," Janice said. "They wouldn't even audition him because he's non-union. So, if he can't go, Matt can't go."

"I agree," Vesta said.

"You don't even have a boyfriend, Vee-Vee," Kayla said.

"I'm already in compliance then."

"Majority wins out, Kayla," Gale said. "Is Matt in the musicians' union?"

"No."

"Too bad. You're all in the same boat, and you'll have to row together. Now, as I was saying, the Monday before Christmas, we're going to be laying tracks on your first single."

"First single?" Janice said.

"Yep."

"What's the song?"

"We haven't seen any music yet," Vesta said.

"Howard's bringing over several songs tomorrow night. Oh! That's the other good news. Howard's coming in to have dinner with you, and go over some other things. He's also bringing your advance checks. Three-hundred and fifty thousand dollars each." Gale expected a big cheer from them, but all the women remained silent with their mouths and eyes locked open. "Hello? Three-hundred and fifty thousand, US dollars? Earth to Chalice?"

Kayla briefly came out of her shock and said, "We heard you, Mum. Can't you see we're stunned." She went back to her stunned look.

"Yeah, right. Back to your songs, one of them we both think is special and will make a dynamic debut single for you. It's called *Lovin' Insanity.* That's the one we'll be concentrating on. A summer hit, and the centerpiece of a hot album, we hope." The women still had shocked looks on their faces. "Are you okay?"

"Three hundred and fifty thousand dollars?" Janice asked.

Vesta and Kayla fell back like they had fainted.

It was Sunday afternoon, and Matt had been on the couch practically the entire day. He rolled over and peered through the window blinds every time he heard a car in the parking lot. So far, no limousine.

For the first time in a week, he was clean shaven. He had on pressed jeans and a fresh sweatshirt. His sandals were in front of the couch so he could quickly put them on and run out to help Kayla with her bags.

He had expected Kayla by nine that morning, but it was after two. A football game on TV kept him from worrying too much about her being in an auto accident or being kidnapped by some mass murderer. He didn't worry about her just leaving him for another man. At least that's what he told himself, but when he heard another car, he sat up and peered through the blinds. He sighed when he found it wasn't her and went back to his football watching position.

Finally, Kayla's limo pulled into the rear parking lot. The

driver opened the door for her, and she stepped out wearing her usual casual clothes, but looking more professionally groomed about her hair and make-up. The few people wandering around the apartment grounds stopped, watched, and wondered about this new beauty in the complex.

Matt came bounding down the stairs with a relieved smile on his face. When he embraced her. She felt so soft and warm he forgot about the bags. He couldn't wait to get her upstairs.

The driver struggled bringing up her bags, but he followed them and set the bags down inside the door.

"Thank you, Herman," she said.

"You're quite welcome, Miss Ross. We'll see you soon." The driver doffed his hat then backed out of the doorway.

Matt closed the door and locked it. He then noticed her changed look.

"Damn. What did they do to you?"

"You like it? They're trying to make us all images of fundamental elements. I'm fire."

"I bet." Matt whistled and circled her, bobbing his head up and down in approval. "You're like a whole 'nother woman." He walked up behind her and embraced her waist, nibbling on her neck and sliding his hand under her belt buckle. "So why don't give me a burn, Miss Fire."

Kayla reached around and gave Matt's hips a squeeze. She then remembered her surprise. "Oh," She turned in his arms. "Hold that thought. I want to show you something." Kayla walked over to her bag and unzipped a side pocket. She pulled out her check, then held it out to Matt. "Have a look."

Matt took the check and saw the amount. He blinked once, making sure he had read the number correctly, then looked up at Kayla.

"I'm seeing this right, right?"

"That's my advance. You can quit your job if you want."

Matt laughed, but the thought was tempting. He looked at the check again and a sinking feeling of fear hit his stomach. "Certified too. Shit. I'm calling in sick tomorrow. We're going to the bank first thing. We can't have something like this lying around the house." He looked at the check again. "Daaamn, gal." He handed it back to her, and she slipped it in her pocket.

"Well. You'll have me for a couple days," Kayla said. "We're going into the studio starting Wednesday. And those will be some long days."

"Yeah, sure. But what about the Christmas shopping?"

Kayla closed her eyes tightly and pushed her hair back. "Right -- bloody hell." She had an idea. "Could you do me a favor?"

"Yeah."

"If I made you a list of my gift ideas, could you get them for me? And you can ship them." Matt nodded silently to her. "Don't forget your gift ideas. You know it's no problem now."

"Yeah." Matt looked down at the sandals on his feet and thought about his most recent paycheck -- $632. "Yeah. No problem. I can do that."

Kayla dragged her bag to the middle of the living room floor and left it there. She turned back to Matt, thinking more about physical business. "Now, sir. About that burn you wanted." Kayla walked seductively up to Matt and draped her arms around his neck. "Any particular place you want this burn?"

Chapter 29

A group of tourists walked by Debra Kastraki's grave marker. To them, it wasn't even worth a glance with all the flamboyant celebrity graves surrounding it. No more flowers adorned her little concrete slab. Even Albert forgot her.

Fourteen-hour work days, six days a week, would make anyone's memory slip. But the producers of *Top This* wanted to get as many shows as possible shot before its debut as a Spring replacement for a failing TV series.

Each night, Albert returned home exhausted. His new Hollywood Hills house was a place he rarely saw in the daylight. It was spacious with cool marble tile floors, clean white walls, and intimate nooks and crannies. Yet, Albert had no furnishings for it. The living room and family room were empty. Nothing was on the walls. The kitchen only had appliances and two high stools at the breakfast bar. In the bedroom, Albert slept on a simple double bed. He had a 50 inch 3-D television and a small dresser that wasn't big enough for all his clothes. So, there were small piles of clothes within his walk-in closet.

He still had plenty of furniture back in Tampa, but shipping them to L-A was one headache he didn't want to deal with now. On top of his dresser were bottles of gin and Scotch, a small glass, an ice chest, and a small picture of Jenny. He didn't want to see her face, yet the picture was there, lying flat. If he happened to walk by and see it, then it was an accident, not something he chose to do.

He had little holiday cheer except what he found in one of those bottles on his dresser. In his off-time, he stayed in his room, watching TV, and sipping on gin and fruit juice. If the phone rang, he never answered it. He only listened to the messages, some from Matt and Milo, and then not return their calls.

Except for the TV show, Albert had withdrawn from the world. He felt safe in the darkness and silence, but each morning, before dawn, he had to go to work and face the temptations of the day.

A week and a half before Christmas, on an afternoon following another morning script reading at the studio, Albert had four hours to spare before his make-up call -- enough time for a good nap. He walked into a spacious dressing room he shared with another of the show's supporting actors. The puffy cushions of a black leather couch drew his weary eyes. The other actor's garment bag was on it, so Albert placed it on the floor to make room for his legs. A bunch of keys fell out of the side pocket. Albert picked them up and placed them back, but his fingers brushed up against a plastic bag inside. He looked down and saw light reflecting off its surface. He separated his fingers, widening the opening and saw the bag contained white powder. He examined it, wanting to open it, but it was a zip-lock bag.

His curiosity kept him hunched over it for minutes. He had hoped it was sugar or flour, but without touching it or smelling it, he knew what it was. In a supernatural manner, it communicated to him a message of peace and invincibility. It was a call to turn back the clock to his carefree youth. It sang to him a song of a thousand melodies, and made him remember the pleasures of a thousand sensations. He then felt the thump of a little girl's body on his car, heard her mother's screams, and faced the scornful stares of her neighbors again.

Albert scooted away from the garment bag, and sat on the opposite end of the couch. He didn't feel comfortable enough to take a nap now.

Roland DeCosta lived in a converted studio prop-shop that was next to his actors' workshop. It was on land once owned by the old MGM studios, but now was an oddity along with his workshop building in a neighborhood of cookie-cutter bungalows and apartments.

The inside was a great room with a kitchen in one corner, living room and dining room in the middle, and on a raised area in the back, Roland's bedroom. The only other room was a bathroom which used to be an old set designer's office.

Wheelchair ramps led to the bathroom, bedroom, and exits. Dozens of gymnastics rings, low enough for a seated man to grab and lift himself, dominated the decor. The rings dangled from metal and wooden beams, framing the ceiling and walls of the old brick building.

Roland's furniture was old, but neat and comfortable. He never had flowers on his tables before Jenny. Now he did. He never felt the need to celebrate any holiday before

Jenny. Now, for the first time, a Christmas tree stood in the middle of his living room.

Jenny stood barefoot on a stepladder hanging gold and silver bulbs near the top. Roland maneuvered his wheelchair around its base hanging bulbs on the lower branches.

She came down for another box of bulbs, then went back up the stepladder. Roland hung his last bulb, then watched Jenny standing above him in her short denim skirt.

Jenny didn't mind giving him such views of herself. She felt his stare and looked down at him. She sensed there were questions mingling with the lust in his eyes. "Something on your mind?"

"Just enjoying the view," he said.

Jenny smiled and flipped her skirt up flashing her thong. "How about that?"

Roland balled his fists tight, and clinched his teeth like an overacting thespian. "Be careful, we may never get this done."

"We're almost finished." Jenny hung the last couple of bulbs, while Roland continued looking up her skirt.

He nervously rubbed his hands, his mind wandering back to a major issue gnawing at his heart. "Have you given anymore thought about that?"

Jenny came down the stepladder and sat on its second step. She crossed her legs and rubbed her knee gently. "Yeah. I have, as a matter of fact."

"And?"

"And -- I still don't know," she said. "I mean, I just came off a relationship like that."

"What about the financial argument. You'll save the rent money."

"I know."

"Then there's the romantic argument. You'll be living with someone who'll be utterly devoted to you."

"I know."

"You're practically here all the time now." He noticed Jenny's thoughtful silence. Her lack of response might have been an answer, an answer he didn't like. "Maybe after spending so much time with me, you're not sure if you want to live with a paraplegic."

"No, that's not it."

"Then what is it?"

"I haven't really been on my own yet. I always had roommates. Now that I'm alone, I kind of like the peace and quiet."

"Peace and quiet, huh?" Roland bowed his head and began pivoting his wheelchair.

Jenny reached out and stopped him. "Dammit. Can't you understand? I am not ruling this out. I do care for you, deeply. I just want us to take it slow."

"The problem with someone like me is that answers like that always feel like rejections."

"No."

"Or at least a loss of interest."

"You're wrong. You are so wrong. The truth is I need to grow up a little -- you know, be responsible for my own life. You're definitely wrong if you think like that." She leaned forward and cupped her hands under his face. "I'm with the only man I want to be with -- you. And we're going to have one of the best Christmases ever, together -- you and me." Her caresses brought a slight smile on his face, but she could tell he wasn't totally convinced. She still had her doubts too, but didn't want to dwell on the issue. "Now, where's the star for the top?"

"It's in the little blue box behind you."

Jenny turned, picked up the box and pulled out a crystalline star. She climbed back up the stepladder, rose up on her toes and placed the star at the top of the tree. "Is it straight?"

Roland never took his eyes off her. "Fine."

"Playback," a recording engineer said.

The Chalice girls held headphones tight on their ears and moved closer to a large microphone. In their ears they heard a mingling of violin-like keyboards and a thumping baseline, hinting of the song's hard driving rhythm. When drums punctuated that rhythm, the women released their four-part harmony.

"Oh-uhhhh -- insanityyyeahhh. Ohhh-uh -- luv-in' insanityyyeahh."

"Cut!" The engineer abruptly cut off the playback in their ears and turned to Gale who sat next to him in the control booth. The women stepped away from the microphone and waited for their next direction.

After a short discussion, Gale leaned in toward the talk-back microphone. "Kayla?"

"Yes?"

"I need you to come a little stronger, honey. Vesta -- Tasha, you're fine where you are. Janice?"

"Yeah, Mom."

Gale rubbed her chin, not quite sure what to do with her. "I want to try something with you. First time around with 'ohhh -- insanity,' stay with your part. Second time around leading into Tasha's opening rap, I want you to go sharp -- not too much. Let's see how it sounds with a little choych -- maybe a quarter or so to start."

"A little choych?"

"A little choych. I'm still looking for that identifiable sound for you. Want to try it again?"

"Yes, Mom," they all said.

Gale backed away from the talk-back microphone. The engineer leaned toward it. "Stand-by for playback."

They tried it again and again, and each time it wasn't quite what Gale wanted to hear. For more than two days she tweaked their sound, and coached their voices -- long hours of experimentation. Each day, they were in the studio from shortly after sunrise to almost midnight.

The girls had breaks, but they spent that time eating catered meals in the studio offices, or training at a nearby fitness center. On the indoor track, they ran dozens of laps together like a four-woman relay team warming up for the Olympics. They certainly were a curiosity to the others who trained there -- four beautiful young women running endless laps in close-order formation. Others were interested in socializing while working out, but the Chalice girls were all business. They just ran, showered, then went directly back to the studios.

It took them three long days, but Chalice had finally finished the backing vocals and chorus for Luvin' Insanity. They still had a long way to go though, and Gale remained patient with them.

With Kayla, Janice, and Vesta watching her from the control booth, Tasha stood at a microphone alone with a lyric sheet on a stand in front of her, waiting for her cue. She heard the instrumental for the song and the four-part harmonies. She heard Janice's voice rise perfectly out of the second part, then began her rap.

"Just loosen you tie -- and look in my eyes. I got you my sights.

"I'm losing control -- I'll go high or low. We wo-don't really -- need the -- shit. Oops." Tasha covered her mouth. "Sorry."

"That's all right," the engineer said. The other three women were falling over each other laughing.

"Tell the three stooges in there to kiss my butt," Tasha snapped. "Mom, is it 'don't' or 'won't' in that line?"

"It's 'don't,' Gale said. "There was a typo there. Let's try it again from the top. Just relax, have fun, and don't pay any attention to the stooges."

"Okay."

The playback started again, but just before Tasha heard her cue, Kayla stood up, threw her hair over her face, and bounced like some kind of caged primate. The shock of seeing Kayla, of all people, acting silly caused Tasha to start late.

"Just loosen you tie -- and ahhhhh --" Tasha couldn't hold it together. She collapsed into a gut flexing laugh, and stumbled away from the microphone.

Before Gale turned around, Kayla quickly straightened her hair and stood next to Vesta as if nothing happened. Gale stared at her with touch of anger in her eyes.

Kayla just shrugged her shoulders. "I don't know what the girl's problem is."

Chapter 30

"Hello?"

"Matt? This is Roger."

"Roger?"

"Doctorow? Roger Doctorow? Your agent?"

"Hey, how are things? I thought you left town or something."

"No, they haven't gotten rid of me yet. I know we haven't talk a lot, but when we do, don't I always have good news?"

"Okay," Matt responded.

"Got another audition for you. A supporting role in a feature motion picture called *Angels in Compton*."

"Angels in what?"

"Compton. It's like that old City of Angels movie, only with a --"

"-- An urban slant. I know."

"Right. It's also charming. You'll love it."

"Why do I keep getting calls for crap like this, Roger?"

"Because I happen to think you're right for these roles."

"How come I never get called for *Black Panther II, Band of Brothers*, romantic comedies or something?"

"This one's a spoof. You're not refusing an audition are you?"

Matt closed his eyes tightly, and stiffened his jaw. "No."

"That's good judgment, kid. You have to pay some dues."

"Some people don't."

"Yeah, right. Remember, I don't get any money when you're not getting jobs. People are getting to know you though. Now, your call time is ten o'clock, Thursday morning at Assurance Films at La Brea and Melrose. You're auditioning for one of the angels. This one has a prison record and can only talk in rap."

"What!"

"Yeah, I thought that was unique too."

It took a while, but excitement over just having an audition soon replaced Matt's negative thoughts about this film. He knew he was due for a win. Maybe he could outshine the material and rise above the expectations of his agent.

Thursday afternoon, Matt emerged from the modest offices of Assurance Films smothering his rage over another lost audition. No film credit, not even a callback, and most heart breaking for Matt, no building block of pride for him to stand on and face Kayla.

He sat in the van with the motor off, watching other rejected actors coming out of the building. Even with their rejections, they all had hopeful smiles. *Must be new to town. Maybe they have a ton of auditions this week. Or they may have great agents.* He was not happy with his. It was time for a change. He pulled out his phone.

"D-S Talent Management," a female voice answered.

"Yeah, this is Matt Redcrop. Is Roger there?"

"Oh sure. He's been looking for you. Just a second."

Matt had never fired an agent. What could he say?

What will he lose? He heard a rather frantic sounding phone grab on the other end.

"Matt!"

"Roger, before you say anything, I think it's time for me to make a change."

"I agree," Roger said.

"Man, these auditions I'm getting are –. You agree with what?"

"I agree with you. Have you ever thought about doing commercials?"

"Of course."

"A friend of mine is producing a national soap commercial, and is looking for African-Americans. I sent him your headshot, and you were the first he called for. Interested?"

"A national?"

"Big residuals, Matt, -- can keep you afloat out here for a couple of years."

"Yeah. I guess so."

"Good. You're set for 2:30 tomorrow at Lawson Casting near the Culver Studios on Washington Boulevard. Is that near you?"

"Not too far from me."

"Great. There are no sides to remember, but wear some swim trunks or bicycle shorts. You're going for a shower scene."

He once thought a truly serious actor wouldn't do such commercials, but the world was full of serious actors who weren't working actors. Matt wanted the work. Considering Kayla's sudden success, he needed the work. So, for the second straight day, Matt called off his job and was at Lawson Casting ready for anything.

"Everyone, this is Matthew Redcrop, SAG-AFTRA-Equity." The casting director backed out of the office and closed the door behind her.

Matt, wearing nothing but a pair of bicycle shorts, stood in front of a group of eight people. With most of the lights shining on him, he couldn't make out their faces clearly, but noticed half of them wore business suits and ties, while the other half wore business dress-suits with open collars. Matt stood under an air conditioning vent and never felt so many goosebumps rising on his skin.

"So, Matthew, tell us a little something about yourself," one of the men said. "Have you done many commercials before?"

"I had done a couple when I was in college – Cleveland State University -- a banking spot and a fast food spot."

"Fine. Are you from Cleveland?"

"Among other places. I was born in Youngstown, went to college in Cleveland, spent some time in Tampa, and now I'm here."

"Fine. I'm sure your agent told you about this spot. What we need you to do is to stimulate – uhhh, simulate a shower scene. We want you to really lather yourself up and enjoy the thrill in using our soap product. You may begin when you're ready."

Matt was briefly paralyzed by his dignity, only standing there with no motivation to move, until he thought about the residuals and Kayla's respect. Slowly, his right hand moved to his chest, rubbing in circular motions as if he were using a bar of soap. His left hand began spreading the imaginary suds over the rest of his torso. He moved the invisible bar under his arms and over his ribs. He scrubbed his face and broke out with a smile. He grunted manly sighs of pleasure, parted his legs and began involving his whole body. He bent low and soaped up each leg, then leaned into a stream of imaginary hot water, rinsing the suds off his face and chest. He then turned to rinse his back.

He thought he was finished, but hadn't heard "cut" so he started doing it again, bouncing up and down, closing his eyes, immersing himself in a world of shower stall pleasures.

"Thank you, Matthew." Matt slowed down and came to a stop. "That was nice. We won't be shooting until after the holidays. We have your agent's name and number?"

"It's on my headshot."

"Good. Thank you for coming down this afternoon. You have nice holiday."

"Thank you. Uh -- you too."

Matt walked out of the office, and closed the door behind him. He put on his pants and sweater in the outer office while the casting director was at her desk on the phone, watching him. He zipped his pants, fastened his belt, and gave her wink as he left.

Matt had missed two straight days of work and had nothing to show for it, but those were the risks he wanted to take. He wasn't emotionally attached to his job, except for the paycheck. That Monday morning, he would lose even that attachment.

He walked into the office early and read his newspaper in the break-room. Other early risers sat around the mostly empty tables breakfasting and relaxing.

Fifteen minutes before nine, Terri walked in and saw

Matt with his newspaper. With the tips of her finger nails, she lightly tickled him on the side of his neck as she passed. Matt flinched and looked around. "Terri?"

"Hello, stranger." She sat next to him, her weighty book bag shaking the table when she set it down.

"Damn. What do you have in that thing?"

"Light reading."

"Right."

She smiled and shyly bit her lower lip. "Missed ya. Did you have some auditions or something?"

"No. I was out sick."

"Right." She nodded her head, knowing better. "Bernie was a little pissed. Four people called off Friday and that left him really short. So be ready for a 'got a minute' meeting."

"Yeah, I know. How was it Thursday and Friday?"

"Dead. I guess no one wants to do anything going into the winter season. It's hard to bonus when it's like this."

"Yeah."

"So, how's your girlfriend?" she asked.

"Fine. They're still working her hard. She went right through the weekend. Hardly saw her at all."

"I know how hard that is."

"Yeah."

She turned her flirty eyes more directly toward Matt, an idea flashing in her mind. "Well, if you ever have weekends like that again, maybe you can come on over to UCLA and catch a basketball game or something. There's a lot of --" Terri looked up to the door leading out of the break-room. Bernie leaned in and pointed in their direction. Terri pointed at herself. "Me?" Bernie shook his head and pointed at Matt. "Matt?"

Matt turned back toward Bernie. Bernie raised his index finger and curled it inward a couple of times summoning Matt to follow him.

"Uh oh," Matt said with a straight face.

"I'll meet you at my desk."

"Yeah." Matt rolled up his paper, stood, and walked over to Bernie. "Yeah, Bern?"

"Got a minute?"

"Sure."

"Follow me, please." He followed Bernie to his office-like cubicle which had the same fabric wall barriers as the telemarketers' cubicles. "Have a seat." Matt sat and Bernie pulled out a file from his drawer and opened it. "I'm gonna have to let you go, Matt. I've warned you twice before about your attendance." He showed paperwork Matt had signed in the past. "Instead, you missed three more days in last couple of weeks. I need those chairs filled."

"Okay." Matt stood. "Do I get my check now or what?"

Bernie was puzzled by Matt's lack of response. "Uh, Friday."

"Okay. See ya then." Matt turned and walked out of Bernie's cubicle.

Bernie sat there with Matt's file open, but wasn't sure if he had finished firing him or not.

Matt walked out of the phone room and passed the break-room on his way to the exit.

Terri saw him passing by and sprinted after him. She caught Matt just as he was about to reach for the exit door. "Where're you going?"

"Home."

"He fired you?"

"Yeah."

"Oh no."

Matt saw Bernie leaning out the phone room. "It's all good, because now I can say, MY AUDITIONS WENT GREAT! I'M GLAD I DIDN'T COME ON THOSE DAYS, SO I COULD MAKE MY AUDITIONS!" Everyone in the hall paused and looked in Matt's direction. Bernie stepped out in the hall with them. Matt waved. "What's up, man?"

"Wait a minute," Terri said. She pulled out a pen and tore a small piece off a grocery store receipt in her pocket. She bent over and wrote on the paper, then handed it to Matt. "I don't know if I'll ever see you again. But I want you to know if you ever feel like hanging-out around Westwood or just want to talk, that's where you can reach me." She took Matt by surprise by throwing her arms around his neck, and giving him a quick kiss on the cheek. "Bye." She hustled back to the phone room.

Matt rubbed in the kiss hoping none of her lipstick stayed on his cheek. He folded the little piece of paper in his hand and slipped it in his pants pocket.

The ten o'clock news was on TV. As he lay on the couch watching the lead story, Matt heard a car pull up in the parking lot. He didn't bother to look. He heard the door shut, and faint footsteps coming up the outside stairway. A key tapped the edges of the door lock.

Kayla walked in with two garment bags in her arms. "Hey, babe," she said, struggling to pull her key out of the lock.

"How'd it go today?"

Kayla closed the door. "They said we're finished with a third track for the album."

"It's moving pretty fast now."

"Yeah." Kayla set her bags on the floor and leaned over Matt to kiss him. She lifted his head and sat down allowing him to rest it on her lap. "Did you have a good day?"

"Yeah. I was fired."

"What?"

"I was fired. Those last two auditions did it."

"Oh, baby, I'm sorry."

"No big deal -- part of the package."

Kayla gently rubbed his right temple as he continued watching the news. She wasn't sure what she could say to pick up his spirits. Telling him that she'll support him monetarily certainly wouldn't do it. This was new to her. She watched the news, but her eyes kept moving back to Matt who never took his eyes off the TV screen. She sighed and gently shifted her legs. "Well, at least we don't have to worry about money right now."

"No."

She had said the right thing. Matt's mood didn't get any worse.

A commercial came on, and Matt yawned. A spot depicting a jazz band caught Matt's attention. He raised his head a little, watching a guitarist strumming his instrument with an animated dancer on its fingerboard. He lowered his head back down on Kayla's lap and relaxed. "Any word yet on when they're holding auditions for your touring band?"

"No." *Shit. Why won't he forget that? He doesn't need to hear the truth now. Maybe when things get a little better for him.* Kayla pulled a scrunchy from her wrist and pulled her hair back into a pony-tail.

"I'm to the point now where I have to try anything for a break."

Kayla continued rubbing Matt's head, staring down at his face. She noticed deepening lines on his forehead and a determined look in his eyes she had often mistook for anger.

The next morning was typical. Kayla had already left in her limo for the recording studio. Sunlight seeped through breaks in the window blinds keeping Matt from going back to sleep. He rose out of bed, showered and dressed, then realized he had nowhere to go.

He ate a simple bowl of corn flakes, then stepped out on the balcony with his guitar enjoying the fresh, chilly air. He noticed a man and a woman having a pleasant conversation on the other side of the parking lot. Matt recognized Milo, but didn't know the woman. The woman tapped, then squeezed Milo's arm in a very familiar manner when their conversation ended. She then walked away leaving Milo.

Matt leaned over the rail. "Yo, Milo."

He looked up and smiled when he recognized Matt. "What's up there, Matthew?" He jogged across the parking lot.

"Nothing much."

"Day off?"

"Yep."

"Ahhh, a star's life. Hey, have you seen Albert lately?" Milo asked.

"No. Not for a while."

"That S-O-B becomes a star, and starts to forget his friends. I've been leaving messages for days."

"Me too."

"Well, if you see him before me. Tell him there's something I want to talk to him about, ASAP."

"Okay."

"So, you getting any work?" Milo asked.

"Lots of feelers for big parts -- little work though."

"Yeah, that's still pretty good. Keep plugging away. It'll come. Ask that girl of yours if we can all ride in that limo. There's some people around here who want to know what she's into."

"Still can't say."

"Yeah, all right. You know I'll find out sooner or later. Check you later."

"Take it easy." Matt watched Milo walk into the stairway of the building next to his. A light breeze buffeted his face reminding him of the beauty of the morning. As special as it was, he never stepped far from apartment that day, remaining indoors with the balcony open allowing a breeze inside. He spent the entire day strumming his guitar, exercising his musical skills for an audition he just knew was in his future.

Kayla came home that night and found him just the way he was the night before, reclining on the couch watching the ten o'clock news. She took off her shoes, laid down her garment bags, and sat with him quietly on the couch.

They didn't talk too much. They both knew how the day went for each other. For Matt, it was blissfully dull, the kind of day that could be spoiling if he had many more like it.

For Kayla, it was another day full of wonders, education, and fun. Music was a dimension of her dreams she had never considered. Her new life was beginning to occupy more of her thoughts every day.

Even as she sat there rubbing Matt's head, she was thinking about the things she wanted to pack for her group's tour. She was rehearsing in her mind the solo track she was going to record the next morning. She thought about Janice, Vesta, and Tasha.

A harmony of women, with a familiar lead voice singing *Who's Lovin' You*, caught her attention on TV. She looked up and saw an advertisement for a new movie. She scooted forward a little bit. There was no announcer's voice, no actor's lines, just that familiar voice, backed by three other women, singing over romantic scenes of a man and woman re-learning love in the Idaho mountains. Her sleepy eyes widened. "Is that's us?"

"Hmmm?" Matt muttered.

"THAT'S US!"

"What?" Matt's eyes widened.

"The song! Oh my God!" Kayla stood up, nearly wrenching Matt's neck. She knelt down close to the TV, and turned up the volume. She clapped her hands and screamed, throwing her arms high. When the commercial ended, she ran to her garment bag and pulled out her phone.

Matt slowly sat up, still not completely sure why she was so excited. He watched her thumb her phone frantically. "What's going on?"

"That old Smokey Robinson -- it's Chalice -- Hello? Janice? -- AHHHHHHHEEEEEEEE! I KNOW! I just saw it!"

Early next morning, Milo used a pass key to enter Jenny's apartment. He leaned in checking for anyone inside. The bookshelves were bare, no pictures on the walls. Only the furniture remained. Jenny no longer lived here, so Milo opened the door wider, allowing in two moving men from a furniture rental company. "It's all yours, gents. I'll be at the office. Let me know when you're done."

"Okay."

Near downtown Culver City, in his warehouse-like home, Roland lay nude in his bed, paralyzed a second time by Jenny's warm hands. From his waist to his shoulders, she pushed her hands over a thin layer of oil, raising a small mound of skin and flesh ahead of them.

She sat upright on his back between two, hanging gymnastic rings, her knees squeezing both his hips. Her face held a sleepy contentment as she shifted the directions of her hands randomly, searching for even the smallest tense muscle.

She had her doubts at first, but she knew this move was good for her. She needed Roland more than she once needed Albert. She needed Roland more than he needed her. Jenny always had a place in her heart for troubled men, and no one had ever filled that void better than Roland.

Christmas and New Years had passed before Matt and Kayla even heard that Jenny moved out of her place. They still hadn't heard from Albert, but only Matt dwelt on the whereabouts of their old friends.

Matt was the only one who had the time to dwell on anything. He was still unemployed, and was getting cozy with idea of not working a regular job ever again. But he still wanted acting jobs so Kayla didn't have to support him completely.

It was disturbing to him that he still hadn't heard anything from his agent about that soap commercial. By this time, he knew he probably didn't get it, but he still had big hopes for the New Year, just like he had last New Year.

Chapter 31

Matt reached into the mailbox and pulled out a mixture of letters and advertisements. After sifting through the junk, he tossed them in the trash and took the letters inside.

The return address of one of letters caught his eye. It was from D-S Talent Management. He had never received a letter from them before. Matt tossed the other letters on the counter top and opened it.

> *Dear Matt,*
>
> *I think it would be best for both of us if I terminate our relationship as per our contract.*
>
> *I know you've been very disappointed in the opportunities I have introduced you to, but things are tough here. There is just too much competition, even among us agents.*

Maybe you'll find another agent better
suited for your particular talents
and needs.

I will return your headshots and resumes.
All the best to you, Matt.

With warm regards,
Roger Doctorow
D-S Talent Management

An impulse of temper pulled his fingers tight crumpling the letter into a ball. Suddenly, Matt felt his stomach twisting and releasing. Diarrhea swept through his system forcing him to drop the letter to the floor. He ran off to the bathroom to both relieve himself, and contemplate the uncertainties of his future.

In Santa Monica, Gale paced in a dance studio in front of Chalice. Kayla, Vesta, Janice, and Tasha were in athletic and dance clothes sitting on a wooden floor, ready to start the next stage of their training.

"Rehearsal," Gale started. "The fashioning, the refining, the polishing of your stage performance. We have to work hard and fast, because your first single is already out in Europe and in select American markets. We're concentrating on Europe first, mainly because the distributor is a European company, and that's the agreement. But that's fine, because if you're successful in Europe, America will go crazy for you. We always love stuff coming from Europe.

"Now, by April, you'll be on tour in Europe too." All the girls gasped, excited smiles filling their faces. "Howard hasn't finalized the schedule yet, but it looks like you'll debut in Berlin, with stops in Prague, Milan, Madrid, and Montreaux. The venues will depend on the success of *Luvin' Insanity,* and your album. But I'm telling you, just between us, you're testing big over there, girls. We're very excited."

"What is this testing we keep hearing about?" Tasha asked.

"Advertising sound tracks, movie trailers, club play, radio surveys -- things like that. It might be paying off. *Luvin Insanity* is already in the top 30 in England and Germany, and you're complete unknowns. That's why we're gonna whip you girls in shape. When you hit the stage over there, I want people to come out of your concerts even more excited about you than when they went in. When you're on stage I want you to remember, your fans owe you nothing." Gale smiled and closed her eyes as if she were reliving her past. "And you owe them everything. You owe them a good time. I want you smiling through the entire performance." She flung her arms wide. "I want you to have fun and take those people with you." She began dancing and strutting. "You're going to be in constant motion on that stage, dancing and playing to the crowd like four fun-loving girls hosting a party." Gale stopped her dancing, and turned to a corner where a frail, young white man sat on the floor quietly listening to her. "I want you to meet Duncan Meredith." Gale gestured to him to come forward. He hopped up in his spacious canvas pants and squeaky sneakers, and hurried over to Gale's side. She draped her arm over his shoulders. "Duncan is one of the finest choreographers in the country. He's going to design your stage performance so it looks absolutely natural. You're in his hands for next few weeks. I'm stepping aside during this time to take a little R & R.

But don't let up, or Sergeant Mom's gonna hear about it." Gale gave Duncan a half a hug, waved at the girls, and walked quickly out of the studio.

Duncan stepped forward, and widened his understanding eyes. His voice was far softer than Gale's. "I've watched some of your sessions in the studio. Very nice. Gale and Howard showed me some of the designs for your stage, and I've listened to all your tracks. So, I'm about as ready as you are." Duncan giggled softly to himself, then looked at the girls. None of them even smiled. They sat there like inactive robots waiting for their first software command. "Look, I want you to know that I am open to your ideas. I'll guide you through some routines I've come up with. But if you have any ideas that can make the routines even more exciting feel free to tell me. I listen." Again, he looked for any response from the girls. There was nothing. "I guess you're ready to work?"

"Yes!" all four of them said.

"Oh my God, you can speak. I was worried." Duncan walked back toward the mirrored wall, and leaned against the rail. "Okay. Everyone stand against the back wall." The girls stood up and did as he said. Duncan pushed his tongue against the left wall of his mouth as he looked at them. He stared at Kayla, because she seemed out of place. "Kayla? Is that right?" She nodded to him. "I want you to stand about five feet to the left of Vesta, actually that's your right. I want you at the end." Kayla walked to the end of the line-up. "Janice, I want you on the other end, five feet away from Tasha." When Janice moved, Duncan paused, tonguing the inside wall of his mouth again while looking at their appearance in this line-up. "That'll work. Let's, for now, call this position one. This is the position you'll be in when you first appear on stage. *Luvin' Insanity* will start things for you. Tasha has the first solo -- a rap I guess, huh?"

"Yeah."

"Okay. Tasha, come down stage about five feet toward the center." Tasha stepped forward. "No. Better still. Step back, Tasha." She went back to her position. "I want everyone come down stage five steps. One, two, three, four, five -- stop. Now Tasha, step out with attitude. Walk diagonally toward Kayla's end, coming down stage five feet or so. Kayla, Vesta, fill in the space toward Janice. Don't worry about spacing right now. We'll change the scale to fit the stage." Everyone did as he said, then stopped in their positions. "Good. That's position two. Now, when we make this move, everyone moves at the same time, and to the beat of the music. What'll happen is Tasha will move freely while she raps." He pointed to Kayla, Vesta, and Janice. "You three will snap off a few choice moves to back her up until the next solo. So, girls, let's go back to position one and start walking this out."

With only breaks for lunch and dinner, Duncan kept them in that dance studio into the night. His directions carved new niches in their brains the more they heard them. "Five-six-seven-eight, step -- touch! Knee -- knee! Step -- heel -- half turn! Shoulder -- shoulder. Come on! I want smoldering women! Stride -- stride. Arms up! Hips --hips. Pop it out, girls. And Kayla's solo!"

On the way home that night, four numbers haunted Kayla's mind, five-six-seven-eight. Though she felt exhausted, she made small movements in her limo seat while mentally reviewing the dance steps.

Matt was already asleep in the bedroom when she came home. She dropped her bags under the kitchen counter, slipped off her shoes, and glanced at the letters on the counter. There were just three bills. She tossed them back, then noticed a crumpled piece of paper on the floor. She stooped down, picked it up, and opened it. It was that letter from Roger Doctorow. After she read it, she balled back up and closed her eyes tightly, feeling the dilemma over whether or not to add to Matt's woes.

She quietly walked into the bedroom, hoping not to disturb him. She removed her blouse and jeans, but when she removed a hanger from the closet, the clicking sound penetrated Matt's deep slumber.

"Kay?"

"Yeah?"

He rolled over and turned on a lamp on the night stand. "Hey, babe. How'd it go today?"

"Rough. They brought in this choreographer, and he kept us in dance rehearsals for twelve hours." She sat on the bed and massaged her calf muscles. Matt pushed the blankets off, scooted up behind her, then began helping her by massaging her thighs. She leaned her head back against his shoulder and closed her eyes. "I accidentally found that letter from your agent. I'm sorry."

"Awe, forget that. You're feeling too good for me to worry about that now. Besides you're my ace in the hole." Kayla giggled softly within his embrace. "Any more news on that tour?"

"Ummm hmmm. It's Europe in the Spring. Berlin, Milan, Switzerland." She yawned. "Places like that."

"Damn. Sounds like weeks."

"More like months."

"Damn," Matt nibbled her shoulder. "I better get my act together for that audition." Kayla opened her eyes. "Can't let you get away from me for months."

Matt kissed her neck, but Kayla didn't feel it. She had to tell him, but not now. Maybe his luck will change in a couple of weeks.

It didn't. Matt's flirtations with other agents ended in repeated rejections. In his mind, destiny was pulling him into another direction, music.

He wasn't putting as much into his acting career as he was in practicing his guitar. He wanted to be perfect for that audition. Every time he asked Kayla about it, she still only had courage enough to say, "I don't know."

It tore at her heart to come home late at night finding Matt asleep on the couch with his guitar on the floor, and balled-up rejection letters from agents on the counter.

On a frosty, gloomy morning in mid-February, Kayla's alarm clock sounded. It was 5:30 in the morning, ninety minutes before her limo would arrive. She sat up and wiped her eyes. Soft guitar sounds from the living room caught her attention. She looked for Matt, but he wasn't in bed.

Kayla swung legs out of the covers, stood, and grabbed her robe. She walked out into the living room and found Matt reclining on the couch strumming random melodies on his guitar. He was wide awake, but there was an unusual peace in his eyes.

"You're up early," she said.

"I didn't sleep well."

Kayla sat in the lounge chair and crossed her legs. With

only six weeks before the tour, she knew she couldn't wait any longer. "Matt, I have --"

"You know when I was out scouting for some agents yesterday, I found an old Hollywood Reporter in one of the lobbies with this little article in the back about the tour band for a new group called Chalice."

"Baby, I can explain."

Matt stopped his strumming, and looked at Kayla with stern eyes. "There's not going to be an audition, is there." Kayla folded her arms across her chest, then shook her head negatively to him. "Why didn't you tell me?"

"I just thought --"

"No, you didn't think! I'm struggling my ass off out here, thinking maybe if the acting thing doesn't work maybe I can have a chance for your band."

"Matt, they had the band set even before the group was formed. And even if there were auditions, the girls voted against having boyfriends on the tour."

"And you couldn't tell me this?"

"I wanted to! But with you having so many problems, I didn't want to add to them."

"So, you think I'm fragile or something?"

"No."

"Or maybe you're not taking my concerns serious enough anymore --"

"NO!"

"Oh, isn't that cute, Matt wants to join my band for my tour. Maybe someday when he's better, but not now."

"What did I say?"

"You told me you didn't want to add to my failures,"

Matt said. "Is that how you see me now? Am I some kind of failure to you?"

"Not at all."

"Bullshit! How can you not look at me like that? I'm dying out here. All the education, the training, the credits -- none of it matters. It's all chance. And here I am living with lady luck herself."

Kayla didn't like being called lucky after all the work she had been through. She unfolded her arms, and uncrossed her legs. "Whatever luck I had was because I put myself in a position to make it bloody well happen. I didn't sit back with my smug attitude about what I thought this business should be. Now, I'm sorry I didn't tell you sooner, but that's all the blame I am taking for your problems here. We both had our chances, didn't we? And whatever we have now is our doing." Kayla stood up and walked toward the bedroom. She stopped and turned back. "Oh, and here's another piece of my luck that I now know you're tough enough to take. In two weeks, I have to go back to that beach house in Malibu. Gail wants the Chalice girls to live together for at least a month before we go to Europe. So, in essence, I have to move out. Now, if you'll excuse me, my limo will be arriving in about an hour." Kayla turned and walked into the bedroom.

Matt stayed silent, simmering like a capped geyser -- explosive words pushing behind his clinched teeth. He remained on the couch listening to her showering, and brushing her teeth. He heard her slide hangers around in the closet. He heard the clicking of her belt buckle, and her legs sliding through her slacks. In thirty minutes, Kayla came from the bedroom looking sharp, and putting on an earring.

She held a serious look on her face until she noticed Matt's silent staring. Her eyes softened, and she sighed. "Aren't you going to say anything?"

Matt turned his eyes downward to his guitar and ran his index finger over it. "You're moving out?"

"I have no choice. I'm going on a world tour. I have no idea when we're coming back." She walked over to Matt and sat next to him. "Remember all those things you told me could happen if we made it? How we could be spending months away from each other? Congratulations, you were right again. There's nothing I wanted more than to have you come with me, but that's not going to happen this time."

"So, you're moving out."

Kayla's eyes drifted downward. "Yes."

Matt inhaled deeply. His exhalation quivered. "All the time we had together."

"We still have more time ahead of us." Kayla reached out and caressed Matt's hand. "You're not rid of me yet."

Matt pulled his hand away from her. "Yeah, two more weeks."

"I mean when I get back."

"You know, things can change over such a long time."

"I'll take it a day at a time if you can. And if something happens, something happens. I'll always love you. That'll never change."

Chapter 32

Two weeks passed like two minutes. Kayla still spent long days at the studio while Matt stayed home struggling through each lonely day looking for options to keep his fading acting career going.

On the morning of her departure to Malibu, Matt and Kayla sat on the couch wrapped up in each other's arms waiting for her limo. They didn't say too much to each other, though they had plenty to say. They had promised this wouldn't be the end, but it sure felt like it.

One of their army style foot lockers was in the middle of the floor with Kayla's two garment bags and a suitcase surrounding it. Small items were missing from their shelves, a crystal clock, some books, and several photos. Kayla decided to leave everything else they shared with Matt.

As she lay her head on his chest, Matt looked down on her face, noticing the blinking of her eyes. He saw a tear rolling rapidly down her cheek and wiped it dry. Seeing that tear caused his eyes to glass up too. He discreetly blinked away the moisture.

"I'm so scared," she whispered.

"I know." He held her tighter, and savored how she felt

against him. He inhaled her subtle lavender fragrance, and felt the involuntary vibrations of her body.

When they heard the familiar sound of her limousine, they both sighed simultaneously, then chuckled. Kayla wiped another tear from her face and said, “Here goes nothing.” She stood and pulled Matt up into an embrace. She tasted his lips and mouth in a way they could only do in private, and continued until the limo driver knocked on their door.

Matt helped the driver load Kayla’s luggage into the car. A small crowd of their neighbors gathered again as they often did every morning when Kayla’s limo arrived. They watched as Matt gave Kayla another kiss.

Just as she was about to enter the limo, Milo pushed his way through some of the people. “Hey! Wait!” he called.

Kayla paused with one foot in the car, and the driver holding open the door.

“I got it,” Milo continued. “I got it now!” He held up a silver CD in a plastic folder, and pointed at Matt. “I told you I’d find out.” He turned to Kayla. “You’re one of the Chalice girls.” Some of the people standing nearby began looking at each other with questions on their faces.

Kayla pulled her foot out of the limo and took the CD from Milo. She examined the graphics and photos. It was the single, *Luvin’ Insanity*. “Where did you get this?”

“A friend of mine who just got back from London. He says this is the hottest thing there. Bodda-bing! Who did I see on the jacket, but Kayla Ross. Look here.” He took the CD back and opened it showing the inside with a photo of Kayla, Janice, Vesta, and Tasha on that rock outcrop in Malibu. Matt stepped in and examined it too. Milo took out his pen and handed to Kayla. "I want to be the first, Kay. And don't forget to date it."

She looked at Matt with a bashful smile.

"Go ahead," he said. "With your messy writing, you'll need the practice."

Kayla shrugged, then signed the CD jacket under her image. After finishing, she glanced out at some of the other people standing around watching her. A nervous twitch ran up her spine. This was a tiny taste of things to come. Little by little, her life was changing, and it would never be the same again. She looked back at Matt who winked at her. She mouthed, "I love you," then entered the limo.

As it drove away, Matt and Milo stood side by side as the small crowd dispersed.

Milo smiled and shook his head. "A star in the making, kid." He slapped Matt on the shoulder. "And living right here too."

"Not anymore."

"Huh?"

"They're touring Europe for a while."

"No shit? Awe man. And you're not going?"

"No."

"Damn. That stinks." Milo looked down at his autographed CD. "Did you hear this yet?"

"No."

"Come on over to the office. I'll throw it on. It's not bad."

Matt shook his head. "That's all right. I have to get ready for some appointments this morning anyway."

"Okay. If you want to borrow it, let me know. You can't find this in the U-S yet. Might be on the Net-Tube, Music-Tube or something. Check the internet."

"Thanks."

There were no appointments, no auditions, and no phone calls. With Albert making himself unavailable, and Jenny playing house with her new beau, Matt really had no close friends to take his mind off his difficulties.

To him, this city seemed even more enormous when alone. During the first few days after Kayla left, Matt wandered its streets in anonymity, finding comfort in its crowds, and its facades of glamor.

Like a tourist, he walked in the footsteps of the famous at Grumman's Chinese Theater, and examined the stars on the Walk of Fame. He stared in the faces of long dead Hollywood immortals painted on countless office buildings, and dreamed about belonging there with them.

Almost always, under every painting, or within a block of every monument to Hollywood success, there were living monuments to broken hearts. For the first time he noticed them, homeless men and women in soiled, smelly clothes, sitting among boxes or pushing grocery carts with everything they had in world in them.

He once ignored them, but found that increasingly difficult. Sometimes he didn't have to see them. He could smell the areas where they had flopped for night. *They may have once been like me,* was a recurring thought for him.

Money was no problem for now. Kayla left a generous sum in his bank account. The bills were taken care of, but Kayla wasn't there. At night, he could still smell her faint fragrance on the empty pillow next to him. Every morning, he woke up on that pillow, but she wasn't there.

Kayla called once a day, but their conversations were

short. They weren't very good phone people. They never had to be while she was there.

Kayla was only in Malibu, and four days after she left, Matt couldn't take it anymore. That day, after talking with her for three minutes on the phone, he came to a split-second decision. Suddenly, he felt settled. Suddenly, he felt ready for the commitment of a lifetime.

He had resisted this final frontier for years. Deep down he wasn't sure Kayla was the one until now. Day after day, month after month, year after year, they were together fighting for a common dream -- Kayla never holding back her love, Matt always holding a little in reserve. Now four days without her, and he was asking himself why? She was the only constant in his adult life.

He sprinted out of the apartment, jumped in the van, and headed down to Santa Monica and the Pacific Coast Highway to Malibu. He wasn't sure where this house was, or even if he could get in the neighborhood, but he had to go to her.

It wasn't too hard for him to find this spit of land with its wealthy neighborhood between a ridge and the brooding Pacific. To his surprise, all he had to do was tell the gate-guard the address of the home he was visiting. The guard wrote down the license plate number of the minivan, then opened the gate.

Matt pulled into this neighborhood of seaside estates, rolling slowly down the narrow street. To his right was the brooding, gray Pacific hurling impressive waves onto the rocks and sand, a danger that would scare away most home owners. Yet, here was a colony of wealth made up of decadent whims, each house, at once, a torment and an inspiration to those with only wealthy dreams.

Near the end of the street, Matt found his destination, Howard Rowe's beach house. He pulled up to the gate, but it was closed. He bent down in his seat to get a better look at the windows in the front. The whole place looked lifeless like the rest of homes of this summer-time community.

Matt lowered the window and reached out for the intercom. It was a little too low for him to reach, so he stepped out of the van, pressed the button, waited a minute, then pressed it again.

Vesta answered. "Yes?"

"Hello? I'm here to see Kayla Ross. Do I have the right place?"

"Who are you?"

"Matt Redcrop. I'm a friend of hers."

"One moment."

Matt heard a brief burst of static, then silence. He began feeling a chilly breeze blowing off the ocean, but endured it. He turned toward the house hoping to see someone looking out one of the windows. If anyone was observing him, he couldn't see them through the mirrored tinting.

It seemed like a long wait. Matt had an impulse of pushing the button again reminding them he was still here, but he then heard the click of a metal crank. The gate swung open. Matt jumped back his minivan and drove inside. He parked it, and locked it, then bounded up the stairs to the front door where Kayla stood waiting for him.

When he took her in his arms, Matt closed his eyes, feeling relief from her absence. He looked up and noticed the other Chalice girls standing just inside the door, their curiosity muting his response to feeling Kayla's warmth again.

"What are you doing here?" Kayla asked.

"Oh, I was just in the neighborhood." Matt laughed nervously.

The other girls smiled and giggled. "Hey Kay-R, we haven't been introduced," Tasha said.

"Don't be rude now," Janice said.

Kayla took Matt by the hand and led him inside the foyer. "This is Matt Redcrop. Matt, this is Chalice -- Janice Watkins --"

Janice shook his hand. "Nice to meet you."

"You too."

"Vesta Dhar --"

"Pleased to meet you," Vesta said.

"Nice to meet you too."

"And Tasha Garcia."

Tasha extended both her hands. "My god, you're gorgeous!" She then slapped Kayla's shoulder. "Talk to me, girl."

"I showed you pictures," Kayla said.

"Yeah, but they don't do justice." Tasha took Matt's other arm. "So, you have a brother or something?"

"Just a sister."

"Yeah? She must be hot too. Too bad my knot's tied straight." Tasha pointed to Kayla. "You better watch out."

Vesta hooked Tasha's arm separating her from Matt and Kayla. "Come on, ladies." She said. "Let's leave them alone." The others walked down a hall off the foyer.

"Congratulations, by the way," Matt said to them.

"Thank you," they responded.

Kayla turned to Matt, and held his hand. "So?"

"So?" Matt's eyes shifted back and forth across Kayla's face scanning every detail. Like an iron filing in a magnetic field his face drifted closer, close enough for his lips to touch hers again, lightly, gently, like desert walkers carefully savoring their first taste of water in days. They leaned their foreheads together. "I missed you."

"Me too," she said.

"Can we go somewhere?"

Kayla lifted her head. "Now? They might hear us."

He smiled. "That's not what I mean. Though I can be quiet if you can. Seriously, there's something I want to talk with you about."

"We can go out back." Kayla looked back toward the living room and lowered her voice to a whisper. "Sometimes they're pretty nosy."

On the beach, the ocean breeze buffeted Matt's thick sweater, and filled Kayla's jacket like a sail. Occasionally, a wind gust would shove her into Matt, but they didn't mind the conditions. Matt had never been here and, to him, the scenery was astonishing its beauty. They held hands and walked about a quarter of a mile.

"She's going to New York just to meet me when we stop over," Kayla said.

"Well, her baby's going overseas."

"I'm not her baby. My mother's acting so interested now. Now, I'm her pride and joy."

"Yeah."

"So, is this what you wanted to talk to me about? -- My mother?"

"No." He stopped, faced her, and looked in her eyes.

Matt took a sigh and seemed ready to say something, but didn't.

Kayla pushed her hair away from her face, and stared back at Matt. She was puzzled by his hesitation to talk. "What?" she asked with a nervous snicker.

"Will you marry me?"

Kayla's mouth dropped open. She stood there motionless, holding her jacket tightly around her neck.

Matt expected an instant vocalization from her, but she remained silent. "Did you hear me?" he asked.

Kayla began moving her mouth, but couldn't make a sound at first. "Marriage?"

Matt nodded. "I love you, Kayla. I've always needed you. I've always wanted you."

"Matt, I -- uh," Kayla bowed her head and collected herself. "Bloody H. Hell. Why do you want to ask me this now?"

"There's a chance I may not see you again if I didn't. You're gonna come back a big star, and your life will be different."

"What do you expect to accomplish by asking me now? Why couldn't you ask me a year ago? Or even four months ago?"

"I should've."

"Maybe the answer would have been yes then." She hesitated and pushed her hair off her face. "It's not now, Matt. I can't."

"Why?"

"I can't leave the group."

"I'm not asking you to leave --"

"Then what kind of wife would I be, being away from

my husband for God knows how long, running around Europe? I'm a little old fashion, you know. I'd like to be with my husband, and have him with me."

"All I know is I want to spend the rest of my life with you. I love you."

"Just stop it!" She held both her hands up in front of her, shut her eyes, then took a deep breath. She walked a couple of steps away from him, then rubbed her forehead. "You really bollixed things up. Do you know how long I've been waiting to hear that from you? It's too late now. I'm already having an affair on you -- with this business, Matt -- this business that you encouraged me to pursue. It's got me now. It makes me feel like I'm really doing something special with my life. It's love, and sex, and power, and it has taken me within its arms and is sweeping me away to other parts of the world. What girl wouldn't have her head turned by such a prospect? I have to see where this'll take me, good or bad. And I can't be worried about being a newlywed. Not yet."

Matt's temple muscles pulsed from the grinding of his teeth. He took a deep breath. "So that's the way it's going to be?"

"That's the way it has to be." She walked closer, reached out and gently touched his cheek. "I don't expect you to fully understand. I know I wouldn't understand if the situation were reversed. I hope you can forgive me. I hope you'll still want to see me again when I come back."

"You'll change," he asked.

"No, I won't."

"Yes, you will. I already noticed a big change in you. There'll be a lot of temptations on the road."

"I know. There'll be temptations for you too, while I'm away. What can I say?"

Matt turned his head toward the ocean and shrugged his shoulders. "Nothing. I guess that's it."

Kayla and Matt didn't say too much to each other as they walked back to the house. Nothing more had to be said. They quietly walked through the house, passing the living room where the other three women were watching a video.

At the front door, Matt and Kayla embraced briefly, kissing with less intensity. The only word they exchanged was "bye."

When Matt stepped through the door, Kayla stayed in the threshold, watching him walk down the stairs. He took another look up at her before entering the van. When it exited the gate, Kayla closed the door, then leaned against it. A smile-like grimace pulled her mouth wide. Her head shook from silent sobs. She turned away from the door and slowly sank to floor, burying her eyes in the palms of her hands.

Tasha, Janice, and Vesta peered around the corner with smiles on their faces, but when they saw Kayla on the floor sobbing, their smiles evaporated. They hurriedly gathered around her, sitting on the floor with her.

"What happened?" Janice asked.

Kayla didn't answer. She just leaned into Janice's chest, her body vibrating from her sobbing.

Chapter 33

It was dingy, silent, and barren, yet nothing had changed in Matt's apartment except Matt. That's how his apartment seemed to him, now that Kayla had ceased to be an everyday physical presence in his life.

He slept late into the mornings and, when awake, had no desire to pursue an agent or even pick up his guitar. During the nights, he stayed up until well after three in the morning, falling asleep many nights on the couch only to wake up to start another cycle of non-existent existence.

Kayla called him a few times before her departure. As usual, their conversations were scarce, mostly focusing in on Kayla's busy days. With every phone call, the time they spent talking grew less -- five minutes to three minutes, to 'I just wanted to see how you're doing today' texts.

On the morning of her departure for Europe, Kayla rang his phone again, but this time there was no answer.

It was just after dawn and the other women were already at the limo's door waiting for Kayla. She had on a ski jacket, slim jeans, and suede ankle boots. She lowered her sunglasses over her eyes and stepped carefully down the stairs while still holding the phone to her ear. Usually, Matt's voicemail would pick up after the fourth ring. She only heard silence, then three quick beeps as if her signal strength was low. She paused on the steps and dialed again.

"Kay-R?" Gale called. "Let's go."

"Coming," Kayla responded. "Answer-answer-answer." Three beeps again.

"Kay-R!" the other girls called together.

"All right!" Kayla click her phone, then bounded down the stairs to the others.

Every five minutes of their trip to L-A International Airport, Kayla dialed Matt's phone, but still couldn't get an answer. Thoughts that she once considered absurd crossed her mind. *Is he in the hospital? Did he kill himself? Not over me. Please God, where is he? Is he with another woman already. No. Or could he?* She dialed again.

"Awe come on," Tasha said. "He's out, aight? You practically told him he could see other women."

"Shut up," Janice said to Tasha.

"She did."

"All right, all right," Gale said. "Does everyone have their passport?"

"You asked us that five times already," Vesta said. "Do you have yours?"

Gale's face lengthened, and her eyes went blank. Gently, she felt the pockets of her coat and slacks. She even drew Kayla's attention away from the phone as she felt around for her passport. She then reached inside her coat and whipped out the little blue book. "Ta-daaa."

"Good," Vesta said. "Now, don't lose it."

Gale playfully stepped on Vesta's new shoes. Vesta retaliated and it quickly became a foot battle.

There still wasn't an answer at Matt's number so Kayla lowered the phone to her lap and slumped lower in her seat.

Gale, noticing Kayla's mood, ended her foot battle with Vesta. "Okay now. Let's get back to thinking about this trip." Gale put an arm around Kayla and patted the side of her head. "Now the video shoot should only take two or three days. We'll be in Potsdam for that. Ernie -- excuse me -- Ernst, he hates Ernie -- Ernst has everything you'll need in place already. You won't have to worry about a thing. They've spared no effort when it comes to Chalice. That's how hot you girls are right now. Now I've also arranged for you to have enough time for sightseeing."

The two limos carrying Chalice and their entourage parked in reserved spaces in front the passenger terminal. It was common to see these kinds vehicles at the L-A airport, yet those who happened to be nearby still had to look just in case it was Barbra Streisand or Will Smith.

The bodyguards, all four of them in dark suits, exited the first limo and walked back to the second where the women waited. One of the men opened the door and Gale emerged with her attaché case. Chalice then emerged from the limo.

Most L-A natives and American tourists didn't know who they were, and barely paused in going about their business. European tourists did notice; many stopped, gawked, and pointed at them.

Two photographers dashed out the terminal doors and began snapping pictures, and there was even a videographer with a reporter following them.

"My god," Kayla said. "What's this?"

The reporter's ear caught Kayla's accent. "You're English?" he asked with a Welsh accent.

"My mother's from Leeds."

"Terrific. Are you excited about going back to Europe?" He shoved a microphone toward her face.

"Well, I've never been --" Kayla thought about what she was about to say. "I've never -- been -- more excited. We're all excited about this tour, right ladies?"

They all crowded around Kayla, "YEEEESSSS," then mugged for the camera.

"Aqui venimos, Europa!" Tasha said.

"Can we take a minute of your time?" a German photographer asked.

The women looked at Gale, and she nodded.

"Sure," Janice said.

"We just need some shots of the four of you together just before your departure."

"You can take a couple out here," Gale said. "Then you can follow us inside if you like."

"Fabulous. Thanks. You're great. Now girls, just be yourselves this is nothing complicated."

It was nothing complicated, but the girls hammed it up anyway. Soon the European tourists who recognized them, but were too shy to approach them, began taking pictures themselves. Some of the teenagers and children even asked for autographs. The girls took turns obliging their requests.

While the girls stirred up a commotion, Howard Rowe walked out of the terminal entry and stepped up behind Gale.

Gale was about to turn around when she was confronted by his brilliant smile. "Howard?"

"All right now, G-Cup!" He grabbed her and kissed her cheek.

"I was wondering where you were."

"You know I had to come here to see my favorite girls off."

"Well there they are, in their element." Gale and Howard watched the young women toy with the photographers, their fans, and each other, displaying one hundred percent of their playful sides. "Where did these photogs come from?" Gale asked.

"I just made a few phone calls. The ball's already rolling over there. I didn't have to sell it. They're gonna be mobbed when they arrive. They're money, baby."

"Now I understand the bodyguards," Gale said.

"Howard?" Kayla called.

"Get over here," Janice said.

"Gale too," Tasha said.

"Get over here." Vesta waved at them.

Gale and Howard hurried over and joined the little party.

"This is our mommy and daddy," Tasha said to the TV reporter in a little girl's voice.

"There are eleven more at home just like us," Kayla said.

"Oh, and there are our 14 half brothers and sisters," Vesta said.

Kayla leaned in front of her. "By Daddy's mistresses."

"And our other 17 half brothers and sisters," Vesta added.

"By Mummy's mister-sers, or something. What do they call male mistresses anyway?"

"Gigolos!" Tasha said.

"Oh yeah."

Inside the terminal lobby the girls continued their informal bantering with the photographers and TV reporter in a lounge area. Their bodyguards were never too far away from them.

Kayla, feeling a little fatigued by the early hour, allowed her mind to drift back to Matt. She looked out the window to the hills along the horizon and a beautiful peach colored sunrise. She lingered on its oil painting like beauty for a few minutes, ignoring the commotion around her until one of the bodyguards tapped her on the shoulder.

"Excuse me, Miss Kay-R." He held a single red rose wrapped in silver paper. "A gentleman wanted me to give this to you."

"A gentleman?" Kayla sat up in her chair and looked around. The bodyguard pointed out toward the edge of the lobby where Matt stood alone among the passing crowds of travelers. Kayla bolted by the bodyguards and photographers, throwing herself in his arms, kissing every part of his face. "Oh God, I thought something happened to you. You had me out of my mind." She slapped his shoulder. "I tried calling you this morning. What's the matter with your phone?"

"I didn't feel your vibration. Maybe my battery's dead."

Kayla lowered her nose to the rose. "Thank you. I didn't think I'd get to see you again."

"I know I had to come out here and uh, I guess -- let you know that I'm very proud of you. Break a leg over there."

She wiped a tear from her eye and pulled Matt into her arms.

The commotion around the other girls died down when Tasha and Janice noticed Kayla and Matt. Janice grabbed Vesta's arm drawing her attention to them. The reporter, noticing the girls looking out there, turned and saw Kayla embracing Matt too.

"Who's that? Her lover?" the reporter asked.

Howard loomed behind the reporter. "That, my friend, is a private matter," he said. "And I hope all of you respect that. I let you in on being the first to talk with these girls, and if you want considerations like that in future, then let them have their private moments."

The reporter looked over his shoulder and nodded in agreement. "Shut her down a moment, Kyle." The videographer lowered his camera, and the photographers did the same.

"We appreciate that, guys," Janice said.

Kayla and Matt walked a short distance away from the lounge, blending in as well as an anonymous couple with a trailing bodyguard could.

They sat in a nearby coffee shop, nibbling on cinnamon buns and sipping a little coffee. They both tried keeping their conversation light, but they couldn't overcome the fact that this was the end. Their lives were already separate. They won't even be on the same continent together.

The bodyguard checked his watch and noticed their time was short. He walked over to their table. "Time to go, Miss."

"Thanks." Kayla never looked at her bodyguard. She

preferred looking at Matt, a man who appeared a little more tired, and a little less confident, but still the man who had churned her chemistry for most of her adult life.

Matt stood and offered his hand. Kayla took it and they slowly walked back to the lounge where the other girls and Gale waited. As they walked, they entwined their fingers, enjoying the feel of each other's hands a final time. He then released it, slowly running his hands across her rear, hooking his thumb on a belt hoop. They turned and face each other. This time their eyes were clear. Each had found peace within themselves.

"Are you all right?" she asked.

"Yeah. You?"

"I'm – Wow. Five years, huh?"

"We'll always have them."

"Yeah." Kayla chuckled. "I had a few cries, but I'm fine."

"Good." Matt pressed his pelvis tighter against Kayla's. Both their smiles faded.

"Thanks for everything," she whispered.

"Kayla honey, we have to go," Gale called.

Kayla heard her. She kissed Matt briefly, but deeply, then scampered to the others. She gave Howard a quick embrace, then she, Gale, and the other Chalice girls entered the jet bridge.

When she disappeared from his sight, Matt put his hands in his pockets and turned away. He drifted through the airport concourses for an hour, wandering through the gift shops, and stopping at a window whenever a departing jet caught his eye.

He waited for the loss of Kayla to overwhelm him, but it didn't. He held firm, and soon felt comfortable enough to go home.

Chapter 34

TV Guide (March 29th-April 4th issue):

ALBERT COLE MAKING BIG COMEBACK IN "TOP THIS."

Los Angeles -- To say Albert Cole had his ups and downs is like saying the space station is only an overblown bottle rocket. Almost two decades ago, Cole was hailed as the next Nicholas Cage. Hollywood heavyweights had their bets on this Yale grad taking his turf.

But on a North Hollywood side street, a little girl died when Cole, strung out on cocaine and booze, struck her with his car. A stint in prison, community service, and several years of probation dropped the budding star from the heavens.

Now he's back, older and wiser, and ironically playing a barkeeper opposite comedian Topper Jamison in his newest series.

Los Angeles Times (June 2nd)

FOX BOASTS HIGHEST RATINGS EVER

Los Angeles -- TOP THIS a surprisingly popular series starring Topper Jamison, Janet Parker, and Albert Cole led Fox's charge to the top in the May prime time sweeps.

Los Angeles Times (June 20th)

PROTEST GROUP TAKING ON CONGRESS

Washington -- Members of a TV watch dog group will be lobbying members of congress for increased standards of decency for prime time TV.

The leader of 'Eye on TV,' Lourdes Thacker, has been a longtime protester against nudity and violence on TV, but now is complaining about a rising number of ex-cons being used as stars.

"Look who's being pushed as role models for our children these days," Thacker said. "There's even a convicted child killer on one of the Fox programs. My God, how much lower can we go."

TV Guide (July 5th-July 11th issue)

TINKERING WITH "TOP THIS"

Los Angeles -- Production has been suspended on the second season of the hit series TOP THIS. Executive producer Benny Arnold says the writers wanted to take the show in a new direction, concentrating more on the domestic side of the lead character's life.

The series, starring comedian Topper Jamison, had been one of Fox's powerhouses, but has recently taken some flack over the controversy surrounding co-star Albert Cole.

Arnold denies the move is in response to the controversy, but sources close to the production say they are de-emphasizing Cole's role in the upcoming season.

Los Angeles Times (August 22nd issue)

ACTOR HOSPITALIZED AFTER DRUG OVERDOSE

Burbank -- Albert Cole, controversial co-star of the popular

Fox sit-com TOP THIS, was rushed to the hospital after allegedly ingesting a large quantity of an unspecified drug.

He was found unconscious in his dressing room on the set of the TV series. Police are investigating, but are ruling out a suicide attempt.

Cole was once convicted of manslaughter after hitting and killing a North Hollywood little girl while driving under the influence of drugs and alcohol. The controversy has followed him ever since.

National Inquirer (September 3rd edition)

CONVICT/ACTOR GOES TO REHAB, AGAIN

La Cresenta -- Albert Cole, co-star of the TV series TOP THIS, has checked into the ultra-private Canyon Hills Rehab Center.

Cole had just recovered from a near fatal drug overdose on the set of his series. He had been reportedly depressed over the reduction of his character's importance to the series.

Though executive producer Benny Arnold denies it, sources close to the series say Cole's disappearance in the series' upcoming season is directly related to the controversy surrounding his manslaughter conviction 16 years ago.

Albert slowly ran a comb through his silver hair. He leaned closer to the mirror and checked the smoothness of his freshly shaven face, then brushed off his shoulders and made sure his shirt was buttoned correctly.

He heard an object slide on the top of his dresser and turned around. Aunt Libby lifted a small, framed picture lying on its back. On it was the image of Albert, Jenny, Kayla, and Matt sitting together on a couch at her house.

"You never heard from these friends of yours?" she asked.

"No. But I haven't been such a good friend myself."

"They should've tried calling you."

"They did. I never called them back."

"Why not?"

"I don't know. Before I left the hospital, I tried callin' Milo. He was off on some shoot. Then I tried callin' Matt, and his number was disconnected."

"And the black girl?"

"Kayla's in Europe last I heard."

"Oh." Libby laid the picture flat on the dresser, walked over to her nephew and straightened his collar like a loving aunt would do for a little boy. She gave him a reassuring smile and a caress on his cheek. "How're you feeling, Dumpy?"

"My body feels so still and peaceful. I almost feel dead."

"Those toxins are clearing out. Now, we have to keep you clean. Ready for your walk?"

"Yeah. But I can only go around the gardens. That's the only area they allow their patients to go."

"Fine."

He put his arm over her shoulders and together they walked toward the door of his little room. "You know what?"

"What?" Libby responded.

"I need go some place where all I am is a simple alcoholic." Albert laughed, but his eyes filled with tears. Libby pulled him closer and massaged his back.

A casting director escorted a young brunette woman into an office. She smiled at the director and his two assistants. The casting director looked at her clipboard.

"This is Claire Diaz, reading for the part of Rachel." The casting director exited the office without another word.

The director rolled his squeaky wheelchair forward. "Hi, I'm Roland DeCosta."

"Nice to meet you, sir."

"Call me Roland. Behind me are my assistant, Jenny Rappaport, and the writer for our film, Carlos Gibson. So, tell me about yourself."

"Well, I'm a California native. Grew up in Chico, went to college at Berkeley, studying physics."

"Really? Every good actor should know quantum dynamics," Roland said.

"Yeah." Claire laughed with an irritating honk.

When Roland heard it, he pivoted his chair and rolled back toward Jenny giving her a sick look. "Go on," he said.

"Well, after college, I got into community theater, and had done several plays as you can see on my resume. And if I get this film, it will be my debut."

"Really? How did you get your union card?"

"My uncle works for the Screen Actors Guild." She laughed again with that hunk.

The writer took off his glasses and wiped one of his eyes.

"Okay," Roland said. "You have your lines?"

"Yes. I wasn't able to remember them though. Can I hold the paper?"

"This is just a cold reading, Ms. Diaz. Jenny will feed you the lines, okay?"

"Yes, sir, uh -- Roland."

Jenny stood with the script in her hands and walked up to Claire. "Let me know when you're ready," Jenny said.

"I'm ready."

Claire held the script in front of her, but stood like a woman waiting to absorb a punch.

"One thing I don't understand is why?" Jenny read.

"Huh?" Claire looked a little puzzled. Jenny pointed to her script. "Ohhhh." Claire looked down at her papers, trying to find her place. "I got it." She laughed again, honk. "Can you say that again?"

"One thing I can't understand is why?"

Claire looked down at her papers and began reading the words with very little feeling or depth. "Because I had no choice. You backed me into a corner and I had to act."

"Uh, Ms. Diaz?" Roland interrupted,

"Yeah?"

"I really appreciate the effort you put into your acting career. But I guess I'm looking for someone with a little more experience for this role. I hope you'll understand."

Claire's smile faded and she took a deep breath. "Was it my laugh?"

"Your laugh?" Roland asked.

"People say my laugh can be very irritating."

"No, dear. It was your reading. But I thank you for coming down."

Claire pouted like a little girl, turned and left the office.

As Jenny went back to her seat. She popped Roland on the head with the script. "That was nice."

"I didn't want to waste her time, or ours."

"Glad I don't have to audition in front of anybody like you."

Billboard Magazine (September issue)

HBO TO BROADCAST CHALICE, LIVE

New York -- HBO announced they will broadcast live the Athens appearance of Chalice. In an arrangement between Howard Rowe of NTA records, his European partners Unique Spin Ltd., and HBO, Chalice will finally make their American television debut.

Chalice, made up of American singers Vesta Dhar, Tasha Garcia, Kayla Ross, and Janice Watkins, has dominated the European charts for months. Their first album 'Cups Runneth Over' is now rising through the top ten on the American charts after staying number one in Europe for ten weeks.

Their second album Sun, Sea, Sky, and Earth is expected to be released in the USA in October.

A live TV camera was outside Chalice's dressing room. A couple dozen security men and stage hands waited patiently for the women to emerge.

Gale came out and pointed to the TV camera. The cameraman pushed the microphone on his headset closer to his lips. "They're coming." He steadied himself. The red light on his camera flashed on.

Gale pointed to two of Chalice's bodyguards. They walked over and held open the double door.

The first one out was Kayla, her fiery hair looking like

cascading smoke and fire. She wore a thin, black, skin-tight suit with Australian Aborigine designs in orange and red covering it. Fabric rings adorned her neck and arms. Her make-up perfectly accented her natural reddish-brown complexion.

She grabbed a microphone from one of the stage hands and waited for the others. Janice, Vesta, and Tasha wore similar costumes, but with colors and designs that reflected the element they represented -- Janice the Earth -- Vesta the sea -- Tasha the sky.

Vesta nervously bounced up and down, then screamed with a big smile toward the camera. Janice and Tasha heard the murmur of the huge crowd in the arena, and put their hands to their mouths like scared little girls.

Kayla turned toward the camera and began dancing toward it, spouting a cheerleader's chant. "Let's-get-fired-up! Let's go get fired up! Here we go now!" Her words kept the rhythm of her bouncing steps as the cameraman backed up keeping her in frame.

The others followed Kayla and Gale toward a long flight of stairs. The cameraman couldn't follow them any further.

Vesta turned around and blew a kiss. "This one's for you, America." She then hurried after the others.

Only a black fabric curtain separated them from the huge stage and the throng in the arena. Janice and Kayla peered through a thin break in the fabric and saw almost 20,000 people waiting for them. "Jesus," Janice said. "This is the biggest one yet."

The lights dimmed and the crowd's thunderous cheer shook the floor. Kayla stepped away from the opening and began breathing hard. "Oh God."

Gale walked up to her. “What’s the matter?”

“I don’t know.” Kayla held her stomach.

“Sweetie, you were a rock until now. Don’t go soft on me.”

“You see that crowd out there?” Kayla asked.

“It’s just like the smaller places, only now you’ll have space to really perform. Now get ready. You’re out there in 30 seconds.”

Kayla bent low, and blew the air out of her lungs. She clutched her microphone with both hands and closed her eyes tight. “Yeeesss,” she whispered. “Let’s go get fired up.”

Outside, Chalice’s band was nestled in a space between two ramps, one descending to the center of the stage, and the other leading to a higher platform on the left side of the stage. Behind the upper stage, a huge video screen hovered high between huge illuminated letters that spelled Chalice on both sides of it.

When the arena’s lights went down, the three keyboardists begin stirring up the crowd with a round of Gothic sounding melodies. The two bassists softly strummed their instruments, hinting of the hard driving beat of the first song. The lead guitarist added his improvisation, racing up and down the scales with sounds spawned in heavy metal.

The chaotic noises all combined on one note that they allowed to fade to silence, but the crowd’s constant cheering filled the sound void. Lightning effects and thunder filled the arena. Stage smoke filled the upper stage and flowed down the central ramp.

The percussionist raced his hand back and forth along a line of tubular bells, simulating the sound of wind. Instantly, a geyser of colorless smoke rose from the upper stage. Tasha’s silhouette appeared within the smoke. She stood with her feet apart, her arms straight down, and her hands turned outward.

A keyboardist added the sound of waves crashing on shore and Vesta's Silhouette appeared in blue light in a second geyser. She stood like a Venus sculpture with her arms reaching for the sky.

A second keyboardist pressed another key adding the sound of a raging inferno. A third geyser erupted with red light illuminating it. Kayla stood within it, posed in profile like an Egyptian goddess.

The lead guitarist added a soaring note that he believed represented Earth. In an orange geyser, Janice stood leaning on one leg in a sexy repose.

The crowd got louder with every geyser. No one was in their chairs. Security men at the front of the stage grew concerned about some parts of the crowd pushing forward.

Seconds after the geysers, the drummer and the percussionist launched into the driving rhythms of their first song. While still in their geysers, the women began singing a chorus in four-part harmony.

"Ohhh-ahhh-ooohhh, in-sanity!

"Ohhh-ahhh-ooohhh, luvin' insanity! INSANITY!" They stepped out of their geysers and onto the central ramp, descending in formation, walking in rhythm with the beat.

"INSANITY!" Half way down the ramp, Tasha broke formation, stepping in front of the other three for her rap solo.

"Just loosen your tie and look in my eyes. I got you in my sights"

"OOHHH-AH-OOHH-OHH!" the others sang out.

"I'm losing control, can go high or low. We don't really need these lights,"

"INSANITY!"

"Call it madness. Call it illness. A complete lack of common sense."

"OOHHH-AH-OOH-OOH!"

"I know what I need. Please forgive my greed. Then drop that little fence. Yeeaahhh!"

"INSANITY!"

Kayla bent low, playfully eying the crowd and sang, "Got to have it!"

"OOHHH-AH-OOH-OOH!"

"Need you luvin' ooohhh."

"INSANITY!"

Kayla stepped out front.

"My urges call! Shed your vaniteee!

"Just us and four walls.

"My only cure --

"You and me making luvin' in – sani - teeee!"

Vesta joined Kayla in a duet. "Don't be afraid.

"Don't want to be serious.

"Come a little closer.

"I'm going delirious."

Janice ran to the front of the stage, and stretched her glorious voice with the others backing her. "PASSION AND JOY!"

"Luvin' insanity," the others sang.

"MY URGES CALL!"

"Luvin' insanity."

"JUST US AND FOUR WALLS!"

"Luvin' insanity."

"COME A LITTLE CLOSER."

"Let's make luvin' in – sani—teeee!"

Kayla charged to the side of the stage drawing huge cheers from those in that part of the arena and began belting out her second solo.

All the physical training, all the mental preparation, all the choreography, and rehearsals worked. Chalice made it look effortless, and no one in Athens felt deprived of the expectations built up by Howard Rowe's hype.

Kayla's smile never looked more brilliant. She had found her place in the business.

And Matt?

A sixteen year old boy was on a chair on a vast theater stage within Tampa's Magnet High School for the Performing Arts.

The boy tilted his head back defiantly, and rubbed his sandy hair. "I need -- I need -- I don't know -- food?" He shrugged and looked at his teacher.

"Good. Continue."

"I want -- I want to get off this stage that's for damn sure."

The murmur of laughter rolled through the other twenty kids in the class.

"Good. You can't yet. Give me one more good one of each and I'll let you go."

"Awe come on, Mr. Redcrop."

"Come on, Frank." Matt strolled out to the center of the stage and stood next to the boy. "Why are you here?"

"Because I can act?"

"You can act in any school. But why are you in this school for the performing arts?"

"Because I figured I'd get better training."

"Is that what you need?" Matt asked.

"Yeah."

"Why?"

"I don't know. Cause I want to go to Hollywood and be star." Murmurs of laughter came from the other students again.

"That's a need and a want. Time to start training seriously or you're not going to make it out of this school. Go back to the audience." Frank left the stage. Matt walked to the edge and sat down facing his class. "Hollywood is good goal, don't get me wrong. But an old friend of mine once said 'Hollywood's like a prude with a whore's reputation. She'll slap down anyone who would test her warped virtue.' I didn't believe it at first, but after trying her myself I can testify that's a fact. Even with all my training she slapped me down and cut a piece of my life away.

"When you're a performer you can't be scared of showing the audience what makes you tick. Whatever you have in your heart and soul is your greatest instrument in acting. That's why I run you through these drills, to get you in touch with your inner self so that you can call upon these feelings to make a scene more believable."

"Let's see you do it," Frank yelled from his seat. A girl next to him shushed him.

Matt nodded his head slowly. "Okay." Matt didn't pause. "I need some sort of tangible success in my life. I want my class to respect my advice. I need old friends and old times." In that moment, he was back on that California beach strumming his guitar with Kayla at his side singing. "And old times." He looked up, and a faint smile grew on his face as a brief tidal wave of Kayla filled his senses -- her lavender fragrance -- soft lips -- her body -- her sensitivity -- her faith in him. "Whew. I really miss some people very dear to me." He inhaled deeply. "I want to not dwell on the past. I'm much too young for that." Some of the students chuckled. "I need something to stomp out the envy I have for some people. I want to not worry about missed opportunities." The school bell rang ending the class. The kids rose out of their seats. "Hey-hey! Get those scene studies together for showcase, gang. Monday, I'm bringing in a real casting director to critique your work, Shelley Isaacson. Have a good weekend."

The students quickly cleared the theater. Matt remained seated on the edge of the stage in silence. He bowed his head low, not noticing the female figure in the sunlit doorway at the side of the stage.

"No day-dreaming in class," she said.

Matt lifted his head and turned to the side. A smile grew on his face when he saw her -- Terri, the woman he first met as a L-A telemarketer.

"I was thinking of you," he said.

"Oh? In that case you may continue." Matt hopped off the stage and strolled over to her. They kissed briefly, careful about their image with the passing students. They walked side by side in the crowded halls, talking softly. "How was your day?" she asked.

"Uneventful. You?"

"I only had one fight to settle, and had to wet nurse three kids who were scared they were about to be kicked out of the program."

"Sounds like you're finally getting comfortable, Counselor."

"Yeah." Terri playfully bumped shoulders with him. "How about if I cook you a good dinner tonight. My place?"

"Sounds good."

(0)

Printed and bound by PG in the USA

USA2018PGIL